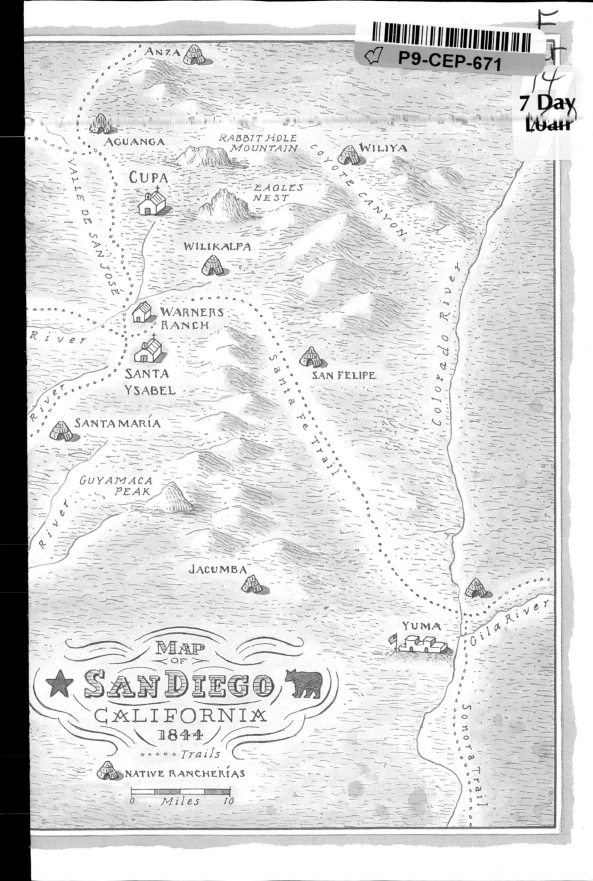

GARTH MURPHY

THE
INDIAN
LOVER

SIMON & SCHUSTER
NEW YORK LONDON TORONTO SYDNEY SINGAPORE

SIMON & SCHUSTER
Rockefeller Center
1230 Avenue of the Americas
New York, NY 10020

For information about special discounts for bulk purchases,
please contact Simon & Schuster Special Sales:
1-800-456-6798 or business@simonandschuster.com

Endpaper map © 2002 by David Cain
Designed by Karolina Harris
Manufactured in the United States of America

10 9 8 7 6 5 4 3 2 1

Library of Congress Cataloging-in-Publication Data

Murphy, Garth.
The Indian Lover / Garth Murphy.
p.   cm.
1. Indians of North America—Fiction. 2. Indians, Treatment of—Fiction. 3. Ethnic relations—Fiction.
4. California—Fiction. I. Title.
PS3613.U73 I5 2002
813'.6—dc21   2002029433

ISBN 0-7432-1943-0

For Euva, my own Indian princess;
for Earl, my fearless scout;
for Stella, who took me to her breast
and rocked me in nature's cradle.

THE
INDIAN
LOVER

PROLOGUE

THE BEGINNING

I L L I A M Marshall first saw California with his eyes squeezed shut.

He rose on tiptoes, hands cupped to ears, tuned in like a bat—transported—as John Trumbull Warner spun his tale of ravishing paradise in that far-away and mythical country. Bill soared on aural wings, buffeted by a jostling crowd of farmers and townsfolk, jammed into the Hartford, Connecticut, meeting hall. California was a magical word in the 1840s and Warner had just spent nine years there.

On the advice of a doctor that exercise and fresh air would cure his asthma, Warner had departed Hartford at age nineteen, heading west on foot to St. Louis. He took a mule train on the Santa Fe Trail to New Mexico and finally to California. There he had remained, traipsing from end to end of the territory, hunting, trapping, trading and exploring, finding health in the untracked wilderness.

Warner had written a story of California, published in the *New York Tribune*, widely copied throughout the States. Now he was back East in person, singing the praises of his newfound home.

"Look folks, it's heaven on earth. That's all I can say. Anything you can imagine is there to be seen: Deserts so dry, when rain falls, it never touches the ground; mountains so high the snow lasts all summer; trees as big around as houses, in forests that stretch forever. A thousand lakes and rivers, with waterfowl so thick you can knock them down with a stick. There are plains of wild grain, teeming with deer, elk and antelope . . . and a fortune in fur to be taken: beaver, bear, lynx and sea otter."

"Did you see any gold?" A trembly voice rose from the front of the hall. Warner paused for a moment. The crowd was silent.

"No need for gold in California; everything is provided for by God's natural bounty. There's nothing to buy; that's what I'm trying to tell you. It's all free: a million acres of unplowed farmland; ranches to fatten a hundred thousand cattle; harbors at San Diego and San Francisco with room for all the ships in the Union.

"The winters are mild and the summers cool. The ocean is warm and calm. It's bursting with sea life . . . all you have to do is dip a net, cast a spear or turn over a rock, and you have a meal.

"The only thing lacking, folks, is people. People like you and me. Americans to make California an American state. There can't be more than a couple of thousand Spanish Californians—they call themselves Californios—they don't consider themselves Mexicans. Most of their leaders would rather be independent, like Texas, or annexed to the States. I've carried letters from them to Washington. All we need are a few thousand settlers to help turn the tide. And the first ones there can get land grants from the governor . . . just like I did.

"All you have to do is swear allegiance to Mexico." Warner chuckled. The crowd laughed with him.

"How 'bout the Indians?" yelled a young voice from the back.

Bill opened his eyes. Warner towered, tall and thin. A dark beard and dark curly hair ringed his pinched but puffy face—visible over the sea of heads and hats—the face of a preacher whose falcon's gaze pierced Bill, and through him to the man behind. It was common knowledge that hostile natives controlled most of the country west of the Mississippi. They were not enthusiastic about American migration. They were savages who killed whites on sight.

"I'm glad you asked," Warner said. A smile tugged at the corners of his thin mouth. "That's the best thing of all. The Indians are friendly and they do all the hard work."

"Hogwash," someone shouted.

Warner shouted back into the ripple of guffaws. "You'll laugh even harder when you know the history: Spanish missionaries controlled California for sixty-five years, from 1769 until 1834. They pacified the Indians, Christianized them and taught them to farm and ranch. They trained them well. The natives are peaceful, they're educated and they'll do any work that needs to be done."

The crowd murmured skeptically.

"It's the truth. I brought one of them with me. He'll tell you himself. I want you to meet Pablo Verdi." Warner turned to pull his good Indian forward. "Tell them in English, Pablo."

A handsome dark-faced boy, about Bill's age, stood next to Warner. He was wearing a short, fitted blue jacket with big brass buttons, a white shirt, dark blue pants with more bright buttons, and a red scarf. He held a leather hat. Next to Warner, he looked tiny, delicate and refined.

"My name is Juan Pablo Verdi," he said with a lilting clip. "I am of the Luiseño People. I went to school for ten years at Mission San Luis Rey, near San Diego, under the direction of Father Francisco González de Ibarra." He rolled the r's like a squirrel's chirp. "We learned to read and write in Latin, Spanish and English. I am a Christian and a citizen of Mexico." He said these words proudly, with a shy smile.

Someone hacked and spat. Warner stared the man down. Pablo spoke.

"As Señor Warner has told you, we are a civilized people. We did do the work of building and maintaining our mission for the Franciscans. Now that the missions are sadly abandoned, we work on our own land, and at those ranchos granted to the Californios by the governor."

He looked to Warner, who patted Pablo's shoulder and nodded.

"It's the truth, folks. I walked the whole country by myself, in safety."

The throng heaved and swayed; Warner quickly took up his pitch.

"A few pioneers and a railroad from St. Louis to San Diego, following the Santa Fe Trail, could bring California straight into the Union. I'd like you all to speak to your congressmen. Stir them up. We can build that railroad. Let's make this whole country ours, from sea to salten sea."

The applause was long. Shouting questioners besieged Warner. "How do we get there?" someone hollered.

"By ship is the easiest, or you can travel overland like I do," Warner called out. The din quieted. "I'm on my way to Washington to visit with the President. Then I'll return to California—to honeymoon at our ranch with my new bride, who awaits me in Los Angeles. You want to walk; I'll show you the way. Meet me at the capital . . ."

There was a rush of noise. Bill wanted to move forward, but the crowd's flow swept him out of the stuffy hall and into cool twilight. When the human tide had ebbed, Bill found Pablo leaning against the wide trunk of an elm tree, deep in shadow. Shiny lines of brass buttons lit his form.

"Pablo?

Pablo straightened. "Yes?"

"I'd like to go with you to California, if you'll have me."

Pablo looked away and replied at length in an Indian tongue. Up close, speaking his own language, he seemed older, more man than boy.

At the end of his speech, Pablo met Bill's eyes.

It hadn't sounded like a no, so Bill stuck out a strong, well-shaped hand.

"The only perfect parts of me are my hands and my feet," he said. "William Marshall, at your service, sir."

ONE

THE
PROMISED
LAND

1

LA PLAYA

BILL awoke to a still and silent ship, not even a sail flapping. The sky was slate gray, solid overcast from horizon to horizon with no breath of wind. The sea was flat as the whole earth used to be, and black as night. Here and there, silver streaks of jumping fish cut through the endless glassy surface, trailing foam like shooting stars, to be swallowed by watery darkness.

As the sun rose, the sea stayed black. The *Hopewell* was surrounded by a thirty-mile-wide shoal of sardines, tightly packed. Swordfish, tuna, mackerel, barracuda and sharks carved joyfully through this endless meal. Bill lowered a small net and the men breakfasted on the bounty. The crisp fish, rolled in flour and fried in fresh whale oil, were devoured whole, head to tail. The gut of the sardine contains vegetable food, sorely craved by the sailor's body.

The day before, the *Hopewell* had been making good time in the breezy Santa Barbara Channel, where half a dozen blue-green chunks of the tumbling California coastal range jutted majestically from a frothy sea. The crew had harpooned a breaching gray whale and spent the day stripping it of blubber and cooking it down to oil. At sunset they had roasted the tender bits of heart and liver—then fallen asleep full and tired, after toasting a toddy of rum to 1845, the new year.

Pablo had slept late and disdained to partake in another fishy meal. With their goal in sight, he spoke longingly of a real Californio breakfast: "Steak and eggs and chorizo and tortillas with spicy salsa and a big cup of lemonade."

He paced the motionless deck, scuffing the oak planks, praying to the dormant sky. "Arise," he shouted. "Awake, four winds. How dare you sleep when I am so near my home—now our sails need your cool breath for just another push. Do not forsake me. I am High Cloud Comes, your friend. I ask but for one final ride, then I will trouble you no more."

His impatient plea met only sulky silence, without a ruffle of the silken sea.

C O M I N G on the *Hopewell* had been Bill's idea.

He had first shipped on a whaler at age fourteen, as a cabin boy. This apprenticeship at sea had begun as a banishment of sorts. He had offended his parents' notion of onshore behavior—for a Puritan farm boy—for a Marshall. To everyone's surprise, Bill had enjoyed living on the ocean. He loved the boundless freedom of an endless horizon, and the cramped, self-contained, disciplined hive of activity—the whale-hunting ship—from which they pursued that horizon.

He was not to be a cabin boy for long. His restless hands and tactile feet were perfectly suited for the endless tasks of a sailor. Bill effortlessly became a seasoned deckhand and expert whaleboat crewman. For four years the ship had been his only home. That was how he wished to go to California: aboard this floating, rocking cradle. To walk would have been too much work, with dangerous distractions along the way. On a ship, you were safe in your own bunk until you disembarked.

Pablo had agreed to journey with Bill by sail. He was greatly curious about the world and wished to see as much of it as possible. They would meet up with John Warner at the end of his long walk.

Mid-morning, the breeze finally snapped the limp sails to attention and the *Hopewell* ran on the backs of sardines all the way to Point Loma, the headland at the entrance to San Diego Harbor. The sky never gave one glimpse of blue, but Pablo and Bill were undaunted, joyful at the prospect of landing, bursting with restrained anticipation, for Bill too planned to leave the ship.

This was a serious offense. He had signed on for a two-year whaling voyage, they were thirteen months into the trip. The ship was just entering the most lucrative phase of the hunt, the slaughter of calving gray whales in the lagoons of the lower California coast. Every hand was needed to process the whale blubber and help sail the *Hopewell* back to Rhode Island before the Straits of Magellan closed for the southern winter in June.

Desertion was punishable by the absolute authority of the captain. Even if he managed to escape, foreigners like Bill were not allowed to stay in California. They were allowed to stop for supplies, and rest, but the sailors could not venture from port. And all hands were required to leave with the ship. This was the official position. Unofficially, what harm could one young American do in this endless land?

The *Hopewell* rounded Point Loma, skirting the huge kelp bed that streamed to the south, tacked into a lighter breeze that wrapped inland around the point where it flattened into the San Diego River's estuary, found the channel and headed for La Playa—a collection of hide huts and warehouses that comprised the barren port, tucked in the shelter of the great headland. There were no trees at San Diego's bayside. The ground was sandy tidal scrubland. The looming bulk of Point Loma held only a light cover of brush and sage; a gray-green background for the handful of hide huts, which displayed the varying deep browns of their weathered wood and cattle skin covers. It was a desolate sight—to anyone but a land-starved sailor.

As the *Hopewell* skimmed up the channel, the shore sprang to life. People ran out of La Playa's low huts like castaways, waving and yelling to stop the boat. Three miles inland, at the pueblo of San Diego, a dust cloud pointed its finger at the bay—the townsfolk racing on horse and wagon to greet the ship. A couple of guns discharged.

La Playa was San Diego's official holding camp for unauthorized non-Mexicans who happened to somehow end up upon these shores. The society was unruly, with Kanakas, as the Hawaiians were called, English, French and Russian sailors, Indian women from various tribes, as well as kids, pigs, chickens and dogs. All the men had arrived by sea—marooned for bad behavior, missing at sailing time or deserting a cruel captain or leaky hull. They were not allowed to leave the immediate area. They worked at the hide-curing vats and acted as a labor pool for undermanned ships. The captain could easily replace Pablo and Bill.

The La Playa residents plunged into the winter-cold sea, swam out to the ship and scrambled up lines to board. Pandemonium reigned on deck. Anchor dropped and the *Hopewell* swung to, a few yards from shore. Then everyone began leaping into the water. Bill jumped in, breaststroked to the beach and ripped off his foul clothes. A native woman threw him a big bar of tallow soap. He rolled in the shallows and scrubbed himself with his soapy shirt, releasing a dark cloud of grime.

Naked, rubbed pink, Bill scrambled back on board to dry and put on the clean clothes he had carefully kept wrapped in oilcloth at the bottom of his footlocker. They seemed to have escaped the rank smell of the ship and himself. He splashed cologne everywhere to be sure.

A WHALER has a stench that precedes and follows it for miles. It is as foul as a full latrine, or a four-day-dead cow, and almost impossible to erase.

The combination of sea water, cooked whale blubber, rancid whale oil in the hold, whale blood and guts, rotting meat, slime, mashed barnacles, bile, seagull and pelican droppings and unwashed sick men permeates the air, wood, clothing, sails, ropes, even brass and iron on a whaler. It will not wash off and you never get used to it. When you leave a whaling ship you have to burn your clothes, shave your hair and scrape off a layer of skin to escape the smell.

Pablo was the cleanest, best-groomed sailor on the *Hopewell*, including the captain. At sea, he bathed at least twice a day, no matter how cold, by dragging a bucket over the side and dousing himself over and over until he was satisfied. Indians must bathe every day, he informed his rank shipmates. At La Playa, he scoured himself with soap and sand until his skin was bright red. But even he couldn't keep the stink off his clothes. As clean as he could get, he still wore the stench of dead whale.

The people of La Playa didn't mind. They lived in their own stink, not as varied or disgusting as a whaler's, but equally strong. Their bayside village was the storage and loading facility for San Diego's only export commodities: tanned cattle hides and tallow. Hides were first field-stripped at the ranches from throat-cut beasts, crudely scraped and dried, then trundled by oxcart to La Playa, where they were tanned and finished, sorted, stacked and stored by the motley residents, to await the next clipper ship, bound for the Boston shoe trade.

The smell of the port was the smell of rotting cattle, wet hides, curing hides, molding hides and animal fat boiling to rancid tallow—further spiced by the usual odors of a fishing village with no sanitary facility save the open ground and hide-flapped privies. It was a unique perfume, intensified by the stillness of the sheltered bay.

BILL had rushed to get clean for the official greeting by the respectable townsfolk of San Diego, who now raced to meet the ship. He was one of the first crewmen ready. Back on deck, sandy hair pulled into a dripping pony-tail, he took a deep breath. He looked the *Hopewell* over carefully, silently saying goodbye to each of his favorite places. He blessed the sturdy timbers that had served so faithfully. He prayed for her safe journey home.

Aboard ship, on the limitless, ever changing expanse of ocean, Bill had found an outlet for all of his physical talent and youthful energy. There was only one great flaw to life at sea: women were not allowed on board. For Bill, life without women was achingly incomplete. He had grown up with three older and two younger sisters. He enjoyed their homey company, their fairness—their gentleness. Womanly sweetness, romance and cheerful work habits made life lighter, less serious and dreadful. He had learned to sleep in the arms of a girl—and that was how he liked to sleep. Bill missed women too much to live at sea forever.

The men assembled, the mate called for order and gave the rules.

"We'll be here a few days to take on water and stores for our trip south. This is our last taste of civilization for a couple of months, so make the most of it. We'll have eight-hour anchor watches. Those of you not on duty may have shore leave. No one but the crew comes aboard. No drinking, fighting or stealing and don't go any further than the town. Come now, man the boats . . . let's take our captain in to greet the mayor."

T H E Y rowed to shore and filed past the now silent La Playans, who were dressed in every sort of rag and skin and old uniform, with hats of stiff cowhide or palm leaf. The Indian women wore long loose smocks, or grass skirts with fur capes wrapped around their shoulders.

The crew marched to the capitanía, or customs house, seventy yards east of the hide storage sheds and residents' shanties. It was more substantial, with thick adobe walls and a thatched roof shading a short porch. The floor was dirt. There were no windows, just a door of heavy oak planks, sagging open on leather hinges. The one room was empty.

In front of the customs house, a growing crowd awaited, horses blowing hard. Some men sat their saddles; others had dismounted. Women and children in rustic carts craned for a look at the newcomers—who drew themselves into a ragged line, the captain in front. A small man, well dressed with a bright-buttoned fitted suit like Pablo's holding a wooden staff topped by a silver ball, rode forward, dismounting gracefully.

"Buenas tardes, señores, soy Juan María Osuna, el alcade de San Diego. Welcome. I am mayor." He smiled at the captain and bowed low.

"Buenas tardes. Captain Ian Saxon, at your service, sir."

He bowed too, but not as low.

"Your papers, please, Capitán."

The captain handed Señor Osuna his protocol from Governor Micheltorena, which he had received at Monterey, the capital of California, always the first legal port of entry.

Osuna opened the packet, closed it as quickly and handed it back.

"He can't read," whispered Pablo.

"Do you have some news or a declaration from el gobernador?" the alcalde asked with a weak smile.

There were titters from the crowd. The southern half of California was in revolt against the appointed Mexican governor. They had established their own governor, Pío Pico, at Los Angeles.

"The governor sends his regards to all of you. And I have a letter for Anita Gale de Warner."

Osuna seemed disappointed.

The captain said, "With your permission, Señor Alcalde, we'd like to stay a few days, to take on food and water, and make some repairs to the ship."

"You are very welcome. And we will be pleased to entertain you by our fiesta. Señor Juan Bandini opens his casa. All are welcome. In good time, we shall take you to the pueblo in las carretas." He opened his hand toward a half-dozen large, two-wheeled, ox-drawn carts that were just pulling up.

Osuna shook the captain's meaty paw, then gave him an abrazo, a hug with two pats on the back. He never let go of his polished staff of office, which had a black ribbon laced through a hole just under the silver globe.

As if by signal, the townsmen descended. Introductions were made in Spanish and English. Then the trading began. Every man, woman and child wanted clothes, cloth and thread. They were well dressed in an old-fashioned way, with nary a fur or skin. The men sported either colonial Spanish waistcoats, breeches and shirts, with tricorn hats, or Mexican cowboy attire: tight flaring trousers with silver buttons, boots with large silver spurs, white shirts, colored scarves, short fitted embroidered jackets and large hats with stiff, flat brims. The women wore long dresses with full skirts, and lace shawls around their shoulders.

The Californios had few means of showing their wealth. Clothing and fine horses were at the top of their list. It was not unusual to see a mounted man and horse wearing two thousand dollars' worth of fine clothing, tack and ornamentation—with silver and gold braid, buttons, buckles, spurs, bits, bridles and saddle tricking. The Californios tried to lead a European life amidst their untamed colony. A Spanish newspaper, a French fashion magazine, a book in any language, and clothing on their backs—instead of skins and furs (the vestments of beasts)—served to keep the wilderness at bay, and to soothe any savagery that may have lurked in their own breasts.

Their small European population, scattered over huge distances, supported no factories or grain mills, no cotton gins or cloth manufacture, no clothing stores, no shopping, no newpapers. Everything was imported at great expense, or homemade—thus the fervent desire for ordinary clothes, and the great value of fine cloth, lace or anything remotely fashionable.

Bill spotted one man dressed like an English country squire, with dark green velvet breeches split at the outsides over long white socks and black boots, a green velvet waistcoat over a white shirt. His green felt hunting hat only partly shaded a mat of gray curls, a pink face and a very red nose.

Captain Edward Stokes was a Yorkshire gentleman and ex–ship captain. He had married Refugio Ortega, daughter of one of San Diego's leading Californio families, and received Rancho Santa Ysabel as a dowry—thirty-four thousand acres of well-watered grazing land and forest, fifty miles northeast of town. He was John Warner's closest neighbor. At Pablo's suggestion, Bill aproached the captain and introduced himself.

Captain Stokes wanted to hear every detail of their voyage and anything Bill might know about events in England—which was very little.

"We San Diegans are desperate for the news," Stokes said. "You have no idea how isolated we feel. It is as though we too have been half a year at sea. We are lucky to see one sail a month. Even then, both news and supplies are usually stale."

"Captain Saxon knows a lot more than I do," Bill assured him.

The physical and geographical remoteness of California was daunting: To the east and north were towering snow-capped mountains, scorching sands and hostile Indian tribes. Mexico City was two thousand miles by land, across inhospitable deserts. The journey by sea from the port of Acapulco required a few months of hard sailing into the prevailing wind, tacking halfway to Hawaii and back, finally reaching the coast near San Francisco, then sliding downwind to San Diego, the last outpost before the thousand brutal miles of Baja California. The voyage was dangerous and unhealthy, with no food and only one stop for water between Acapulco and California. Many died of scurvy on this arduous route, or arrived so weak as to need months to recuperate.

Bill appeased Stokes with the details of their sail to the Marquesas Islands, to Hawaii, then north till they found the west wind and ran quickly to California, sighting land at Fort Ross, north of San Francisco Bay. They'd taken fresh fruit and vegetables at every port on the coast, Buena Ventura, Monterey and Santa Barbara, arriving in San Diego healthy and strong, ready for the lucrative Baja California whale kill, just days ahead.

"Sounds like you're pretty cozy with Cap'n Saxon, for a deckhand," Stokes said, eyeing Bill up and down.

Bill shrugged. "I was his cabin boy when I started. I've been with him for nearly five years."

"So he looks after you?" Captain Stokes's voice was gruff.

"Yes, sir, he does."

"It's prudent seamanship and care for his crew make a good captain." Stokes nodded. "Ian Saxon's one of the best. But 'tis good to hear it from the men."

Bill excused himself. A striking woman had caught his attention, a girl to whom his eyes kept returning.

"Lugarda Osuna," said Stokes, following Bill's wandering gaze. "She's easy to look at. All do. Look but don't touch." He laughed, "Go on, boy. She won't bite . . . just a little sting maybe. I'll see you at the ball."

Lugarda Osuna was wearing a birdshell blue dress with lace trim, a Spanish comb in her long dark hair—accompanied by a woman dressed in pea green, who looked to be her mother, and an Indian girl in a darker blue dress. Warm shawls covered their shoulders.

Pablo had disappeared to carry out his plan of trading clothes for good horses. Bill made his way toward the Osunas alone, introducing himself to everyone, keeping one eye on Lugarda.

He shook the hand of Don Juan Bandini, an Italian-Peruvian and San Diego's most widely respected and hospitable citizen. Bandini was thin as a stick, with a knuckle-crushing grip. He loved music and he loved to dance. His fiestas were legendary among sea captains, reason enough to pull into the harbor for a few days rest. Bandini hosted a ball for every arriving ship, preceded by a feast and some sporting entertainment: cockfights, bronco riding, or a bull and bear battle.

"Today will be the bull and the bear," he confided. "You are lucky. This is a very rare thing, special to California."

Bill felt he already knew Bandini. When Pablo had related stories of his homeland to Bill, Bandini's name constantly popped up. Bandini was wealthy. He owned two large ranches to the south, Tecate and Ti Juan. His home was the social center of the pueblo, and he had four talented daughters near marrying age.

But San Diego was such a small town it was easy to know everyone. The twenty houses of the pueblo were owned by the same families who owned the twenty large land-grant ranches of the San Diego District. All had been carved from the two local missions' estates, since the Mexican Revolution of 1822, when the Catholic Church was accused of being a Spanish puppet, an enemy of republican Mexico, and her missionary assets seized.

The land of Missions San Diego and San Luis Rey had been huge, rich, without boundaries, encompassing all of San Diego. The Franciscan missionaries were finally expelled from California in 1834, freeing their property for distribution. In just ten years, the few impoverished soldiers and colonists of the town, who for decades had looked so enviously at the missions, became wealthy and powerful from the bounty of those lands. These privilaged families now made up the tiny society of San Diego. Their year was measured more by Bandini's parties than by months or seasons. Whenever a ship dropped anchor in the big bay, they all fled their ranchos to converge on the pueblo for the expected fiesta.

Bandini eyed Bill's clean layers of white ruffled shirt, ivory-buttoned navy woolen jacket and blue sailor's ducks. They were about the same size.

"Do you have any clothing to sell?"

"No, sir. I need what little I have." Bill had promised to leave the trading to Pablo.

"Then I beg your pardon. I'll see you at the fiesta." Bandini touched his hat and turned away.

Pablo, whose full Indian name was High Cloud Comes, was partial to the European refinement he had enjoyed as the priests' favorite at Mission San Luis Rey. Educated and intelligent, he cherished his books and clothes. But he also loved to run half naked and roll in warm dust like a puppy. Skins were good enough for High Cloud if he had a fine steed, a knife, a bow, arrows and a lance. He and Bill each wore three layers of shirts and trousers, ready to peel off for sale or trade. Horses, saddles, bridles, food and weapons, they would acquire. But Bill had noticed that Pablo's most finely tailored clothes were carefully folded, packed away and not for sale.

Bill approached the mayor's party. His captain was still there, chatting with Señora María Juliana Josefa López de Osuna, who was fair with scattered freckles and lively light brown eyes. Her face was the only part of her not completely covered in material. When Captain Saxon introduced Bill to her, she curtsied, carefully staying in the shadow of her parasol. She waved toward two of her boys, who wore caballero finery and sat on beautiful black horses. "My sons, Ramón Prudencio and Leandro Inocencio Osuna." They tipped their hats. "My husband, Juan María Osuna, the mayor of our pueblo." She gestured at his back. "And this is my daughter, Señorita Lugarda Dionicia Osuna."

Lugarda was sitting in a parked cart with the Indian maiden, facing the rear. Señora Osuna had neglected to introduce Natalia Pájaro-Azul (Bluebird) Cota, Lugarda's handmaid and lifelong companion. 'Zul, as she was known, wouldn't meet Bill's gaze. Thick black bangs dropped to shadow all but her dark sculpted lips. Lugarda's wide smoky eyes, lit with tiny green flecks, looked into Bill's own for so long that he was forced to break the spell. He lowered his lashes and followed them with a polite bow.

"Mucho gusto," he said.

She replied in halting English, "Pleased to meet you, I hope you enjoy your visit."

Her face was the best possible combination of European and Indian, multicolored eyes, dark brown hair, a long nose, a blood-red mouth parted to reveal small even teeth, and skin the color of ripe wheat. She smiled. Bill stared.

Señora Osuna coughed. "At first sight, every man in California falls in love with my youngest daughter. She is beautiful, no? Don't take it personally, you may be sure that she doesn't. Come, you must greet the mayor." She turned toward her husband.

Lugarda blushed. "Vamos, Santiago," she said, over her shoulder to the driver, without taking her eyes off Bill. The wagoneer took up the reins but did not ask his mules to move. Lugarda crossed her legs. There was a flash of ankle, slim and white-stockinged. She turned to speak with 'Zul, who laughed. Lugarda smiled again.

Bill felt a gloved hand on his elbow. Señora Osuna said to her husband, "Señor Alcalde, may I present Señor Guillermo Marshall." She curtsied.

Bill shook the alcalde's limp hand. "Bill," he said. "Bill will do."

"Mucho gusto," Osuna replied, without enthusiasm. He examined Bill's eager, sunburned face, nodded and turned back to the captain.

Señora Osuna said, "Our mayor is a very important man . . . here." She indicated the wasteland of the sandy plain with a smirk. She shrugged. "We'll see you at the Bandinis', I hope."

"Si, señora, thank you."

"De nada, à bientôt, goodbye for now."

Spanish, French and English: Señora Osuna tossed off the words like an aristocrat, bred for the courts of New Spain. She mounted the wagon gracefully to sit by Lugarda. "Santiago," she said to her youngest son. He clicked the alert team to motion, and they were gone.

" S E Ñ O R I T A María Juliana Josefa López was a blushing fourteen-year-old bride," Pablo had explained, as they lay bundled up on the *Hopewell*'s deck, looking up into a brilliant star-packed winter sky.

"Before the revolution, Juan María Osuna was a Spanish army corporal, the son of a mission guard at Loreto. At least one of his grandmothers was an Indian neophyte, a newly converted Christian at the mission. He had inherited her native good looks. Corporal Osuna had followed in his father's footsteps, and prospered by his own appointment to guard the mission at San Diego. When he was ready to marry, Osuna made a heartfelt offer for Señorita López, a Spanish-Creole from a well-bred but unfortunate San Diego family, very poor and sufficiently fair.

"His offer was accepted and Señora López de Osuna has survived her marriage to bear eleven children. To her intense disappointment, Ramón and Leandro look exactly like their father. Only Santiago and Lugarda could possibly pass for Spanish.

"Señora Osuna has pushed her husband to success, and she never lets Juan María forget it. He's resentful, pompous and greedy. His son Ramón Prudencio lives up to his name, but Leandro Inocencio is anything but. He's mean as a stepped-on snake. Be careful of him," Pablo had warned.

B I L L could see the Osuna boys now, galloping up the road to town. He searched in vain for Pablo among the stragglers at La Playa, before climbing onto the waiting carreta, a crude, hand-hewn wooden freight wagon, with each large wheel a single thick slab of solid oak. He was joined by some of his shipmates and the cart rumbled along the bayside toward the Pueblo of San Diego. With the northwest breeze blowing their dust across ruffled gray water toward the sandy line of the Coronado Islands, they crossed the scruffy lowlands of the San Diego River delta, and headed toward the houses nestled at the base of the first inland hills. It took half an hour to get there.

Bill was pleased. His basic Spanish, taught by Pablo, had held up. He had succeeded in meeting the people Pablo said he should meet—though San Diego was more confusing than expected. There might only be twenty families but there were dozens of aunts and uncles, cousins, children and grandchildren—Bill had forgotten names as soon as he'd heard them—and there were the fascinating people of La Playa, standing at the edge of the crowd, half naked, waving and calling out. But all in all, their plan was unfolding nicely.

Bill had taken the midnight watch on the *Hopewell*, giving them plenty of time to prepare their escape. He wouldn't wait until the ship departed to desert. One more night on that stinkpot was intolerable. At midnight they would be on the way north to Pablo's rancho, Las Flores.

This was their simple scheme: Bill was eligible, by nature of his handsome form, creamy skin and greenish eyes, and his good disposition, to marry a daughter of the Mexican republic; to become a citizen and to receive a land grant. Pablo would introduce him to society; he would fall in love with the right girl and marry. They would have neighboring haciendas and get rich selling cowhides to the Boston traders.

Bill had acquired a beautiful French wedding gown, complete with veil and honeymoon nightdress, from a Boston family—after their daughter was refused marriage at the last minute by her husband-to-be's parents, who learned that she was five months pregnant, and possibly not by their son. The poor girl had poisoned herself. Her abandoned trousseau was now hidden at La Playa, ready to be presented to the prospective bride. And Bill already knew who he wished to see wearing it. He would marry Lugarda Dionicia Osuna, if she would have him.

As the carreta lumbered into town, Bill kept a lookout for Pablo. High Cloud Comes was guide, confidant and protector in this strange new world. Bill couldn't wait to tell him about Lugarda. But where was he? Bill looked to the sky for a sign, but the damp gray ceiling hung low, dark and mute. The carreta pulled up at Juan Bandini's and the men got down to his hearty welcome.

2

THE BULL
AND THE BEAR

ELCOME to San Diego, señores. Mi casa es su casa." Bandini waved at his lengthy one-story adobe house. A big earthen pot of lemonade and a jumble of earthen cups sat on a long table standing in the raked dirt outside his door. Plank benches leaned against the wall. A sweet-looking woman was carefully filling each mug with a wooden ladle.

"Please have a limonada," she said.

"Sit," said Bandini. "We will see something very amusing."

Bill scratched his ankle and knocked a flea off his pants, then sat and slurped a cup of sour lemonade. He had a second cup.

They were in a square, about sixty yards across, with four or five loosely spaced houses on each side. Verandas faced onto the square. Most of the buildings were one-story, made of large adobe bricks, unplastered. The roofs were tile or thatched palm. Veranda posts were wood; their floors were paving stone or packed earth. There were no trees, a few bougainvillea vines and lots of dirt. At the back of the houses were kitchens, woodsheds, lean-tos and animal pens, as well as the ever-present privies. There was nothing else. It was a poor excuse for a town, dusty and flea-infested. The gray sky didn't help.

Most of the crewmen lounged on Bandini's benches, or leaned against the rails of a penned-in space between two houses, on the north side of the plaza. A large long-horned bull stood placidly in the pen, ignoring the men. He was tied to a corner post with a very stout braided rawhide rope, lashed to a wide leather collar secured just above his right front hoof.

Bill was avoiding his shipmates. He didn't want to lie and feel guilty about deserting them. He could see that his relationship with the captain and knowledge of Spanish set him apart from the common seaman, and impressed the Californians. He needed all the help up the social ladder he could devise, for he had arrived to seek marriage and fortune with nothing but the clothes on his sunburned back.

Bill asked Bandini if he had seen Pablo.

"Not since La Playa. Last I saw him he was talking to Señor Fitch, our know-it-all, tell-it-all, buy-it-all, sell-it-all storekeeper. I was trying to beat Fitch when I asked to buy your clothes. We were surprised to see Pablo getting off your ship. He left town two years ago with Juan José Warner. Warner returned without him . . ."

"Warner's here? I met him with Pablo in Connecticut."

"He's not in town. He's out at his ranch. It's a long two-day ride northeast of here—way past Stokes's place. We don't see him that much."

"When did he get back? I bet him a silver dollar that it would be quicker by ship."

"He won that race by a few months. Warner moves fast. Juan Largo, we call him. Long John took his bride out to the ranch and they've already built a big new house. Six rooms."

"Sounds nice. I'd like to go see them."

"You are planning on staying?" Bandini looked at Bill sharply.

"I wish I could. After I heard Warner's talk about California, I had to see for myself. This time I'm just looking. I have to complete my contract with the *Hopewell*."

"Will Pablo be going with you?"

"No. He's had enough of the whaler's life. He's going home to his ranch."

Bandini raised an eyebrow, but didn't comment, so Bill rambled on.

"It was only me talked him into shipping out. We didn't want to hoof or hike four thousand miles. Why walk when you can sail in on the breeze?"

There was a commotion in the square. Four caballeros on mules rode in through an open corner. The Osuna brothers were in front, still wearing fancy outfits. Their two good-looking black mules carried wood-frame pack saddles with a thick pole suspended between them. They rode about four feet apart, as a team. The following mules were similarly outfitted, and between the two pairs of riders hung a large dirt-brown grizzly bear, hog-tied by all fours to a sturdy sapling that was lashed at its ends to the thick poles borne by the pack saddles.

The bear was alive, making snuffling noises; glaring upside down, his head nearly dragging on the ground. The blindered mules were frightened, but as all were lashed together in fixed positions, could neither advance nor retreat from the bear. They pranced and brayed and flattened their ears. All the horses in the town began to stamp and whinny. People poured out of every door and leaned from the windows or rushed to the balconies. Lugarda and her mother appeared in a high corner alcove. Señor Osuna came out a lower door of the same house.

By the time the sixteen-legged litter stopped in front of his pen, the bull was pacing, pawing and snorting. The two Osuna boys slid easily off the necks of their mounts. One held the mules' heads. The other, larger, brother unlashed the bear pole, hoisting it on his shoulder while the first two mules were led away. He dropped the pole and the bear smashed nose first to the ground. The grizzly roared and the two still connected mules reared, lifting the bear and dropping him again. Both Osunas went to help unlash the other end of the pole, the mules were led away, and the bear was left lying on his side, mouth full of slobbery dirt, panting. All four of his feet remained tied to the sapling. People were shouting, making and taking bets, the square filled with onlookers.

The four men lifted the bear pole and swung his heavy body around, to face the bull. They attached a leather collar to the bear's left front paw, above the elbow, and pulled it tight. Then they tied the loose end of the bull's tether to a ring on the bear's leg collar and lashed it snug. The bear and bull were strung together like convicts. Only the bars of the corral gate separated them.

G R I Z Z L Y bears are native to California, and were the undisputed kings of the land until the Spanish arrived. The native peoples revered them, not as gods to worship, but as equals. They left each other alone, respected each other's territory, ate the same foods, suffered the same shortages of game, droughts, or fires and enjoyed the same abundance. There were thousands of bears when the first conquistadores arrived. Every deep California canyon still held a family of grizzlies.

The invading Spanish brought cattle for mobile fresh meat and to raise, once settled. The bears and cattle avoided each other. Steers would trot off immediately at the smell of any bear and stampede at first sight of a grizzly. A bear might occasionally catch and kill a young calf. They also ate the abandoned carcasses of cattle skinned on the range and left to rot by the Californios. But they would rather eat roots and acorns and berries, or catch fish and mollusks. Cattle were neither natural prey nor enemy. The grizzly was king but he was outnumbered, and he would not willingly fight a bull.

For the Californios, bears were a source of sport. A grizzly was brave. He would not run, but stand and fight. A boy could prove his manhood by killing a grizzly with only a lance and a knife. Or he might rope a bear and drag him home to taunt and torture . . . or pit against a fighting bull, the most aggressive and fearsome creature in the Spanish world. Since first setting foot on California soil, the Spaniards had regularly matched their toro champions against the local king of beasts. But the unnatural enemies had to be tied together to ensure a battle to the death.

M E N stood at the corral bars and at the bear's front and hind legs. The onlookers took positions giving easy access to flight. Many climbed to the balconies or roofs or into animal pens. Someone yelled, "Suéltelo!" and they cut the ties at the bear's feet and yanked the pole free. He looked confused and licked his paws. They pulled the bars of the corral gate down and dragged them away. The bull snorted but didn't want to leave the corral with the bear in front of him. He backed to the rear of the corral, pulling the bear in. The grizzly leapt to his feet and ran the other way, dragging the bull along. He tripped on the rope, tumbled, and roared.

They wanted nothing but to escape from each other, but tied by their front feet with twenty feet of rope, there was no escape. They were of equal weight, so neither could drag the other far. The bull finally charged, gouging with his left horn. The bear stood up to his full height of eight feet and came down on the bull's back, riding him to the ground, biting his haunch and clawing at his belly.

They were both bleeding, the bull bellowing, the bear moaning, rolling in the dirt. The bull scrambled to his feet first, stomping the bear with his hind hooves, and lurched off. The bear ran after, howling, enraged—both going the same direction now, moving at high speed. They crashed into a veranda post, splintering it. People scattered and roof tiles rained on the combatants. They bolted from the wreckage, bull on the run and bear under him, clinging with both front paws, gnawing at the pulsing throat with bloody yellow teeth, raking the bull's underbelly with razor-sharp hind claws. The bull bucked and twisted. The bear held on.

The bull corkscrewed and dislodged the bear, which fell under his pounding front hooves. The bear rolled, the rope tangled, the bull somersaulted and came up dangling a broken leg. He was bleeding from the neck and sides and lengths of his gut hung from his torn belly. The bear bounced onto him, growling. The onlookers cheered as he gnawed at the bull's backbone and raked at his exposed entrails. The bull bellowed in terror and folded to his knees. He lowered his hindquarters and lay down, then rolled up the rope and onto the bear's arm, pinning it. The bear roared, whined in pain, bit at the rawhide, whimpered and roared again as the bull bled to death. Everyone was shouting, "Suéltelo, suéltelo! Turn him loose." Someone cut the rope with a single slice of a long-poled lance.

Everyone fled indoors or climbed to high ground, but the bear just lay there whimpering, licking his wounds and gnawing at the rawhide collar on his arm. He got up after about a minute of this, looked around, saw an opening between the buildings and lumbered through it, heading north. He stopped to chew at the collar again, then disappeared in dense scrub by the edge of the river, about a quarter of a mile from the pueblo.

Bill nervously gulped another cup of lemonade and walked over to look at the broken veranda. Men were propping it up with a temporary pole. The captain was measuring the splintered post with his large hand. It was a solid trunk about nine inches thick.

"Captain Saxon, sir, have you seen Pablo?"

"Probably run off to the hills. I haven't seen him since the beach."

"Some fight."

"Sure, but nothing compared to fighting a whale."

"To tell the truth, sir, they both make me feel ill."

One of the mule teams was brought in, hitched to the bull, and they towed him out of the plaza.

"It takes getting used to killing, especially with the larger creatures. They don't die easy."

"Pablo says the real test of a man is killing another man, an equal. The Indians believe that. They give even more credit to striking an armed man in combat, and getting away clean."

"I haven't done either, so I can't say. Don't forget your twelve o'clock watch. There'll be a wagon to take you back at midnight."

"Yes, sir."

ACROSS miles of estuary, a pale-faced sun sank through thick overcast into slate gray sea. Bandini's table lay heaped with food. Don Juan sat on a bench by his front door, smoking a cigar. Roast-meat aromas wafted, mouth-watering. Bill strolled through the dust to sit with his host. Everyone who entered Bandini's house was stopping to whisk their legs with a short broom with long flexible bristles. They did it at each passing.

"What are they doing with that broom?"

"Knocking the fleas off their legs, I hope. Damn fleas are that thick here. Got to try to keep them out of the house or they'll drive you mad. Hope you're hungry. Did you ever see anything like that bull an' bear fight?"

"Nope. Wish I'd bet on the grizzly."

"The bear will win most every time. He won't give up. A bull will just quit at some point. To win, he has to get a good horn in at the beginning, then stay away and hope the bear bleeds to death. It's always exciting either way, but you can bet on the bear."

Something moved at the corner of the house—Pablo motioning to Bill.

Bill jumped up. "Con permiso, Señor Bandini. Excuse me."

"Of course."

Around the corner, Pablo was leaning against the wall, his face haggard, his cheek tear-stained.

"Pablo, what happened, where've you been?"

They hugged and leaned back against the building. The light was fading and Bill's flea bites were itching. His belly gurgled.

"I've lost my ranch. The governor, Pío Pico, took it while I was gone." Pablo gasped as if he'd been kicked in the ribs.

"What! How could he? This can't be true. He'll have to give it back."

"I'll kill him first. It would be good to cut that cabrón, piece by piece." Quick breaths rasped in Pablo's throat.

"Tell me what happened. You can't kill the governor. They'll string you to the nearest tree."

"These Californios all know, but they won't say a thing to me," Pablo spat out bitterly. "It is true. I heard from some Kumeyaay and I rode out to the mission to ask the priest. He told me this: After I had been gone a year, Pico appeared with a receipt, supposedly signed by me, deeding Las Flores to himself. Pico has joined Las Flores to his Santa Margarita property."

He sobbed, took a deep breath, exhaled.

"My family has left Las Flores and gone to live with friends at Cupa, in the mountains near Warner's ranch. We now have nothing. Nada. I should never have left."

"Pablo . . ." Bill's stomach roiled and contracted. He felt wobbly, as though the earth were folding under him in one of those earthquakes he had heard about.

Pablo took Bill's arm. "I must go to my family; to Cupa. I have traded for four good horses, two each. We should leave now. Everything is ready."

Bill could smell Bandini's table laden with food, the like he hadn't seen in seventeen months. He pictured Lugarda's ankle, her face.

"We'd best wait till just before midnight," he protested. "The captain's looking out for me. I just talked to him. They could follow us if we leave now. Let's eat, dance, act like sailors on shore leave, and slip away, just as we planned.

"We might learn something useful," Bill added hopefully.

It was too dark to see Pablo's expression, but he was still; so still he didn't seem to be breathing. It occurred to Bill that Pablo might just leave; leave him here to reboard the ship or fend for himself. It would be so much simpler to go on alone. Bill quit breathing too. Finally Pablo touched his shoulder. Then he gripped it.

"Bueno, Bill, you are right. I'd forgotten our plan. But I can't face these people tonight. I'll get some food from the kitchen and take my rest with the horses. If you see 'Zul, Lugarda's handmaid, ask her to come here, to me."

Bill's strength flowed back with a lungful of fresh cool air. He hugged Pablo and held on. He spoke into the back of his friend's neck.

"Don't worry, Pablo. We'll get a new ranch together. Better together anyway. What do I know about ranching? If you get your ranch back, I'll come there to live. If not, you'll come to mine."

Pablo laughed then and wiped his eyes. He smiled.

"Give me two shirts and two of your pants. I need them to pay for the horses."

Bill stripped them off. Pablo shook them out and folded them, carefully pressing away the wrinkles with his palm. Damp air penetrated Bill's single remaining layer of clothing to the skin. He stamped his feet and put on his wool coat.

"Now I've got to eat," he said. "I feel light-headed. Did you see how that grizzly ripped the bull apart?"

"And to what end?" Pablo sighed dejectedly. "I stayed with the horses. The roaring and bellowing had them frenzied. They nearly broke out of the corral."

B I L L was sorry he'd mentioned the bear. Pablo hated to see a creature tormented. He would have to pay close attention to Pablo. It would be a terrible blow, if the ranch were truly lost.

Pablo's extended tribal family had been living at Las Flores forever. They shared a large adobe house, built under the direction of the padres. Pablo had described it in detail. It was like a miniature mission, with dormitories around an interior courtyard and a chapel with bell tower at one corner. Nearby was a reliable stream. Irrigated fields lined both banks. Rich grazing land extended for miles to the north and east. About one hundred thirty Christian Indians had lived and worked there. There were forty-three families in all. Those Indians who did not live in the ranch house occupied a village downstream, on the way to the beach, a half mile west.

Las Flores was only one of seven well-developed Indian rancherías that had once belonged to Mission San Luis Rey. When the mission lands were broken up, the Mexican governor had deeded Las Flores to the Luiseño (as the Indians who lived in that mission's territory were called), as a free town, or pueblo libre. The deed was in Pablo's name, since he was young and the best educated, most trusted of the Christian natives attached to Las Flores. It was the governor's intention that the Luiseño should own this productive land—and thus be able to take care of themselves after the departure of the Franciscans. In the eyes of Mexico, it was the natives' just due.

But Mexico was far away and Pío Pico was the new governor of southern California. Yesterday Pablo had been a prince, a privileged head of family who controlled a ranch as large as any other in San Diego. He was on his way home to his kingdom. Today he was homeless. The governor himself had taken the cherished tribal land. He would never get another land grant from Pico, and he couldn't marry into a Californio ranch. No one wanted Indian blood darkening the family tree.

Now it was all up to Bill. He had to marry well and receive land as a dowry or a wedding present, as they'd planned, as Warner and Stokes had done. He was more determined than ever to succeed. Then they could deal with Pico.

A T the heavily laden table, Bill mounded his earthen plate with steak and tamales, tortillas, beans and a hot tomato and chile sauce. He sat on a bench and stared at his steaming food. Their plans were unraveling fast. The drama they'd rehearsed for a year, on board the rolling ship, had a new plot and an uncertain ending.

Bill dejectedly considered rejoining the *Hopewell* and dropping the whole California adventure. But he believed in California. His sources of information, Pablo and Warner, were certainly partisan—most people think they live in the best place in the world—just as he had once felt about the family farm in Providence. But Bill had seen enough of California by land and sea to believe it might be as wonderful as described. He had to find out.

The smell of food finally penetrated his gloom and Bill took a desultory bite of tough steak. Succulent, wood-roast flavors burst on his palate, obliterating every other consideration. He ate ravenously, without pause, strength and purpose flowing back with each bite.

When he'd finished—plate licked clean and another large cup of lemonade emptied—cool evening dew had settled on the plaza. Bill buttoned up his coat. Bandini called the diners to his door.

"Come, my friends, let's dance. Vamos a bailar."

3

FANDANGO

A VIOLIN scratched inside the house, warming up. Bill headed for the trough to wash, skipping out a dance step Pablo had taught him.

"You have to learn our dances," Pablo had insisted. "Everyone takes part. It is a good chance to show off and the main source of entertainment in California. You must be a good dancer to win a señorita."

Before the Spanish, the natives had led a leisurely life, rising late, bathing, eating acorn flour stew prepared by the women and a handful of pine nuts; hunting or fishing in the afternoon; then smoking a wild tobacco, telling stories, singing and dancing until late in the night, every night. Legends, language, history, knowledge of people, plants, animals and the land were recorded, taught and remembered in song and dance. Dance and music were pleasures that bound a tribe together, educated and kept traditions alive.

The padres had tried to change this unrestrained life, to get the natives to rise early, work hard, grow their food and go to bed at dark. The church would provide education and culture. Dancing especially bothered the priests: naked dancing till two or four in the morning. But dancing was a habit that proved impossible to break. The Indians kept dancing, naked or clothed. The best the padres could do was to introduce European instruments and teach the neophytes to sing Christian hymns.

Settlers, arriving from Spain, also loved to dance, fully costumed, and to Moorish or Gypsy guitar melodies. Many took Indian wives—ninety percent of the first colonists were men—forced by the padres to marry their native mistresses. In a marriage of traditions, dancing became a necessary part of Spanish-Californio life. The music of guitar, violin and accordion synchronized with the rhythms of Indian rattles and drumming feet. New ways of dancing evolved with this new music—and new versions of old dances.

The fandango was the most popular. It combined energetic native stomp-ing with Gypsy display and formal Spanish courting ritual. Watching Pablo, Bill had mastered the basic steps on the *Hopewell*'s rollicking deck.

Bill stutter-stepped around the water trough, taking deep breaths of cool night air, thinking of Lugarda. He whacked the fleas from his boots with the whisk and slipped into Bandini's house.

The din was deafening. It assaulted the senses. It raised the hair on his arms. The men were stomping their booted feet to the sounds of the band. Dust rose from the wooden plank floor, suspended like a haze. The women were clapping time, seated on chairs and benches placed against the two long walls of the room. The band was at one end of the dance floor, the men at the other. A bright yellow glow warmed the room. Whale oil lamps cast eerie shadows. The air was thick, loud with laughter, shouts and whoops. Bill took his place in line with the men.

Each man in turn went onto the floor alone, stomping, strutting, twirling and clapping, stopping in front of a woman with whom he wished to dance. She might flutter her fan, or hide her face behind it, giggle and point to the next woman. If she liked what she saw, she would rise and dance with the man, lifting and flouncing her full skirt, raising her arms, snapping her fan and fingers, kicking and stomping, taking a full turn around the room before returning to her seat to fan herself cool.

One woman, with a clay pot of water balanced on her head, danced con-tinuously. Her hair was braided, coiled and pinned with a large comb at the crown to make a bed for the water jug. Her upper body remained still; hips, legs and feet kept constant motion. Her arms moved to an entirely different rythym, smoothly, unearthly—now at her sides, now over her head, then extended, fingers snapping as she slowly twirled—the movements mesmeriz-ing. Her grace, at half the speed of the other dancers, was the grace of a god-dess at play. It was Lugarda—Bill's eyes never left her.

He tried to catch her glance, but Lugarda never broke her trance, and then Bill was given a shove. "Vaya güero," someone yelled. It was his turn. He handed off his coat and tap-danced down the line of women, never stop-ping long enough to invite a partner, twisting and turning to keep Lugarda in sight. She seemed to be following, in slow-motion mimicry of his steps.

Bill recognized 'Zul and paused in front of her to jump and stomp like a man possessed. She hid behind her fan. To his relief, she finally rose, folding the fan with a nervous laugh. 'Zul was more delicate than she had appeared at La Playa. She had made up her lovely face and done her hair in braided coils. Her smile was sweet and shy as a twelve-year-old's. She matched Bill's manic step as he leaned close enough to shout.

"Pablo's out back with the horses. He wants to see you."

She blushed and snapped open her fan to hide her delight. They finished their turn, Lugarda hovering behind like a wind-up doll, automatic and emotionless, perfect. Bill said, "Gracias," and bowed. Then he resumed dancing down the other line of women, one eye always on Lugarda.

She had positioned herself at the end of the chairs, her back to them, giving an occasional glance Bill's way, her eyes downcast, dancing for the shouting group of men. Bill worked his way up the row of women, old and young, married and maidens, stepping at double time until he was only three feet behind Lugarda.

There he stopped, keeping his feet pounding, and began to mimic her arm movements, swaying upper body and head stillness. Lugarda had on the same light blue dress as at La Playa, but the shawl was now of loose dark lace and tied around her waist. Her arms, neck and half of her shoulders were bare. Fine free strands at the base of her hairline tapered to a dark down.

Lugarda could hear Bill stomping behind her. She knew he was waiting for her to turn. She let him wait. "Baile," the men shouted, clapping even louder. Bill had given up following her arms; now he concentrated on her hips, trying to match their movement. Lugarda finally turned, slowly, first with head and neck, looking over her shoulder, then her body twisting to follow, hands held high, fingers snapping. The tops of her breasts swelled, stretched upward by her raised arms. Her mouth opened to take a deep breath. Tiny beads of sweat clung to her upper lip. She met Bill's eyes, she smiled and he could see her teeth and tongue, white and pink and wet.

Lugarda turned twice more in front of him, slowly round, never losing her rhythm, giving Bill a smirk the second time, serious the third. Then she moved back to the center of the room, looking toward the band, encouraging them to keep going. Bill was tempted to follow her, but took his place with the other men, panting, waiting for a turn again.

He stood, still swaying; his heart raced; dust tickled his throat. The noise was deafening. The house vibrated like a thing alive. He found his coat and ducked outside for a drink and some fresh air. Sweat-damp clothes stuck to his skin and were quickly cool in the night breeze. He wondered if the Indian dances were as wild as this. He could faintly hear drums, or the vibration of the stomping, off the close-shadowed hill.

Bill was full of Lugarda. There was no other way to express how he felt. He had taken her inside, possessed her like a vampire, and now she was his. He prayed she felt the same. He would marry her if she did. He would ask her no matter what.

The dance had cleared Bill's head. He would stay in California. He had to. He ducked behind the building to seek Pablo's counsel. It was Pablo who had so lyrically alerted him to Lugarda's charms. It was Pablo who had taught him to dance. He would know the next step.

PABLO was leaning on the corral gate, talking to 'Zul. She had pulled her shawl tight around her head and shoulders. She rested against him.

"I want to marry Lugarda," Bill blurted. He took a breath. 'Zul stood back. "Lugarda Osuna. I want to marry her," he told them.

'Zul put her hand to her mouth but it was too dark to see any expression. Pablo snorted.

"Bill, you have met 'Zul, yes? We were just talking about Lugarda."

"What were you saying?" He looked from one to the other.

Pablo was silent for a moment. He laid his hand gently on Bill's trembling arm.

"Amigo, here is the truth: Half of the caballeros, even the oldest, and all of their sons want to marry that woman. She flirts, she dances like a dream, she'll show an ankle, flutter her fan, smile, whisper in your ear, maybe even sneak out for a ride, and let a man kiss her hand or cheek or throat. But Señorita Lugarda Dionicia Osuna will marry her childhood sweetheart, José María Alvarado, the ex-governor's son and owner of Rancho San Marcos, right next door to Señor Osuna's Rancho San Dieguito. The families will be united, the ranches will be united; they will have many children, and hopefully a daughter as beautiful as her mother. They will live happily ever after. Just like in your fairy tales."

There was bitterness in Pablo's tone. 'Zul said something and they spoke quickly in Luiseño.

"I still want to marry her. I have to try," Bill protested.

"There is no place for you in this happy scene. You can surely marry one of the other girls, maybe even a Bandini daughter. You made your debut. You have danced handsomely. I will have 'Zul listen among her sisters to see which muchacha covets you for herself. I will find out who wants his daughter to marry a fair and green-eyed American. We will make a good match, one that brings a ranch with it as a dowry."

This was not what Bill wished to hear. He turned to 'Zul. "When does Lugarda go home to San Dieguito?" he asked in Spanish. "I could maybe see her there. We were leaving tonight—it is on our way."

"Mañana, early, with her mother and Señor Osuna," she said, head down, hiding behind her bangs.

Pablo corrected her. "Tomorrow in the afternoon. Osuna is trading with the captain in the morning."

"Pablo, I must do this. We can stop by for just a moment on our way to your ranch. I'll ask her father and then we go on. Yes or no, we have nothing to lose. I have to ask him. She is in here." Bill patted his breast over his heart. "I feel her everywhere." His arms fluttered. "She is all I see . . . I am possessed," he muttered, as surprised as they were.

Bill could see them better, now his eyes were adjusted to the dark. They were staring, wide-eyed, mute.

"Pablo, it was you who filled my head with visions of Lugarda. Now I've found her, you want me to forget her?"

'Zul looked at Pablo and he shrugged. He shook his head, but said, "I will take you to the Osunas tomorrow. I never knew she was engaged to José María Alvarado. A lot happened while I was gone."

"Thank you, that's all I ask."

"But we leave now. I do not want to be here. I must find my people. Everything has changed." Pablo hung his head. "I am sorry."

'Zul took his hand and put it to her lips.

She had surely confirmed the loss of Pablo's ranch, but Bill couldn't think about that now. He said to her, "I brought a beautiful French wedding dress with me, for my bride. Now it is for Lugarda. Tell her we will visit tomorrow afternoon, please."

Pablo translated this proposal, and 'Zul slipped away with an Indian word of goodbye, never looking at Bill.

"We'll have to get the dress."

"It's here," Pablo said impatiently. "I brought it. Everything is ready."

They checked the saddled horses, stood with them silently while the band took a minute's break, then led them away as the music started up. About three hundred yards down the trail toward the ship, they mounted and turned north on a well-worn wagon road.

4

EL CAMINO REAL

I T WAS too dark to see where they were going, but Bill could make out Pablo's trailing horse in the gloomy glow of the cloud-and-fog-enshrouded half-moon. The horses knew the road, which led along the east side of the estuary of False Bay and up Rose Canyon to Sorrento Valley, then on through the hills to San Dieguito River and the Osuna ranch.

This was the old El Camino Real, or King's Highway, which linked the missions of California, all of which were inland, where the soil was richer and water more reliable than along the coastline. There was a shore trail, but it was broken and there was little pasture or sweet water for the horses. Pablo planned to ride on the open beach from San Dieguito to the Santa Margarita River. "This is actually a shortcut and will let us arrive at Las Flores without being seen. I want to surprise the Picos. They will think they are being visited by a ghost." That was all the plan he had.

Bill hadn't been on a horse in a few years. He was tired and sore after an hour. They pulled off the trail to the right, riding up San Clemente Canyon in a running stream to cover their tracks. It was even darker there, the banks choked with huge trees, but the horses never faltered. Upstream, they rode into a clearing, unsaddled, tied the animals to graze and fell to the ground. It had been a long day.

Pablo had soft cured deerskin sheets to wrap in, rabbit skin blankets for warmth and tanned cowhides to lay on the ground: a good trade for a pair of sailor's duck trousers.

Bill fell into a deep sleep, his first on California soil, a deep grateful sleep, scented by live oaks and sage, mustard weed and soft new grass.

/ / /

When he opened his eyes, it was well after daybreak. The sun was up, pale behind the gray curtain of overcast. Pablo was chewing on a grass stem, staring at Bill. He looked like he hadn't slept much.

"This is a taste I've missed." He sucked the sweet stem.

"You should have woken me. It's late."

"Sleep is good. You'll need all your strength today. I would have slept if I could."

They were in a meadow of wild oats, up about a foot after an early rainy season. The big trees along the stream were towering sycamores, devoid of leaves in winter, and encinos or live oaks, with dark gray trunks and small prickly evergreen leaves. The largest oaks were about four feet in diameter at the trunk, with a heavy canopy sixty feet in circumference.

Oaks provided the natives with their staple food of acorns—to be ground, blanched and roasted as a kind of bread, or boiled as mush. The acorns were gathered and stored whole in elevated baskets, to last the year in their hard shells. The big trees also offered shade, shelter, a bed of leaves and plenty of long burning firewood. To Pablo, every oak was campground and larder. And California was covered in them.

Near to any oak grove, set in a large stable granite rock, were ancient grinding holes, ready for the acorn gatherer, who had only to take a round stone from the stream, fill the hole with acorns and pound them to a pulp. This pulp was cleaned of hulls, soaked twice overnight in water, then mixed with sea salt, or deer fat or just a bit of fresh water, and roasted on a flat rock in the fire. The patty was eaten with whatever greens or roots or nuts or meats were at hand. A simple, satisfying, and in California, a bountiful existence— with dancing every night to insure a long dreaming sleep.

As they left the camp, they passed a series of grinding holes in a big black rock by the stream. When Bill asked Pablo to show him how acorns were ground, he sniffed, "That's women's work, and these nuts aren't ripe. Let's get going so we arrive in time for lunch."

B I L L was expecting to see an abundance of game in California. He was not disappointed. That second day he saw herds of deer and antelope, rabbits, frogs, thousands of ducks, geese, quail and doves. There were also the animals to eat them: puma, bobcat, bear, golden eagles, great condors, hawks and small wolves they called coyotes. And snakes.

Pablo wanted to show him every kind of snake in California. He would leap from his horse to race off and return with a gopher snake, black and tan and mustard, which was always angry; or a king snake, striped or banded dark brown and white, docile and unconcerned. The king could beat a rattler in a fight. He had antivenin in his blood.

There were racers, striped or yellow, barely visible as they streaked through the grass, shy and nervous to the touch. In the streams or on the riverbanks were garter snakes, common to the entire United States. The rattlesnakes Bill had known in other forms. The California rattlers were small and gray with diamond patterns. They were fast and deadly, the only California snake that was dangerous.

Bill humored Pablo by handling the friendlier reptiles. A snake's skin was wonderful to feel; every bit of it its clean, cool, dry surface as sensitive as your fingertips, and more responsive. A snake can move across your arm by flexing its coils, or by "walking" with its underbelly, gliding along in a straight line through scale control. When a snake's skin gets too beat up and rough, he sheds it by crawling between tight branches, or through a crack in a rock, pulling it off from head to tail, emerging bright and smooth, shiny as a new hatchling.

Snakes were Pablo's boyhood toys and pets, colorful and active, wild but tameable. In the winter, on cold mornings they would snuggle docilely with him to warm up, then want to escape to catch food, or hide and glide through the grass. When they were lost, you found another. Like the oak trees, they were never far away. They transported him back to childhood and happy times.

His favorite snake was one he called a rosy boa, less than two feet long, pink, black and silvery with a stubby tail. When frightened, it would make itself into a tight ball, head hidden inside. Then if you left it alone, it would slowly uncurl, crawling over your arm or leg unconcerned. These boas were tame, dainty, nocturnal and beautiful. They were the rarest of the local snakes and prized. Pablo often carried one in his pocket for company.

Beside the delays for snake hunting, Pablo had to show Bill the Torrey Pine grove on the seaside bluffs at the head of Sorrento Valley. The Kumeyaay, the tribe that "belonged" to San Diego Mission—called Diegeño by the Spanish—would come in pine nut season to gorge on ripe nuts, and to harvest abalone, mussels, clams and scallops that lay in profusion on the rocks, on the sandy beach and in the estuary.

They skirted a ranch called Penasquitos, avoiding contact, and finally began to descend from a sage-covered hill into the San Dieguito River Valley. It was about a mile wide, with a floor covered in grass and oaks, divided by a winding sandy riverbed. From the hilltop, they could see about five miles up the valley and one mile across an estuary to the beach and a gray sea. The grassland was dotted with grazing cattle.

"All stolen from San Diego Mission," said Pablo. "There must be four or five thousand. Each hide is worth two dollars."

"How could he steal five thousand of them? They're not exactly hidden."

"He stole the ranch. Just like Pico. Most of the cattle came with it." Pablo turned his horse down the hill toward the river. "Osuna was in the Spanish army, guarding the mission at San Diego. During the revolution the Californios supported Spain. They were not Mexican. They were a faithful Spanish colony, abandoned by their defeated country when Mexico won its independence. Juan María was forced to cut off his long monarchist braid, and pledge allegiance to the republic. If he had been born in Spain, he would have been deported." Pablo raised his eyes.

"Corporal Osuna took advantage of the chaos of the new republic and the breakup of the mission system. He knew the right people. He had intimate knowledge of the workings and wealth of the missions. He got himself elected alcalde; he assisted Juan Ortega, the first civil administrator of San Diego Mission." Pablo waved his rein-free hand in a circle.

"In 1839, after five years of blatant corruption on the part of Juan Ortega, Governor Alvarado removed Ortega from this post and installed Señor Osuna as mission administrator. This was the same Governor Alvarado whose son will marry Lugarda," Pablo added with a grunt.

"Ortega had stripped the mission of its flocks and given himself the two finest ranchos, Santa María and Santa Ysabel. You met Captain Edward Stokes, who married Juan Ortega's daughter and was given Santa Ysabel as a dowry. The only honest thing Ortega did was to establish eighteen Indian rancherías on mission pastureland in the San Dieguito River Valley . . . just like at Las Flores."

Pablo stared up the wide valley. It was beautiful. They crossed the sandy river and rode through belly-high grass. The horses tore at it greedily, chewing around their bits. Pablo yanked at his mount's head and picked up the pace.

"Not to be outdone by his predessesor, Osuna melted down the remaining silver and gold relics from the church, sold the stores of wine and grain to his friends, forced the Indians at San Dieguito further inland to salt-poisoned land, and took over this lush pasture for himself. He built a ranch house, furnished it by stripping the mission, then drove all of the mission livestock he could round up out to his new rancho. All this he did in the guise of mission administrator." Pablo spat out the words and reached for his water jug. He swigged and spit that out too. He swung to look at Bill.

"When Governor Alvarado approved Juan María's application for the title to Rancho San Dieguito, the cattle were marked with the Osuna brand. Those are the steers you see. His fortune was made . . . and everyone knows exactly how he made it. Just as they know about Pico."

Pablo struggled to control his emotions, then jerked his head to the east.

"The Osuna house is about two miles up the valley, on the north bank of the river. Vamos."

Anger had rendered his normally soft voice brittle and deadly.

When Bill had ridden away, Pablo muttered, "If those pinché Picos took my cattle . . ." It sounded just like a rattlesnake's rattle.

5

THE OSUNAS

P A B L O walked his horses leisurely upstream, letting them eat, calming himself. Bill felt like galloping, racing straight to Lugarda's heart, but he followed meekly, drinking in the scenery. The farther he came from the barren bleakness of San Diego Bay, the more he liked California.

"Will the sun come out?"

"I doubt it. You'll see the sun when we get inland another few miles. These are coastal clouds. San Marcos is sunny." Pablo turned to Bill. "The Alvarado ranch."

"I know." Bill didn't want to hear that name. He trotted ahead to wait under a big oak.

He stood beside his horses in the shade, resting his sore back and legs against the wide trunk. There were two horses to ride, but only one of him. He was exhausted and they were fresh. They had been still for a minute when a group of six antelope came browsing by. Two were bucks, with short curved horns. They were the size of a goat, only more delicate. The females were smaller and softer-looking, without the antlers. They were tan, white-bellied with black markings on the nose and tail. All were very alert. They saw the horses; Bill was sure they saw him, but they didn't shy.

When Pablo rode up the antelope trotted off about a hundred yards and continued grazing, amazingly unconcerned.

"I'm surprised they're so unafraid." Bill had heard how tasty they were. He remounted with a groan.

"Mexicans don't eat game. The antelope know this. They're a little more wary of an Indian." He gave a whoop and galloped after them. They bolted with great graceful leaps and disappeared up a slope into the brush. Pablo rode back.

"Beef is the Californio man's meat. Wild animals are only fit to feed the savages. These ranchers think steak three times a day will make them strong like a bull." He held up his hands as though weighing two oranges. "Huevones." He laughed sourly. "Big balls."

"Americans eat everything. We love to hunt," Bill said, to cheer Pablo.

"Good. I traded a shirt for two beautiful bows and a quiver of arrows."

"I'm not much good with a bow."

"It's easy. As you've noticed, the game is tame."

"Except for the bears."

"They're tame too. Only they do the hunting."

T H E Osuna ranch house nestled against a hillside, in the shade of three huge oaks. It was one long single-story building with unattached stables, storerooms and a bunkhouse. The walls were of unadorned adobe, the roof clay tile. A veranda swept the front, with one door and two small glass windows facing the grasslands and river. The house had a humble look. It was a frontier cabin, everything handmade, the woodwork rough and unfinished.

They saw no one as they rode into the yard, dismounted and tied the horses by a trough. Bill washed his face. Pablo stuck his whole head in the water and shook it dry. He ran a comb through his wet hair, slicking it back. It was cut straight at the jawline.

Señora Osuna appeared, framed in the open central door. She stepped onto the porch.

"Hello, Señor Marshall, welcome. You're just in time for lunch. You too, Pablo. How was the ride? We came after the dance, sleeping in the carreta, I couldn't spend another night in that flea-infested town. Come in, come in. Adelante. We were expecting you."

Pablo took the horses to the stable. Bill followed her in, stomping his boots on the veranda to release the dust, and any fleas. She was right. The fleas were a problem in San Diego. He tried not to scratch.

Inside, the house looked richer, with a polished tile floor, a Persian rug and European furniture as well as homemade pieces. A round table was set with real china, delicate blue and white, on a starched tablecloth with linen napkins. There was a matching tea set. Bill sat in a chair that seemed too slight for his frame.

"Buenas tardes, Mamá, Buenas tardes, Señor Marshall."

Lugarda came through the room's back door to sit next to Bill. He felt himself blushing. A wave of warmth surged from his heart to his head, down his back and into his legs. All aches dissolved.

"Buenas tardes, Señorita Lugarda." He rose carefully, feeling huge, bobbed his head, and sat back down.

She was wearing a white embroidered blouse with long sleeves and a high neckline. A long tan riding skirt covered her dark brown boots. Bill could smell a waft of perfume. Jasmine? Should he have used her first name? He didn't look directly at her.

Señora Osuna called out the door, "Pablo. Por favor. Please come."

Lugarda said, "He'll take his lunch with 'Zul, Mami."

Señora Osuna turned and came to sit at Bill's other side. She removed her kid gloves and folded them into a skirt pocket, rubbing some color into her smooth white hands.

"That's a shame," she was saying. "Pablo's such good company. A bright boy and always knows the best gossip. I'm very surprised he sold the family ranch to the Picos. He was so proud of it." She watched her guest with the corner of an eye, opening her napkin with a snap, placing it precisely on her lap.

"He didn't sell it." Bill saw her eyebrow rise in an arch to wrinkle her smooth brow. "Pico somehow forged the papers while Pablo was gone. He's on his way to find out exactly what happened."

Bill looked at Lugarda. She was so close that his thoughts scattered. He let his eyes speak.

"How could Pico do that?" Lugarda asked her mother. "'Zul says Pablo is heartbroken." She looked to Bill for confirmation.

He smiled weakly. He was considering his own pounding heart. Señora Osuna rang a blue and white porcelain table bell.

She answered her daughter matter-of-factly. "Pío Pico promoted his brother, Andrés, from sergeant to general, and he moved the capital from Monterey to Los Angeles. Pico is the governor. He does what he wants."

She rang the bell again. The tinkling brought Bill back. "What about the law, Señora Osuna?"

"What law? If there could be a law, it is in Mexico City, two thousand miles distant. You saw San Diego; you rode from there to here. Did you see any policía or soldiers or lawyers? My dear illiterate husband is the only official in all of San Diego. El Alcalde: mayor, justice of the peace and judge. Ha."

"Mamá, what if Pico did forge the papers? That's not fair. We could tell everyone. Pico would have to give the ranch back." Lugarda's mouth curved angrily. Her feet kicked, bumping Bill's under the table.

"Who would make him? Your father? Pico elected him alcalde, and he can just as easily dismiss him. Andrés Pico controls the pathetic army. Gossip will not affect him. And many people were jealous of Las Flores, not just Pico. Pico doesn't really care about the ranch. It is Mission San Luis Rey he covets. He had it once. He wants it all."

She looked at Lugarda meaningfully. Lugarda bit her lower lip.

"Here, there is no law. On our ranch my husband and his sons—your brothers—are the law. You know that. That is all the law we have."

Turning to Bill, she said, calmer, "There are no fences in this land. The map of our ranch is a piece of paper with a square outlined by drawings of hills. Not even we know where the borders are. Fortunately, it is signed by Governor Alvarado."

Bill winced, hearing that name again. 'Zul came in with two full plates; she left without a word to bring more.

"The next ranch is the same, and the next, and beyond that the Indians roam and say they own everything. Who knows? Here one is happy to be alive, clean, with food to eat, and occasional company from the civilized world."

'Zul brought a deep soup bowl and a pitcher of lemonade, which she poured. When she had gone, Señora Osuna said, "Please let us give thanks, and eat. Lord, thank you for your blessings. Amen."

The meal was hearty: a beef and onion broth; corn bread tamales filled with pork, olives and mild chiles, all tied in a husk; and the ubiquitous steaks of tough beef with a very mild green sauce that Lugarda said was made from tomatillos, something like a small green tomato. A covered basket with a linen liner held a warm pile of thick corn tortillas.

When they had finished, an herb tea was poured.

Señora Osuna wanted to know all the news from Europe and America. Bill did his best, but did not know much more than she did. Lugarda was quiet.

"And what brings you to our ranch, Mr. Marshall?" Señora Osuna sipped her steaming cup, looking innocently at him over the blue rim.

"I am riding with Pablo to Las Flores." Bill could feel Lugarda's eyes. He surrendered his to hers. "I was hoping to see your daughter again."

Lugarda widened her eyes and opened her mouth in mock surprise.

"And your ship? The *Hopewell* sails day after tomorrow, doesn't it?" Señora Osuna was tapping her teacup with a fingernail.

Bill took the plunge. "I'm not going with the ship," he said to Lugarda. "I'm staying in California."

Now her surprise was real.

"That's wonderful," said Señora Osuna. "We need colonists like you. You'll have to declare allegiance to Mexico."

"How do I do that?" Bill sought safety with the mother.

"Pico. You petition the governor for citizenship."

"Oh."

"And you must belong to the Catholic Church. The priest will—"

"Pablo can arrange that," He said quickly. "That's all?"

"That's all. Then you'll need some land to grow cattle . . . and a wife."

Señora Osuna held his eyes. Lugarda was looking too, amused. This was Bill's chance. Be bold, had been Pablo's advice. Be bold, you have nothing to lose.

"I brought a wedding dress," Bill said, not daring to look at Lugarda. "A beautiful French wedding gown with a veil and train."

"Smart man. That's half the price of a bride in this lonely corner of the world. I wish you luck."

"I was hoping that Lugarda would wear it."

Mother and daughter looked at each other, then at Bill. They were obviously confused. He flushed red as a beet.

"If it fits her, then she may have it," he backtracked in embarrassment.

Neither mother nor daughter said a word. Lugarda's blush was just as deep as Bill's. She kept her eyes downcast, twisting her napkin.

Finally Señora Osuna sighed. "Then this is a serious matter."

She looked from one to the other. They were both watching her.

"I suppose we had better have a look at this famous dress, Lugarda," she said lightly. The situation amused her. She sat back, sipping her tea.

Lugarda waited a moment, searching her mother's face. Then she nodded and gave Bill a tiny smile, her first real sign of encouragement.

"It is a generous offer you have made to my daughter," Señora Osuna said formally. "Please show us the dress. I would be very interested to see what new fashion the Paris designers have invented."

When Bill didn't move, she said, "You may bring it now."

He jumped. With a "Con permiso," he flew out the door.

PABLO and 'Zul were eating at an outdoor table near the bunkhouse.

"I'm going to show them the dress," Bill shouted. "Where are the pack saddles?"

'Zul spoke to Pablo.

"'Zul wants to see the dress too," Pablo said, disgusted.

Bill returned to the dining room with 'Zul and the tightly tied bundle, unopened since packing a year ago. When they entered, mother and daughter were speaking intently in rapid-fire Spanish. They went quiet. Bill held up the bundle and handed it to Lugarda with a flourish.

"Never open a gift for a woman, my mother always told me. The opening magnifies the pleasure."

"So this is really a gift?" Lugarda smiled slyly.

"If it fits, it's yours."

She tore at the strings, unwrapping the outer oilskin and then the old white muslin sheet used for protection. She held the crumpled dress up to her breast and pulled it to her shape. It smelled of staleness, and a whiff of whale, but not too strong. The dress was silk, and so white it colored Lugarda's yellowed-ivory complexion.

"Oh, Mamá, please, could I try it on? It is beautiful. Feel how soft and light it is. Please."

She handed the dress to her mother and knelt on a chair, her arms draped over the back.

"Por favor, mamá, don't say no. I so want to try in on."

Señora Osuna examined the fabric, stitching, lace and hem. She looked at the veil and train and at the sheer nightdress that had come with the wedding gown. Then she turned to Bill with raised eyebrows.

He nodded and said, "Yes."

"Well then, yes, try it if you must. 'Zul, you had better help. Be careful not to rip anything."

They rushed from the room. Bill sat and sipped his cooled cup of tea. When he looked up, Señora Osuna was staring at him.

"So you want to marry my daughter." She shook her head and smiled sympathetically. "You've only known her two days . . . but that is not unusual. Men ask for her hand the moment they meet her. Why do you think you want to marry Lugarda?"

"She is very beautiful," he offered.

"Is that it? I think not. A man does not want to marry every beautiful woman he meets. He must have a vision of himself with her, and the children they will have, and the life they will lead. It is a whole fantasy that Lugarda somehow calls forth. An idyll, in which the poor man sees himself living happily ever after. Beauty may be the trigger, but there must be more, much more."

"Yes, there is more." Bill said faithfully. "I feel . . ."

"Think," she said. "Maybe it is you; it is the man who has within him the capacity to create this happiness he imagines, not Lugarda. Maybe she only shows him what is possible for him to achieve. My daughter is—"

Lugarda walked deliberately into the room, stepping as to a wedding march. 'Zul followed, carrying the train. The bride stopped before them. She stayed still, serious. Lugarda looked like a goddess in a Renaissance painting, luminescent in white, pale behind her veil.

She lifted the gauze so that they could see her enchanted face. "I think it fits, no?"

She removed the veil carefully and handed it to 'Zul. Then she slowly turned. It was a fitted dress, not bell-shaped like the California style. It only opened wide at the ankle-length hem and was trimmed there with white ermine. The bodice was cut low and trimmed with the same white fur. The arms were wrist-length and tight at the ermine cuffs. The dress was simple, elegant and fit her perfectly.

'Zul and Lugarda both beamed. Bill beamed back.

"It is absolutely gorgeous, beyond words," he said. "I have never seen it worn by anyone. It fits you perfectly. It must be yours."

Lugarda smiled. In that smile Bill did see the promise of eternal bliss.

"It's scandalous . . . beautiful," declared Señora Osuna. "The French—"

"Thank you, I accept," Lugarda said. She smiled haughtily at her mother, turned and walked regally from the room.

"When she returns, you must tell her of your true intentions," Señora Osuna said to Bill coldly. "I'm sure you already know she is engaged to José María Alvarado. If you do not marry, and there is very little chance you will, then she will give back the dress." She held up a finger to still his protest.

"I will take my siesta in the next room and leave you two to talk. I should, of course, chaperone, but . . . I know you must . . . we must, as they say, nip this in the bud. I trust my daughter and I am willing to trust you with her. I do not want you to mislead each other. You must both tell the truth. As far as my husband is concerned, I will have been with you all afternoon."

She stood and offered her hand.

"Please tell 'Zul to bring the tea to my room. And could you please ask Pablo if he brought any books. I would love one to read, in any language."

"Of course," Bill said. "We did bring a few books."

"Good afternoon, Mr. Marshall. Good luck."

The door closed. Bill poured another half cup of tea and swallowed it. He walked to the window. The sun still shone weakly through the overcast. He looked down the valley, across the silver strip of river, into the haze where the sea must be.

When Lugarda and 'Zul returned, he repeated Señora Osuna's instructions. 'Zul cleared the table, taking the teapot and a clean cup last, then shut the door behind her.

Bill was alone with Lugarda.

"Your mother . . ."

"My mother is a witch," she said irritated. She sat on an armchair and crossed her legs. Tall riding boots came almost to her knees.

"Do you ride?" he asked.

"Yes, nearly every day."

"I have to get used to it. I'm still sore." Bill stood, nervously rubbing his hip.

"Here everyone rides. The distances are great and the roads rough. Wagons are slow and uncomfortable. Only my mother takes the carreta." She wrinkled her nose.

"The dress is beautiful."

"There was another with it, very fine, almost transparent. Is that worn under?" She lowered her eyes and blushed.

"No. That is for the bride to wear the night of her wedding. The French call it a peignoir. It is only to be seen by her husband."

Their eyes locked.

"Do you give that to me also?"

"Only if you will marry me. I want to marry you. You may wear it on our wedding night."

Lugarda leapt to her feet and went to the window.

"Are you mad? You're joking." She looked out.

"I am proposing. I came here to ask you to marry me."

She turned. She was not smiling. "You can't be serious. You've only known me a day. I'm already promised. My father would never approve. It is not possible."

Bill sank to his knees and took her hand. "Please, you must marry me, Lugarda. I loved you the second I saw you. We will be happy. I will be a perfect husband."

She pulled him up with both hands, very close. He could see the heartbeat on her throat. He wanted to kiss it.

"Your proposal is very kind. The dress is beautiful, precious. I did try the night dress." She blushed. "I . . . it . . . I am not sure I could ever wear it, even for a husband."

Bill searched her eyes for a sign. She looked down, then up again. She gave each of her words space and weight.

"I will consider your proposal in my heart, yes, but as you know . . . in California you must have the father's blessing . . ."

He kissed her then, first on the throat, then the cheek and finally the mouth. His arms slipped around her waist. He wanted to touch her skin, to feel her pulse, to know her with his hands, to possess her by such knowledge.

She let him kiss her. She felt his lips, soft and smooth, his teeth, his tongue. Her eyes closed. He tasted like tea.

His hands slid down to rest on her buttocks, small and soft.

She pulled back. "Only my husband may touch me there," she said sharply.

Bill kept his hands where they were.

"We'll marry," he said. "You'll be my wife."

She could feel him bulging against her, and where they met, a strange spreading sensation of infinite pleasure and warmth.

"You have to court a woman. You don't just . . ." She searched for the right word. "Marry her."

She held his shoulders and leaned back to arm's length, which only increased the pressure at their hips. He could see her nipples' outline on her blouse, where her breasts had pushed against him.

"You talk, you dance, you kiss her hand. Then maybe a week later you kiss her wrist," she instructed

"Lo siento," he said, which was not right. He meant to say excuse me, which is perdóname or discúlpame, but he said "Lo siento," again, softly, which means I feel, I sympathize.

Somehow this was the magic word. She smiled and quit pulling away.

He turned his head to kiss her hand. He kissed her wrist.

"Then you kiss her shoulder, but weeks later," she sighed, and he kissed her shoulder. "Then her neck or the top of her breast," which he did too, through the cloth. "Then, months later you kiss her on the lips."

"It feels like months," Bill said, and kissed her on the lips, hard, then soft and sweet. This time, Lugarda kissed him back.

As they were kissing, he was kneading her buttocks, which felt like two large breasts. She couldn't think to stop him. She was coming apart where they touched in front. He was tugging at her skirt. Her whole body was covered in cloth from wrist to throat to ankle. There was endless material and underskirt and finally pantaloons with an opening where her legs met, and warm skin at last. He stroked the back of her velvet thigh.

She took her mouth away. She was melting everywhere.

"Then you become engaged, then you plan the wedding, then you marry, and then, only then, you may touch me there," she panted.

"How long does it all take?"

"About a year, more than a year," she breathed into his ear.

He caressed her inner thighs, one by one with the back of his hand and then his fingertips, just stopping before they met. Lugarda was watching him, questioning. She was very still. Then her long lashes fell and her eyelids closed like a clamshell. She leaned into him and pressed her mouth to his.

Bill kissed her lower lip, bit it and felt deeper to slipperiness. He swirled around her mouth and stroked and tapped until she too was nibbling his lips and pushing against his fingers. She smelled her own sweet womanly scent. She was leaking, sinking, falling, floating, whirling around his touch, edging into delirium. He held his breath. She gnawed his upper lip. A horse trotted by, then another, a third. They froze, eyes opened. Bill let her skirt drop and put his guilty hands behind his back. Lugarda took two deep breaths. She looked frightened, then pained. He thought she might cry.

Instead she hissed fiercely. "And first . . . first you must speak to her father." Then he was alone.

Bill took a last breath of the air they had shared. He found his hat, checked for any signs that might be incriminating, and went out into the dim, cool evening. He could hear the household noises clearly now, cooking, voices, horses, dogs, chickens, and in the distance a coyote.

He wanted to hear a bear growl, or a puma howl. He felt like howling himself, as he found some brush to pee behind—he felt that good. He splashed his face at the water trough, washed his hands. When he was done, Bill could still faintly smell the sweet luxury of her jasmine-scented flesh.

Then Pablo was there, 'Zul just behind. Pablo looked worried. The dusk shadowed his eyes. There were deep circles under them.

"Juan María and his sons have arrived. They have eaten on the road and are too tired to entertain us. This is good, for we can leave without offending." He looked hopefully at Bill, who said nothing. He looked down. "Or we can stay in the guest rooms and 'Zul will bring us some corn, carne asada and tortillas, and we can leave in the morning."

"That sounds better, I'm hungry. I need to speak to Señor Osuna."

"You could see him at breakfast and meet afterward," said 'Zul, in Spanish.

"Bueno," muttered Pablo and turned to go. Bill followed.

"I will bring the supper," whispered 'Zul.

They strolled toward the guest rooms, along the north wing of the long house. Pablo was nervous.

"You are crazy, amigo," he almost shouted. "This family is bad. We should leave now and take 'Zul with us."

"Pablo, I have to talk to Señor Osuna. Lugarda . . . we kissed . . . She told me to ask her father for her hand. I want to marry her. She has my dress."

"She'll never. She's a tease. She's engaged to José María Alvarado. José is her childhood friend. You just arrived from nowhere, you're not part of her life." Pablo looked sick with worry.

"I am now. I will be. You're the one who told me I could be."

"Her father is compadre to José María's father. They are like brothers."

"Her mother likes me."

"Do not mistake hospitality, that is given as a matter of pride and duty and boredom, for affection."

"I like her too."

"No one in California likes her mother."

"I do. And you do too. You said so."

Pablo shrugged. "Everything has changed for me," he said sadly.

"For me also."

'ZUL came in with the food and Bill dug in. Pablo pushed his plate away. He sat back and watched Bill eat. 'Zul spoke to him in their language. She cheered him and he began to pick at his food. When she left with the empty plates, Bill asked Pablo what she'd said.

"She said, 'Don't worry, Pablo, Señor Osuna will have his balls for breakfast.'"

They blew out the candles and lay on their hard beds. Bill was picturing Lugarda in the peignoir; her curves and points veiled and revealed at once. In the wedding dress, she had seemed an apparition, unearthly, unrecognizable until she lifted the veil. In the night dress . . .

"She's no Virgin Mary, you know—loco," Pablo said to the dark.

"Go to sleep, High Cloud."

Pablo didn't respond.

"Who else?"

"'Zul told me her brother was playing with her when she was a little girl. God knows who else she allows."

"Which brother?"

"Leandro."

Bill pictured that for a while.

"With 'Zul too, till Lugarda made him stop. She threatened to tell her father—about herself, not 'Zul. 'Zul doesn't count." Pablo grunted. "Huh."

"You going to marry 'Zul?"

"She's married to the Osunas. She'll never leave Lugarda."

"Neither will I. We could have a double wedding."

Pablo exhaled with a growl. "Good night, tonto."

"Señora Osuna would like a book to read."

"My books are for Father González de Ibarra. They will be in the library at Mission San Luis Rey. Tell her that."

AFTER a mountainous dawn breakfast of scrambled eggs with spicy chorizo, tortillas, orange juice, liver with onions and roasted ears of corn sprinkled with red chile powder, Señor Osuna and Bill had their talk. Pablo had avoided the breakfast, saying he needed to prepare the horses. Lugarda and her mother did not attend, due to the early hour. The brothers had kept their heads to their plates, then excused themselves, Osuna acknowledging with a nod.

'Zul had served in silence and they had eaten mostly in polite, uneasy silence. Bill wondered if they all knew; if Lugarda had spoken to her mother, her father?

"I'm sorry we have no coffee to offer, only the native herbs with which to make tea. Please try. Yerba buena, it is called." Osuna poured two steaming cups.

It was too hot, even to sip, so Bill left the cup in its saucer and blurted out the only line he had, "Señor Osuna, with your permission, I would like to ask you for permission to marry your daughter, la Señorita Lugarda."

Pablo had written out the proper Spanish words to ask for Lugarda's hand. No misunderstanding possible. No way to avoid an answer.

The men locked eyes. Osuna took a gulp of tea without looking away. Either he was burning his tongue or just faking the drink, playing macho, taking his time. He put the cup down, wiped his mouth with the back of his hand. His eyes followed that hand to the table. He replied in halting English, without looking up.

"Señor Marshall, that is your name, I . . ." he searched for the word.

"Presume," Bill said.

"Presume, yes, presume . . . all the world is wanting to marry my pretty daughter. Every man is loving my Lugarda." Now he looked up. "Every man and maybe every boy too, no? She is so beautiful, she contain so much vida . . . so much life and joy of life, no man could say no to her.

"And here are many men, and no so many women." He nodded his head and looked into the palms of his hands. "The rest of us must marry Indios. You understand. My own grandfather married a Christian India de la mission, God bless her, my grandmother." He closed his weathered eyes and crossed himself.

When he opened them they were composed and clear and cold.

"By God's grace, we now have opportunity to marry with women of our own race. Here, the value of a woman like Lugarda has no limit. She is the best of California. Since her tenth year, I have received wedding offers for her, from friends, neighbors and strangers. So many offers. Excellent offers," he added disdainfully.

"I have accepted the wishes of the ex-governor of California, Señor Juan Bautista Alvarado, my benefactor and compadre; my friend. Lugarda will marry his son José María, in the spring. They were promised since childhood, and in my country, to men of honor, she is already married. The rancho of San Marcos will go to José María, and then to Lugarda's sons. We will be neighbors together. Our two ranchos will be the richest in San Diego, equal to Pío Pico's Santa Margarita y Las Flores."

Bill glared back at him then, hearing that name. Osuna examined his hands again.

"Too bad Pablo lost his ranch. You can never leave something so valuable. Hay que . . . you must guard it. Guard what has value with your life. Like my daughter, like my precious little daughter."

He looked Bill hard in the eyes, hard and dangerous and unmovable: the look of a predator, guarding his kin.

"But what if she loves me?" Bill pleaded, evoking that magic word, slashing with it like a sword, hoping to sunder that awful spell. "What value does love have here in California?" He slapped the table hard.

Osuna laughed, a genuine laugh. He slumped back in his chair. He knew he had Bill, right then and there, and so did Bill.

"Love! What is love? The love of a man for his daughter, of the daughter for her father, and for her mother. What could be stronger than that? Lugarda loves her family, her life, this ranch, her friends, her horses, even the land itself. And she loves José María since a little girl. Him she truly loves." He sipped his tea.

"If she loves you also, for two days, bueno. Buena suerte, you are a lucky man. But this love would be like a flea next to my biggest bull, compared to her love for her family, for José María. Just like a flea."

He reached down and caught one of those loathsome insects off his boot, rolled it to crush between thumb and forefinger, and flicked it back to the floor.

"Your ship will leave in two days, Señor Marshall. You will be on it. Foreigners are not allowed to stay in California. Lugarda will forget you, we will have our lives as before. Tranquilo, with no problems. I am sorry. I wish you well."

He got up, rang the bell, shook Bill's hand and said, "Please take oranges from my huerta, beef machaca, pigs and chickens if you like, for your voyage. Whatever you need we will be glad to give you."

'Zul came in, and stood.

Osuna told her to give Bill whatever he might want from the ranch stores. "Anything," he said. "Adiós, Señor Marshall."

He went into the next room, and closed the door.

"What would you like to take, señor?" 'Zul asked sympathetically.

"Only Lugarda," Bill snapped.

She shook her head sadly. "Nothing else?"

"No, nothing. Gracias."

He walked out and down the veranda to his room, slowly. His heels struck the rough boards like hammers nailing the lid on a coffin. The sky was still as gray and solid as a sheet of lead liner. The sun only made a white circle in the draping cloud. The horses stood ready, by the trough, heads down.

Pablo was in their room, sitting on one of the beds. He handed Bill his jacket and a cloth bundle.

"Lugarda sent back your dress."

"I gave it to her."

"She gave it back."

"Did you see her?"

"No."

They left the bunkroom. 'Zul was with the horses. Ramón and Leandro sat on the top stair of the veranda. There was no one else.

"Give my regards to Señora Osuna and your sister," Bill said to them.

"Bueno," Ramón answered softly.

"Adiós," said Pablo.

Leandro pushed back his hat. He had a long whip in his hand.

"Don't worry, güero, you'll find a nice Indian girl." He glanced at 'Zul. Ramón laughed. Pablo froze.

"Just like you," Bill said, and kept walking toward the horses.

The whip lashed out and the split rawhide tip flicked his right ear. It didn't take it off, like Bill knew it could, but it stung like a wasp and his cheek went hot. He faced Leandro and inclined his other ear. "Try this side, huevón," he taunted.

The whip snapped and Bill got his left hand up, took the cut as it curled around his fingers, held on tight and yanked hard. Leandro jerked forward and the whip flew as Bill ran toward him. He caught the butt in his right hand and hit Leandro with the weighted end, twice on the head, and twice on the neck as Leandro crumpled to his knees.

Bill raised the butt again. His free hand clutched a hank of oily black hair. Ramón had not moved. He shrugged. Pablo was still frozen. 'Zul shook her head slightly: a no. A backlit figure filled the doorway. No way to tell who. Bill took a few steps back and lashed Leandro as hard as he could across the shoulders. He threw the whip at him. Trembling, he turned away.

They got on their horses and rode. 'Zul didn't wave. No one did.

A S soon as Pablo and Bill were out of sight, the ranch house door flew open and Juan María Osuna burst out onto the front porch.

"Leandro," he screamed at his son. "You whipped a guest in my house? You picked a fight with a guest on my front porch? A man who had politely come to ask for your sister's hand, had offered a beautiful dress, had asked for no dowry? A man whom I had reduced by words of refusal to the size of a flea, who would take nothing, not even a tortilla, who was crawling from this house like a belly-kicked dog . . . You whipped our guest!"

Leandro rubbed his bruised neck. He would not look up. Osuna grabbed a riding crop that hung on a peg and began to lash his son methodically across the shoulders. When Leandro tried to protect himself, the crop came down viciously on his hands and arms until they retracted. Osuna continued with easier blows to the upper body, all the while yelling, "In my house. You whipped a guest. You disgraced me in front of my family, in my own house."

Ramón sat still as a stair, watching his brother take his medicine. When Leandro began to whimper, he said, "Papi, the Yankee touched our sister."

It was meant to be a defense and Osuna did pause for a second, whip poised. Then he brought it down again hard on Leandro's shoulder.

"And how do we know this?" Osuna sounded deadly. He had his eyes on Ramón, and Leandro shifted to take the blows in a less thrashed area.

"We heard the sailor tell Pablo Verdi."

At the doorway, Señora Osuna and Lugarda had been watching, 'Zul had come around to stand behind them. The mother, who was poised to rescue her eldest son, turned and slapped Lugarda on the mouth. She hit her again, grabbing her arm to pull her close and struck once more. Lugarda's lip began to bleed.

"No, Mami, he's lying. Please. You're hurting me. He's lying," she sniffed and tears began to fall.

Osuna kept slashing at Leandro.

"You heard something like that and you didn't tell me? When could this thing have happened?"

"In the afternoon," offered Ramón.

"It's a lie," Lugarda wailed.

Her mother yanked her by the hair and pulled her to the porch.

"We'll see who is lying," she said to her husband.

When they drew near, Osuna turned, and with his free arm backhanded his wife on the ear hard enough to knock her down. He never slowed his blows to Leandro's back. Señora Osuna scrambled to her feet.

"And where were you when all this took place?" Osuna demanded, finally leaving Leandro. "You can't even chaperone my own daughter in my own house. You let some cabrón Yankee ship deserter, in his second day on dry land, touch my daughter?" He slapped her again and she sank to her knees. Both hands covered her face.

"Don't, Papi. Don't hurt her," sobbed Lugarda. "It's not her fault. It's all a lie. Nothing happened. It's Leandro himself who always wants to touch me. He's jealous of any other man who comes near me." She stabbed her finger at Leandro, and helped her mother up, brushing off her dress, tears still streaming.

The porch went silent.

Osuna stared at Leandro, who shook his head and moaned, "No." Ramón gaped at Lugarda. His mouth flapped. He wouldn't meet his father's eyes.

Señora Osuna gasped for breath and began to shake Lugarda.

"You're lying," she said. "Admit you're lying."

Osuna glared at his wife and daughter. He turned to 'Zul. 'Zul was practicing the Indian art of making herself invisible. She had dropped her bangs, eyes on the cracks in the floorboards, willing her body to flow down through them into cool darkness. Osuna jerked her up by the braid and pulled her face to his. 'Zul slowly nodded her head once, glancing at Leandro, her eyes naked and defiant; an unmistakable yes.

Osuna flung her from him. He began to kick Leandro with toe, then heel of his polished boot, muttering, "In my house, my own son, in my house." Leandro grunted with each blow.

"Tell him you're lying," Señora Osuna kept begging Lugarda. She let go of her daughter and tried to hold her husband. "No more," she pleaded.

Lugarda watched Leandro's punishment for a few more kicks. When Osuna switched feet, she said, "That's enough, Papi." She held his arm. "The sailor never touched me and neither did my brother. Leandro only came into my room once with his thing out and waved it at me, to scare me."

Osuna shrugged her hand off. His boot tapped the floor. All eyes were on Lugarda.

"You never told me? You never told your mother?"

"I promised not to if he would leave 'Zul alone. He was making her do those things with him."

It took Osuna a second to know where first to strike. He started with a wood-chopping blow to Lugarda's outstretched arm.

"What do you think the maids are for," he hissed, as she staggered back and cried out. "Leandro can do what he likes with the whole heathen lot of them. Idiota," he croaked.

Then he turned to Leandro. He started in with the crop again, this time not sparing the head and neck. "I'm going to beat some respect into this son of a whore." He jabbed his bloodshot eyes at his wife. Leandro made himself into a tight ball, head buried.

Lugarda leapt from the porch and ran toward the stable, 'Zul close behind.

When they emerged, mounted, Osuna was pacing the veranda, cursing to himself. "In my house, my own son," he kept saying.

Ramón and Señora Osuna were unwinding Leandro, trying to remove his jacket to examine the damage. They made a long shadow, like some six-armed, three-headed monster. As she rode by, 'Zul carefully spat on Leandro's section of it.

His lips were moving. "I'm going to get you, putas," they whispered. "You too," he told his brother Ramón.

The crop swung ready from its peg on the porch.

L U G A R D A rode and did not stop until she reached San Marcos, where she threw herself into José María Alvarado's arms.

"Marry me now, I'm never going home again," she sobbed.

She clung to José María with all her body, so desperately that she frightened him, and when she tried to kiss him, he shrank from her hungry mouth, full of salty tears. But he held her and prepared a guest room for her, and sent a hand, a cousin of 'Zul's, galloping to inform Señor Osuna that his daughter was safe with the family of her betrothed, and would be returned on the morrow.

6

ENCINITAS

BILL and Pablo trotted for a long time, then walked in silence. Bill's hand still stung whenever he flexed it. There was a raised red welt where the whip had wrapped around it. He didn't enjoy fighting. But he was glad he'd been able to whack Leandro a couple of times for 'Zul and Lugarda. He took steady deep breaths through his nose to calm himself. Sometimes you had to fight a bully, win or lose, to stop him picking on you, and sometimes you just fought instinctively, as he had with Leandro, no thought but to give harm for harm.

Bill smelled the oaks as they passed, sage and wild rosemary, a pungent skunk so strong his horse laid back his ears. He breathed the moist thick air, aromatic with cow dung, the sweating horses and his own rank body—two long days without a bath.

Pablo had retraced their path to El Camino Real, then turned north. They crossed a marshy stream called San Elijo, and stayed on the road for three more miles. Then they left the wagon track to climb a toyon-and-sage-covered hill, on an animal trail, for about half a mile. They descended along a rivulet into a little valley choked with oak trees, whose dark canopy completely blocked the still overcast twilight.

They went single file. Pablo gave his horse his head and ducked low to avoid any sweeping branches. Here the smell was of damp and decomposing oak leaf, layered on rich black mud. Frogs croaked and splashed, doves flew from their nests. Twice Bill heard owls. In half an hour, they emerged at the valley's mouth, between two gentle hills separated by about one hundred yards of sand and a pebble bar, where the brook gurgled to disappear beneath the fine-grained beach. Beyond was the sea.

Bill inhaled the briny air. There was seagrass in the sandy valley. They turned out the horses to graze, hobbling two of them.

"This place is called Encinitas," Pablo said, "because the oaks are so thick. The land has been granted to Ybarra, the La Playa grog shop keeper," he added with a twitch of his nose.

"Encinitas is one of the few places the People can harvest acorns by the sea. We would come in late summer when it was warm, to play in the water; to pick acorns; to eat fish, and to gather clams and mussels at the rocky point about a mile south, where the waves are always big. There are lobster and abalone in the tide pools. Tomorrow we will take some at the early low tide. Then we can ride up the beach as you wished."

Bill was too tired to talk. He rolled out his skins and stared at the gray sky, brightened by the reflection of long lines of white water that flowed from crashing waves over the shallows to the shore.

There came a stiff breeze down the canyon, falling from night-cool land to warmer sea. They bundled against it and slept to the crack of breakers, their rumbling wash to the beach, and the tumbling of the pebble bar at high tide. Bill dreamed of whales.

"Great gray whales swimming in pods of ten or fifteen, jumping and splashing for joy, chasing each other, babies following their mothers who followed the fathers who followed their fellows. South, they flowed south and we followed them in our little boat, the mate standing at the bow with a barbed harpoon attached to a long rope with floats. He darted the harpoon at a whale close enough to touch, and we stroked furiously away as it sounded with a huge whack of its tail, surprised, stung.

"Then we went for a ride. A Nantucket sleigh ride. Towed by the whale for miles until it tired, and surfaced to lie puffing through its blow hole . . . as we slipped up to it.

"Now the mate had a razor-sharp lance in hand and he drove it between the whale's ribs and into its heart. The lance had no barbs. It was meant to slice its way out, a fountain of blood gushing through the hole it left; gallons of blood, barrels of red blood, and the whale went still. Then came the sharks. They slashed through the gore, tearing off great hunks of whale, turning the water to a bloody froth, a froth of pink bubbles . . . and someone was calling, saying, Bill, Billy."

"That was me." Pablo laughed. "That was no dream. That happened, remember?" It was barely light and the fog lay damp around them. "Let's go get breakfast. I can smell the seafood."

"Wait a minute, I need to wake up. Where are we? Did you dream too?"

"California, Encinitas. On the beach, low tide. No dreaming. Lobster and abalone for breakfast, then a bath."

"I never liked to kill a whale."

"Nor I. Before the whalers came we used to swim with them in the cove at La Jolla. They played like big dolphins. And they never ran into anyone. We didn't think to kill them: too much life to kill; too gentle, and too dangerous to provoke."

T H E Y snatched red spiny lobster from the tide pools, two big ones, and pried abalone from under the rocks with their knives. Pablo made a drift-wood fire and threw the whole lobsters on it until they turned brick red.

He scraped the abalone from their hand-sized shells, cut off the guts, then pounded the meat, which was about an inch thick, between two flat rocks until it made a thin tender patty the size of a tortilla.

He placed two washed stones at the edge of the fire, put the abalone on the stones and let them cook until they turned from translucent to white. They peeled them off the rocks with a knife and ate them hot. The pounding made them melt in the mouth. The flavor was delicious, delicately salty, like eating the sea itself.

The lobster they pulled to pieces, sucking the meat from the legs and body and chewing on the tougher tails. Bill thought they tasted like the ocean floor where they crawled. Unlike Atlantic lobster, they had no claws.

Pablo wanted to bathe in the sea, even though it was freezing. When Bill protested, Pablo teased him about his ripening odor. He insisted that Americans were just as shy of a bath as the Californios—who thought that ague and fever were the penalties for bathing. "La gripa," they called the illness that came from getting wet. Native People found this lack of cleanliness disgusting.

Californio women would ask their Indian servants to spend hours washing clothes, then put the clean garments on without bathing. They might crush a few flower petals and place them between their breasts, or splash on a few drops of rosewater, but that was it. Everyone knew that they did not even dis-robe to have sex, but wore pantaloons open at the crotch under a nightdress. It was possible that a Spanish woman was never, ever naked. Handmaidens reported that their mistresses even changed pantaloons without removing their skirts.

The men were even worse. No Indian had ever seen a Spaniard bathe. The good side to their foul odor was that no Spaniard, boss or soldier, could approach an Indian without being detected.

Bill had danced and ridden all night, slept, then ridden again, sweated through his interviews with the Osunas, slept, fought Leandro and ridden again. He needed a bath, even a freezing one.

They warmed themselves by the fire, piled on more driftwood and plunged into the sea to wash. It was stinging cold. Scrubbed pink, they ran back to the bonfire to dry.

Five Indians emerged from the oaks and came to stand by the blaze. They stripped their ragged clothes and skins and ran screaming to bathe. Bill had hastily turned to put his pants on when they appeared, and looked away when they stripped. They came out of the sea in goosebumps. A man, a woman, a young girl and two boys warmed by the fire, naked and at ease, chatting with High Cloud.

Bill went to catch the horses, saddled them and loaded the bedrolls. The fire had burned down. The Indians were wrapped in furs of rabbit and fox and bobcat. Their ragged clothes had been washed and were drying on the rocks. They looked wild and natural and were shy with him.

High Cloud made the introductions in Spanish. "Bill, I present you to my amigos, New Moon, Flat Nose, Coyote Jumps, Night Bird Owl and Cries at Night. She will have a new name when she is older."

He repeated the names in English with sign language flourishes of both hands. Bill tried not to laugh, but when he did, so did they.

"I told them your name means "Falls In Love Easily," Pablo said. "That's what got the laugh."

Bill and Pablo bade them "Adiós," and they all said, "Adiós, que les vayan bien."

That was to become Bill's favorite Spanish phrase. "That you go well," literally, or "go thee well." He loved to hear those words and feel their blessing.

7

LAS FLORES

N O W they rushed north, riding with the wind, everything lashed tight to the horses, the beach flat and hard with only a few small cobbles to dodge. The air was cool; a light south wind blew at half the horses' speed, a sea breeze that Bill breathed gratefully. The swim, the seafood, the air, the undulating ocean filling the whole left side of his vision, were restoring him. They cantered along high sandy cliffs, then past Batiquitos Lagoon, more high cliffs to Ponto, and on for about seven miles before Pablo slowed. The horses were blowing. Bill's legs were tired; he needed a rest.

They threw down the saddles, cooled and watered the horses. Bill lay flat while Pablo switched tack with the other mounts. Now it was Pablo who was restless, possessed. Bill stretched his legs, rubbed his back on a round rock and they rode again. This time the pace was a fast trot. The horses could go half the day at that speed and Bill settled in for some backside torture. But Pablo soon pulled up at the mouth of a river that smelled of rotten eggs, sulfur, rotting muck, something foul.

"Agua Hedionda," he said. "Stinking water. There's a nice ranch here; a sister of Lugarda is married to the owner."

Pablo wheeled his horse and set off again. By now there was no need to lead the extra mounts. They had gone too far to run home. Untied, they followed, like herd animals are supposed to follow.

The beach was uniform, flat with fine gray sand. The sandy cliffs were ruddy or golden, tall or short, and broken every couple of miles by a stream or an estuary. A feathered blanket of waterfowl covered the estuaries: ducks, teal, geese and pelicans in profusion. They endlessly flew overhead, landing to take off again, at times in formations thick enough to shadow the weak sun.

The estuaries were full of shrimp, scallops, breeding fish, fingerlings, crabs, weeds and every other form of bird food life that thrives in brackish water.

"We could live on ducks alone," Bill said. "Or abalone, or deer. This is the California I dreamed of: not a land to work like a farmer, dawn to dusk, but a place to harvest the natural bounty at leisure. Just like you say the Indians have always done."

Pablo gave Bill not a glance, trotting north, drawn to his home like a swallow, not to stop till he got there. And what then? He didn't have a plan. He already knew the answer to any question he might ask. He just had to see for himself and feel what he would feel. Like Bill with Lugarda.

The hair on Pablo's neck bristled and his sweat chilled. He spurred his horse. Damp gray sand, flecked with fool's gold, flew from his steed's hooves to splatter Bill, who dropped back a pace or two. He noticed the gold glitter and imagined how his life might unfold if only it were real.

A R O U N D noon, they crossed the San Luis Rey River and rode on two miles, to another, larger, river mouth. It was about a half-mile across, with water covering fifty yards in two channels. Pablo slowed to a walk, crossed the channels, turned in on the north bank, jumped down under a huge oak and lay on the ground.

"This is the Santa Margarita River," he said. "Rancho Santa Margarita is on the south side; Las Flores is at the next stream, just to the north."

Bill tied the horses to a low branch to cool before allowing them to drink. Pablo stripped to bathe in the river. He took out tallow soap and a little round mirror. He cleaned his slender body carefully, soaping from hair to toes. He rinsed, combed his wet hair, cleaned his nails with a knife, brushed his teeth with the smashed end of a stick, rubbed some crushed red berries on his cheeks and then took a brand new set of clothes from his saddlebag. He shook them out.

The pants were bright blue, like American cavalry pants, but with silver buttons instead of stripes down the sides; the shirt snow white, open at the neck with long sleeves and ruffled cuffs. He had a short tight jacket with gold braid on the shoulders, silver buttons down the front, and gold braid on the cuffs. His hat and dark boots were scrubbed and polished. He affixed large embossed silver spurs to his boot heels, and slipped a silver-studded band on his hat.

Bill brushed Pablo's black horse, slipped on a new red saddle blanket, dusted and cinched the saddle. Pablo attached silver disks to the halter sides and buckled on new reins with silver studs. He mounted. His horse sidestepped.

"Do I look like the owner of this ranch?"

"You got all that silver for our clothes?" Bill grinned. "You look like you own the whole country."

"Then get dressed and let's go find out exactly who owns what."

He was glowering, puffed up and fearless, and Bill gained some courage. He put on stiff clean clothes, combed his wavy hair and brushed his teeth. Bill gave Pablo a red silk scarf he had brought to trade, tied one on his own neck, and off they pranced like two dandies going to a dance.

P A B L O rode through Las Flores like a duke in his fiefdom, greeting those he knew or didn't regally, with a "buenos días, como están," and a touch of his hat. They trotted right up to his front door, tied the horses to a veranda rail and walked into the imposing two-story adobe house without knocking.

A stocky man sat at a rustic table in the main room, eating a bowl of soup. He had the drumstick of a chicken or a duck in one hand, a large spoon in the other. A rumpled military jacket hung open from thick shoulders, half covering his gray-stained undershirt. He didn't seem surprised to see them.

"Pablo, welcome, sit, have some caldo. María, dos platos más," he called out for two more bowls. He pushed back the nearest chair without getting up. Pablo didn't sit, so Bill didn't either.

"What are you doing here, Andrés, in my home." Pablo's voice trembled. He opened his arms to take in the room and maybe more—the whole ranch, earth, river, trees, grass and sky above.

Andrés Pico kept his elbows on the table. He chewed the bird leg. He tossed the bone to a dog. He wiped his hands on his napkin, wiped his mouth and got up. He and Pablo were about the same height but Pico outweighed him by forty pounds. His hair was filthy, and plastered to his big head except at the ears and back, where greasy curls sprang loose. His ears were large and furry. His gut sagged over dirty low-slung black pants.

"Pablo, go to your father. Do not make a problem for yourself. Pío Pico bought this ranch. He paid your mother, bless her heart. Your cattle are with them. We only bought the land. It is no longer yours."

"And who signed the papers?"

"You did, before you left. You don't remember?"

Pablo just stared at his enemy, willing the lie to nonexistence. Andrés Pico raised his hands in a surrendering gesture.

"If you loved Las Flores so much, you should never have left it. Like a good horse or a young bride, you cannot leave one or the other for two years and expect to find them waiting when you return . . . can you?"

It was the same line Bill had heard from Osuna.

"How much did you pay?" Bill glared, as mean and hard as he could.
Pico ignored him.

"Who is this Americano, Pablo? Does he have a letter of conduct to be here?"

"How much did the governor say he paid?" asked Pablo quietly.

"Two hundred pesos, in gold."

"I will buy it back."

"It's not for sale."

"Then it will be two hundred pesos plus two lives. That is my price."

Pablo turned to go. "Adiós," he spat over his shoulder. Bill followed.

"We all pay with our lives, Indio," grunted Andrés. "Go to your people. Take your friend. He will be arrested the next time I see him in California." He sat back down, heavily. "María," he shouted.

They were out the door by then, but Bill heard Andrés say, "Give the soup to the dogs."

They were moving fast to a symphony of sounds: Their boots on tile, then on wood, then dirt; the dogs scrapping for the soup, a chicken clucking; the saddles creaking, the horses' hooves on packed earth; the caw of a crow and the rustle of wind in the oaks.

Pablo was silent, his face emotion-free as a stone. He walked his horse without guiding it. They turned east out of the ranch yard, heading toward some foothills, keeping to the north bank of the river, which ran deep, clear and fast. The horses seemed to know where they were going and Pablo let them go. The wind came stronger from the south.

Soon they were once more on El Camino Real, heading back into the wind. The horses forded Santa Margarita River where it ran over a wide gravel bar. After a couple of miles easy riding, they came to the valley that held the San Luis Rey River. Their horses picked up the pace.

Up ahead, clouds were taking on definition, billowing low and wide instead of the solid gray matte of the last two days. Silent thunderheads loomed tall and dark, ready to break and rain. Around a bend in the river the riders entered a broad stretch of the valley, a good mile wide. It was flat. On the far side was a hill and on that hill was the biggest, whitest building in all of California.

"The mission," Bill shouted. "Mission San Luis Rey. Look at that. Will you look at that."

Pablo was smiling. Tears flooded his eyes. He could only nod.

A ray of sunlight struck the chapel dome for just one second, and was extinguished by cloud. It began to sprinkle and they trotted the excited horses across the valley in a refreshing mist.

8

SAN LUIS REY

PABLO'S grandfather had worked most of his adult life building the mission. Pablo's father, Francisco Verdi, was born the year of San Luis Rey's founding. The padre had instructed the Indians—stone by stone in the foundation, brick by adobe brick on the walls, tree by cut and hewn tree to form the rafters, doors and windows, and tile by clay tile, pressed to the curve of a bare thigh, baked and assembled to complete the roof. Then they mixed and applied plaster and paint, a thick whitewash of crushed cactus and limestone. Finally they formed thick, square tiles to cover the floors. Young Francisco had learned all of these skills at his father's side. They had gone on to work together as carpenters, making simple hand-carved furniture for the mission.

At each step of construction, the native laborers had only known what they were doing that day. They learned to build as they built. They never had an overall concept of the monument they were creating. They only knew it was to be the house of God.

Eight years it took to complete the main building. For Pablo's father and his tribe—who had never made more than conical brush and palm huts, to be burned and rebuilt when they finally rotted—Mission San Luis Rey was a miracle. Before the mission, the local natives had been known by their village names, Quechla, Guajome, Temecula or Pauma. Forever after, they were called Luiseño, proudly linking themselves with the mission they had helped to build.

Every native within a hundred miles came to see the house of San Luis Rey—that the People had created, the Luiseño. The wily padres conceived most of their new Christian conversions by the power of this awesome temple.

There it stood, like a castle of Spain, a piece of Europe in the vast wilderness. The town of San Diego was a peasant village compared to this master-piece of design and construction. It was the biggest building Bill had ever seen, and appeared even larger in the picturesque and lonely valley.

The padres had also turned their attention to the land. With their army of converts, they had planted the wide fertile plain with groves of lemons, oranges, grapefruit and avocados. They had sown a thousand grape vines; planted hundreds of acres in corn, wheat, tomatoes, chiles, chayote, squash, cabbage and artichokes; bred thirty thousand cattle and an equal number of sheep, pigs, goats and horses. They were to share this agricultural and animal bounty with the Luiseño: a fifth to the church, a fifth to the Spanish crown, and three fifths to support the People, as the natives called themselves.

The mission system the Franciscans created in California strung from San Diego to San Francisco, twenty-one in all, connected by El Camino Real. Pablo had been born to this system. He had traveled with the padres on the Royal Highway to every mission. He knew the Bible in Spanish and Latin. He was proud of Mission San Luis Rey, and as possessive as his forefathers who had created it.

THEY clattered into the cobbled courtyard, slick with raindrops. The padre was standing in the shelter of a wide corridor of pillars and arches that ran around the entire plaza. He rushed into the drizzle to embrace Pablo.

"Pablito, my son, I thought you were dead." He hugged Pablo and patted him on the back.

"And many wished it so, it seems, mi Padre. I'm pleased you're still here. This is William Marshall, my friend from Providence, Rhode Island. May I present Padre Francisco González de Ibarra, my teacher and spiritual master."

"Mucho gusto, Padre."

"Señor Marshall, the pleasure is mine." He vigorously pumped Bill's hand. "Let's get out of the rain. No sense soaking such fine clothing. Pablo, you look splendid."

"Once I was, Padre. But no more." Pablo was unbuttoning his wet jacket. "I'm sure you've heard."

"Come, come." The padre hustled them to shelter. "We have plenty of good homespun cotton pants and shirts here. Please, out of these wet things and into something clean and dry. You're staying, I hope. We have so much to talk about. Come this way, please."

The guest room he took them to, down a long hallway, was white, with a blood-red polished tile floor. It held two narrow beds with roughly squared timber frames and thick straw mattresses. There were clean cotton sheets folded down over loosely woven woolen blankets, dyed a rusty brown. A washstand of hand-hewn timber with a clay bowl, a cup and a clay pot full of water, stood between the beds. There was one small window with sawn wood shutters.

A young boy brought warm sheepskin moccasins, clean homemade shirts and pants of white cotton. Pablo and Bill stripped their wet clothes, hung them on wooden pegs embedded in a wall and donned the loose-fitting homespuns. Exhausted from the morning ride, Bill lay flat on his back, closed his eyes and breathed a deep sigh. It was nice to be in a bed. Pablo shut the door gently and padded up the familiar hall to the padre's dining room.

Father Ibarra was standing at the head of a long, elbow-worn, food-oiled table, lighting a tallow candle. His bulky shadow loomed on the unadorned wall behind.

Before he could utter a greeting, Pablo burst out in anguish.

"Oh, Father, how could it be that God allows a pig like Pío Pico—who has already more property than he can possibly use, who has broken every commandment and thrown each and every one in your face, who has mistreated you and every priest of this mission, who has violated the very sanctity of your church—how could he be allowed to take the only home and land of us Christian people, who worked so faithfully in God's name for more than forty years? How could this possibly be the will of God?"

"Pablo . . . buenas noches. Come here; sit. Of course this is not God's will. It is the work of the devil. But there it is and what is done cannot be undone. Even God cannot undo what is done."

He made the sign of the cross and poured two cups of wine from an earthen jug. Pablo sat. He thumped his elbows on the table, and held his head in his hands

"My parents, what say they?" he said, without looking up.

"Your mother, Ladislaya, only grows stronger." Ibarra mimicked her voice. "So now we finally get to live like our grandparents, before the coming of the sosabitom—with their hairy beards and slave animals and crosses and fleas and disease. We have nothing. We lack nothing. We want nothing. We will be happy. That is what she said."

Pablo smiled. "How I miss Mami."

"I miss her too . . . Ladi . . ."

"And my father?"

"Francisco took it hard . . . and so he should. He built Las Flores with his own hands. All of the woodwork, the doors, the furniture . . . he made it all and they took it from him "

"I never even thought of the furniture. When we were there today, Andrés Pico was eating lunch at our table, sitting in a chair made by my father."

Pablo beat Ibarra's dining table until the cups jumped and rattled.

"I will kill Pico and his brothers before another day passes."

"This you cannot do, my son. It is a mortal sin to kill another man. They will die. Every man will die. It matters little when or how or why."

"Then it matters little if I take their lives now."

"To them, no, but to you, yes, it matters. To hate and to kill are not God's will. It is forgiveness He asks."

"This crime is too cruel to forgive, Father. I can never forgive them until it is undone."

"There is always an excuse to hate. Never an excuse not to forgive and forget."

Pablo dismissed these words with a wave of his hand.

"You always have an answer that is no answer. Why must we lose our lands? Why must we work like slaves or starve to death? How can I forget? How can this be God's plan?"

"I ask this question myself, each and every day," Ibarra replied sadly. "Never have I received an answer. I have prayed for days and months and years and now one of my most fervent prayers has been answered—for you have returned to me alive—and for this I thank God. How I prayed for you Pablo. Let us rejoice."

Pablo said nothing, but his face softened and he took the padre's thin white hand and held it.

Ibarra spoke first. "Let us not spoil this homecoming in bitterness and recrimination. What is done is done. We must be happy to be alive, together again after all this time."

"Oh, Father, I'm so happy to see you I could cry."

And Pablo loosed his dammed tears.

W H E N Bill awoke, it was dark. The moon was up. It had stopped raining and the patch of sky through the little window was clear and starry. Pablo was asleep in the next bed, his face washed clean, lying at peace on top of the blankets. In his mission clothing, in a mission bed made by his father, he looked like a ten-year-old boy. The door opened a crack and the priest stuck his head in. He had a candle. Bill put a finger to his lips, found the sheepskin slippers and went out to join him.

They traversed the hallway, passed ten or twelve doors and went into the dining hall.

"Will you eat? Pablo and I supped together. I can bring you something."

Bill sat and Ibarra brought four burritos of spiced dried salt beef called machaca and two cups of wine. The jug was placed on the big table, in easy reach. The padre talked while Bill ate.

"Pablo will sleep. I mixed some powders in his wine. He was distraught."

Bill kept chewing. "His ranch? His parents?" he said when he had swallowed.

"The family is fine. You went to Las Flores? You want to know what happened there?" Bill nodded. "I will explain."

Ibarra spoke slowly and clearly, in accented but excellent English.

"I begin at the beginning. Before we Spanish came, the natives had no concept of individual land ownership. Each tribe had its traditional hunting, collecting and fishing territories. But there were no boundaries or fences and drought or a severe winter might drive groups to share an area they normally didn't use. No individual native owned a particular spot of earth. The land belonged to the gods. The People were only the caretakers.

"The Franciscans' concept was similar. God owned the land. We were the caretakers, in the name of God's chosen representative, the Catholic Church, and the Crown of Spain—which was sworn to that church. We made the native lands productive where we could, and gave that produce to the Indians. The church and God were new, but the lands were still theirs to use. For this reason twenty-five Franciscans, armed only with their faith, were able to peacefully settle California with its quarter of a million Indios.

"The problems we had were always with the Spanish colonists and soldiers—who came from an ancient feudal country where every square inch of land was owned by king, count, duke or lord—who dreamed of nothing but to own a piece of California. And, to a man, they were infected by what we call the Spanish caballero's disease: They did not wish to work. Work was beneath their station. Riding out to manage his cattle was as much as a gentleman could do without demeaning himself. Manual labor or working in the fields? Never. But the land and cattle belonged to the mission and the Indians. Though we fed the soldiers and settlers as part of our obligation to the king, the colonists were covetous of what we had.

"Would you like some more burritos," he asked Bill, who was picking crumbs from his earthenware plate.

"Please, If it is not too much trouble. They are wonderful."

"I hope I'm not boring you," said Ibarra when he returned.

"To the contrary. I'm fascinated. The more I learn the better."

"Good. Let me fill our cups."

The wine was poured, dripping in its travel between the mugs.

"In 1822 the province of New Spain became the republic of Mexico. To Mexico, the missions were the spoils of war. We Franciscans in California were given ten years to complete our work of civilizing and converting the Indians, to mold them into citizens on the Mexican model. By the end of these ten years, we were to transfer all of the mission property back to the Mexican Indian citizens, to own and operate for their benefit. Then the foreign-born priests should go back to Spain. This was one of the more noble goals of the revolution." Ibarra took up his mug.

Bill finished chewing and said, "But it never happened . . ."

"The natives were not ready for self-government, as the Mexicans understood it. When Friar Antonio Peyri, who founded San Luis Rey in 1798, and governed it for all of its independent existence, would deed a tract of land to the freed neophytes, as ordered, they would sell it or gamble it away to the land-greedy Californios. Then the Indians would simply take their cattle, which they truly valued, and move to the hills. They had never experienced private land ownership, and there seemed to be plenty of land. It took a while for them to understand the consequences. By then, it was too late. San Luis Rey Mission was in the hands of their enemies."

Padre Ibarra sipped his wine and watched Bill eat. Bill was content to listen, mesmerized by the food, the wine and the mission, whose massive walls lent mute testimony to the priest's story.

"Las Flores is not an isolated incident. This has been happening apace, ever since Peyri retired and returned to Spain in 1832, and Pío Pico was named secular administrator. Friar Peyri could not bear to witness the destruction of his creation, his lands in the hands of the Mexicans, with his converts becoming virtual serfs to the landlords, or forced to leave. He had dragged his feet on land distribution, allowing Pico to inherit a relatively intact mission. Pico immediately began handing out the best of the mission's estates to his friends and family, with the help of Alcalde Osuna, who had to approve each grant.

"Las Flores is just another piece of land to Pico, a step toward retaking the mission itself, which has been his goal since the day he was forcibly removed by Governor Alvarado, for corruption, nepotism and thievery in the disposition of mission assets. That was four years ago, but most of the damage had already been done."

Ibarra gestured to take in the room and all that surrounded it. He toyed with his cup, finally thumping it to the table.

"You have no idea what a trial Pío Pico has been for all of us," he complained bitterly, losing all composure. "On the very day of his appointment, Pico moved into this building, treating it as his personal hacienda. He lived here in splendor for five years, while I was confined to my spiritual duties and occupied a cell at the back of the chapel. Pico whipped the Indios who refused to work, or put them in the stocks. He turned out the female converts to live in sin where they may. He made my dining room a den of drunkenness and gambling. At cards, he lost the things he stole, and stole more to pay his debts. He impregnated at least one neophyte and even performed illegal marriages, in my church." The priest's voice shook. Bill was speechless.

When he was a little calmer, Ibarra said, "As governor, he wishes to steal even more of the mission lands. We yet fight him on behalf of the Indios, for the ranchos of Pala and Temecula. I am thankful to have limited him to Santa Margarita and Las Flores.

"That is the truth," Ibarra said softly. "No one can control him now. There is nothing Pablo can do." In the flickering light, the priest looked old and tired and beaten.

Both men were silent. Everything about the Picos was bad. Bill could only think to flee their influence.

In a minute Ibarra rallied and addressed Bill again.

"Pablo wants to join his family at Cupa. He says he'll try the old ways and see if they still bring joy, as the wild ones claim they do." He sighed dejectedly. "Pablo was my best student ever. I hope the things I taught him will not go to waste."

"Speaking all the languages must surely be an advantage."

Ibarra waved his hand in dismissal of what he took for granted.

"And what will you do? Pablo says you want to be converted to Catholicism and become a citizen of Mexico."

Bill was slow to reply. "I'm not so sure now. I'll stay with Pablo, till he's safe with his family. Then I'll decide."

"I'm glad you're going with him. I've never seen Pablo this dispirited."

"In San Diego, he was like a ghost. I'll make sure he gets to Cupa, then we'll figure out what to do."

"He told me you asked for the hand of Lugarda Osuna."

Bill spread his hands and shrugged. He guessed the whole world would soon know. Father Ibarra waited for him to compose an answer.

"Yes, I asked to marry her—I fell in love our first day in San Diego—but her father said no."

"You should have told Señor Osuna that your family owns boot factories in New England, and offered to buy his hides at double the current price."

Bill blushed. It embarrassed him how naive he'd been. The padre patted his arm.

"It was an impossible arrangement to stop, no matter what you may have offered. The Alvarado boy is a good match. The two fathers are fast friends and tied together in the hide business. I plan to marry them in the spring."

Bill was shaking his head.

"Does she love him?" he demanded. This, a priest might know.

Ibarra ignored the question.

"There are other women and you are young. Come to see me when Pablo is settled. I am a good matchmaker."

"I will, thank you, if I get the chance." What chance did he have with Lugarda? She had already spoken to the priest and set a date.

He excused himself and slipped outside to walk around the buildings in the moon- and starlight. It was crisply cold after the rain. The fresh damp air smelled of clean wet leaves and grass and earth. The oaks were big dark mushrooms on the hillsides and out in the valley the river sparkled and gurgled over the cobblestone bar.

The wine had gone to his head. He breathed deeply, concentrating on the air, taking in the fields and orchard, the church and buildings. He tried to add up all the work it had taken to make it, but Lugarda kept intruding. Bill relented and held her there in his mind until cold and exaustion drove him in to bed.

PABLO slept most of the next two days, coming out for lunch, then taking a long siesta until dinnertime. Dressed in his simple tunic and trousers, he seemed to wake up younger with each nap. The sun came out after the rain and stayed out, lightening everything. He spent all of his waking hours with Padre Ibarra, talking of their old life together and current events at the mission. They were enjoying each other's company, laughing and switching languages whenever Bill came around.

Bill rode steadily to get in shape for the journey to Cupa. He spent the days exploring and spying on Andrés Pico, when he could locate him. Andrés Pico was not lazy, rising early and riding out to tend the cattle, returning for lunch, then going out again till dark. But ranching was dignified work, and cowhides the only cash crop in San Diego. He had no time for fruits and vegetables, so the gardens at Las Flores had gone to seed, overrun by weeds, mowed down by cows and goats. Pico kept a handful of vaqueros to tend his herds, fed them beef and bought or traded at the mission for corn and tortillas.

By contrast, the fifty remaining mission acres were a manicured, spotless agricultural machine, turning out every necessity of life from wine to goat cheese to cotton. The mission too had cattle, and individual Indians had herds and hides to sell for cash, but the emphasis was on living well by creating every necessary product themselves.

San Luis Rey was wonderfully complete, with its tall, thick-walled building, five hundred feet on a side, housing workshops, dormitories, library, infirmary and a beautiful chapel. Though Pablo and Father Ibarra assured Bill it was a crumbling shadow of its former glory, the impression of wealth, power and intelligent planning was inescapable. It was easy to see why the Picos coveted it.

Bill sympathized with the Picos' prejudice against farm labor. He had had enough of it as a child. The days of riding at the mission gave him a pleasant taste of the cattle rancher's life. How foolish he'd been to think he would be given grazing land and a Californio wife of his own. All the good land he saw was spoken for, as was the woman he wanted.

This was a tight-knit society. Even though the distances were great, everyone knew everything that went on, and quickly. Ibarra had heard of the *Hopewell's* departure by the afternoon of the day she set sail from San Diego. Bill felt a pang of guilt for leaving Captain Saxon, but no regret. It was common knowledge that he had jumped ship, but no one seemed to care. Andrés Pico had come one day to buy corn flour. He nodded to Bill and chatted amiably with Padre Ibarra as though nothing were ill among them. Bill was amazed at how well the supposed enemies got along.

When he commented to the priest, Ibarra patiently explained, "We Spanish are a polite society. We have an ironclad code of hospitality that originates with the seven-hundred-year Moorish domination of Spain, ended in 1492 by Isabella La Católica, God rest her soul. In the Moslem code, every man is to be treated like a brother while he is a guest in your home—friend or enemy. Not until he goes outside your walls can you slit his throat." He chuckled.

"Besides, we are a very small community and gossip is our first source of entertainment. Andrés Pico is my closest neighbor, and not as despicable as his brother. He is an amusing man, from whom I have learned many useful things. What he has done does not make him any less entertaining. Here, if you are not cordial, life will be very lonely."

This attitude was unnatural to Bill. In New England, farmers can live next to each other and not speak for decades—over some slight, or a disputed cow. Grudges are taken seriously, feuds go on for generations, and impoliteness to your enemies is the rule. That's what enemies are for, his father once told him, to focus your anger and keep you from lashing out at your friends.

Bill had already made one enemy. He did not think polite gossip would work with Leandro Osuna. And Pablo had sworn to kill the Picos. Politeness could not affect that vow.

9
A JOURNEY INTO THE PAST

N THE third morning, Pablo rolled out of bed at dawn. "Today we leave for Cupa," he said with renewed energy.

They descended fifty adobe steps to the brick-lined washing pool, had a bracing cold bath, dressed in riding clothes, ate the usual big California breakfast and left just as the sun poked out of the morning haze. Padre Ibarra saw them off, inviting both to come and live at the mission. "I'll put you to work." His long face rounded into a grin. "You won't get rich, but you'll live like princes, and I'll find Bill a wife."

"We would be sweating like plow horses," snorted Pablo, as they rode east along the south bank of the San Luis Rey River, at a leisurely pace. "The padres firmly believe that an idle man is the devil's disciple. Only a guest is treated like a prince."

The mission's agricultural projects extended along the loamy riverbed for about six miles, in varying states of disorder now that they were in private hands, and ended abruptly at a wall of trees, tules and tall grass. They followed a wilderness trail obscured by a dense canopy of willow and oak. Sycamores towered another level above.

They emerged at a narrows in the river, where the current ran swiftly over a cobbled bottom. Pablo stopped. He disrobed and told Bill to do the same.

"We'll spear some fish in these rapids," he said. "An oceangoing trout or small salmon called steelhead returns to this river each year to spawn." When Bill pointed to dark shapes in the shallows, Pablo said, "Yes, those."

At the mission, Pablo had procured two hefty lances with razor-sharp steel points. They were serious weapons for large game and hunting on horseback. They took the lances from the packhorse rigs and walked quietly to the river's edge.

"Follow me and do as I do."

Pablo waded into the river where it flowed shallow and swift. He stood very still until a fish swam right to him, coming upstream. His arm flashed, he held the fish speared to the bottom, reached down to haul it up with the spear and walked back to shore. He pulled the fish off and returned to Bill's side. Bill had made two attempts to strike fish and missed both times.

"The water refracts the fish's image," Pablo said. "You have to know where to aim. It's easiest to spear a fish coming directly at you. Keep the point of the lance underwater. Then it too will be refracted and you can aim by the position of the tip. Wait until the fish is almost touching the point, then plunge it in. It's very sharp, so no need to strike a hard blow. You have to pin the fish to the bottom to hold it. There are no barbs. Then reach down and bring it up with the spear."

Bill stuck his lance into the current. The shaft had a bend, just as described.

"Now stand still facing the sun. If you move or cast a shadow, the fish will also move, even in these rapids."

Bill did as he was told, waited until a large trout was at his spear point, stabbed down and felt the fish thrash against the bottom, pinned. Excited, he plunged his left arm up to the shoulder to seize the trout. The racing current grabbed his arm, and the rest of Bill tumbled into its flow. The fish wriggled free and Bill was dragged fifty yards downstream before he could regain his feet.

Pablo had caught another trout and was walking back to shore. He did a little dance of exaggerated guffaws and waded back out to the bar.

The next fish Bill speared, he braced himself securely with the lance, stretched carefully to his fingertips and managed to hold the trout without being swept downstream. "I got one," he yelled. Pablo gave a whoop. Bill dashed ashore to discard it, flopping, on a thick bed of oak leaves. They speared another dozen quickly.

"This is easy, High Cloud, like picking abalone off the rocks. I hope they taste as good."

"It's all easy when you learn from a master," Pablo boasted. "I'm going to teach you to be an Indian. By the time we reach Cupa, you'll be hunting like a native."

They cleaned the pink-fleshed trout, which were about a foot and a half long, then split them along the inside of the backbone, leaving the flesh attached to the skin and the heads on. Each fish was skewered vertically by two sticks, which were stuck upright in the ground around a small fire, flesh side in. The ring of fish was about five feet across. They kept the low fire going all that day and night.

In the two weeks it took to travel to Cupa, Pablo taught Bill to hunt deer with bow and arrows, to catch rabbits with a bent throwing stick or thong snare, and to shoot quail with a very slender reed arrow that held a sharpened wood point. They also knocked ducks down with the throwing stick, hurling it into the thick of a flock as they were just about to land on a pond.

All of the game was roasted on the spot or cleaned and dried by slow fire, to store in the packs. At night the packs were suspended high on a branch, far from camp, out of the reach of keen-scented grizzlies.

The smoked trout were a delicious treat. The second morning, when they awoke, the circle of fish had brazed to a golden brown with a dark hard crust. Pablo ceremoniously handed one to Bill. He stripped the flesh from its skin and ate it like candy, sweet and oak-scented. The rest were wrapped, putting two fish together, skins out, and bundling the pairs into packets of six. Every morning, Pablo and Bill would peel off a dried fish to present to the other for breakfast. An Indian hunter did not eat the animal he killed. If he did, he would ruin his chances to kill again. The successful hunter had to trade or give his catch to his companions. This insured that everybody hunted and ate well.

Bill learned to walk very quietly, avoiding sticks and loose stones, and to stand motionless for up to an hour, which was most difficult. He liked to chase things, not wait for them to come.

Pablo told him to be patient, to hunt the way animals hunt, to wait until the prey was touchable, then strike. Pablo rarely lost an arrow or missed his target, always waiting until an animal was no more than a few feet away to shoot his bow or thrust with his lance. He believed that the animal dies willingly, with respect, if you can touch him before you kill him—animals were always him or her—because he has been fairly outsmarted.

This was the opposite of what Bill had learned as a kid. Hunters always bragged that they had killed a deer at three hundred yards or shot a squirrel in the eye from a hundred. It was more sporting. Hunting whale had been Bill's first experience of stalking to kill at lance tip range. Now he learned to hunt every animal in the same fashion: to hunt to kill.

It did no one any good to have a wounded creature stumbling, flying or swimming off ten miles to bleed to death, far from where he was needed. It was not respectful to the animals. It was wasteful, an insult to God.

Pablo made Bill track a deer he had wounded, that fled halfway up the steep south slope of Mount Palomar. Pablo followed for two days, helping track and grumbling until Bill had made the kill, apologized to the deer and carried the meat and hide back to camp. That was the last long shot Bill took with his bow. They were lucky the horses were still where they had left them hobbled to graze.

When they weren't hunting or preparing skins or smoking meat or making arrows, they lounged in camp, bathed in the river, or basked on a dark rock. It was dead of winter in San Diego, but the sun was warm by mid-morning, like summer weather in New England.

Pablo had been reading since he was young and many of his ideas came from books. *Don Quixote* or *Ulysses* he mentioned constantly, and the Bible and Sir Walter Scott's *Lancelot*, which he had read on the ship. Pablo spoke of the characters as though they were real. He learned from them and tried to pattern his life from what he learned. He liked men who had a plan, a quest.

Pablo had come up with a scheme for his new life, and Bill's, if he wished to follow: He would go back to being what he truly was, a native; an Indian. He would return to a traditional way of life, as led by his forefathers, before the Spanish arrival.

"In my travels from here to New York, I saw natives, Spanish and Americans living their chosen lives as hunters, farmers, ranchers, laborers, traders, shipbuilders, sailors, soldiers and outlaws. I have read every book of Europe that I could borrow. I have been a Christian and know the ways of Jews, Moslems, native People, Romans and the Greek philosophers. From what I have seen, no one way of life is any better than another. People live well or not, are happy and unhappy, grow fat or starve, get old and die."

Pablo shook his head and looked intently at Bill.

"I once loved my life at the mission. I was proud of my life as a rancher. I thought that to be a caballero was a great achievement. I dreamed of nothing else and you entered into that dream with me. It was a good dream; it is no longer possible. Now I will try to live as my ancestors did. They say it was a good life. I will find out how good."

"We could still have a ranch," Bill protested. "You may even get yours back." This he had not given up.

"I can no longer hope for that. If it happens, yes of course," Pablo added quickly when Bill opened his mouth to protest. "But I would not do it like the Spanish or Mexicans, all cattle or nothing. It is as silly for us Indians to want to live like them as it is for them to pretend they are in Madrid. Nor should we want to dress like them. You've seen how serious they are about their European clothes. We shall use dress like costumes in a drama, according to the part we must play."

The first day out, Pablo had carefully folded his riding pants, shirt and jacket, and packed them in the saddlebags. He told Bill to do the same. They wore only the breechcloth and robes of the wild Indians. This was the out-ward sign of their metamorphosis.

It occurred to Bill that it might be more difficult for Pablo to be an Indian than for himself. He had grown up as a backwoods boy, farmer, hunter, fish-erman, and then a whaler. This was not far from the Indian way of life. Pablo was raised in the mission, immersed in books, in church, in a polite and edu-cated society that valued "civilization" above all but their belief in God. Pablo knew the Indian customs because they surrounded him, but he had never lived them—even bows and arrows had been banned at the mission. He was relearning the wild ways as he taught them to Bill.

I N the afternoon, they passed through an Indian village, or ranchería, at Pala, about thirty miles up the river. Pala was mostly Christianized. There was a sub-mission, or "visita," with a chapel where the padres could come at regular in-tervals to hold services. The people of Pala were called Luiseño, after the mission, but were of a different tribe than those on the coast. They raised crops and cattle and also engaged in some traditional hunting and gathering.

At Pala the People lived in one-room adobe houses, or woven-reed-walled, thatch-roofed huts. They dressed in ragged versions of Californio clothing, mixed with skins. The town was full of fleas. They looked poor.

"Strip them of their rags, burn their flea-ridden hovels, bathe them and dress them in furs, and you'll see they're not poor at all. They're only miser-able because they want what the Californios and padres have. Those who live as tenant serfs on the ranches are the only poor in California," Pablo said.

"Look what bounty we have extracted from their lands in one week." He gestured toward their packs, heavy with animal products. "If what you have is what you want, you are wealthy." He looked at Bill hard. "If you want some-thing you don't have, then you are poor."

Bill could only think of Lugarda. He was impoverished in just that way.

"The People have everything where we are going: land, plentiful food, cat-tle, good company, and a hot spring to sit in on cold nights," Pablo declared, echoing his mother. "You will see, my friend."

Pablo had greeted those Palans he knew and flown on his way, begging the need to see his parents. But he was in no hurry to get to Cupa. They rode about five miles each day, not necessarily in the right direction.

10

PAUMA

T H E native clothes Pablo insisted they wear turned out to be extremely practical for their new way of life. The skins were a natural camouflage for hunting. Animals would often stare, just long enough to allow you to get off a shot with bow or throwing stick. If you had to move fast you threw off your robe and went tearing away. To relieve yourself on the trail, you lifted the robe. To rest, you threw it on the softest pile of oak leaves or pine needles at hand. If it rained you pulled the robe over your head, and to sleep you wrapped up in it.

"Even the Roman senators wore robes," Pablo said, sitting proudly in his saddle, wrapped in a cloak of rabbit skins trimmed with spotted lynx.

They rode into the next village thus: draped in fine robes, hair shining, horses decorated with feathers and abalone shells, pack animals laden with the fruits of their hunting. People rushed from their huts in surprise. Shouts of, "Pablo, High Cloud, welcome," echoed through the valley. It was Pauma, ancestral home to Pablo's father's tribe, a small group of about eighty who had occupied this sunny upland meadow forever.

Pauma ranchería was neat and organized, with small sturdy stone or adobe houses on a cleared slope. There were also tule or grass huts tucked in the corners of the valley. The open space was a mile long and three hundred yards wide. Hills and big oaks lined the sides. At the center was a stream that gurgled through the grassy meadow of the valley floor.

Pauma Valley was the last big level step on the way up to the high plain of Valle de San José, Warner's ranch and Cupa. Around this step, mountains rose to the north, south and east, wooded but not steep enough to be threatening. It was a beautiful self-contained world: stream, grassland, oaks and woods all within easy sight and reach, in pleasing proportions.

In the middle of the valley, a large adobe building sat on a rise with a view to the river. From there, this whole compact world could be observed with a swing of the head. Pablo headed toward the big adobe. Bill rode close behind.

Manuelito Cota was the Pauma chief, or capitán. Like Pablo's mother and father, he was mission-educated and spoke a few languages. He had been Pauma's majordomo, or foreman, at the mission and now managed labor forces for two of the offshoot ranchos. Manuelito was well respected by the padres, Californios and Indians. He always took his pay in cattle and had amassed a fine herd. The big adobe was his nearly finished new house.

They walked the horses with a growing throng through the dry meadow and up to the construction site, where Manuelito was overseeing the work. He ran out with a shout and Bill lost Pablo to his people and their strange language.

It reminded Bill of turning a favorite saddle mount out to pasture with a herd of loose horses. One minute you are his whole world; the next he disappears among his kind and they move and swirl together until he is no longer distinguishable as an individual. When you try to find him in the herd, the horse looks so right with his fellows that you lose heart, and doubt that he will ever commune with you again.

At Pauma, the language barrier was impossible to penetrate. The sounds were strange and flowed together so that Bill could not even differentiate the words. There were four other distinct native dialects in San Diego plus the overlays of sign language and Spanish. There were priests speaking Latin and Greek, English, Italian, German and French. There was Hawaiian at La Playa. Most people spoke at least three of the varied tongues; everyone threw in words from any idiom that came to mind. Anyone wanting a private conversation just switched to a language the others didn't know. In Bill's case this meant everything but English.

But it was nice to sit back and observe without being expected to speak. Bill found that by studying people, without knowing a word they uttered, he could still fit together the puzzle of their personality and their niche in society. He never missed anything important: He knew when it was time to eat or hunt, dance or sleep. He knew who was in love, or depressed, or insulted. He could observe a pecking order. He knew who was interested in him, and whom he wanted to know better.

"The silent one sees all," he said to himself. "Who needs the blather of gossip or bother of philosophy? Not I."

But he would have to master Spanish. The padres had dealt with the multiplicity of native tongues by learning enough in each Indian language to teach them all Spanish. Spanish was the uniting idiom for both Indians and foreigners. Bill's Spanish was rudimentary—learned from another sailor and then Pablo—one had only to speak fast to lose him. What was really maddening, was twisting his tongue to come out with the right phrase in bad Spanish, only to have the conversant look at him blankly and say, "You can speak English, if you like."

Manuelito did that on Bill's second day in the village. "Excuse me," he said smoothly, "I thought you knew Spanish and some of our Pauma language." His accent was light. "Pablo has been explaining your training with him to become one of us. I assumed that speaking the dialect would be part of becoming a native. Wouldn't that make sense?" He grinned at Bill.

"Not at all," Pablo defended his methods, "I'm waiting until we reach Cupa. As you know, they speak a different language. Bill is still learning Spanish. It would not do to confuse him, and besides our Pauma tribe is one of the best educated. We all speak Spanish."

"And some of us act Spanish." Manuelito giggled. "Pablo has been lecturing me on the Higher Path that you will be taking, the Indian traditional path he assumes is still the way of life in Cupa. The Cupeño do speak another language, but they live as we do. You won't meet any wild Indians until you encounter the Cahuilla. Then look to your life." Manuelito made a throat-slitting motion with the side of his hand.

The chief dressed as a Californio: hat, shirt, trousers, boots and scarf. He didn't wear a fancy silver-studded outfit like the one Pablo had in his pack, but he looked every bit as Mexican. His herd of cattle, horses, sheep and goats was large and he was building a three-room house with a stone chimney. He was a native caballero, which literally means a horseman, but also implies the status of a gentleman.

Not that he was comparable to Andrés Pico or Juan María Osuna. As capitán, Manuelito shared everything with his fellow Paumans. In the Pauma herd were many cattle belonging to Pablo's father and the refugees from Las Flores. Manuelito was quick to offer Pablo a home at Pauma and a share of the grasslands for his stock. He agreed to take Bill in too, if he wished to stay. They demurred.

Pablo had given gifts to every single member of the village: clothes, shells, dried steelhead, beads, candy, salt, tiny mirrors, cloth, scarves, a pocketknife for Manuelito and his last book, a Bible in Spanish for their chapel. By the rights of the giver, they were in his debt. He had to collect or they would be offended and burdened by their gifts until they were repaid. One way to even the debt was to return the item given. The other, to give something in exchange, something of equal or greater value. Pablo accepted skins of bobcat, sea otter and coyote, some arrows and two long lances with razor-sharp iron blades. He thanked Manuelito and the others for their generosity, then bade them goodbye.

"These people are my own flesh," he told Bill as they saddled the horses. "But they are cattle ranchers and sheepherders. Wild game eats the grass cattle need to grow, bear eat the sheep, mountain lions eat the goats. For them, the native creatures have become a problem. The Pauma dress like poor Mexicans, pray to God for rain, for many calves and for good prices for their hides. I have left this life with Las Flores. There is another way. Where we go, we may truly let ourselves be men, as the gods meant us to be . . . Vámonos."

11

VALLE DE SAN JOSÉ

T HEY had been climbing steadily since leaving the coast. The trail out of Pauma Valley climbed steeply, zigzagging, while the river below plunged over boulders through the narrowing canyon between Mount Palomar and the hills to the south. This gorge was choked with trees and undergrowth, and extended for about three miles. Big clouds towered overhead; the air was brisk from the southwest, the usual sign of rain. Four or five huge birds soared high in clear sections of sky, condors and golden eagles, each with an eight-foot wingspan.

"That is Manuelito and my father, Francisco, watching over us. They have been best friends since childhood. My father is the Eagle of Gold and Manuelito is the Condor with the Hooked Nose. Their fathers too were best friends, compadres, first from their village to heed the call of the Franciscans; to help in building the house of God. They ran off as rebellious youths to do this forbidden and unheard-of thing. Like us now."

The visit had revitalized Pablo. The gifts given and received had lightened the burden of responsibility that lay heavy as consequence of the loss of Las Flores. He had heard not a whisper of blame for having left the ranch vulnerable to Pico's duplicity.

"Manuelito helped us to set up Las Flores. Many of the Pauma lived there. He has taken them all in. They were able to bring their share of the cattle, and my father's too. These people are happy to be back in their homeland. All has not been lost. I am free," Pablo said gratefully.

"I'm free!" he screamed loud enough to echo from the rocks up into clear sky, all the way to the circling birds.

"You say it," he said.

"I'm free," Bill shouted into the heavens.

They had walked, leading the horses, emerging from dark green shadows to find themselves on level ground, at a meadow's edge in a new and distinct climate. The air was crisper, the haze of the coast had lost itself in the lower twists and turns of the gorge; the wind was dry and smelled of oak mulch and manzanita with a hint of sage and red shank. Pablo even imagined he smelled the desert, still fifty miles to the east. They rode over a final wooded rise, the hills ahead dropped away to the left and right, and they entered the wide-open, big-skied, grassy bowl of Valle de San José, home to Cupa and Warner's ranch.

The valley was really a high plain, twenty miles wide by forty miles long, mostly flat, with a slight tilt toward the ocean. San Luis Rey River began here—in hundreds of streams, creeks and rivulets that fed to the west and came together in the vast shallow plain, leaking through a single crack in the rim to flow to the sea.

After their confinement in the gorge, the spaciousness of the valley was balm to the eyes. They dismounted, turned the horses loose, and unpacked a breakfast of beef machaca burritos that had been pressed on them at the village. To the northwest, hulking Mount Palomar was a gray-green, cloud-enshrouded mass. To the south and east, lower hills and mountain, thickly forested with oaks and pines, also held puffy gray clouds. To the north, across thirty miles of grassy rolling plain, lay Eagle's Nest and Rabbit Hole Mountain, the granite-clad peaks of Cupa, as yet clear, reflecting the mid-morning sun.

Cattle and herds of deer and antelope grazed on the plain. Ahead lay a llano, or shallow lake, a wide grassy depression, awaiting the winter rains. Short green shoots poked from the dark soil of the llano. The dry grass of the valley itself was a dirty straw color. Huge black shadows, from great raptors soaring in high-altitude orbits, swept across the plain at speed; fearsome specters for prey animals, spooking the horses whenever they came near.

Pablo calmed the flighty beasts, while Bill lay back on his robe to doze. They were still in no hurry. This was the valley where Pablo would make his home, and he wanted to savor the scenery. He would allow time for word of his approach to reach Cupa before he made his entrance.

N O W he taught Bill to collect acorns, grind the flour, leach it of tannic acid by soaking twice overnight in water, squeeze the water out, form it into patties and roast it on flat rocks by the fire. The flour could also be boiled as mush or dumplings. The taste was bland and slightly nutty. It was filling.

This was hard work—woman's work—but necessary for survival if game were scarce. Washing the flour was the critical skill in preparation. Heavy cramping was the result of improper blanching.

"All the more reason to know how it is done so that your wife doesn't poison you when you anger her! Washed in the hot springs, the flour will taste even better," Pablo said.

Wife? Bill was haunted by visions of Lugarda in the wedding dress. He wanted to see her lovely face again, to smell her scent and feel her skin vibrate to his touch. He ached for her. She was all the wife he wanted. Manuelito was planning to harvest hides in February, when the coats were thick and shaggy. They would take the cured cowhides to San Diego by packhorse. Bill had been invited to help. He could see Lugarda then.

"Does Manuelito have sons or daughters?" Pablo hadn't mentioned any. A son would have to be a best friend.

"He has daughters. Two are married. 'Zul is the third."

"You should have told me. We could marry 'Zul and Lugarda together. That would be perfect. We could bring them to Pauma."

"You can forget Lugarda. She has already asked José María to move their wedding date forward."

"Says who?"

"Manuelito told me. A nephew who works for the Alvarados told him. Lugarda appeared one afternoon in tears and—"

"Forward to when?"

"Now. She begged José María to marry her now. She said she never wanted to go home again."

"Something must have happened."

Pablo turned to look hard at Bill.

"A lot happpened, tonto. You fell in love with Lugarda at a dance. You followed her home and asked her to marry you. You tried to bribe her with a French wedding dress. The first minute you were alone together, you molested her. Then you asked her father for her hand, and when he said no, you beat her brother, Leandro, to his knees with his own whip. That's what happened."

Bill concentrated on his acorn grinding. Pablo watched him.

"I . . . I meant something else must have happened," Bill said lamely.

Pablo took up a stone and beat another handful of hulled acorns into the deep hole.

"I don't know anything more. It's all thirdhand gossip anyway. Lugarda will marry José María Alvarado and 'Zul will go with her to San Marcos." He shrugged. "You and I will met our wives in Cupa. Beautiful native women who will make us feel like men, not twist our balls and drain our brains."

He tried to make it sound good, but a shade drew over Pablo's face and Bill knew he was thinking of 'Zul, in the Osunas' twisted clutch.

They had been circling the plain to the southeast, staying close to the edge of the forest and exploring any inviting-looking side canyons. They passed one large valley with a well-worn trail, which Pablo said led some fifteen miles south to Santa Ysabel, a large Indian ranchería with a mission chapel, and the home of Edward Stokes, the fancy-dressing English ex–sea captain Bill had met. From Santa Ysabel there was a shorter way to San Diego, downhill to Rancho Santa María, then through the San Pasqual Valley to the San Dieguito River, the Osuna ranch and the coast.

Pablo smirked and Bill gave the trail a good hard stare. That would be his shortcut to Lugarda.

T H E Y saw large numbers of coyotes lying low in the shadows just out of bow-shot range, ears alert, with luxurious gray, brown, beige and yellow winter coats. When the riders approached they would lope off in a pack, but not too far, then slink low to lie in tall grass, soaking in the sun's welcome heat.

"Are they following us?" Bill wondered. "Or are there dozens of coyote packs in this valley?"

"Both. They're waiting for the winter hide harvest, which they know comes soon. They'll feast on the carcasses for weeks, then den up to have their pups." Pablo studied one of the leaders.

"We'll make some traps when we get to Cupa and harvest pelts for winter robes. Nothing is warmer than coyote, except bear, which is too heavy. And the bear does not give his skin so easily."

They had seen almost as many grizzlies as people, snatching trout from the river, gorging on berries, ambling through the woods, or sitting in a sunny meadow playing with their cubs. The bears hadn't given chase, though they had watched the riders closely. Their attitude was that of a king in his domain. Though the men knew different, they were not about to issue a personal challenge.

When the grizzly did move, at top speed he was fast as a horse, mowing down bushes and saplings like a runaway cannon. The Indians were right to revere them. Bill had to respect the courage of those Californios who defeated a bear alone with only a knife and spear, or roped a bear from horseback.

A bear was the one animal horses would not abide. Just the scent of bear made them snort and stamp and rear. The roar of a big grizzly on the move would send them galloping, riders hanging on as best they could, the packs bumping and flapping, terrifying the frightened creatures even more.

On one of those wild, bear-fleeing gallops, a valley opened broadly to the east. The horses pounded up a sandy streambed that wound down from rocky ridges to lose itself in the flattened plain. A mile ahead, on the north bank of the stream, they saw buildings: a house and barn, corrals and a couple of sheds. Warner's ranch.

Pablo spurred his horse with a yell and Bill did the same. About halfway there, a packhorse lost his saddle, and the pack burst open. Bill circled back to pick up the mess. The saddle-free horse kept going after Pablo, who had not slowed his breakneck gallop.

It had been raining off and on for two days, big heavy clouds marching majestically off Mount Palomar to the rumble of thunder and crack of lightning, soaking the plain and lofty peaks, then dripping east into the desert. The sun had emerged bright. The contents of the pack saddle were strewn over thirty feet of wet, bent brown grass. Tiny green shoots sprouted bravely from the under soil—a soft, sandy, decomposed granite that quickly absorbed any moisture—gambling that the next rain would not be a freezing snowstorm.

Bill was on hands and knees, picking up scattered seashells, when he heard a rifle shot. Shouts followed, then silence. This was the first shot he'd heard since their arrival at San Diego. He'd seen only a few guns in California, old muskets and blunderbuss shotguns. There was no gunpowder or lead to buy even if you had a gun. The shot must have come from Warner. Pablo said Juan Largo always traveled with a few rifles, the best he could buy, and was a crack marksman.

Bill imagined Pablo galloping into Warner's yard, dressed like the wild Indian he wished to become, to be shot down as an intruder. How easy to mistake Pablo for a Yuman or Cahuilla brave—out to prove himself in solitary combat.

He scrambled to his horse, leaped on without touching the stirrups and took off toward the house. Halfway there, a horseman rode out. Bill recognized Pablo. Just as they met, two other mounted ponies detached themselves from the barn.

"What happened, Pablo? I heard the shot," Bill choked. Their excited horses circled.

Pablo had a huge grin. He was breathing hard.

"I nearly lost my heart." He put his hand to his chest. "Warner is out riding the range. He left his wife and a young Yuman boy at home alone. She took a shot at me. I heard it go by." He was laughing, wiping away wind tears.

"They were scared to death. The kid was ready to loose a couple of arrows when I called out. He's a nasty little thing. Keep an eye on him. I'm sure Warner told him to protect her with his life."

The startled pair trotted up as Bill and Pablo dismounted to retrieve the strewn belongings. Both riders rode bareback, on small painted horses with braided rawhide halters. The boy was tiny, about ten years old, and scowling his meanest scowl. He was armed with a large knife stuck in his belt and a short bow with a fistful of arrows. He didn't come close. The girl jumped down, releasing her horse, who snorted and galloped off toward the barn. "Calico, you get back here," she yelled. The boy watched the horse; then glanced at her. "Go get him," she said, then an Indian word and a jerk of her head. The boy took off like he'd been whipped.

The girl turned to Bill with a curtsy and said, "I'm Anita Gale de Warner." She stuck out her small hand.

"Bill Marshall. My pleasure."

He gripped her fingers, then let them slip out. She was staring at Pablo excitedly, breathing in quick little gulps.

"Pablo, please forgive me, don't tell John I tried to shoot you. I thought you were . . ." She looked at Bill again. "You two are dressed like savages: wild Indians. Why, Pablo? Oh, I could have killed you, and John would have sent me back to Los Angeles . . ."

She wept for a second, then saw the strewn contents of the pack in the moist trampled grass.

"Let me help you, please." She fell to her knees and they started the task of retrieving shells, pocketknives, dried meats and skins, clothing and other trading treasures.

Pablo assured her that he had been riding too swiftly to be hit with a bullet, even by Warner, and it was his fault anyway for coming up so unexpectedly and looking so dangerous. He was secretly pleased at his effect. He kept catching Bill's eye and chuckling. Bill was crawling and collecting as best he could without exposing himself to Mrs. Warner, which was not easy wearing a breechcloth.

She was dressed in a clean blue and white gingham dress, long to the ankles, with a gingham ruffle and an inch of white lace around the high neck. Her coat was of wool; a sailor's coat dyed a dark blue, with navy blue buttons. It was open. Anita was young. She looked sixteen at most, and her dress was getting muddy at the knees. She had brown sun-blond hair, tied with a thin ribbon in a ponytail, blue eyes and a tanned freckled face.

She wrinkled her nose. She picked up Bill's bundle of clothes and smelled it with a deep inhalation. Then she grabbed the cloth bundle with the wedding dress and took another more delicate sniff.

"You came on a whaler," she shouted. She jumped up. "It's the stink of a whaler. I'm the only person in the world who loves that smell. I'd know it a mile away. That's the smell of my entire childhood. Let me smell your arm." She took Bill's hand and stuck her nose against his forearm. It tickled the hairs.

"It's clean. You must have really gone native, bathing twice a day and all. A whaler should return to his ship before the stench wears off him, my father always said. You must not be going back. Oh Bill, Pablo, do you have any news of Captain Gale? You were on the *Hopewell*, right? Captain Saxon is one of my father's best friends."

Pablo said, "We saw him in Lahaina Harbor. He was fine."

"What else. Did he mention me?"

"He said to give you his love and his blessing for your marriage. We didn't stay long because there was a syphilis outbreak in the town and an epidemic of measles. No one went ashore."

"My father never leaves his ship anyway." But Anita looked worried.

"I do have a letter for you in my pack. I left it at your barn," added Pablo.

"Oh, let's go get it . . . Luna," she called the boy, who had returned with her horse. Anita tucked her full skirt between her legs and mounted like a man, in a leap astraddle. They raced off, her skinny ankles and white calves only partly covered by short soft boots.

Pablo mounted and followed. "I'd better go. They'll rip my pack to pieces before they find the letter."

"I'll be right there."

Bill gathered the last of the valuables and tied them to his saddle. He balanced the broken pack saddle on his horse's neck, and walked the rest of the way to the ranch house.

12

WARNER'S RANCH

I N T H E shallow valley, the homestead was safely set on a rise about one hundred yards from the river's unstable sandy bank, well out of flood range.

The house was of adobe, low at the sides with a high peak, as long as wide, with the veranda facing west and the ends pointed north and south, up and downstream.

The roof was made of palm thatch over heavy logs. A trail of smoke at the south end marked the fireplace and kitchen. It was lunchtime in California, the single universal activity of all resident humans.

Behind the house, across the yard, was a barn of wood, very American-looking, with a steep two-sided shingle roof, almost no overhang and upright plank walls with batten-covered seams, weathered gray. A small open window was tucked high under each eave. Large double doors sagged ajar at the western end.

Two small corrals stood river-side of the barn, on a sunny flat. The whole yard—house, barn and some chicken and sheep pens—was fenced with split pine, lashed to upright posts with inch-wide strips of rawhide. Fieldstones were piled at the base of the wood fence, giving it a solid effect. Bill imagined that Warner, being a good Connecticut Yankee, would make a stone wall when he had collected enough rock.

He put his horse in the corral with Pablo's and pulled off the saddles, hanging them on the top rail. Anita came to the door at the north end of her house to call out to him. "You may put them in the barn. Change into some civilized clothes and come to the house. John will be here soon and then we'll eat."

Inside, the barn was dark. There were four horse stalls on one side, a tack room, a storeroom and a room that looked like Luna's bunkroom on the other. The storeroom had a ceiling, with a loft above, and a door with an ancient padlock. Bill put the saddles in the tack room, left his pack on the floor of the hall, in the light, and went back out to wash in the water trough.

There was a bucket beside the trough with cleaner water. He used that. In rumpled trousers, shirt and jacket, he crossed the yard to the house, checked his boots for fleas and entered.

At the end of a tall dark hall, noise came from the kitchen. It was well illuminated, for a ranch house. A shuttered window on either side let light in and the open doorway filled the shadows. Anita was at the fireplace with Pablo, freshly dressed in his fancy caballero's suit, still wearing a wicked grin.

The rough table in front of them was set for four. There were six wooden chairs tucked under; a couple more stood by the hearth, flanking a long bench with a cushion of furs. A tall grandfather clock with chimes hanging in its open front—which must have once held glass—hugged the adobe wall. The time was five till two. Bill looked forward to hearing the sound it might make on the hour.

Anita said, "Sit, please." She was extracting the news from Pablo, who wasn't offering much.

"Bill's from Providence. It's not far to Nantucket and you may have folks you know in common. I just passed through with John, and don't know a thing he hasn't told you."

"It's your turn, Bill," she said. "Tell me everything about the last nine years in the U.S. I haven't been there since I was eleven."

That made her twenty. Here preparing the meal, she seemed more her age, but when she turned to the light, her unlined, fire-red glow was again that of a child. She looked closer to Luna's age than Bill's. He wondered if the little Yuman was rifling their packs.

Before Bill had exhausted his store of U.S. news and political gossip, the chimes rang twice, deep and friendly. They heard John Warner ride up and all rushed out to greet him. Luna appeared from behind the house like a spirit and took his horse. Warner shooed the others back into the kitchen and proceeded to the barn to wash.

"Where's your pack?" Bill held Pablo back as they reentered.

"I don't know. I gave it to Luna and told him if anything were lost I would remove his thumbs and send them back to Yuma." He chuckled.

"Good, I left my saddlebags on the floor of the barn."

"Warner bought the boy from the Yumans for a bushel of corn. He's a slave who was captured further south in Sonora. I don't know if he understands a word I said, but he knows sign."

Pablo drew the edge of his hand across the base of his thumb like a knife. He opened both eyes with his fingers, in imitation of the boy's reply. That meant, "I see clearly with two eyes, I understand."

Warner stomped in, ducking his six-foot-five frame under the low door jamb. Juan Largo—the Indians and Californios had named him well. "You each owe me a dollar," he said. Then he kissed Anita on her rosy cheek, gave her a pat on the small of her back and folded his frame into a chair at one end of the table with a grateful sigh.

"Long ride today. I'd rather walk. Not as tiring, though slower. But you can't chase cattle on foot. Let's eat, honey. Then we can fill in the blanks of our lives over fresh coffee."

They ate venison stew from a big earthen pot, on a nice set of glazed clay plates from Mexico. Whole chunks of corn, a green vegetable of some sort, onions and short fat carrots thickened the stew. Cornmeal dumplings with the texture of tamales floated on top. It tasted too good to talk.

"I heard a shot," Warner said between bites. Pablo pointed at Anita and kept chewing. She blushed and waved her fork at her husband, rolling her eyes.

Luna slipped in, Anita filled his bowl and he slid out the door with a side-long glance at Pablo.

"Why do you call him Luna?" Bill asked Anita.

"We couldn't pronounce his Indian name, which means moon god. The Spanish name he chose is Santos de la Luna. Saints of the Moon. Everyone calls him Luna, or Lunito, little moon."

After lunch, Pablo and Warner sat on the porch sipping hot coffee and talking, while Bill helped Anita clean up. They took the dishes out to the trough to wash. Bill went to the hand-dug well beside the river for more clean water. The rinsed dishes were placed on a wooden rack in the kitchen to dry. Anita and Bill chatted excitedly, searching for mutual friends, exclaiming over life on the whaling ships, and confiding about their experiences in California.

Anita Gale had been the only child of the lonely wife of a whaling captain. When she was four, her doting mother died of scarlet fever. Grieving, Captain Gale took Anita to sea with him. That year, and the next and the next, and every year he told her that this would be her last voyage. But he always gave in and took her again, for so she pleaded, and she was such good company.

Anita raised the spirits of the sailors with her joy at each day's work, scampering over the ship like a kitten, swinging from the rigging like a monkey, or hiding to spring out with a shout from any nook or chest or cupboard. She became her father's cabin boy and learned to cook.

In her seventh year at sea, when she was eleven, Anita fell in love with one of the crew, a boy of only fourteen. She began to spend time with him, to bring him treats from the galley, to hold his hand. The rest of the crewmen set to grumbling. She was a pet to all of them. They were jealous and protective. They knew the boy saw her as a woman, well before her father did.

One night, the captain awoke to find Anita gone from their cabin. She was on deck in the moonlight, kissing her boy, lying on a coil of rope.

Captain Gale was furious. Cursing himself for a fool, blaming no one else, he put her ashore at Los Angeles—to be the ward of Señora Eustaquia Pico, Pío Pico's mother. The Picos treated her as a daughter, she learned Spanish, and adapted to frontier town life. There she met John Warner, who ran a store in Los Angeles and was a friend of the Picos. Warner was naturally paired with Anita, as a rare fellow American to whom she could speak English and talk of home. They grew to be friends. They fell in love. After her quinceañera, or fifteenth birthday, which is the year of coming out in Mexico, and just before Warner's trip to the East, they were married at San Luis Rey Mission.

Upon his return to California, Warner took Anita to live at his new ranch, the most remote in southern California. The nearest neighbor was fifteen miles away. (The Indians didn't count.) It was one hundred thirty miles to Los Angeles, eighty to San Diego. Here she lived, pretty, sweet and lonely— in the way that only someone who has spent their life as the center of attention for a large family, or a ship's crew, can be.

Anita's world at the ranch was John Warner, Luna, a nearly four-year-old daughter named Mary Ann, a native servant girl called Fanny (also bought from the Yumans), their animals, and the endless wilderness under an immense, thin-aired sky. Anita was thrilled that Bill would be staying less than an hour's ride north, at Cupa. He was happy to have her as a neighbor. They knew they would be friends.

O N the porch they could hear her husband yelling at Pablo, "You can't go backwards, you fool. The Americans are coming. You were there. You saw what they're like. You're twice as educated and twice as smart as ninety percent of them, and all of these Californios. You and Bill should stay here, work with me. I'll give you a share of the land. You already have cattle. When the Yankees come we'll be kings."

This was the third such offer they had received. Each one had sounded good to Bill, but Pablo was adamant.

"No, Señor Warner, I must go first to my family, to my people, to Cupa."

"Those aren't your people. Old Chief No'ka is a fake. Manuelito will tell you. The Pauma are your people, not these wild throwbacks. Your father is very old and not well. To him it doesn't matter."

He put his hand on Pablo's shoulder, as Pablo's face went stubbornly blank. Pablo stiffened and shrugged it away. Warner sat back.

"Go to your father and see what he says, then come back to me and we will speak again." John's voice was gentle now, and Bill could understand how Anita might love him in a daughterly way. At thirty-seven, he seemed too old to be her husband.

Warner retired for his siesta to a room that adjoined the kitchen. Pablo and Bill went to the barn to fetch a cow skin to throw on the ground. They walked to the river and dozed under the weak sun.

It was very open around the Warner ranch, which Bill thought was strange. He had grown accustomed to camping among the huge oaks. The shelter of their leafy living rooms had become his extended home. It would be nice to have a house among them.

Pablo said security was the reason Warner had built his house far from any trees. There was nothing nearby for man or beast to hide behind.

T H E Y awoke to a chilly breeze; the sun falling pale over Mount Palomar. Pablo paced, flattening the dry grass. He had seen enough of the Warners. He had paid every debt of conscience. He wanted to saddle up and push on to Cupa. He was worried about his father.

They readied the horses and bade goodbye to John and Anita, both of whom seemed truly distressed by their departure.

Warner had not said all he had to say: "It's a shame about Las Flores. The Picos have gone too far this time. Next they'll want to take back the mission." He looked disgusted.

Pablo said not a word. He stared at Warner.

"You stayed away too long," Warner protested. "Now I feel bad about ever taking you with you."

Pablo still didn't reply.

"It's a nasty business, cheating a man of his land," Warner said to Bill. "But there's nothing any of us can do about it. The Picos cannot be denied. They're too powerful."

Anita kept quiet, her eyes on her boot toes. Pablo watched them both intently, mute.

Warner fidgeted. "If you insist on going now, I'll have the boy show you a shortcut to Cupa."

Pablo only knew the way by the Santa Ysabel road. The village was at the base of a tall granite face called Eagle's Nest. He had only to keep the mountain in sight to get there. But it would be dark before they arrived. He nodded. Warner barked out, "Luna," and they followed the wary little guide across the river and into the hills.

Two

Kuupiaxchem

13

CUPA

T H E Y traveled at a steady trot, barely looking to right or left, eyes on the rump of the boy's paint pony, or on the tail of the horse ahead, pushing their mounts as they had not done since the run on the beach to Las Flores. The Yuman knew exactly where he was going. In the gathering dusk, every blind canyon or insurmountable cliff opened obligingly before them. They heard the clip-clop of hooves, on rock, in sand, then on dirt, then in grass.

The smells of equine sweat, sage, the oaks, and finally pines accompanied their progress north.

About half an hour on the trail, they were enveloped by a foul stench of rotting flesh. It must have been a dead deer or steer. Coyotes yelped, growling and feeding, but the men saw nothing. The stink faded and was replaced by the pungent wet-muck odor of a tule-lined stream. A cold wind wrinkled Bill's nose.

Luna turned up a soggy path. They were walking now, close to Cupa, not wanting to surprise anyone. The sun had set, but colors held to wisps of cloud that hung on the summit of Mount Palomar. Up ahead, slim streaks of very faded pink kissed the crags of Eagle's Nest. A glimmer of light reflected from the granite face, way above the dark tree line.

"Cupa," said Luna. He spun on the trail and brushed past, fading like a ghost into the dark.

"Adiós, chico," Pablo muttered.

He nudged his horse forward and called out in his language, "Father it is I, your son, High Cloud Comes, also known as Pablo Verdi, who seeks to visit you. I am here. If you are here, answer me." He said this twice as they clattered up the main street of the village. People ran alongside, shouting. Torches appeared to spook the horses. Murmurs came from houses they passed. Doorways filled with people, and finally a woman ran out an open door, shouting, "Pablo. It is I, Ladislaya, your mother. We are here. We welcome you, High Cloud."

Bill held the horses in a growing crowd while Pablo embraced his mother and entered the house. The doorway filled with curious people, and Bill lost his chance to witness the homecoming.

They had changed back to Indian garb for the trip to Cupa. In the dimness, Bill was inconspicuous. He hadn't uttered a word and couldn't tell if anyone addressed him, so unfamiliar was the tongue he heard.

He waited until Pablo appeared at the door and called out in English, "Bill come in, I want you to meet my parents."

Bill handed the horses to the nearest man, and entered the house.

"Bill, please meet my father, and my mother, Ladislaya. This is Bill Marshall, my compañero."

Bill said, "Pleased to meet you, Ladislaya. Mucho gusto."

She laughed at the way Bill said her name. "Ladi," she told him, shyly touching his hand. "Everyone calls me Ladi."

She was small and slim, like Pablo, of the Ipai, a coastal tribe. She wore a fur wrap over a long homespun wool dress.

"And my father . . . Francisco Verdi."

Francisco was lying on a raised bedstead that looked as if it came from the mission. It was covered in soft furs. A fur was draped over him. Bill walked forward and bent to take his cold hand. Francisco held on and looked closely at Bill's face, then at his clothes. He dropped Bill's hand, a laugh rattling in his throat, his wicked grin a skeletal version of his son's.

"You too? You're an American not an Indian. Did you make him dress like this?" he asked Pablo.

"That's the way we both want to dress. When in Rome do as the Romans, remember."

The sick man coughed and choked. He put his hand out in refusal when Pablo went to help him. "I'm fine, just a bit cold. Ladi, please . . . a couple of sticks on the fire."

An open fire glowed in a circular stone depression at the center of the single room. The floor was made of river stones, more or less flat and set in the earth. The walls were a basketry of flexible sticks about the diameter of a thumb, placed horizontal and woven in and out of larger vertical posts. Mud had been plastered against the weaving to keep out the wind. The fire had baked the mud in place. It was cracked here and there and cold air filtered in through the fissures. The roof was thatched grass with a hole at each eave, high against the peak to let smoke out. There was a box made of straight lashed sticks hanging from the ceiling for food storage. A couple of bundles, some cooking utensils and two handmade wooden stools completed the furnishings.

Francisco cleared his throat with a gargle.

"I should warm these old bones in the hot pools." He shivered. "The chief will want to see you," he said to Pablo. "And you should also pay your respects to the chief, Señor Marshall. We've heard about you for days. What took you so long?"

"I was teaching Bill the ancient timeless ways, Father, and relearning them myself. We were hunting and camping, drying meats, moving through the land as our grandfathers did."

"Your grandfather spent most of his life building the mission. His father, my grandfather, yes, he was a native man." Francisco was sitting up. He looked dangerously thin. Ladislaya wrapped him in a long coyote skin robe.

"And how did you find the ancient ways?" she asked.

She was looking at Bill. He stood uncomfortably tall, too big for the room.

"I enjoyed them. Pablo is a skilled hunter and excellent teacher. He even showed me how to do the work of a woman." They didn't laugh. "He taught me to grind acorns." When no one commented, he nervously said, "I have a lot more to learn."

They helped Francisco to his feet, Pablo on one side, Bill on the other. He was so light Bill could have carried him in his arms like a child. No one knew what was wrong with him.

When they left the house, Pablo chirped in Cupeño to the man holding the horses. They walked through the town and a few yards down a trail to a little stream running in a rocky ravine. There were pools giving off steam, but it was too dark to see much else. As they helped Francisco across the rocks, heat rose from the flowing water. Francisco pointed to a pool and they led him to its edge. There were two others in it, submerged to the neck. Francisco dropped his robe and lowered his naked skeleton gingerly into the steaming water. He sighed and spoke to the two in the pool. They laughed and looked shyly at Pablo and Bill. There was just enough moonlight to see that both were women, similar-looking. One said something to Pablo, who shrugged and dropped his robe on his father's. He untied his breechcloth and slipped into the water. Ladislaya folded her robe and dress and followed.

Bill looked behind and saw others coming to the pools for a bath. They were going to different parts of the creek, above and below. He put his robe on a rock, shivered in the cool air and went in without removing his breechcloth. The water was hotter than expected and he jumped back out to ease in slowly. His legs burned.

The women laughed and asked Pablo something. He translated.

"They say, why does he have his clothes on? Is his equipaje so ugly it would frighten us?"

Bill blushed. "No," he said too loudly. "I'm shy." They all giggled.

"Americans do not undress before strangers," offered Pablo.

Bill was finally all the way into the pool. Heat permeated his skin; spread to muscles and bones; there was a strong sulfur smell; he began to sweat.

"This is a very hot pool," Francisco said softly. "Some are less hot, some cold. You have to find the temperature you like, or go from hot to cold, like I do."

The two women left the pool and scrambled over some rocks to another close-by spot, with a separate stream of water. One was older, Bill thought, from the slightness of her form and careful way she moved. "Water is cold," said the younger in halting English.

Pablo introduced them in Spanish and then English. "Bill, these are the two most important women in Cupa: White Fox, the wife of Capitán José No'ka, and Dominga Falling Star, their daughter. Please meet my *mom-nawechom* brother, William Marshall, known as Bill."

Bill said "Mucho gusto" twice. They mimicked him. Then White Fox spoke rapidly to Pablo in Cupeño. Clicks, grunts and sighs punctuated the phrases. Impossible to learn, Bill thought dejectedly. They mercifully switched to Spanish. He understood that the chief had retired and shouldn't be disturbed.

Francisco crawled to the cold pool, submerged to the tips of his hair, and floated, holding his breath for a minute. He came up gasping and sputtering, got his breath and crawled back to the heated water.

"After the cold it doesn't feel so hot."

Bill took the hint and flopped into the cold pool, splashing the ladies and three others who had slipped in. He yelped at the shock of the icy water and submerged as the old man had. The cold made his temples ache, but he tried to stay down. When he burst the surface, sucking in air, he was alone. Everyone had scrambled into the hot pool. They were chuckling at his screams.

Bill cannonballed into the hot water. Strong arms held him under for a boiling second. They let him up and Pablo said, "You nearly drowned my father."

Francisco went back to the cold pool. He stayed a minute, then got out.

Ladislaya wrapped him in his robe and led him up the bank. He had gained strength and walked steadily on his own.

Pablo asked White Fox to give their regards to her husband and to inform him that he wanted to ask permission to stay in Cupa. She wondered, "How long," and he said, "We want to stay. We have no plans to go elsewhere." She said "We?" and he said, "We." A meeting was set for the morning.

The women unselfconsciously left the creek and walked up the path. They didn't have any robes on the bank and must have walked down as naked as they returned.

In the dark their bodies looked perfectly sculpted and hairless. Bill wondered if they thought hair was ugly, like the Chinese. He was hairy of arm and leg and had a full beard, grown out since his first day in San Diego. It was less than a month, but seemed like years. "Time flies when you're busy," his father always said, to steer him to his chores. "Time flies when you're having fun," was Bill's unuttered retort. He would shave in the morning at the hot pool before greeting the chief.

Pablo and Bill stayed in the stream another hour, until their muscles turned to jelly and their sun-dark skin had wrinkled white, then they too went up the trail—to fall asleep in furs piled around the fire on the floor of Francisco's house.

14

MOURNING

B I L L arose at first light. He gently rummaged in his pack for a razor and a lump of soap, and slipped out the cowhide door into the chilly morning. The Cupeño slept late. He wanted to get a look at the town and visit the hot spring without causing a commotion.

Cupa was two rows of houses set in an oak grove, separated by a cobble and packed-earth street about thirty feet wide. There were twenty or so houses on each side of the street, with a large oak closing off the upper end. Beyond the great oak were more oaks and a few scattered dwellings. The northern row of houses backed onto the bank of the noisy stream with its steaming pools.

The little river ran through the town in a rocky gorge, about twelve feet below the level of the houses, then flattened out after two hundred yards, to wander into a tule-lined meadow. On the north side of the stream were other houses, and on a bluff just before the land flattened stood a small chapel, about twenty by forty feet, made of adobe, stuccoed and whitewashed. The walls were tall and the peaked roof was of tile. This was another Franciscan visita. Padre Peyri had determined to build a chapel near any Indian population center, even if it were to be unmanned by priests ninety-nine percent of the time.

The houses of Cupa's main street averaged twenty by twenty feet. They were mostly made of woven brush. The roofs were grass-thatched, with two slopes and gable ends. Some of the homes were unadorned adobe. All of them had a shady ramada—a flat-roofed porch—on either the street or back side; some had both sides protected. The ramada was made of poles and covered with brush.

The town had a friendly, tidy and well-maintained look. There had to be latrines, corrals for cattle and sheep, and horse stables nearby, but not close enough to smell or fill the town with flies—downwind, southeast of the town, toward the Warners'.

Bill walked the deserted street and descended to the hot pool to soak and shave his whiskers. The pool seemed smaller than the night before but was just as hot. It scalded the tender skin of his thighs. He tried a couple of pools further downstream and found one that had hot water on one side and cold on the other.

He washed and shaved, then sat in the pool absorbing the heat, moving to the cold side and back, enjoying the steam that enveloped his face in the cool air. A few kids climbed down to the pools to bathe, looking like little Eskimos in their furs. They leapt naked into the heated water.

A piercing scream shattered the air. Mournful wailing arose from the village. It didn't stop. Bill left the pool and hopped rocks back to his robe. The children stared with open mouths at his bright pink body.

He hurried up the bank. There were people crowded in front of Francisco's house, the source of the spine-tingling lament. He pushed his way to the doorway and in. Pablo slumped cross-legged on his robe pallet, sobbing. Ladislaya rocked on the edge of her marriage bed, holding Francisco's bony shoulders, his head cradled in her lap, her hair crudely hacked off to fall where it may, keening at the top of her lungs.

Francisco had died peacefully in the night, hanging on to life just long enough to bless and be blessed by his returned son. The People at the door began to sing—a mournful chant that spread throughout the village. The melody was eerie, atonal, with just a hint of familiarity, akin to one of the sad Christian hymns. The chant grew in volume to permeate the great oak grove surrounding the village. It scaled the granite face of Eagle's Nest and filled the air—until it seemed to issue from the sky, sung down by immortals.

Pablo's father had asked to be buried in the traditional manner—not buried at all, but placed on a pyre of saplings piled high in an open space on the mountainside. He had been wrapped in his best robe and laid gently on his handmade bed. Laid with him were lance, bow and arrows, dried venison, acorns and other seeds—and a rosary and crucifix, should the Great Carpenter wish to recognize his former disciple. Hammer, chisels, saw and nails were spread out at Francisco's feet.

The fire was lit and fanned Ladislaya added her hacked locks to the blaze. Chants mingled with the dense cloud of smoke and rose high, to spirit the dead man into the blue mystery of the heavens.

/ / /

FRANCISCO had first doubted his Christian faith when the Franciscans lost their missions and land. "If this God cannot protect His own servants in His own house from the Spanish, who are now called Mexicans, who want to steal everything from them, then He is a weak and ungrateful god and not worthy of our respect." Pico's subsequent administration had only proved the helplessness of God to protect his flock from the enemy.

The loss of Las Flores to Pico had been the final blow to Francisco's shattered faith. From that day, he had left his life's work at the mission to live with his old friend, José No'ka, in the still mostly traditional village of Cupa.

Over the decades, Capitán No'ka, and his father and grandfather before, had resisted the mission of the Franciscans and the arguments and entreaties of the priests and converted Indians.

"Let this new God prove himself," they said. "What has He done but to make us sick with his secret diseases.

"Look at us. Our gods have been good to us and to the other creatures, to the plants and to the very earth we stand on. Why should we be unfaithful to our gods who have been so faithful to us? Who have treated us so kindly?"

The exclusivity of Christianity especially rankled. "How could the new God be so jealous and insecure that you had to renounce all other gods in order to embrace Him?" they asked.

"It would be like turning out your old, faithful wife, whom you dearly loved, to the coyotes, every time you embraced a new wife. What kind of a man would do that?"

This was the argument closer, for that was exactly what the priests had demanded that they do: to choose one from among their wives, and to reject the others.

So the Cupeño remained faithful to their traditional beliefs. They had allowed the Franciscans to build their chapel on the gentle rise across from the town—because it could not hurt to have a house for this new God nearby. The priests always brought gifts and goods to trade. They were pleasant, respectful and sang beautiful songs. It was right to be hospitable to those who came in peace. Many had submitted to baptism. But one need not heed the many tenants of Catholicism, or every word the priests uttered.

When Las Flores was sadly lost, Francisco had been embraced by the Cupeño, with nary an "I told you so." Now he lay at rest; his soul, or chamson, departed to Tolmar—where all People united to live in joy—or to heaven, though Pablo and his mother agreed they were probably one and the same.

By midday the village was back to normal. Ladislaya had stayed by the ashes of her husband to chant and keen. She was his only wife and Pablo the only surviving child. The weight of mourning was on their shoulders.

Pablo couldn't sit still. He decided to ride immediately to his father's people at Pauma, to bring them the news and to pay his respects. But before he fled, he wanted to have his meeting with Chief José No'ka. Pablo wished to secure Bill's place in the village. If allowed, Bill would remain at Cupa to look after Ladislaya until Pablo returned.

15

THE KUUPIAXCHEM

T H E Y met the chief under the ancient oak at the east end of the main street. The consultation had become a tribal meeting, partly to honor Pablo's father, partly to make public their request for residence, which was unusual because of Bill. The entire village attended, close to two hundred people counting children, mostly dressed in the traditional manner: breechcloth and fur cloak or coat for men, and tule-grass skirt with deerskin apron and a fur cloak for women. The women also wore shell-embroidered belts, shells braided into their long hair, and jewelry of shells or beads, with bits of silver and gold. Both sexes kept their hair long, from shoulder length on down to the ground. Bangs, cut straight across the forehead, were a popular style.

The Cupeño looked healthy and strong. Their bodies were muscular; most were stocky with well-rounded forearms and calves, thighs, shoulders and buttocks. Their faces too tended to round, with slightly oriental eyes. Skin varied from brown, lined and leathery, to light tan and baby smooth. All eyes were dark and hair black.

Pablo and Bill sat with Capitán José No'ka, his wife, White Fox, his daughter, Falling Star, and his son, Jacobo Stomping Deer. They faced the semicircle of curious faces, looking down the neat street of Cupa, over the oak grove to the plain beyond, and on to the blue-green bulk of Mount Palomar.

The chief was a dignified man, about forty-five years old, with a strong, weathered face. His head was large, his nose thick, his eyes deep set and widely spread. His mouth was supple, surrounded by laugh creases. Long gray hair rested on the ceremonial cape of hawk and eagle feathers that adorned his shoulders. He had smiled, his eyes twinkling merrily, when Pablo and Bill met him. Now he was serious. He raised his hand for silence.

No'ka gave a short eulogy for Francisco Verdi, a man who had dedicated himself to the mission; who had mastered the *sosabitom* art of carpentry; who had returned to die among friends and fellow spirits, among his brothers—to die as one of the People.

"Huh!" shouted the crowd.

The chief welcomed Pablo, to be known in Cupa as High Cloud Comes. He commended High Cloud for honoring his father and the tribe; for renouncing the Franciscans and Mexicans to embrace the ancestral way of the Kuupiaxchem. High Cloud could take his father's place in the village, living here as Kuupiaxchem. "Huh!"

Kuupiaxchem was the Cupeño's own name for their tribe. Pablo told Bill it meant "Those who dwell at Cupa." If he were accepted, Bill too could eventually claim to be Kuupiaxchem, by virtue of living there. He could be adopted. Pablo nodded at the chief's words.

"High Cloud has been traveling in the East for the last two years, spying on the Americans and learning what he can of their way of life. We will speak at length of these things, after the mourning for his father is complete. He has assured me that he saw nothing to compare with our way of living. He is honored to share our life and ways."

A spy? Bill couldn't catch his friend's eye. Pablo nodded again.

"We shall also consider the matter of High Cloud's compañero, Guillermo, who requests to live among us as a brother." The chief had switched to Spanish for Bill's benefit. He did not speak English and neither did anyone else, save his daughter.

She looked long at Bill with a shy smile, and the rest of the Kuupiaxchem looked at him in astonishment. No foreigner had ever asked to live with them. Never. Warner had come to live in a corner of their land as its owner, not with them. Murmurs rippled through the crowd; hurried whispers. A hissing undercurrent bubbled and burst into a hundred conversations, cut dead by the chief's powerful baritone.

"I recommend we allow him to stay, so long as he learns our language, respects our customs and abides by our rules of conduct. He must also marry one of our daughters within the year." He paused and every eye was upon Bill. "If there are any objections, I will hear them now."

The babble resumed.

"Where will he live?" said a man's voice. This was crucial. Warner had been banished to the other side of the valley.

"Here in Cupa, with Ladislaya and High Cloud. Then they will build a house. Or some father might offer him a home as a lure to his daughter." There was a lot of chuckling. The chief smiled.

Bill caught Falling Star's eye and she looked away, blushing.

"What if he is a spy for the Americans, like High Cloud has been for us?" Stomping Deer fiercely challenged Bill and didn't look away. He was wiry, a taut, teenage version of his father. "What if he should claim our land like Warner?"

"I'm not a spy." Bill said.

"But you are a *momnawechom*, a Yankee who lives on the sea, a whale killer and a ship deserter. The Mexicans may come to take you." Stomping Deer accused him directly.

"They're too busy counting cattle," said Pablo sarcastically. "Bill means nothing to them. And Warner already claims all of this land. What is there for Bill to claim?"

This was a sore point and the crowd rumbled. No'ka held up his hand.

"It is said that he bull-whipped Leandro Osuna," Stomping Deer said stubbornly. "This cabrón will not forget. He will seek revenge."

The chief cut in, "And how many of the People have the Osunas flogged? This was a brave thing Guillermo did. We do not fear the Osunas."

"Tell us why you left your home on the sea," said Antonio Garra, capitán of one of Cupa's most powerful clans. His hands traced the words in sign language.

"I came to . . ." Bill looked to Pablo.

"Women are not allowed on sea ships," Pablo told them. "He came to marry."

"Hmm," nodded Garra.

A handsome woman stood to speak. "If he will stay, he should have a Kuupiaxchem name; a name we can all say. Everyone here has a tribal name."

"My name is Bill, not Guillermo. Bill Marshall."

"A traditional name would be good." The chief smiled encouragingly, happy to move to a safer topic. Bill shrugged.

"We can name him now," said Stomping Deer, baring his teeth. "What shall we call this paleface?"

"Pink Pecker," said one of the kids from the hot spring.

Laughter flowed in waves until some were crying and pounding the ground. Others slapped the backs of those in front of them. Names came fast and loud from every direction.

Pablo tried to keep up, translating, "Big Nose, Big Foot, Red Butt, Hairy Balls, Spotted Face, White Cloud, Whipping Boy, Woodpecker, Running Nose," until he could no longer speak for laughing.

Chief No'ka stopped the hilarity with a raised hand. By then, Bill had turned a shade of crimson. Chuckling still broke out if he looked at anyone.

In the relative quiet, Pablo said, "Bill is English for the beak of a duck or the sword of a swordfish. He too has a long nose. And he swims like a fish. He can be Duck Beak Bill or Swordfish Bill. Then we can call him Bill for short."

"That is a good solution," the chief quickly decreed, looking pleased. The laughter had broken any resistance to his wishes. "Duck Beak Bill is a good name. He can later earn another by his actions, as is our custom." There were murmurs of assent.

"Then it is settled. He shall live in Ladislaya's house until he finds a wife. Now we must excuse High Cloud, to go to his father's people, to bring word of their brother's death. We Kuupiaxchem will take sustenance, and by the weight of the earthly food we ingest, celebrate the lightness of Francisco's spirit flight."

No'ka closed the meeting by raising his two arms high and shouting "Huh." Everyone joined him in this exclamation.

They celebrated with a feast, singing and dancing. The chanting kept building until late in the night, the singers warmed by four great bonfires. Then a light snow began to fall, the first of the season. There was a great cheer, as though the celebrants had created the snow by their own energies.

Everyone rushed to the hot springs. The singing continued there into the wee hours, until the last of the People glided up the snow-covered path to their homes and a warm pile of furs—and their well-earned dreams.

As the snow began to fall, Bill had left the bonfires to go to Ladislaya at the funeral pyre, to bring her back to the house before she froze. He found her already sleeping, exhausted; a small fur-wrapped bundle under a snowy mound. He picked her up, light as her dead husband but exquisitely alive, and carried her home.

Bill gently tucked Ladislaya between soft coyote pelts stacked where her marriage bed had stood. She whimpered once, moaned like a child, and fell back to reverie.

He stayed with her, worn out too, bundled up like a furry animal, digesting the day until sleep overcame him.

16

FALLING STAR

T THE meeting, No'ka had assigned Falling Star the task of making Bill comfortable in the village. "Translate and answer his questions and make sure he is well fed," were No'ka's exact instructions. "See what he is like, find out why he's here. Maybe you'll like him. It's time you married."

She had said, "Papi . . ." and shook her head negatively, but did as bidden.

Next morning, at the hot pools, Falling Star was prodded to tell all by her best friend, Melones.

"Is he hairy all over, or only on the arms and legs?"

"I don't know, Meli, his chest has hair too. That much I saw."

"Is it soft like a puppy or bristly like a pig?"

"Soft on the arms. It tickles."

"You touched him?"

"Only my arm against his."

"He didn't touch you?"

"He put his hand on me a few times."

"How did it feel?"

"Tingly."

"Tingly good, or creepy-tingly?"

"Tingly tingly, Meli. Nice hands. Tingly tingly."

No'ka and White Fox gently lowered themselves into the hot water next to their daughter.

"Tingly tingly?" asked her father.

Melones chortled and Falling Star splashed her.

"Tell, tell, tell," commanded White Fox.

"I'm going to the cold pool," said Melones. She stood and clambered over the rocks using both hands and feet. She was extremely voluptuous. They watched her, until she submerged in a cooler pool with a shout.

"She is pregnant?" White Fox asked.

"She has missed a bleeding."

"Is the Pauma boy the father?"

"She hopes so."

"Tell us about the Americano," said No'ka.

"There's not much to tell. He likes to eat. He watches. He says little."

"Who does he watch?"

"Melones . . ."

"Every man watches that one," said White Fox. "What else?"

"Everything else. He watches everyone."

"Do his eyes change color?"

"No. Yes. It depends on the light."

"Did he say why he came?" No'ka interrupted.

"He came because Pablo came. They travel together."

"And why did he come to California?"

"Warner told him to come."

They were silent for a while.

"Do you want to marry him?" No'ka asked.

"Papi, I just met him."

"Well, do you like what you have met?"

"He is pleasant and polite."

"Your father offered you to the white boy," said White Fox. "He offered cattle too. Lots of them."

Falling Star looked at her father in disbelief. The Kuupiaxchem did not give dowries.

"Why not," he said. Who else will you marry? You have turned down half the men in the village and Bull Bear twice. What have you been waiting for . . . but for this gift, our guest? Why else has he come?"

Falling Star's mouth fell open, but soundless. Her hands came up.

"Daughter, do you like him?" White Fox took both flapping hands and held them. "Or not."

The answer was slow to come. "I think so . . ." She took a breath. "Yes, I think so."

"Good," said No'ka, as though that would be the end of it.

"It's too hot, Mami. I have to get out."

Falling Star joined Melones, who was just standing up. "I'm cold now. I'm going back to the heat."

"Did you hear what they told me?"

"They want you to marry the green-eyed guest. We already knew that."

"But Papi offered him cattle . . ."

Melones plopped herself into the hot pool, raising a wave.

"The *momnawechom* will have to ask her himself," she told the dripping parents. "The sailor must offer her a gift, as is the custom. If she accepts, she will marry him. She doesn't like your bribing."

"I told you, tonto," White Fox accused her husband. "You are just like a Mexican, trying to peddle his ugly daughter. Leave them be. It will happen if it will happen."

"It will happen, wife," No'ka retorted, heading for cooler water.

He hummed an ancient boy's puberty rite song, not daring to speak the words: "Looking looking, touching touching, tingle tingle, dangle dingle."

B I L L awoke with a start. It was light out. He had slept late. For just a moment, he didn't know where he was. Ladislaya was gone. His memory returned and with it the chief's words, "Marry one of our women within a year." Bill had been dreaming of Lugarda. A good dream, but here in the bright of day, a faint fantasy. This was real: Capitán José No'ka wanted Bill to marry his daughter, Falling Star. He would give one hundred steers, with one hundred cows and calves, as a dowry. They were to be pastured on tribal lands.

Bill knew the cattle would not really be his. No'ka would only give them when he took Bill into the family. The cattle would come back to the tribe with Bill. The offer was meant to impress, and it did. But it scared him too. Refusal would mean loss of face for the chief and embarrassment for his daughter. No'ka had made the offer too rich to gracefully turn down. Bill would have to accept or leave. The chief had sprung a trap.

Falling Star was beautiful by any standards. Her skin was a rich tan, soft and blemish-free. Thick black hair hung shiny to her waist. Her eyes were wide-set over prominent cheekbones and glowed with spirit. Her nose was strong. This, she had inherited from her father. Her lips were full and often parted in a smile or laugh, her teeth perfectly white and even. At repose, her lower lip was fatter than the upper. It looked like it would be good to chew on.

Falling Star had been solicitous all afternoon, bringing a bowl of venison stew, bending close, her robe open, inviting Bill to see and smell her sweet flesh. She had danced before him in her grass skirt, leaping and bending, athletic, strong, muscled like an acrobat, toned, smooth and balanced.

At the hot spring, standing erect, ready to drop into the cold pool, she looked like wet carved ivory, hairless and slippery smooth. When she emerged, waist deep, water streaming, her belly button a deep dimple, her breasts taut, nipples extended, her mane a dark cascade, she could have been the model for every mermaid ever carved on a wooden ship's prow.

Falling Star was not delicate like her mother, whose beauty was subtle and refined. She was physically more like her father, handsome and solid. She looked as if she could wrestle. Her smile told you she would win.

She, her father and mother all had an air of serenity that was infectious. It enveloped Bill and made him feel at home. But marriage was serious. Bill wanted to fall in love, like he had with Lugarda. Then nothing else mattered. It was Lugarda he wished to marry, if only he could.

He felt trapped and he didn't like the feeling. He needed to talk to Pablo, or Warner and Anita, someone anyway, to help him see through this new predicament.

17

NO'KA

BILL decided it would be best to start with Capitán José No'ka, to be sure he had understood him. The chief had been very straightforward. Bill would be so with him. They had all been naked together in the pools: the whole tribe. Bill felt he had nothing he should hide.

He had seen another young woman he liked—a cartoon version of a woman, like those little statues of fertility goddesses they dig up in Macedonia, all chest and buttocks and mouth. This girl was round in every direction and dimension; breasts like honeydew melons, belly like a pregnant woman, ballooning buttocks, her head as spherical as a pumpkin. She had told him her name with a beautiful welcoming smile . . . Melones. The possibility of a proposal to her might defuse the situation; give him room to maneuver.

Bill found the chief in a good mood. The snow had given everything a clean white coat. The big granite rock above the village glistened. The sky had reverted to blue and the sun warmed anything it touched—not unusual after a southern California snowstorm.

No'ka was sitting by the stone fireplace of his cozy adobe house. A window at his back with its wooden shutter propped open lit the single room. A sleeping mattress of pine boughs was covered in elk skin, with folded furs piled at the ends. Behind the bed was a wooden seaman's trunk that once had a padlock, and an elevated stove of solid adobe about two and a half feet high. It had three slots for three different burners, separated by adobe bricks, open at one end to feed in small pieces of wood.

Four three-legged oak stools stood by the hearth and two fur bundles were thrown in a corner. On the walls hung bows, arrows, rawhide halters and ropes, saddles, traps and hunting lances. From the solid logs of the pitched ceiling, two wooden platforms were suspended on braided leather ropes. One held food and blackened pots; the other eating utensils: cups, bowls, plates and serving dishes, all of fired clay. Baskets hung from the rafters and walls, tightly woven, light and flexible. Axes, a pick, a shovel and a brush broom stood in a corner.

Here was tack room, armory, bedroom, kitchen, living room and shed, all in a space twenty by twenty-five feet. The stone floor was gray, the walls gray-black from smoke, the pine ceiling beams blackened and cracked.

White Fox had let Bill in as she slipped out, leaving the wooden door half open for light and air, and maybe eavesdropping. The chief motioned Bill to a stool. It was warm by the fire. He wore only a breechcloth. He looked strong for a man of his age, with just a bit of belly.

"Welcome Duck Beak Bi'." A smile came with the name.

"Thank you. I hate Guillermo. Bill is easy."

"Yes it is. How was your sleep?"

"Fine. With good dreams."

"I didn't expect to see you so soon. Have you decided to accept my daughter?" The chief looked at the fire. They were speaking in Spanish.

What Bill had to say could only be simply stated. "I'm considering the offer."

"Have you seen someone else? I heard you were looking at Melones." No'ka accented the "o," and it hung round in the air.

"I looked at one with that name. She is nice to look at."

No'ka locked his eyes on Bill's. "There is but one Melones and many look her way." He sighed. "She is pregnant."

"The father?"

"One of the men." He evaded Bill's eyes.

Bill blushed. "I'm sorry, I shouldn't have asked that question. Excuse me."

"I will say this: If the seed of my dreams could find a way to her womb, then it might be me." His eyes twinkled. Bill blushed again. "Since her thirteenth summer, Melones has had her pick of the young men, but she has chosen a Pauma boy." The chief shrugged his heavy shoulders. "You looked upon my daughter too, she tells me."

"I looked at her. She is easy on the eye."

No'ka held his gaze.

"Where the eyes go the soul and body will follow. Here among the People it is not polite to stare. Looks mean something: that you want to challenge a man, or join with a woman, or exchange thoughts to understand. We go naked but we do not stare. It is rude." He chuckled when he saw Bill's embarrassment. "With Melones, of course, this is not possible—a wondrous being." No'ka paused, then said seriously, "Is the number of cattle too small? I did not want to anger Stomping Deer by giving them all away."

The trap opened, yawned at Bill.

"It is not that. The dowry is not important. It is a serious matter, a big step for me. I need to know more. That is all. I need to know Falling Star better."

"With the Kuupiaxchem this is not a problem. You may take another wife if she doesn't please you. Or simply put her things outside the door and she will return to her family. Of course, then you must return the dowry."

"And if she leaves me?"

"Then you must beg her to return . . . if you should want a woman back who wishes to leave you."

"I have met a Mexican woman who is much in my dreams." Bill looked at his hands.

"Yes we know . . . Lugarda Osuna. She dances in the minds of many San Diego caballeros. I have heard of her. I have not seen her, but I feel I know her. She pulls men in and pushes them away at the same time, until she becomes the unattainable idol of all and most coveted woman-prize. She is a mirage. She will marry José María Alvarado. It is written. They will unite in March."

"And, if she were to love me?" It irked Bill to hear it put that starkly. It irked him that everyone knew about his dream of Lugarda. It irked him that no one gave him the slightest chance of success.

No'ka grunted. "She will still marry Alvarado."

"Why do you want me to marry your daughter?"

"He wants a grandson with blue eyes."

Bill had not heard White Fox enter. There had only been a moment's shadow at the doorway. She sat on one of the stools and put her hands to the coals. She looked at the chief.

"My eyes are green," Bill said.

No'ka grunted again. "Yes, my wife speaks true. Blue or green, what matters is that you are American, and more important, that in her twenty summers, Falling Star has not found a mate among the Kuupiaxchem. Big Bull Bear is the latest to ask her. She has twice refused him."

A large and handsome Cupeño had given Bill a long look at the pools: a challenging look. Big Bull Bear was a fitting name for him.

The chief seemed puzzled. "What has she been waiting for, I ask myself?" He took his wife's hand. "Now you have appeared, and our daughter looks upon you favorably."

No'ka looked to his wife for confirmation. White Fox nodded her head. No'ka shrugged. "Perhaps she has always awaited your arrival.

"Then there is the manner of your coming, you a *momnawechom*, an ocean dweller, thrust naked from the bosom of the sea to ask to live among us. This is not a common occurrence. The only American who ever came here to stay is Juan Largo. And he came with an American wife, to live not with us, but next to us, in his own custom, in the way of the *sosabitom*, the Spanish, who came by land to conquer." No'ka sighed.

"There is much you do not know. You have met Warner here. You met him at your home in the East. He went to see the secretary of war in Washington, to give a report on Mexican strength in California. He has presented a plan to build a railroad from St. Louis to San Diego, following the Santa Fe Trail, passing through this valley. He has received a deed to our land, including all you can see, from Pío Pico. He builds a store here, at the trail's crossroad to Los Angeles and San Diego. He became a Mexican citizen for the acquiring of this land, but he is an agent, a spy for the Americans."

Bill sat still, his mouth open.

"You think we do not know these things? Warner himself has told me this. He says the Americans are like the million leaves on an oak, and strong winds blow them westward." No'ka fluttered his ten fingers, mimicking leaves floating sideways in the breeze. "Soon they will be here."

"Yes," Bill said. "It is possible. They are many, and restless."

"Yes, and if it be so, then we must ally with the Americans, and here you are. I like the idea of mixing our blood with yours. If you stay in Cupa, you can teach us your language and represent us to your people. A child will bind you to the Kuupiaxchem. A child will grow up to help us commingle. And a child of mixed blood may be very beautiful. Like Lugarda Osuna, whose grandmother was pure Indio." He smiled at Bill fondly.

"Now I understand," Bill told them. "A blue-eyed child . . ." He laughed and shifted uncomfortably, looking from the chief to White Fox. "I hope green will do." She gave him a sweet smile and nodded.

"I do not know why you appeared," said No'ka, "like a deer who has stepped from the forest into my path. I must loose my arrow. If I have missed, please do not take offense. I would be a fool to have lost the opportunity."

"Your arrow did not miss," Bill heard himself say. "If Lugarda Osuna marries José María Alvarado, as they say she will, I shall marry Falling Star."

White Fox had risen to take some red-hot coals from the fire and place them with a few sticks of kindling in one of the stove burners. She shot Bill an angry look, under furrowed brow. But before she could speak, José No'ka, capitán of the Kuupiaxchem, had risen to embrace Bill in a powerful hug. "Then you will marry our daughter in March. I am happy. I will tell Falling Star."

White Fox spit out a couple of sentences in Cupeño and No'ka answered as swiftly. From the look on her face, Bill was glad not to understand. She was tiny, under five feet, weighing less than ninety pounds, but perfectly proportioned. She never looked small, unless you stood right next to her. When she was angry, she seemed enormously dangerous—especially if you were sitting and she loomed over, fire tongs in hand, glaring with menace.

No'ka's translation tempered her outburst. "White Fox is delighted that her daughter will marry an honest man; a man of his word who does not hide his thoughts from his mother-in-law."

She banged down a pot and threw something into it. Bill was certain she had roundly cursed him. Her full name was Fox Who Protects Her Kits in Their Den. She was living up to it.

"I would not tell Falling Star the condition of your agreement," White Fox hissed, turning her back. Both braids swished as she tossed her head. The single thick clump of white hair that had changed her name vanished in a black blur.

"She already knows about Lugarda, wife of mine. This is a challenge to a daughter of good breeding." No'ka reached to hug her from behind. She tried to shrug him off but he held tight.

"You must offer my daughter a gift, as is our custom," White Fox warned Bill. "Only if she accepts, will you marry."

"Of course," he said. "Gracias."

"Pásale," said the chief, nodding at the door.

Bill slunk out the door into brightness. He looked up into brilliant blue depths of sky and took long chill breaths of mountain air. He needed Pablo. He remembered Ladislaya, still mourning on the mountain, slapped his face, and slunk back in to beg a bowl of stew to take her.

In the afternoon Pablo returned with Francisco's sister and Manuelito's wife. Between the drumming at the hot spring and the chanting and crying of the mourning women, it was a restless night.

Dawn found the ladies and Pablo in exhausted sleep. Bill pulled some clothes from his pack, bathed and shaved at the spring, dressed and rode to visit the Warners.

18

THE WARNERS'
ADVICE

B I L L took the well-worn trail leading south down the broad grassy valley toward Santa Ysabel. In a couple of miles there would be a branch to the left that led to Warner's. The morning was crisp and clear, empty of humans. Rabbits, antelope, deer and cattle were his company. Quail would rise in little clouds when he surprised them; rabbits ran, then stopped to stare. All else ignored him.

Bill had been practicing with a throwing stick that the Cupeño toss at small game with deadly accuracy. About two and a half feet long, curved, and sharp on the inside edge of the curve, it sweeps through the air parallel to the ground, revolving like a windmill. A skilled thrower can knock a rabbit over on the run, and down quail on the fly. But the stick is not easy to master. Quail were beyond Bill's capabilities.

He managed to hit two fat rabbits and tied them to his saddle to take to the Warners. Their bodies felt unusually warm in the crisp morning air.

The valley was open prairie with hardly a tree for miles. The Indians had created the parkland by repeated burnings of the brush, and the sowing of different grass seeds, over the centuries. Only the great oaks survived the fires, leaving rich grassland and scattered shelter for grazing animals—and the People who came to hunt them. It was like managing the pastures on a farm, only the animals were wild and there were no fences.

W H E N Bill trotted up to Warner's barn, Luna popped out and shouted. Warner emerged to greet Bill. They took his horse and sent him to the house, where Anita was making breakfast. They would be right in with fresh milk.

Bill gave John the two rabbits. Warner handed them to Luna, who looked them over with a questioning glance. Bill pointed to his throwing stick, tied to the saddle, and Luna smiled shyly.

When Bill stomped his boots on the veranda, Anita appeared.

"Oh, Bill, the sailor. I'm so glad you've come." She jumped up to stand on a rough-looking rocking chair with a cowhide seat. Holding her long skirt, bracing one knee against the back, she swayed to imitate the roll of a ship.

"Thar she blows! All hands on deck! Lower the boats," she cried, jumping nimbly back to the floor. "You're just in time for breakfast, come in."

They were talking ships and sailing when Warner brought the milk. Anita laid out a breakfast of scrambled eggs, strips of tough steak with a sauce of onions and chiles, beans, chorizo and coffee.

Warner wanted to know what was going on in Cupa. Bill told him, leaving a few things out. When he mentioned the possibility of marrying Falling Star, there was an awkward silence. Anita was the first to react.

"I've been teaching her English. No'ka asked me to. She's smart. Oh, Bill, are you sure you want to marry an Indian girl? They're so different. There are lots of girls in Los Angeles. John knows everyone there. It would be easy to find you a nice wife."

John took over. "She's right. No'ka's tribe are good people, but the old chief likes to keep things traditional. Don't be hasty. I was going to offer you a job with us. We need someone to watch the ranch when I go to San Diego or Los Angeles, and to mind the store I'm setting up. Anita knows every girl her age within a hundred miles." There was concern in his voice.

"Pablo and I want to live in Cupa." Their doubts had somehow made Bill more certain. "I like it there. No'ka will let me stay if I marry a girl from the village. He has offered a generous dowry if I marry his daughter. I have agreed, but asked for a couple of months to be sure. I'll marry no sooner than March."

"That's sensible. A lot can happen in two months," Warner said guardedly, after exchanging looks with Anita.

"Will you go naked in the village, as they do?" Anita was wide-eyed. "We stayed there while we built this house. I saw more naked men than a women should ever see. And they stayed up all hours dancing, and singing and drumming. We never had a good night's sleep."

Bill suppressed a chuckle. "Once you get used to it, it doesn't seem to matter."

"I asked No'ka to have the men dress, but he refused." Warner frowned.

"He told you to ask them yourself," said Anita.

"That's one of the reasons we built our house way over here. The other is to be astraddle the trail up from Yuma, so we're the first civilization folks see when they enter the valley. I'm enlarging the house to make a general store. We'll sell everything; trade horses and mules two for one; have a blacksmith shop for shoeing and wagon repairs."

"You think Americans will come? This way?"

"I'm betting everything I have on it. It's the only all-weather trail in from the east. That's why we're sitting here in the middle of nowhere, when we could be in Los Angeles, running a store in a comfortable society." Warner took Anita's hand.

"When?"

"This year, next year the latest. This is no secret. Thomas O. Larkin, the U.S. consul in Monterey, has been working with the Californios, who mostly would welcome us."

"The army or settlers?"

Warner looked away. "One leads to the other."

Bill sipped his coffee. It was hard to imagine wagon trains of Americans rolling by.

"I'll have to see it," he said. "Meanwhile we have it to ourselves."

"We sure do," said Warner.

"I'll be happy when they come," Anita nearly shouted.

"No'ka says you own this whole valley . . ."

"Forty-eight thousand acres of it," said Warner proudly. "I have the deeds signed by the governor."

"Does that include Cupa?"

"And all the land around it, to Rabbit Hole Mountain at the north and Palomar to the west."

"What about the Indians?"

"I offered to give sixteen square miles of my ranch to No'ka—four by four miles around the hot springs. Told him to build a stone wall, or at least pile rocks to mark it. You know what he said? 'Is the fence to keep you out or to keep us in?' Warner chuckled. "No'ka's no fool."

He should make that wall, Bill thought, biting his tongue.

Warner said, "He's a good man. He runs his cattle all over the valley; uses it as his own, which is fine by me. I need the Indians to work. If you do stay at Cupa, you could be a big help to us. Right now I need about twenty men for the hide harvest. You could help me organize it. Be my foreman."

"I don't know much about it."

"It's easy. All you've got to do is strip the hide, scrape it clean, fold it in half—two dollars a hide—that's all you need to know," said Warner. "We just need some manpower."

19

HIDE HARVEST

B U T it wasn't as easy as that. The difficulty lay in catching and killing the steers. This dangerous task required the cooperation of the entire village. Bill had to convince the Cupeño to help.

"So now you're working for Warner," grumbled Pablo when he heard the plan.

"I'm working with him, Pablo. We can all make some easy money."

"Warner always pays with goods at the store," No'ka grizzled when he was consulted. The normal arrangement was to split the hides fifty-fifty with the harvesters.

"I'll deliver the hides to San Diego myself. We'll get cash for our work."

"In that case, we should sell some of our own hides too," White Fox urged at the tribal council called to consider the proposal. "We could use some hard money this year." The other women murmured assent.

Bill had been surprised by their inclusion.

"The women have always been on our councils. My wife is their capitána," No'ka had informed him. "They do most of the hard work, especially at hide harvest. Without their consent, nothing happens."

"Two hides apiece will buy our needs," suggested an elderly woman.

The young men were excited at the prospect of a hunt, except for Stomping Deer and Big Bull Bear. They sat stonily silent until Stomping Deer leapt up to shout, "How does this *momnawechom*, who has been a Cupa visitor for only a few days, sit on our council? He is nothing to us and we consult him like a capitán. How can this be?"

No'ka let the meeting break into discussion for a few minutes.

"It is a good idea," Antonio Garra called out. "Why should we care who brought it to us?"

"Duck Bi' can help us to deal with Juan Largo and the *momnawechom* who buy our hides," No'ka said, raising a hand and looking hard at Bill. "He can get us money so that we do not have to depend on Warner, who only pays with goods."

"Things are cheaper in San Diego," Pablo explained. "We can get what you want from Fitch's shop. That is where Warner buys to trade to you at a higher price."

"This will be a good test for Pablo and his sailor friend," No'ka argued. "We lose nothing by trying. It is time to harvest cattle, to make room for the young deer and antelope to graze and grow this spring.

"Huh," he shouted and the council echoed him.

Stomping Deer and Bull Bear remained silent, exchanging frowns.

"Don't worry about them," No'ka reassured Bill. "They are the best hunters and would not miss a harvest even if Warner kept all of the hides."

But Bill was worrying about the triangle of scowls and smiles that had passed between Falling Star, Bull Bear and himself during the meeting.

P A B L O steadfastly refused to do any work for Warner.

"His lectures back East ring in my ears," Pablo griped. He mimicked Warner's drawl. "'And folks, this is the best thing about California. No need for slaves; the Indians do all the work. The padres broke and trained them. Isn't that right, Pablo, you tell 'em.'

"When I saw the black slaves that Americans buy and sell, working on the roads and in the plantations, it made me ashamed. Is that what my father and grandfather, who labored their whole lives for the padres, looked like to Warner? Is that what these landowners think of the natives who live and work on their land? Are we some kind of captive labor force? Is that what I am . . . a slave?"

Pablo spit. "I will not work for that man. I'll help you with our cattle."

Bill had pledged half of any dowry cattle to Pablo. Pablo had agreed to take only the usual half share for doing the harvesting. They talked No'ka into letting them have some steers before the wedding.

"I don't care about the cattle," No'ka told them with a twinkle in his eye. "You will see how much work it takes to get your two dollars out of them. If you don't marry, I'll take the money."

Pablo and Bill strolled down the embankment to the hot pools just after twilight. It was cold and clear, the stars twinkling sharply in their black mantle. They could hear people chatting at the pools. The village murmured behind them. Pablo led down the dark trail. Bill followed carefully, thinking that he should refrain from sex with Falling Star until they were married, if they did. That way he could be true to Lugarda and avoid premature entanglement. A foot snaked out, silently tripping him into Pablo. Bill fell with a cry to the rough gravel. He rolled to rest against a large rock, losing his robe. Bull Bear stood straddling him, laughing, blotting out the stars.

"What happened, whitey," he grunted in harsh Spanish. "Let me give you a hand."

He reached down to jerk Bill up by the biceps with a powerful grip. Bill came up naked, and Bull Bear wrapped him into a bone-crushing hug. He was naked too. Bill smelled the flesh at his attacker's throat, a clean child's smell. He couldn't get a breath. His heart strained to beat. Bull Bear was squeezing him to death.

Bill bit down on the collarbone that was smashing his mouth, and kneed Bull Bear as hard as he could in the groin. Bull Bear kept up the pressure. He backed up the trail with Bill, blocking attempts to knee him again, ignoring Bill's tearing teeth. When they reached leveler ground, he threw Bill down with a growl and dropped on him, one knee on the chest and one at his throat. Bill was smashed to the earth, his single gasp of air knocked back out with a mouthful of blood and Bull Bear's flesh—no breath allowed back in.

Bill grabbed the Bear's balls and twisted. He punched with his other fist, but Bull Bear just bore down harder on Bill's throat. It was hopeless. A moment before he blacked out, Bill went limp and patted the strangling leg twice in surrender. He noticed it was hairless. He fainted.

Pablo spoke, his lips brushing Bull Bear's ear.

"You have won, Bravest of Bears, no need to kill him now."

The big man was silent.

"Killing him changes nothing. Falling Star turned you down twice before this one came. You will only anger her and her father. You gain nothing. It was the capitán chose Bill. He has use for this man."

The knee on Bill's neck let up a bit and Pablo heard a gurgling breath.

"You are our mightiest warrior. To destroy a helpless man brings no glory. You have struck him down fairly in hand-to-hand combat, and live to tell the tale. Let him survive to wear the shame of his defeat and remind the People of your prowess."

"We should kill these foreigners now. They bring no good," Bull Bear grunted. Pablo was relieved to hear him speak.

"You may kill them when we have done with them. For now we need him," he said softy, patting the Bear on the shoulder.

Bull Bear stood up. Bill lay there gasping. He put a hand tenderly to his throat. He felt the gravel embedded in his back.

Bull Bear loomed over Bill's tiny rescuer.

"Those are the same words No'ka spoke," he grumbled, "about Warner and his blondie bride. We should drive them out now, as we did Portilla and Pico, the *sosabitom* who also came to take our land and cattle. How many Americans do we need among us to learn that they are no good? Warner has been no better than the *sosabitom*, huh!"

Bill sat up and brushed the stones from his back. "I come to do no one harm," he tried to say, but the words caught in his damaged throat.

The Bear turned his bulk toward the squeak. His eyes were black holes.

"You have already harmed me, unwelcome guest." He took a breath and exhaled. "We shall see who else he harms," he spit over his shoulder.

Big Bull Bear faded into darkness.

"What do you mean by, kill them when we have done with them?" Bill croaked as he was helped to his feet.

"Don't try to talk. I was buying your life. That's all. You're cold. Let's get you to the hot pool."

But Bill didn't like the sound of it. He wondered whether Warner, with his Yankee self-confidence, suspected that his life hung on a thread.

T H E morning picked to start the harvest was icy-cold, the air crisp with big snowflakes, the sky obscured by a solid blanket of high gray cloud, the earth cushioned with six fresh inches of snow. The daylight was eerie, the valley a shadowless space, dim gray above, bright white below, with black dots in between.

Some of the black dots were cattle. Others were coyotes. In the air were buzzards, condors, eagles and hawks. Somehow they knew a feast was about to be served. The largest black splotches were hunters, stalking on horseback along the edges of the plain. They rode in two loose columns. Pablo led one; Stomping Deer and Bull Bear the other.

Valle de San José was surrounded by forest and canyons with thick brush that provided refuge for any animal who felt threatened. Deer and antelope would disappear up little paths at any sign of pursuit. Cattle would stay in the plain longer, but were just as wild, and would take to the hills in a mad rush, once frightened. The harvest strategy was to cut off and kill as many cattle as possible before they all stampeded. This was to be a hunt, not a roundup. It required many men to act in concert.

There were two accepted methods of killing cattle for hides, both danger-ous, both using the lance, with its thick ten-foot shaft tipped by a foot-long, razor-sharp steel point. The method of the most skilled and daring horsemen was to charge a running steer, and drive the lance into his heart through the chest cavity. It was difficult to make a clean kill this way. Like a bullfighter's sword, the lance had to be directed perfectly, so as not to strike any large bones, to slip through and pierce the heart. Even if this feat were accom-plished, the steer often as not fell on the lance, breaking the shaft, leaving the point deep inside the animal. The successful lancer thrust and jerked his blade back out in one smooth motion.

But if the blow were off target—and this was common because of the speed of the chase and the wild turns of the steer—the enraged animal would escape to gallop off to the bushes, or turn on horse and rider, lowering its horns for a desperate charge. Then the beast would have to be stuck again and again, ruining the hide in the process.

The surer kill was accomplished by a team of two or three riders who would rope a steer, trip or throw him to the ground, and toss a second rope onto one or more of his legs, holding him fast by backing their horses up on the ropes. One rider would jump down to cut the steer's throat with his lance, or in some cases, a sharp knife. The steer was held until he bled to death.

This took an equal amount of skill, roping expertise and physical courage. It resulted in cleaner hides and fewer broken or lost lances. The downside was that someone had to deal personally with an angry eight-hundred-pound bull, on foot, at arm's length. If the monster pulled loose from the ropes, or another wounded steer came at you when you were on foot . . . it was a race to your horse, or a lucky plunge of the lance, or you were trampled and gored.

T H E excited men rode slowly into the ten-mile-long plain, horses blowing steam from their nostrils, men bundled against the cold. The riders split into twos and threes and strung out, keeping between the cattle and the hills, Pablo's group to the right, the others to the left. Then, silently, they descended on the hapless beasts.

The cattle bellowed, their hooves pounding the snow-covered earth. But the hunters came from too many directions for them to organize a stampede. One by one they fell, spurting hot blood.

As quickly as one steer went down, the hunters would race after another, kill it, and then another. In five minutes the horsemen were spread over two miles of plain. Dark lumps of fallen cattle littered the snow-white ground. Here and there big blood-red stains stood out like candy ice, and smaller scarlet trails led to a fallen animal, or into the tree line.

Behind the hunters came the skinners, also on horseback, followed by the butchers: Both groups were women from the tribe. Then came coyotes, the birds of prey and the carrion eaters. Every carcass was covered with creatures, cutting, pulling, tearing it to pieces; spreading gore around each humped corpse as it disintegrated.

Bill was not skilled enough with rope or spear to kill a cow. He rode as safety man to any nearby hunters. He would cut off cattle trying to escape to the brush, redirect wounded beasts, decoy charging animals, or pick up any-one on foot who needed a ride to his horse.

Pablo did the same thing but with much more skill. He had been harvest-ing hides at the mission all his life and was an expert cow handler. He kept the steers away from the brush, bunched and milling confusedly in the open, until they could be picked off by the slaughterers. His pony seemed to be pos-sessed, plunging and turning, slathered and foaming at the mouth, working tirelessly without any instruction from Pablo.

All the horses were excited to madness by their wild gallops, the bellow-ing, the blood and the wounds they received from the horns of frightened cattle. Some would take off the minute their rider dismounted. Bill would race to grab their flying reins before they disappeared for the day. As a result, he saw action all over the plain. But he found myself pairing again and again with Big Bear and Stomping Deer.

They were a killing machine. One had only to direct a cow their way and it was dead, either impaled on Bull Bear's lance, or throat-cut by Stomping Deer after being leg-roped and tossed to the snow. Stomping Deer would loop a front hoof at a gallop, take a couple of turns around his saddle horn, slip off as his horse put on the brakes to drop the steer, race up on foot, jerk one horn back with his left hand, and slit the exposed throat with a slash of his big knife. He'd unloop the rope from the hoof, coil it as he ran to his mount and be off to do it again.

Bull Bear simply put his lance under his arm like a medieval knight and spurred his big horse at top speed toward the nearest steer, sinking the red-glistering blade of hardened steel into softer flesh or bone with sickening force. He would drive the impaled beast into the ground, back off, withdraw-ing his lance with a jerk, and dodge the sucking gush of blood that pulsed from the hole. If a steer was not mortally struck, Big Bear would impale it once more. What few got up again to run, Bill would haze back toward the big lanceman, or chase until they dropped from loss of blood.

After the night of Bill's beating, the Bear had been cool but cordial. Now he smiled and shouted at Bill as though all had been forgiven. It was inspiring to watch the big man at the hide taking. He used every ounce of his great strength with utmost precision. He did not tire at what was exhausting work for everyone else. But Bill hadn't forgotten his scare. His throat still hurt. He thought his voice box might be permanently damaged.

At day's end the sky was still gray, the light even dimmer. Over three square miles of white plain were scattered the carcasses of two hundred twelve steers, each a dark bloody pile surrounded by blood-trampled snow.

The men and women had left the field. Packs of coyotes tore at the steers; great condors ripped hunks of flesh from the bones. Golden and bald eagles lorded over several gory piles; turkey buzzards darted in for a taste, dodging the snapping beaks of larger birds and snarling coyote teeth. Crows dropped from the sky to snatch scraps. Three grizzly families dared the animal kingdom to challenge their choice of cows to feast upon.

Only the big cats, the pumas and bobcats, were too shy to partake until nightfall. They snarled and growled in the brush at the edge of the plain, spooking the horses, licking their lips in anticipation, whipping their tails in frustration.

The Cupeño had stripped as much choice meat as they could carry from the beasts. Liver, heart, tongue, filets and rump were sliced off and wrapped in heavy bundles with fresh cow skin. These were loaded on long drags made of saplings tied to either side of a horse's saddle and lashed together behind the tail with cross-sticks. The bundles were hauled back to Cupa, the meats to be roasted, dried and smoked. Even with most of the village working, only about half the dead cows could be butchered. It was a colossal waste of good meat; a grand feast for every beast in the valley.

The skins were stacked on the snow in a central location, one pile for Warner and one for Cupa. There were about twenty skins with Manuelito's brand in a third pile. Warner's brand was on fifty-two hides. No'ka claimed all of the rest for Cupa, about one hundred forty.

The chief had ridden out late in the morning to observe the hunt. He sat on a bearskin, spread out on a snow-covered hill with a good command of the valley. John Warner and Anita had joined him in the afternoon.

When the hides were counted, fires built by each stack and guards posted for the night to fend off hungry animals, Bill trotted up to report to his two benefactors. He had never seen them together—the two lords of the valley. He was curious to see how they would get along.

They were laughing as Bill dismounted. They watched him in amusement.

"So what do we have?" Warner's Yankee drawl cut off any small talk and Bill's chance to find out what was so funny.

"Fifty-two for you, one hundred forty for the Cupeño," Bill rasped in Spanish. He pinched his throat.

"Darn," spat Warner.

"Only fifty-two," echoed Anita.

They had agreed to give the Cupeño half the hides as pay for culling them. This was the standard wage. That left them twenty-six.

"Fifty-two, you can check them."

No'ka wore a satisfied smirk. "I told you this was not the best place to raise cattle, Juan Largo. There is too much competition from the game."

"The cattle do fine. You know they do fine. I just have to set my brand on more of my young'uns," Warner said irritably.

No'ka made no comment. The arrangement he had made, when the Warners first arrived in the valley, was that Juan Largo should brand his cows. All mission brand and unbranded steers belonged to the Indian herds. But cattle here were as wild as deer, and calves about as easy to brand. Each year the chief's herd had grown disproportionately. Warner was not a rancher. He had been a fur trapper, then a shopkeeper in Los Angeles. Cattle were a sideline, but for now he depended on them because of the lack of customers at his new store.

No'ka too was a reluctant rancher. It was his goal to rid the valley of cattle and restore the game herds. Cattle had flourished in the valley under the padres. But the huge herds were sensitive to drought and disease. They stripped the grasses and starved out the game. The Picos had slaughtered them by the thousands, just before secularization of the missions, reducing the herd to a few hundred. The cattle were readily replaced by hardier native game—deer, antelope, rabbit and elk further north. Wherever there was fodder, game flourished—due to the decline in the native hunting population by exposure to infectious Spanish diseases, and because of the Spaniards' distaste for any meat but beef.

No'ka enjoyed eating beef, but he objected to the wastefulness of the hide trade. When a ship came from Boston, it had to be filled. Capacity was about forty thousand hides so a lot of animals were killed at once. Most of the carcasses were left to rot. The hide-for-money exchange did not inspire a traditionalist who had little need for cash. No'ka preferred to cull a few animals at a time. Only what could be eaten. The Indians liked to use every bit of a hunted animal, down to the guts and bones. But if hides were to be taken, better they be Cupa's than Warner's.

Luna galloped up on his pony to shout out, "Cincuenta y dos," to Warner. He wheeled and shot back to guard his fifty-two hides.

"You see, we do not cheat like your patron, Pío Puerco," said No'ka.

Anita blanched and bit her lip.

"We need to cull more hides," Warner said to Bill.

No'ka turned to Anita. "Pico came twice to take hides for Father Ibarra of San Luis Rey Mission. Each time he slaughtered more than three thousand cattle, reported two thousand, took half of that as his share and kept the unreported thousand as well. That is why we call him Pío Puerco."

Anita blushed, but said, "I don't believe that's true." Warner glared.

"The plain was covered with rotting bodies for months. It stank like a whale boat," No'ka said with disgust.

"Poof," spat Anita, with a magician's wave of her hand. But No'ka did not disappear.

"I need to buy goods for the store," Warner told Bill. "I'd like to get another fifty hides." He ignored No'ka.

The chief crossed his arms and stared Warner down. "Enough cattle have been killed for the winter," he said firmly. "We have meat to last till summertime."

There was no way to harvest Warner's hides without the help of the tribe. Even then, it was impossible without killing Indian cattle too. It was difficult to see the brands at a gallop. And the herd had gone into the brush and canyons and would not be back to the plain until the smell of death subsided.

"I tell you what," Bill said, looking from Warner to No'ka and back. "We'll just take twelve of your hides to pay the vaqueros and leave you with forty. I've got plenty of my own to make up the difference. That way we don't have to kill again and you get the money you need."

"That's very generous of you, Bill," said Anita with a scowl at No'ka.

"Fine by me," said Warner.

No'ka's expression was unreadable. Bill knew he had overreached his authority.

"You still have the hardest work to do," was all the chief said. "Now let us go eat some of this fine meat, before I freeze to death."

No'ka stood to stretch. He bade goodbye to John and Anita, nodded to Bill, walked to where his horse was grazing, jumped on nimbly and rode off toward the village at a trot.

"What an unpleasant old man," said Anita.

"A good man, Anita," said Warner. "He just speaks his mind. We're lucky to have him as chief, and not one of the hotheads."

"How could you let him say those things about Tío Pío?"

"What he said was true."

"How can you say that? After everything he's done for us . . ."

"What has he done? He only gave us this ranch because he knew the Cupeño would never let him use it. It's worthless without No'ka's blessing."

"I'd better get going," Bill said. "I don't know my way that well in the dark. Goodbye, Anita, John."

"Goodbye, Bill, we'll see you tomorrow, I hope." Anita gave him a smile.

"Thank you, Bill," said John.

When Bill had mounted, he walked his tired horse back to the Warners'.

"What does *sosabitom* mean," he asked them.

"That's what the Indios call the Spanish," Anita said.

"I know. But does the word have any other meaning?"

"They'll never admit to anything else," Warner said. "But you know what I hear every time they say it? The way they spit the word out, sounds to me just like *son of a bitch.*"

T H E next day was spent preparing the hides to ship to San Diego.

The morning dawned cold and frosty. The sky had cleared during the night, letting frigid winter air down upon the sleeping valley. The hides had frozen stiff as boards. The first task was to spread them out to thaw in the weak sun, hair down on snow-flattened grass.

Two hundred hides cover a lot of ground. When they became flexible, the whole village started scraping every bit of meat, fat and sinew from them. Any flesh left on the leather would rot, destroying the value of the hide.

While the skins thawed, Pablo rode to Pauma to recruit some hands to prepare Manuelito's share. Warner arrived with Anita, Luna, Mary Ann, Fanny and Sally, the Yuman sisters whom he had purchased for nine bushels of corn at the same time he bought Luna. They had a lot of hides to clean.

Bill worked with the men and women of Cupa. They each took a hide, and painstakingly scraped it clean with a knife or a sharpened stone or a seashell, removing every scrap of gristle, meat or fat. It was hard work, as No'ka had said, and occupied most of the day. Everyone chewed on roast meat the women had packed. They ate fresh snow when thirsty and chatted or joked to pass the time. For Bill, the day went quickly. It felt good to be part of a busy community.

The clean skins were folded in half, hair out, loaded on pole skids, stacked twenty-five hides high and dragged back to the village. The Pauma who had come rode along to spend a night at Cupa. They planned to leave with Bill and Pablo the next day, in caravan for San Diego and the hide processors of La Playa.

Warner's wagon was piled high with his forty skins. He drove home with Anita, Fanny, Mary Ann, Sally and Luna perched on the stack. He would take his hides to La Playa in the wagon and bring back goods for his store.

No'ka had stayed at home. As Bill wearily dropped from his horse at the village corrals, the chief said, "You were right. We didn't need to take any payment for killing Warner's steers. But with the tribe, we always talk things over before making an important decision. It takes longer but prevents squabbling later."

Bill let his head droop. "I'm sorry. I just . . ."

"Go, go, don't worry. Go to the hot waters. I'll take the horse."

All evening, aching bodies were gratefully soaked in the sulfured pools. They were a luxury Bill was becoming attached to. Falling Star attended him to the point of obsession, massaging his shoulders and neck, rubbing his tired feet and hands, and bringing bowls of fresh melted snow when he was thirsty.

She teasingly slid her slippery body against him at every opportunity. She nestled her breasts against his back; she rested her head on his shoulder. It seemed she wanted to possess him now, this night, before he left for San Diego and a rendezvous with Lugarda. Bill was sure she knew his plan, with that instinct women have for a rival's proximity in time or place or mind.

Then she did something that embarrassed Bill; done so quickly, he barely had time to open his eyes in surprise and cry out, before she silenced him with her lips.

20

THE BACK TRAIL
TO SAN DIEGO

ALLING Star awoke to Melones's singsong voice and her mother's soft-spoken replies. They watched her stretch and yawn.

"Come, sleeping beauty, arise," Melones sang as she brought her friend a cup of tea. "We want to hear all about your evening. Come, sweet sister, we want to know how you bewitched Bi'o, how you made him forget his Mexicana bitch."

Falling Star held up a hand and sipped the desert-flower tea, letting her memory flow.

"Nothing happened until we were too hot to be in the pool. We sat together on a cool rock. We warmed the cold air and I sent my hands flying over his body like a flock of butterflies, landing lightly here, there and here. He spoke to me, his voice falling softer and lower and softer, until I heard no words, only sensations; goosebumps outside and melting inside."

"Was he up?"

"Up, up, up. It kept banging against me. I finally touched it. I said, what is this? He was embarrassed. Nothing, he said."

"Nothing?"

"Nothing! I was so angry, I yanked on it hard, one, two, three. He cried out and I kissed him on the lips. He kissed me back and kissed me again."

"Did he look into your eyes?" Melones wondered.

"He closed his eyes."

"Dreaming of the Mexicana," said White Fox.

"Then what?" said Melones.

"He held me and we breathed together. He said, thank you, sweet princess, and he went to bed alone."

"Princess? I wouldn't have let him get away."

"The daughter of a queen," White Fox told them, patting her womb.

"We should poison the Osuna señorita," Melones whispered.

"I liked that he was faithful to her; if I should win him, so should he be faithful to me."

A T dawn, Pablo and Bill had departed Cupa alone; the Pauma had stayed up all night dancing; they would follow at their own pace. Dressed in civilized clothing for their passage through the Californio ranchos, they led six horses, each dragging a load of hides lashed to poles and cross braces. Saddlebags held camp gear, weapons, food and spare clothes.

The trip to San Diego would take three days if they kept moving. Pablo and Bill were in the mood to move. The excitement of the harvest had only temporarily eased the pain of Pablo's father's death. Bill's evening with Falling Star had unfolded in such a natural way it seemed not to have happened. They were comfortable together; they had been from the first moment they met. Lugarda was different. She made him uncomfortable. The itch she gave him had lingered. He was determined to scratch it.

They crossed the Valley of San José and took the trail to Santa Ysabel, arriving at mid-morning for a late breakfast in the native ranchería with Ignacio, the village chief, who was Pablo's friend.

The Indian ranchería at Santa Ysabel was larger than Cupa and had been missionized. The priests had constructed a chapel with native labor, which was assigned to the mission at San Diego. Behind the spacious chapel, the Cuyumaca Mountains rose sharply, with thick pine woods and a good head of snow. Santa Ysabel Valley was narrower than Cupa's and more thickly wooded, but equally bountiful in pasture, stock and game.

The People were Kumeyaay. Though closely related to the Cupeño by marriage and proximity, they spoke a different language. Capitán Ignacio also spoke English, Spanish, Luiseño and Cupeño. He was a cattleman, in league with Captain Edward Stokes, who held the grant to Rancho Santa Ysabel, and Cockney Bill Williams, Stokes's majordomo. The Englishmen had gone to San Diego the preceding day with their own load of hides.

From Santa Ysabel, the trail passed through Rancho Santa María, which belonged to Stokes's father-in-law, down the San Pasqual Valley to Rancho Bernardo, then over low hills, bypassing San Dieguito, to Penasquitos and on to San Diego and La Playa.

On the trip to Cupa they had seemed to be journeying back in time. On this route to San Diego the clock thrust forward. Mile by mile, the Indian world receded, giving way to Spanish-Californio civilization. Game grew more scarce; cattle, sheep, goats and horses more numerous. The condition of the Indians went downhill as the path wound down from the mountains to the sea. Kings in Cupa; equals in Santa Ysabel; the natives were slaves in San Diego, hungry, dressed in tatters of discarded rags, working on ranches or in the town for scraps of food, whipped for the slightest infraction.

The forests thinned out, then vanished, replaced by sage and toyon, mustard weed and scrub oak. The sky itself shrank back from the earth, hiding behind a thick gray blanket of cloud, casting its pall of gloom upon their weary caravan of pack ponies. It was easy to understand why the Cupeño declined to make this too short journey into the grim future.

As Pablo and Bill emerged from Rose Canyon to a view of False Bay, Point Loma and the harbor in the distance, their spirits sank even lower. There were no ships in sight. San Diego without a ship was sad, barren, dusty and deserted. Bandini was at his ranch, Ti Juan, to the south. The Osunas, Alvarados, Ortegas and the rest of the Californios were off tending their properties and harvesting hides.

Tumbleweed blew in the square and piled against the adobe houses of the flea-infested pueblo. They only saw the storekeeper, Fitch, who called a foul-mouthed greeting and threw stones at a pack of dogs that harried the horses. Without a ship there would be no money to spend at Fitch's store. They didn't even bother to dismount, proceeding directly across the gray sands of the bayside to La Playa.

There they found life. The Kanakas were busy curing hides. The People helped them, half-breed, half drunk but still the People, Tipai and Ipai. And there was *momna*, the ocean, blue and cold and clean and beautiful. Bill missed the sea. He really had become an ocean dweller in the past five years. The hot springs would have to serve as his tiny port, if he remained at Cupa.

Two of the Hawaiians were lounging in the shade of a storage shed, strumming ukuleles—tiny guitars—singing a plaintive song. After greeting Pablo like a brother, they said that two ships out of Boston were in California waters, gathering hides. The captains had left the Hawaiians in charge of the tanning process and gone north to collect more skins at San Juan Capistrano, which had a passable anchorage in a nearby cove sheltered from winter swells.

Bill dropped the drags from the tired horses. The Kanakas unloaded the hides, counting them carefully, and stored them in a large shed belonging to the Boston company. The tally was entered into a ledger and payment promised on the ship's return.

The Bostonians always paid. Sometimes it took a year to gather the forty thousand cowhides needed to fill a ship. They didn't want to lose a single one to a competitor. To them, California's hide trade was a miracle, made possible by the huge number of cattle on the ranchos, and the scarcity of people to buy and eat them. Nowhere else in the world would a rancher slaughter a cow for two dollars, much less forty thousand of them. The profit on a full hold, docked in Boston, was one hundred thousand dollars, a fortune.

All hides ended up at San Diego, because it was the only harbor calm enough for loading the cured leather without exposing it to salt water. The skins were collected up and down the coast, stacked, cured, tanned and stored in La Playa until there were sufficient to fill a clipper. Only then did a captain jettison the ballast in his ship's hold, line it with clean brush to keep the bottom skins from wetting and moldering, and stack and compact the hides until his ship could hold no more. He paid for the hides as they came in, if the ship was in the harbor. He also paid on the spot if his men went to a ranch, or he picked them up somewhere on the coast with one of his smaller boats. But it was not unusual for the hides to be dropped at the company shed and paid for later.

Pablo asked the Hawaiians to have the money sent to Cupa with Manuelito, who would come in the next two weeks. Failing that, it could be left with Fitch. Pablo didn't want to spend a single night in San Diego—with its gloomy overcast, army of fleas and deserted adobes. And Bill couldn't sit still, this close to Lugarda. They bathed quickly in the cold calm harbor, strung their lighthearted horses together and headed north, up Rose Canyon, through Sorrento Valley, over the hills and down into Valle de San Dieguito.

At the river, Bill took the spare horses and went downstream to the coast, then up the beach, staying out of sight, to camp again at the mouth of the pretty little valley of Encinitas. Pablo had the delicate task of arranging a meeting with Lugarda and 'Zul, without alerting the Osuna men. He had already heard, through the Indian grapevine, that Leandro had sworn to kill Bill on sight. Whether machismo or not, there was little chance of Bill seeing Lugarda at the ranch.

Bill was amazed by the quality and speed of Indian communication. If a ship were sighted at Dana Point, sixty miles north, they would hear of it the next day at Cupa, ninety miles inland. Casual gossip spread by the same system of word of mouth, drumbeat and smoke signal. Everyone knew who was sick or pregnant, or had died or fallen off a horse or fallen in love—as in Bill's case—as soon as it happened.

There was only a little sharing of information with the Californios. The ranchers had their own system of gossip by daily contact with their neighbors. They would think nothing of riding twenty miles for an afternoon chat. There was always a good meal and a fresh bed for the bearer of news.

After two months in San Diego, Bill had resigned himself to the fact that there could be no secrets here, especially among the Indians. Only his thoughts, those told to no one, and his own actions, those no one else saw, were private. All else would be public knowledge sooner or later.

"And even your thoughts may be read if someone wishes to," Pablo insisted.

PABLO did not go to the Osuna ranch. He rode to the Kumeyaay ranchería that was farther up the valley. There, an auntie of 'Zul told him the girls were still at San Marcos with the Alvarados. She gathered a basket of quail eggs to sell and rode to San Marcos Ranch, where she was able to speak to 'Zul. They settled on a meeting place and time, and the auntie returned with the answer. Pablo thanked her and, having no gift, promised to bring her a calf. He circled the Osunas', keeping to the bushy hills. Just after dark he emerged from the oak-tunnel trail that led to Bill's camp.

Pablo's smile said everything. They embraced.

"I've been worrying all afternoon," Bill cried. "I was about to sneak over to San Dieguito to rescue you."

He threw some driftwood on his sputtering fire and they sat on the rocks to eat a dinner of roasted abalone, lobster and clams Bill had gathered in the afternoon. 'Zul had sent Pablo some fresh corn tortillas wrapped in a small white cotton lace handkerchief. As Pablo passed them to Bill, he said, "They're still at San Marcos. But they sent these for us."

Bill's frown turned to bliss as he took a deep breath of the scented cloth. It smelled of jasmine . . . Lugarda. He closed his eyes and inhaled again.

"The tortillas are to eat 'mano. There is no sustenance in that snot rag."

"Oh yes there is." The scent was invigorating.

"I'll bet you ten dollars she marries Alvarado."

Bill had to take the challenge. Indians loved to gamble, as did the Californios. Fortunes were won and lost on far more trivial wagers. Bill didn't usually bet because he hated to lose, and felt sorry for the loser if he won. This wager was different. If he won he would need the money. If he lost . . . he wouldn't care about anything.

"Ten dollars and the handkerchief."

"Done," said Pablo.

Bill stuffed the kerchief into his shirt pocket, pressing it to his heart. He said a prayer to every God who might be watching over them.

They stared at the fire, listening to the waves roll the pebbles. Pablo carefully cleaned his teeth with a twig, and told Bill the gossip he'd heard while waiting for 'Zul's auntie to return.

"Every rancho is slaughtering cattle. There are probably twenty thousand carcasses between here and Cupa. Everyone is fat on fresh meat. The coyotes and bears are so bold they don't even leave a steer when men ride up. They just snarl and keep eating. The stench of rot is foul in the lower valleys, and along the coast where there is no frost."

"I thought I smelled something deathly."

"The Kumeyaay are sad to see so many animals die at one time. They complain of the waste and that the ranchers do not give them their share of the money. The cattle belong also to the Indians, but here, where the ranchers claim huge tracts of land, they also claim all animals found on their land. The Osunas, Alvarados and Picos are the stingiest." Pablo spit and the fire crackled momentarily. He picked his teeth for a long time and watched the coals.

Pablo flung the twig into the fire where it flared and died. When he looked up, his face was emotionless.

"After tomorrow we go straight to Cupa. I know a shorter way. It is too depressing here for me. I will visit Father Ibarra another time."

Before Bill could reply, Pablo had rolled up in his skins, back to the fire. He took a couple of deep breaths and nestled into the sand.

Bill was not depressed. He was elated. He would be seeing Lugarda tomorrow. They were on a beautiful beach with bellies full of good food and a nice fire to warm them. But he was surprised that Pablo had canceled his planned stop at the mission.

He rolled down into his own furs to stare at the only two stars bright enough to penetrate the haze. If Lugarda said yes, he would take her away with him, then and there. What he knew in his gut was this: Like Pablo, he had no life here on the coast with the Californios. In Cupa, or at Warner's ranch, there was a chance for him to flourish.

21

BOX CANYON

T H E meeting place was to be a jewel-box canyon, six miles inland from Encinitas, about halfway to San Marcos, up a narrow valley that wound to the east out of Batequitos Lagoon. You followed a stream, passing through a dense twisted forest of stunted oaks, and emerged to a tiny meadow of new green grass. Rusty-gray cliff walls rose one hundred twenty feet on every side, and a dark cool pool nestled at their base.

The waters of the pool lapped at the shore of the meadow. Smooth granite boulders studded the grass. The pool was very deep. "Bottomless," said Pablo.

There was only one long way in and no other way out of the canyon by horse. No one would happen by this place. 'Zul knew the entry trail; Pablo doubted whether the Osunas had ever been there. It was perfect.

To be absolutely sure, Pablo's plan was to leave their horses in the brush at the top of the cliffs. "We can enter by jumping into the pool and leave by climbing up the rocks. We could escape if we had to."

They left Encinitas early in the chill of morning. A thick fog blanketed the coast. They only knew that the day would be fine when they crossed the hills into the valley of El Camino Real, the main north-south road. There, a weak sun warmed the dewy grasses, filtered through thin mist still drifting in from the sea.

They climbed out of El Camino Real onto an undulating mesa, following cow and deer trails through thick brush. After two more miles of this, the earth opened up as though God's wayward chisel had gouged a deep slot in it. At the bottom of the gorge, which was only eighty yards wide, was the miniature lake. A dark green line of trees pointed west through the outlet cut in solid rock. You could have ridden by fifty yards away and never see the canyon.

They tied the horses by a vernal pool trapped on the mesa. It was freshly wet with two inches of water and filled with tall bunchgrass. The horses nickered. Frogs and toads croaked and hopped out of their way. Mockingbirds scolded the intruders, then went back to singing their complex songs.

On foot, the lovebirds made their way cautiously to the edge of the cliff. They perched on a boulder to bask in the sun and await their mates' arrival. It was a long way down, looking much farther than one hundred feet. Bill wasn't too keen on jumping.

"I don't know, Pablo. It looks like we could get hurt."

"You see that jutting rock?"

Pablo pointed about forty feet below, to a ledge that thrust precariously from the cliffside. "We climb down to there, then jump. It's only fifty or sixty feet. I've done it before. You can't miss."

They scrabbled down more like crabs than birds, leaving their clothes at the top, and alighted on this rock platform. The perch was hard and cold, shadowed by the sheer wall above. Luckily the women soon emerged from the choke of oaks into the glen below. 'Zul was riding ahead, astraddle a thick fold of animal skin, wearing a yellow cotton dress and what looked like a man's jacket. Lugarda rode sidesaddle, in the same pale blue dress she had worn for their arrival at San Diego, wrapped in a dark shawl.

They dismounted and 'Zul spread the fur she had been using as a saddle pad on a sunny patch of grass. They led their horses to the pool to wet their throats, then tied them to a bush at the edge of the meadow. Lugarda walked to the fur and sat on it, unlacing her riding boots. 'Zul took off her moccasins and stuck a toe in the pool. "Ay," she cried. It echoed up to the tensed jumpers. She helped Lugarda pull off a boot.

When her back was turned, just as she tugged on the second boot and Lugarda's slim leg showed, disappearing into a white petticoat, Pablo let out a wild whoop and jumped. Bill flew a second behind. He wanted to watch Lugarda react, but the fear of falling flat kept his arms and legs flapping and both eyes on the water. He hit with a harsh slap that bruised his feet and stung his arms. Water rushed up his nose as he went down, down, down, to where the pool was dark and cold.

He stopped without reaching bottom, hovered a second, opened his eyes and stroked furiously for the lighted surface, propelling himself into the air to the waist, then dropped back to thrash breathlessly to shore. He emerged, dripping and gasping, hobbling on tingling feet, mad with the shock of the fall and the cold water. He could hear Pablo chasing 'Zul down the canyon trail. Bill was alone with Lugarda, for the second time.

"Buenas tardes, Señorita Lugarda."

"Buenas tardes, William Marshall. Do you always enter by falling from the sky or leaping from the sea?"

"Once I limped from the back of a horse to your front door," he reminded her. "That was not so romantic."

She blushed and handed him a large cloth with red and white checks. It looked like the tablecloth for a picnic. Bill dabbed at the drops of water on his chest. Water immersion is the ultimate touch and Bill tingled from his hair down to his numb pink toes. He wanted to leave the water exactly where it was for a while.

"You are cold."

"I'm not cold. The water is. I'm warm."

"And undressed like an Indian."

He wore only a breechcloth.

"My clothes are up on the cliff. I didn't want to get them wet."

"Very sensible."

The thought of his clothes made him feel the cold. He rubbed hard to dry and warm myself.

"I'm so glad you came. You have been much on my mind," he said. His face was level with hers as he bent to dry his legs.

She looked at him carefully, meeting his eyes.

"And you are much on mine. I had to find out what makes it so."

"Everyone says we only want what we cannot have."

Bill wrapped the cloth around his waist.

"Do you believe this?" She leaned back on the coyote skin rug, crossing her ankles, and patted a spot next to her. Bill followed her down.

"It would be easy to find out," he said, brushing her lips with his own.

She laughed, a single "ha."

"If you could have me, you wouldn't want me? Is that what you think?"

"No, I would want you more."

"So this could not be all of it."

She sat up and wrapped her elbows around her knees. Her bodice opened a bit and Bill could see down the tops of her breasts, into their shadow. Her face was very close to his, her eyes shining.

"Oh Bill, I came because with you I experienced a rapture. This I cannot explain."

"The rapture is love. Lovemaking begets rapture."

"Then I should have this feeling with my husband?"

"Yes you should. That is why I want to marry you." Bill held his breath.

"I will marry José María Alvarado. You know that." She leaned back and looked up at the pale blue sky. "I only pray I will feel this way."

Bill let his breath go in a hiss. "You will if you love him; if you are lucky. If he is good to you, then . . . You haven't tried?" He felt numb all over. He hated the question.

"Your voice is funny."

"I was beaten." He tilted his head back to show the bruise. She touched it with a fingertip.

"We kiss, that is all."

"How does it feel?"

She tried to think. It was hard with Bill this close. She remembered a ten-year-old José Maria, closing his lips to her curious mouth. He still did it.

"We have been friends since childhood. We are comfortable together." She didn't look Bill in the eye.

"Comfortable is not enough," he said and kissed her roughly. They watched each other as he smashed her lips. She seemed to be analyzing what sensations she might be feeling. He wanted to overwhelm her, as she overwhelmed him; to break all barriers to union; to devour and be devoured by her. When finally she closed her eyes, she kissed him back just as fiercely.

He pulled away first, breathing hard. Her perfect silken skin had flushed bright pink. Her throat was splotched and he had left red handprints on both shoulders. Bill bit the base of her neck and looked at the teeth marks. She touched the spot with her fingertips wondrously. Her eyes were tearful.

"Is this the rapture you felt?" He wanted to hear her say it again.

She pulled him to her, resting her forehead in the curve of his collarbone. "Yes, Bill," she said. "Yes. Yes," and she wept.

WHEN she had calmed, Bill wiped her face with a damp corner of the tablecloth. He held and kissed her hands.

She tried to smile and said, "I'm sorry. I shouldn't have come."

"No . . ." He was shaking his head.

"Because I'll want to go home . . . and I will." She was imploring him to understand.

"You don't have to go home. We could just take our horses and keep going. Wherever we go, rapture goes with us." He loved the sound of rapture. It was like a blissful form of capture.

"I would miss my family. I love them, and my life." She felt like crying again.

"I once loved my family, but to leave them was the greatest thing I ever did. I felt strong and free. Like a god or a mountain. Alone and invincible."

"And rain fell like tears on the lonely mountain," she quoted, sad and serious. "I couldn't leave my family . . . or José María."

There, she had said it. Teardrops welled in her lovely eyes. "I am not like that."

"Then what are we to become?" Bill asked. "Frustrated lovers, like those in some tragedy, to long for each other and never be?"

"What other choice do we have?" She raised his hand and kissed it. "Bill, sweet Bill, I did not choose it to be so. You fell into my life like this," she waved toward the cliff, "and I am trying to find a place for you."

"So you do love me?" Bill kissed a tear from her lashes.

"If love is what this feeling is, then yes. You make my heart leap." She patted her chest above her left breast. He rested his ear there to hear it thump. She smelled of skin and jasmine. Bill imagined her crushing the flowers; rubbing them on her neck and bosom.

Lugarda stroked his shoulder. "I cannot give myself to you. A Spanish señorita is owned by her father and brothers, who may give or sell, or pay to pass possession of her to a husband, and then to his sons. I cannot disobey my father. If I were to go with you, they would hunt us down, kill you and drag me back as stolen, damaged property." She wiped her eyes and swallowed back tears. "My heart is the only part of me I truly own. My heart is all I have to give."

She lifted his wet hair from her dress and draped it on his shoulder. There was just enough sun to keep him warm. She lay back and put her arm around his waist.

"Would you like to hear a poem of mine? A funny poem?" Bill asked, still listening to her heartbeat.

"Yes," she said. "I need to laugh."

"A breast is white, or brown or pink,
and round and smooth and soft and sink
your teeth, but not too hard, and tongue,
and, oh their praises must be sung."

Lugarda giggled.

"A breast will feed you when you're young,
A breast's a comfort when you're stung.
A breast can take your breath away,
Can turn your head, may gently sway . . .

And yes they're white or brown or pink,
and round and smooth and soft and sink
your teeth, but not too hard, and tongue,
and, oh they're great to be among."

She sat up and clapped her hands. "Bravo. Were you inspired by the women of Cupa?"

Bill shrugged. The poem had been written one longing evening at sea and forgotten.

"The eye of man rests easily on bare bosom," he replied, lifting his eyes to hers. "You inspired me to remember."

She looked at Bill from under arched eyebrows, head down, thick hair spilling forward.

"We Californio women have our own way of revealing our bosom."

She leaned toward him and brought her shoulders together. Her blouse fell open until he could see down to the dark tips of her breasts. She moved so they swayed softly. Her nipples were still conical from a lack of suckling.

"It is a good custom," he whispered.

She pulled her shoulders back and the blouse snapped shut. When he looked up she was laughing. He took her head in his hands and kissed her mouth.

She lay back down with a dark toss of her hair. Bill followed. She felt deliciously mischievous, lying on the black and tan coyote skins, watching him; admiring her own breasts pushing at her blouse.

"They are a sign of the life force of a woman," Bill said, brushing her there with the back of his hand.

"Tell me the others," she teased.

Bill lifted his head. "Your beautiful eyes," he said, and kissed them one by one.

"The Moors cover their women's faces. They say the eyes are the windows of the soul."

Bill quoted No'ka. "And where the eyes go, the body will follow."

She kissed him then, softly, both eyes open. Where they met, in that bottomless kiss, what was revealed in soul-searching bliss, was this: They would not be partners in their lives ahead, but go their own ways instead.

Bill lay back next to Lugarda, his fingers intertwined with hers, and stared into the unending sky.

He too would be comfortable. He would marry Falling Star as soon as he reached Cupa. For the first time, it felt like exactly what he wanted to do. He missed her. No'ka had been right. He missed him too. He missed the whole village, the great valley, the hot springs, Eagle's Nest, Rabbit Hole Mountain and hulking Mount Palomar: It was there he would make his home.

P A B L O and 'Zul found them dreaming, lying in the weak sun like two lost children. They were in a love coma, not dead like Romeo and Juliet, but equally thwarted and relieved of earthly care.

Lugarda didn't let go of Bill's hand or sit up. She pointed her feet for 'Zul to slip on her boots. She stood proudly and wrapped her shawl around her shoulders. Señorita Lugarda Dionicia Osuna, daughter of Alcalde Juan María Osuna, betrothed to José María Alvarado, governor's son, was radiant. She thanked them for coming. She kissed them both on both cheeks. They helped the women to mount and watched them ride down the trail and disappear into the oaks.

Up they scrambled, up the rocky cliff, dressed in the cold and turned their horses toward San Marcos, Pauma Valley and home.

Pablo was glad to be returning to Cupa. He didn't tell Bill how much 'Zul occupied his mind. But she wouldn't leave Lugarda. They had made a pact. She would not break it.

When they had ridden enough to settle the horses, Bill said, "I'm going to marry Falling Star and live in Cupa. That's enough of Lugarda for me."

"What?" Pablo swiveled to face him.

"She's marrying Alvarado."

"Then you owe me ten dollars," Pablo yelled and kicked his horse. They raced toward home, the packhorses trailing behind.

When Bill caught up, Pablo said, "No'ka will say, I told you so."

"Don't tell him right away. I want to let him wonder."

San Marcos was littered with cattle carcasses in various stages of decomposition. They passed three or four thousand piles of bones and rotting meat. At the conjunction with Rincon del Diablo, the other Alvarado ranch, the carnage spilled out to the southeast, away from their path.

"Looks like José María made a big kill, to pay for his wedding," Pablo commented, with a sidelong glance.

"I hope she bankrupts him. Spends every penny, and he has to sell the ranch."

"Then what?" Pablo grinned viciously.

"Then maybe he has an accident." Bill grinned back.

"A bear? Lightning? A rattlesnake? What do you have in mind?"

"I don't have a picture. Just something as painful as this broken heart." Bill made a theatrical grab at his chest, heaving a stage-worthy sigh.

Pablo laughed and clapped his hands, startling his horse, who laid back his ears and bucked and spun.

"The hero shall live, the villain must die," Pablo shouted.

His words carried over the grassy valley, through the oaks and into the wooded hills. Coyotes feeding on rotten carcasses looked up and hunkered down. A couple of buzzards took off to circle and land again. A huge brown bear shot a disdainful, beady-eyed glance, and kept chewing.

22

MELONES

I T W A S chilly when they arrived late at Manuelito's Pauma ranchería. Manuelito's wife had a big fire throwing dangerous sparks in their cozy adobe. He was gone, on the way to La Playa with his load of hides, but Pablo's mother was there. Ladislaya looked happy; beautiful and free of grief. They had made tamales with stringy beef and chiles wrapped in corn dough, tied in corn husks, then boiled. Pablo's aunt came in and they ate the steaming tamales, warming their cold bodies from the inside. Bill fell asleep snuggled deep in a cushion of furs on a bed of pine boughs, lulled by the chatter of the three ladies and High Cloud. The scents of burning wood, wild tobacco, cooked food, animal skin and pine needles perfumed his dreams. He slept the deep sleep of a wanderer safely returned.

In the morning Bill was fresh and ready to go, anxious to get to Cupa. Pablo had talked late. He wanted to sleep in and spend the day with his mother. There was a slight chance that Manuelito would appear with their money. Bill could take the string of packhorses and ride at a leisurely pace. Pablo would gallop on his pony to catch up later in the afternoon.

Melones had come with the ladies from Cupa to see the father of her child. He was very attached to his mother and had not been willing to move to Cupa. Neither did Melones want to leave her tribe to live at Pauma with her mother-in-law. There had been no new resolution. They would not marry. After a sleepless night, she had broken with him.

Melones didn't want to spend another moment at Pauma with her momma's boy. While Bill readied the horses, it was decided Melones should go with him. He would be traveling at an easy pace. He could carry her double on his big bay riding horse, a comfortable walker. The packhorses were too wild to mount in her condition, four or five months pregnant, and she had returned the horse Momma's Boy had given her. Bill laid a folded coyote robe across his horse's rump, behind the saddle. Ladislaya helped Melones up, and they set out to climb the canyon trail to Valle de San José.

The morning was crisp and cold, the last day of February, a leap year. The sun had not yet risen high enough to penetrate Pauma Valley, although it looked warm and clear above the mist and smoke of the village. Muffled in furs, they rode in comfortable silence to the sounds of the horses' hooves, birds singing their morning songs and the river rushing past wherever the trail came near. Once in a while they heard game, or a bear, rustling in the brush, getting out of the way. When the path was steep, the horses puffed and blew steam from their nostrils.

After about three hours of climbing, they topped the ridge that rimmed the big plain of their home valley. They left the tree line and rode on grass into the midday winter sunshine. The snow of the hide hunt had mostly melted away. Bill headed north, cross-country, up the west side of the plain. The main trail ran parallel, three miles east. At three thousand feet of elevation, the visibility was perfect. Pablo could easily spot them. If they were hidden by a rise, or a cluster of oaks, all he had to do was follow their tracks in the soft ground.

They saw not a soul, only deer, antelope and cattle returned to the plain to graze, and the omnipresent big birds, and coyotes.

B I L L had made the passage from San Diego to Cupa three times, each on a different trail. He was getting a feel for the country. It appeared to him as a grassy sea, with little private islands dotted here and there, like Cupa, or Warner's, Pauma or the mission at San Luis Rey. The rest was open territory. Anyone could travel freely, man or beast, more or less doing as he pleased in the wide-open spaces between private islands. There simply were no fences or borders or signs or markers, no sheriffs, armies, police or bandits to tell you otherwise.

And the grassy sea was great in size in comparison to the little private places, no more than forty in number for all of San Diego. On this inland sea, there was plenty or room for a sailor like Bi'; plenty of oaks to anchor beneath, plenty of food to please his taste. And welcoming women in the lively island towns, with whom a sailor could bed down.

This is what he was thinking as they slowly walked the horses, allowing them to snatch at tufts of dry grass, meandering in the general direction of Cupa. With the sun rising higher to warm their right sides, robes were soon shed and Melones added them to her saddle pad. They had dressed as Cupeños for the trip home. As Melones shifted around, pulling up to get the robes under her, her breasts pressed into Bill's bare back. She settled down, her hands on his hips, and rode with her nipples lightly brushing against his ribs. Sometimes she would let go, then smash against him as they jounced downhill, or press tight when they climbed to keep from sliding off. But with every move of the horse, her breasts and belly were the bumpers between them. She said not a word. Bill was dizzily aroused. The rocking of the horse kept him that way. He began to sweat and either she did too or his wetness was enough for both.

They slid and bounced like this for at least an hour. They were nearing Cupa. Pablo had not appeared. Bill didn't want to ride into the village with a hard-on and Melones naked at his back. He pulled up under a spreading oak by the side of a tiny stream with a sandy bed. There were snow patches in the shade. He would switch to one of the packhorses; give Melones his bay. They could cool down, let the horses graze, wait for Pablo and enter the village in a dignified manner.

When they stopped in the shade, Melones slid off, taking the robes with her. Bill let his horse walk to the stream, leading the others. He dismounted carefully, not wanting her to see his protrusion. He knelt to drink, splashing water in his face and lowering himself until he hung in the icy water, instantly shriveling and shrinking. He tied the lead horse to a bush, freeing the rest.

When he turned to look, Melones was lying high on the robes she had carefully stacked in a sunny spot. She had taken off her skirt, and lay on her back with her legs slightly open, propped up on her elbows, looking at Bill over her breasts. She grinned, trying not to laugh.

"Ven," she said in Spanish. "Come."

Bill did as he was asked.

By the time he reached her side he was growing again. She took his hand, lifted his breechcloth to look, and pulled him down. She undid his belt and pulled his covering away from her bulging belly, watching him intently. With the sweetest smile, she whispered "Hórale," on an exhalation that transformed it to a moan. "Now."

Bill sank onto and into her cushioned form with a sigh of resignation, lust and contentment. He rocked gently on the fulcrum of her belly button, her breasts pressed to his, eyes closed. It was over in seconds. He laid his head on her shoulder and would have stayed there, but she slapped his back and he rolled to lie next to her on the robes.

Bill stared into the limbs and leaves of the great tree; the sun sparkling through as the breeze moved the branches. This is like a cathedral, he thought, a living cathedral.

He felt Melones turn to face him. One of her breasts spilled over his arm. She put her hand on his belly and stroked it lightly, round and round. He remembered her pregnancy. Bill was glad she couldn't conceive.

"Do you have milk?"

"Try me," she said.

He did and there was none, but her nipple was big as a ripe olive. Bill guiltily thought of Lugarda's, barely formed.

"When it does come, it's yours," Melones promised.

"That is one of the nicest things anyone has ever said to me," he told her in English.

"Sí," she answered.

She slid her hand down to touch him, found sufficient firmness, threw her leg over and pulled forward onto his stomach, then let herself back onto him.

She sat up with a little grunt, put her hands on Bill's chest and swished her hips experimentally. Her belly was distended like a Chinese Buddha. He supported it with both hands and tried to picture the baby inside. Melones didn't want to look at him. Her eyes were closed, her face scrunched in concentration. She rocked harder. Her swollen breasts began to bobble and lunge. She took Bill's hands without stopping, and placed them just beneath her nipples to control the wobbling.

They were heavy, pliable; full of what, if not milk, he wondered. Her nipples protruded between his thumbs and forefingers, dark and distended. Melones held her breath for a moment, then let it out in a groan. She flopped down onto his chest, covering his face with her hair. It tickled his eyes, nose and mouth. He could feel her heart pounding against his ribs.

She rolled off to lie on her back, breathing hard, damp with perspiration. She touched her tender breasts gently. They both looked into the shifting patterns of light on the leaves above and let the breeze cool their wet skin.

"Gracias," she said. She was looking up, not his way, thanking heaven, wondering what to say to Falling Star.

"Gracias a tí," he replied. Bill thanked her and her alone.

She rose, walked to the rivulet, washed, sitting in the icy water, then rubbed herself in the breeze until she was dry, her skin rosy. She put on her red bark skirt; arranged her hair; pulled her robe around her shoulders. Taking a finely woven basket that had been folded in her knapsack, Melones started to collect acorns. They had littered months ago and she sorted for the good ones. Bill dozed.

He woke up chilled. Pablo had not appeared. He put on his deerskin apron, rolled up in one of the robes, and started to arrange the easiest riding packhorse for the short trip to the village. Melones stowed her acorns on one of the others. She wanted to ride sidesaddle like a señorita, so he put the coyote rug over the saddle on his big bay. She hung one knee around the horn, and he handed her the reins. It didn't look comfortable, but she balanced herself perfectly. Giving him a regal nod, she set off.

They walked slowly across the valley to the trail, where a breathless Pablo joined them, just outside the village.

"I waited for Manuelito, but he never came," he gasped.

They rode in with Melones at the lead, holding her belly with both hands, as delicate and demure as a Madonna, a smile illuminating her sweet round face. Pablo came next, his horse blowing and steaming from the run. Bill was happy to bring up the rear with the pack train.

23

HOMECOMING

T H E Y were welcomed like sailors returning home from a two-year voyage. It had been less than a week, but time was not the issue. They had gone into enemy territory and returned successful, alive, with Melones, a favorite sister who had strayed, reason enough to celebrate.

Melones was helped down and bundled off. The horses were taken, Pablo and Bill were patted on the back, embraced, kissed, questioned, ruffled and passed from person to person like rag dolls. Even Big Bear and Stomping Deer gave Bill bone-crushing hugs. But no one had asked about the money. And Bill worried about what Melones might say or do.

"I had to try out your sailor man," Melones told Falling Star as she slid off the big horse and passed the reins to her friend. "I tried his horse too," she added when she saw Falling Star's mouth drop.

"What?"

"Don't worry. It's you he likes. He never ever looked me in the eye. No kisses. He just stared at my fat breasts like they all do. Pure lust . . ."

"Meli . . . how could you . . . you knew he was mine . . . did he . . . ?"

"He didn't do anything. I made him do. I was feeling low after Momma's Boy refused me again. Bi' was suffering too. The Osuna señorita rejected him. We comforted each other. That's all."

"That's all?"

"Better me than her."

Falling Star turned away, sputtering, and Melones touched her arm.

"Don't be mad. I wanted to get to know him for you; to make sure he was not still dreaming of the Mexicana, and is not just marrying you for the cattle or because that bitch is marrying someone else."

"There are other ways to get to know a man, Meli."

The horse nickered and Falling Star turned away with him. Melones followed.

"Yes but they take too long. My way is sure and fast. I wanted to make sure that Bi' was . . ."

"Was what?

"Was good enough for you. Not strange with us, like Warner."

"And?"

"He is normal. He was quick. He is sweet." She bit her tongue to keep from saying, he let me do what I wanted. "He wants to marry you," came out instead.

Falling Star broke into a trot and Melones gave up following.

"I did it to see if I could. To be sure he wasn't still being faithful to her," she called out. "I would never do it again," she promised. "I won't."

"Thanks, melon-head," Falling Star growled under her breath, without looking back. "You'd better not," she said, louder. "Ever."

W H E N Bill got to the end of the greeting line, Falling Star, Chief No'ka and White Fox were waiting. He hugged and kissed Falling Star. She felt light and strong and smelled of sage. She sniffed for signs of Lugarda—or Melones. When No'ka gave him a bear hug, Bill couldn't wait to whisper "Father-in-law" into his ear. No'ka laughed and slapped Bill's back hard.

He called out to wife and daughter in their language. They looked at Bill and then each other, faces blank. No'ka dragged Bill toward their house, saying, "Come tell me everything, come, come," he motioned to his family. He caught Pablo by the arm and pulled him along too.

As Bill went through the door with the chief, he realized he hadn't given a thought to Lugarda all day . . . just the one. With a pang of guilt, he silently thanked Melones. Somehow she had freed him to give himself wholly to Falling Star. That was a secret he hoped would keep.

No'ka and his family were too discreet to ask about the Osunas. Pablo told them everything else in a rush, using Spanish, English and Cupeño, depending on his level of excitement and whom he was addressing.

Bill lay back by the fire and watched Falling Star as she and her mother cooked. It was warm and they had laid down their robes. They both had muscular athletic bodies, Falling Star heavier, fuller of breast and softer of expression. Their hair was weighted down at the ends, starting at their shoulder blades, with little shells braided in. The heavy tresses swung when they moved. Their tule-grass skirts were red, also held down at the ends by shells. The belts were shell-studded in geometric patterns. Their beauty was stunning. Bill felt blessed by association.

When he could catch Falling Star's eye, she would look away shyly. White Fox was all business with the cooking, asking an occasional question of Pablo or Bill; calm and collected as though this were any evening. But Bill had said that word. They were now bound together. They would be a family. Excitement permeated the house.

Bill wanted to be married tomorrow, to marry Falling Star before Lugarda's wedding, to show his devotion, to silence wagging tongues. But most of all he wanted to be with her now, before anything could intervene.

After dinner Bill announced this intent. Everyone kept quiet for a second; then all spoke at once. They argued about the ceremony. Falling Star wanted to be married in the chapel. No'ka and White Fox wanted a traditional ceremony. White Fox was the singer of the wedding song and lead dancer among the women. She wanted to perform. Bill was for the native ceremony. Falling Star wanted the church, so she could wear her dress and walk down the aisle. Pablo said Father Ibarra was too old to come this far. No'ka wanted time to summon all of his friends and relatives for the feast. He had to notify the other chiefs: Ignacio at Santa Ysabel, Chapuli at Los Coyotes, Mocate at Wilakalpa, Manuelito, of course, and Antonio and Baupista of the Cahuilla.

In a moment of silence, mother and daughter exchanged looks and White Fox said, "My daughter has not yet accepted this man. He must present her with a gift. If she keeps it, they are married by our custom. Whatever else we do, will only be for our pleasure."

Falling Star stood expectant, hands on hips, a stubborn pout on her lips. She had heard about the wedding dress from Pablo. Bill hadn't yet mentioned it. She wanted to see it, to know that he hadn't given it to Lugarda.

"The dress," whispered Pablo as Bill rushed out the door.

Bill brought it to her. She shook it out. She dropped her skirt in front of everyone and signed him to help her. Bill thought she might have searched it out and tried it on while they were delivering hides, but she seemed so unsure of what to do with it that he discarded the notion.

White Fox and Bill helped pull on the pantaloons and slip, dropped the dress over up-stretched arms, buttoned up the back, flounced the skirt to relax the wrinkles, and installed the veil with its lacy train. Pablo and No'ka, arguing by the fire over the details of the ceremony, looked up at a word from White Fox.

They all exclaimed in Cupeño. Bill turned Falling Star for them. By the firelight, she was breathtaking. She filled the gown to overflowing. Tight at the waist, the skirt swirled at the floor in a scalloped circle three feet in diameter. The train, held by White Fox, stretched out across the cabin. The bodice pressed her breasts up so that they bulged into the open neckline, barely contained.

With the veil down she looked mysterious, ravishing and virginal—exactly as the dressmakers in Paris had intended. It was a gown designed to stun the courts of royalty. Here in Cupa, in White Fox and No'ka's humble cabin, worn by their lithe girl-child, it was unearthly, ungodly, heavenly.

Capitán José No'ka, king of this wild world, was equal to the occasion. He pulled himself up to his full magisterial height and faced his daughter.

"We shall have both ceremonies. We start with my daughter on my arm, coming down the aisle of the chapel like a señorita. Pablito will say the vows in Spanish and English. After twenty-five years he should know his God well enough to ask him to bless this simple union. We will wear the costume of our people so that no one feels left undressed. Only Falling Star will dress as this angelita." He waved the fire poker at her, like a magic wand. "Then we will proceed to the sacred oak where White Fox will sing the marriage song and all guests shall join her. We will enjoy a feast that leaves hungry no man, creature, or god who looks upon us. After the feast, we sing and dance and retire to the pools while the newlyweds begin the creation of my grandchild. This is what we will do."

Falling Star lifted her veil and nodded to her father. She touched her mother's arm, carefully picked up her dress and motioned Bill to follow.

They moved to the shadows behind the stove by the beds, where she could stand on fur rugs while he worked on the buttons, stays and laces that held it all together. She removed the veil, folded it, put it on the bed. Then she stood like a child while Bill undressed her, love and utter trust radiating from her to envelop them both.

"Falling Star," Bill whispered. "Such a beautiful name."

"When I was born, in her pain my mother looked to the sky, and a star fell to comfort her." She glanced down to caress the dress, and Bill was able to examine the length and breadth of her eyelashes. "I am that falling star," she said, shyly raising her eyes to his.

When the dress slipped to the floor, she stepped out of it and stood in the pantaloons while he folded the separated petticoats and stacked the fluffy pile on the bed. Bill loosened the cord that tied the pantaloons, noticing as they slipped down that they were open at the crotch. While he folded them she stood watching, still as a statue, the firelight and shadows lending definition to her sculpted form. She could have been carved from some tawny golden marble block by a Roman master; every muscle and curve perfect, symmetrical, hard, eternal.

Bill wrapped his arms around her. He held her tight until she came to life, warm, soft, molding to his embrace. In that moment, she knew she had fallen just for him. They kissed and clung to each other. Bill could hear the fire popping and the voices of Pablo and White Fox, only a few feet away. They were in that bubble of privacy Indians will allow, living as they do in such close quarters, eyes averted, their whole body language saying "I don't see you," and they won't.

"I want to marry you now," Bill whispered. "Let's ask your father to wed us tomorrow."

"The next day, Bi'. He needs time to send riders to notify his friends. I would have my mother sing the song right now and here." She was kissing his nipple, nipping at it.

"But let's tell him. You tell him. I don't want to wait any longer."

"Papi," she called out. "We will marry pasado mañana."

"What is the hurry? That gives little time to prepare."

"My husband has ordered me thus." She looked up at Bill with such fierceness, a tear sprang to his eye and slid down his cheek. She laughed and wiped it away with her thumb. "I cannot disobey him." She hugged him and grinned at her father.

"Of course not, my daughter. To obey is the first duty of a wife."

"Ha!" said White Fox.

"Pasado mañana it shall be," pronounced No'ka.

Thus was William Marshall, late of Providence, Rhode Island, married to Dominga Falling Star, daughter of José No'ka, chief of the Kuupiaxchem.

24

THE CELEBRATION

N O'KA sent invitations by rider to Pauma, Santa Ysabel, Los Coyotes, and the Cahuilla in Anza. The men hunted; a couple of cattle were butchered. Acorns were ground and blanched, roots dug, greens cut.

The chapel of Saint Francis was swept clean, a path cleared to the great oak, the village tidied, firewood stacked, two cooking pits dug. Latrines were torched, their holes covered, new ones dug and new grass huts built over them. Mangy dogs were killed; fallen brush, scraps of leather and any other trash piled and burned.

Every house was cleaned; new bedding boughs were brought in from the pine forests; rugs were shaken and aired. The street was swept by a line of women, then wetted with gourds of water from the stream. Corrals were repaired, horses curried, ramadas patched. The whole town was given an early spring brush-up.

The Kuupiaxchem took pride in their tidy village. Of the guests, only the Cahuilla and Los Coyotes still lived traditionally. But their towns were scrappy by comparison: just a collection of conical straw huts scattered together. And Cupa had the chapel.

When Falling Star walked up the aisle on the arm of her father, who was equally resplendent in his cape of alternating eagle and condor feathers, with a ruffle of pheasant plumes and a matching headpiece, the assembly went silent. Drums softly thudded; Christians crossed themselves; mouths fell open. Someone whispered, "La Virgen. La Madona." The words rustled through the crowd like a gust of wind on leaves.

Falling Star floated, virtually invisible. The afternoon sunlight was winter bright, streaming through the windows from the west, illuminating the white apparition she had become. Her veil was down, the train carried by two tiny girls in bright red tule skirts. She had pulled on the short white gloves that came with the dress. Not a patch of skin showed below the fur cuffs of the sleeves. All of her was entirely covered in white.

No one had ever seen a dress like this one. Surprise, delight, wonder and some nervous fear flitted on the faces that turned toward Bill, as she and her father approached the altar. Pablo and Bill were dressed in new deerskin aprons with shell-studded belts. The aprons had been dyed red. They wore matching rabbit capes trimmed in fox. Falling Star stopped at Bill's side. She looked nervous under her veil. No'ka was sweating along the edge of his headpiece. A dignified, satisfied expression graced his handsome, lined face. Bill smiled at Falling Star and took her offered hand. Pablo was tense. He wasted no words.

"Do you, Dominga Falling Star, daughter of José No'ka, capitán of the Ku-upiaxchem, and White Fox Who Protects Her Kits In Their Den, capitána, take William Marshall as your husband, to have and to hold, to cherish and obey, till death do you part?"

"I do," she replied softly, tears making her dark eyes shine.

"Do you, Bill Marshall, take Dominga Falling Star, daughter of the Kuu-piaxchem, to be your wife, to have and to hold, cherish and defend, till death do you part?"

"I do."

"You may kiss the bride."

Bill lifted the veil, kissed the tears from her eyelids, kissed their trails from her cheeks, and kissed her slightly parted lips, softly. Then he dropped her veil and took her by the right hand while she carefully turned, avoiding stepping on her train. They walked back down the aisle and out of the chapel into the sunlight.

Pablo and No'ka followed, then White Fox and Pablo's mother, Ladislaya, then the chiefs: Antonio and Baupista of the Cahuilla, Chapuli of the Los Coyotes, Ignacio of Santa Ysabel, Manuelito from Pauma, Antonio Garra, and Mocate of Wilakalpa, a small Cupeño village east of Warner's ranch. Each wore the feather cape and helmet of captaincy. The rest of the assembly trailed after, talking excitedly, happy to be out of the chapel and on familiar ground.

Falling Star walked as on a cloud. Across the wooden bridge she led the throng, up the main street of Cupa, shiny with its wet stones, up to the trunk of the Great Oak. The two little girls carrying her train stumbled a couple of times, but managed to keep it out of the dirt.

To this point they had been about fifteen minutes in ceremony. Now they stood with White Fox and No'ka, facing the crowd. There were drummers and flutists to one side of the big tree trunk. No'ka announced, "My wife, White Fox, will sing the marriage song." Tortoise-shell rattles swung smartly into a steady rhythm. Reed flutes began tentatively to play. Everyone shuffled from one foot to the other, in place. The flutes trailed off and White Fox began her song.

She sang in Cupeño, using melodies totally unrecognizable to Bill. She sang for about two hours, covering every topic and phase of marriage, using an amazing variety of calls and moans, high notes, clicking sounds, chants and spoken passages, wails, screams and lullabies. Whenever she would pause, the reed flutes and rattles would pick up, and all the while the People danced their trancelike stomp.

When she wanted to sing, she would look at the flutists, they would stop and she would take off. At times her voice soared to the heavens, bouncing in waves off the granite of Eagle's Nest; at others, it would be a bare whisper, or whimpering, or a rhythmic humming. Wild tobacco was stuffed in pipes made of clay, smoked and passed around from hand to hand. The feet kept walking, going nowhere.

Bill closed his eyes and surrendered to the trance created by her song, lulled by the rocking motion of his feet. Just when he wearied and longed for the finish, the rattles and flutes joined White Fox for a soaring crescendo. The whole crowd shouted a final "Huh!" into the sky, and showered the newlyweds with seeds. Everyone began to talk. The party broke into groups and spread throughout the village.

Bill thanked White Fox. She said, "Oh, this is only the start. After we eat, I will sing you the rest."

"There are five or six more hours," said No'ka with a giggle. "Marriage is a complicated relationship. Come, sit with me and we shall receive gifts while the food is prepared."

Bill sat with Falling Star and No'ka on furs laid over the cushion of oak leaves. They leaned against the tree's wide trunk to rest, and accepted congratulations from the villagers and guests.

Bill looked on apprehensively, as the mountain of presents grew. By now he knew that every gift is a debt.

Falling Star patted his hand reassuringly. "Don't worry, Bi'. It has nothing to do with you. My father will redistribute all of the gifts to those who can best use them. We keep only a few things we cannot do without: like this fine sea otter cloak, the cooking bowls, a bow and arrows for you, a throwing stick and the two painted ponies Antonio and Baupista gave to me."

"Pablo gave us his parents' house," Bill said doubtfully.

"That too we need," she said. "We will invite him to live with us, of course."

She was still in her dress, veil down; the two little girls curled up at her side. People looked at her curiously, trying not to stare.

Manuelito said, "Falling Star, is that really you?" He presented No'ka with the money from the hide ship. He gave another eighty silver dollars to Bill for Warner, who had also left his hides at La Playa.

She giggled, "And who do you think I might be, Tío? One of the señoritas in disguise?" No'ka laughed. Falling Star squeezed Bill's hand.

Manuelito blushed, saying, "No, no, it's just that you look . . ."

"Like an angel," said No'ka.

"Yes. We do not recognize you like this. The people are saying . . ." Manuelito searched for the next word.

"They are saying what, Tío?"

"La Madona." He looked embarrassed. "La Virgen."

"You Christians are so superstitious," she teased. "It's only me in a white dress. They will see me naked in the pools soon enough." But she didn't lift her veil.

No'ka clapped Bill on the back. "You didn't know you were marrying La Virgen." He grinned wickedly. "Perhaps you should see if she can make a child without sex."

"If she has a child, it will be mine," Bill said. "If you want green eyes, it is up to me."

"A husband is the only god a woman needs," Manuelito concurred.

Falling Star silenced them with a wave of her white-gloved hand.

"When he gives me a child, then I shall worship him."

AFTER the gifts, they feasted on spit-roasted beef, machaca of deer tamales and acorn dumplings. Tortillas were the edible plates. White Fox and others sang. Everyone danced around a huge bonfire. Later, people drifted to the hot pools to bathe and converse. No'ka had politics to discuss with the other chiefs; men talked hunting, cattle and women; the ladies spoke of the wedding, children and lovers; the young ones splashed and passed out to be carried to bed. Bill stayed close by the sculpted side of Falling Star, who had finally appeared naked, as promised.

At first light, the newlyweds trudged wearily up the path toward their house—to the sound of catcalls and crude remarks from those still awake.

They dove into the fresh bed with its piney scent and pile of furs, held each other close, and fell into a deep slumber.

When Bill awoke, about midday, he was married. Falling Star was lying next to him, watching with a sleepy-eyed smile, her hand on his chest possessively. She kissed him.

"How did you sleep, husband?"

"Like a baby, wife." Both laughed.

"And like a baby, did you awake hungry?"

"No, thirsty," Bill mumbled and took her nipple in his mouth. She rolled away, sat up and patted him on the head.

"I'll get you some water, Bi'."

She dipped into the earthen water pot that sits by the stove in every home in California, filling a cup that hung from a knob on its side, and brought the cold water, which Bill drained without pause.

"What shall we do today, sweet husband?"

"Today we make a baby," he ordered, pulling her down. "We don't leave this house until we have accomplished this difficult task."

It was a first for both of them and they were not scientific in their method. They chewed one another, plunged in and out, bounced off the bed, floors and walls, sweated, passed out, awoke to eat and try again. Neither had ever made love with the purpose of causing pregnancy. It had always been the opposite. Falling Star had only tried it once, painfully, with Big Bull Bear.

"Painful," her mother had scoffed. "That's not pain. Wait until you feel your baby's head forcing its way out through that same little opening. That is pain. Then you will be happy to have had it stretched a bit by a man."

But it had been enough pain to discourage her from sex and make her fear pregnancy. Bill was naturally easy and patient, using fingers and tongue to bring her enough pleasure that she relaxed and felt no discomfort when she first fearfully took him in—only a burning desire for more and more and more of him. He gave willingly, the potential for pleasure seemed to be unlimited.

But by evening they were spent. They could take no more, even if they had wanted to. They bathed at the pools, answering compliments and vulgar innuendoes with smug smiles. They returned to the cozy house to stand by the fire. Pablo came in to get some of his things, then left them alone.

Bill had been holding back the peignoir that came with the wedding dress. He kept it deep in his pack, and with it his memories of Lugarda. He had imagined her elegant form silhouetted by candlelight, pushing at the diaphanous gauze wherever she had curves or points. This potent image carried her jasmine scent and the feel of her soft slim body.

Bill wanted no more fantasies. He wanted to cancel Lugarda's spell. He emptied the pack and pulled out the nightdress. He held it behind his back.

"I have a present for you, my wife."

In a moment of panic, he wanted to untie the bundle himself, in case Lugarda's scent, or some essence trapped in the dress, should escape and be detected by that sixth sense women surely have.

But Falling Star was upon him, wrapping her arms around to snatch it from his hand. She sat on the bed, carefully untying the string. She unfolded the red and white striped cloth that was its wrapper, and took the feather-light roll of silk in her hands. Bill leaned in to kiss her, distracting her, blocking her view. She jumped up and shook the roll out in front of the fire, looking at him curiously.

"It's a peignoir, a night dress. The French ladies wear them on their honeymoon."

It was totally transparent by the flickering firelight, even doubled. He took it from her; he said, "Raise your arms." He slipped her hands into the sleeves and dropped it over her head to fall on her shoulders. It caught on both breasts, held aloft by raised arms. Bill gently eased the soft pink folds over her nipples, flounced the flimsy material to cover her bottom, and took a step back to look.

Falling Star did a turn. Desperate to see herself, she searched for her little mirror and had Bill hold it to her from all sides and angles. She had again been transformed into an angel—this time, an unchaste one. Bill asked her to get the veil. She put it on and faced him.

With the pink peignoir and the white veil, all of her was covered. She looked like a ghost, yet simultaneously every detail of her form was visible, exaggerated by the folds of the garments. It was eerie, erotic beauty: palpable, alluring and accessible.

"If you go out now, you might scare the people to death," Bill said, shaking his head.

"Is that how I look to you?" She lifted the veil and tossed it on the bed.

"To me? To me you look like a ghostly goddess, a goddess of love." In her perfection, her complex-curved form could only be compared to a Venus or Aphrodite. "It is impossible that I should possess such beauty."

She took a couple of steps toward him, stopping when her breasts pressed lightly against his ribs. "And yet you do. Possess me," she commanded.

She rose on tiptoes, aware of her nipples brushing his chest; aware of the cool gown sliding silkily down between them, warm on her shoulders where her hair held it close, as she rose to join her mouth to his. In that moment she forgave Melones—forgave her for going down with Bill and anyone else—feeling as she did how heavenly it could feel, and she forgave Bill.

She crushed her mouth to his. They fell back onto the bed and he gave himself to her, but it was she who possessed him, spellbound by her own powers.

25

SHADOWS

BILL rose early, dressed in his caballero outfit, and tiptoed out to ride with Pablo to the Warners, to deliver the money from the hides. They wanted to catch Juan Largo at breakfast, before he left on his daily rounds of the ranch. This also meant enjoying a good meal. Bill was famished.

He felt a little guilty at not having invited John to the wedding. But both No'ka and Pablo had opposed including their neighbor. The guests would not have been at ease with Juan Largo looking on.

They trotted out of the village into a clear cool morning. Dew dripped from the grass. Rabbits scurried from their path, leaving wet trails. They kept to a trot, arriving in less than an hour, just as the sun climbed out of the desert to warm the high valley.

Anita came out on her porch and waved as they rode up, shouting, jumping and clapping. Warner was at the barn, tending the milk cows and checking his cheeses. Luna, the wild little shadow, was at his side. They went to the house together and sat down to a bountiful breakfast: eggs, beef, sausage, tortillas, tamales, coffee and milk.

The Warners wanted to know all about the wedding: who was there, what gifts they brought, the dress, what they ate. John was a trader in information as well as goods, always keen to add to his stock in either.

When Bill gave him the money from his hides, eighty silver dollars, Warner shook the bag like a musical instrument.

"Oh, Anita, what a friend we have here," he said. "Now that you're a permanent resident, I'm begging you to be my ranch foreman and handle the store when I'm gone. I'll pay you a dollar a day in cash or goods."

"Say yes, Bill. I hate to be here alone, when John is away." Anita took his arm pleadingly.

Bill looked to Pablo, who showed him nothing.

"I'll think about it," he said. "I'll have to ask the chief."

"You're your own man," Warner said sourly. "It's not for him to decide."

"You know what I mean. I still have to talk to him about it. He is my father-in-law. He may have work for me too."

"By all means, do talk to him," Warner agreed, still frowning. "Pablo, what do the capitánes have to say? Will they support the Mexicans if war comes? Any warpaths planned?"

"No war dances were mentioned. You're safe for now," Pablo said, with a smirk at Anita.

Everyone in the mountains was afraid of the Cahuilla, including No'ka. They were numerous, warlike and had never been subdued by the Spanish or Mexicans. They occupied the desert areas of Anza, Borrego and Palm Springs, and the mountains to the north up to San Jacinto. They were right next door, more than a light threat, but Juan Antonio, their chief, was content at the moment.

The exciting news was that the Mexican general, Santa Anna, was engaged in a losing battle against American settlers in Texas. New Mexico and California could be next. The chiefs had discussed this very subject. Warner's nosiness irritated Pablo, but he answered at length.

"We spoke of the war in Texas. Manuelito, No'ka, Ignacio and Chapuli favor the Americans. The Cahuilla under Antonio and Baupista will side with the Mexicans, if war should come to California."

"What reasons did they give?" Warner was all ears.

"The Cahuilla gave no reasons. I believe they like an enemy they know. The Mexicans never touched them: they don't covet their barren lands, or bony cattle. Since the sacking of the mission at Yuma, more than fifty years ago, the priests have kept their distance. The Americans are a new threat, best repulsed.

"As for the rest of us, we have all suffered enough contact with the Spanish to hate and mistrust them. The Americans are unknown, except for you and Bill. We are convinced, and Bill agrees, that the Americans will win, no matter whom we support. I have seen their cities. They are many, they are near; they are fierce and fearless. If they decide to come, they will cover California like a blanket of snow. It behooves us to welcome them. Those are the thoughts of all but the Cahuilla."

"And right thoughts they are, Pablo." Warner had information to exchange. "I made a quick trip to Los Angeles while you were gone. The word is that the U.S. will annex Texas, after it has been a republic for a year or so. That will cause Santa Anna to declare war. Then the U.S. will invade California. I got this tip from Thomas O. Larkin, the U.S. consul at Monterey."

"When will it happen?" Pablo asked. "How soon?"

"A couple of years, at most. It has to play out this way, so that Mexico will be the one who declares war. That way the Europeans will most certainly stay out of any conflict."

"Oh, John, must we always talk politics and war, it scares me," Anita pouted. "Let's give Bill his wedding present." She took Bill's hand and pulled him from the table. "You're going to love him."

Warner unfolded from his chair and joined them, followed by Pablo, looking worried.

When they got to the barn, Anita called out, "El cachorro, Lunito."

The boy emerged from the darkness carrying a gray bundle of soft fur about the size of a bobcat. He handed the pup to Anita, who gave him to Bill. The puppy lay still in his arms. He had a short smooth coat like a seal, dark gray from nose to tail, with floppy ears, a square face, and huge eyes, head and paws. Bill placed him on the ground. He grunted like a piglet, taking a couple of shy steps.

"Isn't he sweet? His name's Shadow. He's a mastiff from Italy. John says they were bred to fight lions."

"He is beautiful." Pablo bent to touch him. "His fur is like silk." He lifted an oversized paw and put it down. "He's going to be big if he grows into these feet." Shadow lifted his other paw and waved it at Pablo.

"At least a hundred fifty pounds," said Warner. "I got him in Los Angeles from a French frigate that had his mother aboard. She was the biggest dog I've ever seen."

"Thank you both," Bill said, shaking John's hand and giving Anita a hug. "Falling Star will love him. I won't have to worry about anyone bothering her with this fellow around."

"I got him for Anita's sake, to keep watch at the farm," said Warner, a little peevishly. "She thought he would be a nice wedding gift. So now you'd best come to work here with us. You can bring him along."

"I'll let you know as soon as I can. Right now I should get home to my new wife. Thanks for the breakfast."

Bill picked up the pup, cradling him in an arm, mounted, and followed Pablo back down the trail. He turned to wave to Anita and John, who watched until Bill passed behind the first hill.

"Don't feel obligated to work for that Yankee, just because he gave you the dog," Pablo grumbled, with a scowl at Shadow. "I'm sick of that turncoat

Juan Largo. He plays friend to everyone; sells information to anyone; and pledges loyalty to no one. What kind of a person would leave his own beautiful land to come to live here alone, in the middle of nowhere, with no friend or family? And what right has he to own slaves. Slavery is outlawed in Mexico. Big Bear is right. We should give his spying face a couple of new eye holes, then sell his wife to the Yumans."

Bill let Pablo fume. He hoped it was just talk.

At the fork in the trail, they turned north, trotting toward Eagle's Nest. Bill felt lighthearted, with little Shadow nestled under his coat, riding home to his new wife in their cozy home.

"If I work for Warner, I can keep an eye on him," he placated. "His information may be useful. And his wife sure cooks a good breakfast."

"Phh!" spit Pablo. "If you work for Juan Largo, don't ask me to help."

They rode in uneasy silence. Pablo was usually quick to cool. Something had happened between him and Warner on their trip to the East; something that ruffled Pablo's hackles and wouldn't go away.

When Pablo finally spoke again, he was calmer.

"I can't help thinking that Warner lured me back East to give the Picos their chance to seize Las Flores."

"Didn't you say Father Ibarra introduced you . . . he arranged the trip?"

"Yes, he did. But Warner and Pico go way back . . . to Los Angeles, where Warner had a store. Juan Largo saved Pico's life in some quarrel with a sergeant. Pico gave him this ranch. And when I met Warner, he said that he had heard nothing but good things about me, from his buen amigo, Pío Pico. What things, I wonder?"

"John says he now wishes he hadn't taken you. He feels responsible for what happened."

"So he should. Did he know in advance? That's what drives me mad. If I find out he did, I'll kill him."

"They might have killed you if you'd stayed," Bill said. "Ibarra told me Pico would have taken Las Flores even if you were there."

"Maybe, maybe not."

At that moment, Pablo looked so fierce, Bill could not imagine him giving up his ranch alive.

Just as they entered the village Pablo turned to Bill, his expression grave.

"It is not just Warner. It is what he foretells. When he said, two years till the Americans come, it made me sick to my stomach. I pray this gossip he passes is wrong."

"Right or wrong, the more we know the better. At least we are warned."

"Speaking of gossip, I must go to San Luis Rey to explain to Father Ibarra about your wedding. I don't want him thinking I performed an illegal marriage."

"I noticed you didn't pronounce us man and wife."

"I couldn't. I am not a priest. That would have been sacrilege. But who knows what lies the father will hear? I must tell him myself."

"I'm sorry I put you in that position."

"It's my own fault. I never thought of it until I was standing there uttering those sacred words. Then all I could think of was Pico. Of all the sins that that pig has committed, performing marriages in San Luis Rey's chapel upset the padre the most."

Bill would not let Pablo's depression get to him. Shadow burrowed deeper into his shirt, nosing for a teat. They were alive and thriving. That was all Bill needed to know.

T H E Y found No'ka sitting in his ramada, warming himself in the afternoon sun. Pablo recounted the conversation with Warner, word for word. No'ka said not a thing; only closed his eyes and kept them closed, opening them to look from Pablo to Bill at the end.

"That's exactly what he said," Bill offered.

"We should drive Warner from the valley, right now," Pablo exclaimed.

"What have you got under your arm?" No'ka reached out to take the pup, who had fallen asleep. Shadow was heavy, soft, floppy and warm. He grunted and settled into No'ka's lap.

"Anita gave him to us as a wedding present. He's a mastiff, an Italian guard dog."

No'ka stroked Shadow's silky coat. "He's beautiful, I'm surprised that old fur trapper, Juan Largo, didn't lift his pelt. You know he came to California to trap beaver and shoot sea otter? In 1831, fourteen years ago."

"He bought the pup for Anita, for protection. She wanted us to have him. His trapping days are over, I think."

"Yes, they are—for him and for all of us. There are no more beaver, or sea otter, where once there were many. What is the dog's name?"

"Sombra," Bill said it in Spanish.

"Sombra." When No'ka said the word, a cloud passed swiftly over the sun, darkening his face momentarily. Bill's spin tingled; the hair stood up on his arms.

"Warner is a visionary." The light had returned to No'ka's face. He remained serene, his eyes half closed. "It is not for nothing that he has come to this little corner of our world, to sit in his store, stocked with goods, and not a customer to cross his door."

Bill had to chuckle at this picture of Warner. No one else did.

"That is why we have allowed him to stay. He is waiting for something; something he is positive will come. He is betting his life, his wife, children and money on this thing to come." No'ka paused. He looked Bill hard in the eyes. "If and when this invasion, this thousand-headed creature he calls 'the Americans' arrives, I want him here to meet it. I do not want to face it alone. I would not care to greet such a thing."

"But what if he is calling for them, bringing them here by his very presence?" Pablo protested.

"The road is an ancient one. We People came north by it. Anza and the Spaniards followed. Warner's party first passed through here in '31. Warner is here because of the trail, not vice versa."

Humbled, Pablo said, "Yes, you are right. But Warner advertised the trail, I was with him."

"Of course. But who told him? This trail is no secret. Many have passed this way, but only Warner has the vision of what will come to pass. I do not. He also has eyes and ears in Los Angeles, Monterey and Washington. We will let him sit there in his store, staring into the east, waiting for customers. If they come, we will be the first to know. If not, he will grow old and tired and blind from watching the burning sun rise off the desert. Then we will steal his sons and daughters and sell his wife to the Yumans."

No'ka grinned at Pablo, who turned to Bill, embarrassed. But Bill hadn't mentioned Pablo's earlier outburst. This seemed to be a common idea.

"Bi', you have my blessing to work for Warner. You can be my spy at his lonesome outpost. It will be good for you to get out of the house and give my daughter a rest from baby making. You may even be able to steal me a little coffee and sugar when no one is looking." He winked and patted Bill's arm.

Bill had stayed inside all day after the wedding. He knew the village would notice and give credit to Falling Star, for being irresistible, and for her husband's insatiable appetite, though they both had plumbed their limits.

"I am glad you approve," Bill said. "I like to keep busy."

"Do you share this vision with Warner?" No'ka was serious.

"I can only think of today. My life is full every day. I do not see into the future."

"You are lucky. That is the way to live. Two years become a lifetime, lived thus."

Pablo was silent, disapproving.

"Take this little Sombra to his mistress." No'ka handed Bill the pup. "May he guard her well. A Shadow is a good thing if it belongs to no one else. Pablo, sit here with me. We will talk some more."

He patted the warm earth affectionately, and Pablo took his place there with a sigh.

26

A DAY'S GOSSIP

T H E wedding had not gone unnoticed in the pueblo of San Diego.

"Bill has married Falling Star, daughter of No'ka, the Cupeño capitán," 'Zul told Lugarda.

Lugarda gasped. "When?"

"Yesterday."

"Oh . . . I was supposed to marry first," she sobbed. "Is it legal; binding?"

"He gave her the dress. She accepted. By custom they are married."

"He gave her my dress? The same dress he gave me?"

"She wore it at the celebration, in the chapel at Cupa."

"They have a chapel? A priest married them too?"

"No priest. Pablo announced the marriage before all of the capitánes."

"Then he's not really married."

"I say yes. He sleeps with her in a house given to them by Ladislaya, Pablo's mother."

"Oh . . . is she . . . is she beautiful?"

"So they say."

L E A N D R O Osuna said to José María Alvarado, "You should be a happy man—now your rival has gone and married an Indian."

"That cabrón is not my rival."

"Every man is your rival, hombre. Every man."

L E A N D R O Osuna said to Lugarda Dionicia, " . . . and now your sailor boy has left you for a squaw. I could teach you how to keep a man, little sister."

///

J U A N María Osuna shouted at his wife, " . . . to a wild Indian. What did I tell you; you should never have let that Yankee deserter in my house."

"At least now he won't dare show his face," Señora Osuna replied.

J U A N María Osuna said to Padre Ibarra, "Your favorite fakir, that Indio Pablo Verdi, performed the marriage—in the chapel of Saint Francis."

"I can't believe Pablo would do that."

"Believe it, Padre. His novia, our servant girl 'Zul, told my daughter. A hundred heathens witnessed the vows."

A N I T A Gale de Warner said to Refugio Ortega de Stokes, her next-door neighbor, "And Refie, the gown was from Paris, absolutely the latest style and most gorgeous. She floated down the chapel aisle, like an angel."

"In the chapel of Saint Francis? You were there?"

"No, but I heard all about it from Bill. He's going to be our new ranch foreman. He's really sweet and so much fun. And he's not a drunk."

C O C K N E Y Bill Williams said to his boss, Captain Edward Stokes. "Ignacio saw it all. Even the Cahuilla were there, in paint and feathers and not much else."

C A P T A I N Edward Stokes said to Henry Fitch and Juan Bandini, "All the chiefs came in warpaint, everyone naked but for the bride. She sported a wedding dress the sailor had given to Lugarda Osuna—same one our little alcalde made her give right back. Don't be shy with that brandy, Fitch."

"Good for Bill," said Bandini. "I liked the boy. He can always quit that ship too, when the time comes."

Stokes banged his mug on Fitch's counter. "Captain Saxon let him go. Capitán father-in-law could be a lot tougher."

Fitch poured the drink. "The lucky bastard's buried to his balls in tule skirt and all we can do is talk about it," he said. "Bottoms up."

"Lucky he is Lugarda turned him down, or he'd be getting it once a month, straight up, Doña Mexicana style like we all do," said Stokes.

"Speak for your self, Captain. My Mexican screws me more bloody ways than you can shake your stick at."

"Hear, hear," chimed in Don Juan Bandini.

"Bed steady, my old man always said, you got to marry a lass who's bed steady."

"An' you shoulda listened to your pa." Fitch leveled a wagging finger at Stokes.

"That's it for me," said Bandini. "Put this stuff on my account, will you, Fitch?"

A N I T A Gale said to John Warner, "I pray he'll stay and work for us. With Bill helping, we'll get more than our share of calves branded."

"He can't leave now," said John. "Where could he go with an Indian wife and the half-breed kids he says he's making? Who else would have him?"

M E L O N E S said to Falling Star, "Of course Bill didn't hurt. Big Bear's thrice the size. Even I wouldn't want to take that sword."

"It's not just the size, Meli. Bill was so . . ."

"After I have my child, Big Bear might fit just right," Melones teased, patting her belly and puffing her cheeks.

"Meliii . . . you're making me sick."

"You're not pregnant are you?"

"Probably."

F A L L I N G Star said to her mother, "I hope Bill doesn't ask me to live with him on the ocean."

"We'll have to make his life here so good, he never dreams of leaving."

27

MAJORDOMO

FROM the moment she saw his silky, square face, Falling Star loved the puppy. She loved Bill, she loved their cozy straw house, she loved being married; she made their life a joy. And Bill loved her as much as his restless soul would allow.

His days were spent at the Warners', or on the range, or in the woods; nights with her at the village. Sundays were always a day of rest at the Warners'. That was Bill's day to be with Falling Star, riding to picnics, playing with Shadow, swimming, making baskets or lying around the house. This routine only changed when Warner went to San Diego or Los Angeles. Then Bill would spend both days and nights at the ranch.

Falling Star hated those days. She was jealous. She accused Bill of sleeping with the "little blondie," called him a deserter, a traitor; feigned illness, loneliness, and desperation, but always let him go with a kiss, keeping Shadow. She secretly enjoyed those evenings alone, visiting with her mother or Melones; staying up all night talking to her father.

When John was gone, Bill stayed close to the ranch house and slept in the barn. Anita was great company, full of talk, jokes and laughter. She fed him like a prince, followed him at his chores or sat with him in the store; or she would ride out with Bill to check an injured steer, or to round up the milk cows.

Luna became Bill's shadow. Where Bill went, the boy followed, at first suspiciously, later for company, finally out of friendship. He rarely said a word, simply watched Bill and helped if needed, or got out of the way. When Warner was around, Luna followed John in the same way, but a bit more warily, alert for a cuff.

Fanny and her sister took care of the house and Anita's daughter, Mary

Ann, a shy, serious girl, tall and slim, with her father's face. Anita was too young, or acted too young to be a devoted mother. Fanny was her surrogate.

They were seven, plus a few of the men from Cupa who worked under Bill, growing corn, chiles, potatoes, watermelons, asparagus and wheat, making butter and cheese, tending the cows, carrying water, braiding rope or building sheep sheds, chicken coops, a blacksmith shop and the rest of Warner's projects.

Bill became an integral part of the Warner family. His life revolved around his job as Warner's majordomo, or foreman. He enjoyed it, he was good at it; the Warners appreciated and depended on him.

28

AGUANGA

I N 1 8 4 5 , Bill's only long break from work was a trip with the tribe to Aguanga, at the head of the Valley of Temecula, to harvest acorns. This expedition took place in late October.

Aguanga was at the northern border of Kuupiaxchem territory, the southern for the Cahuilla. It was traditionally a shared resource, with its great stand of the best variety of acorn-producing oaks. The Indians recognized six types of oak trees and had a distinct name for each. Bill could never differentiate more than three: the scrub oaks of the chaparral and dry gullies; the canyon oaks of Encinitas and other streambeds; and the great oaks of the major valleys like Aguanga, with their trunks five feet in diameter and branches to a circumference of sixty feet. All produced acorns, but the best were found on the biggest type of tree.

When they ripened, the Cahuilla, the Cupeño, the Los Coyotes, the Kumeyaay from Santa Ysabel, and often the Pauma People would journey to Aguanga to fill their baskets from the mass of acorns littering the ground beneath the huge trees.

There was no specific date to meet at the grove, but usually the tribes were there at about the same time in the fall, gathering fallen acorns before the animals got to them. It was a camping trip that everyone looked forward to; a chance to mingle in a beautiful neutral setting, meet potential mates, compete in games of skill, tell stories, gamble, race and trade horses, and to take home six month's worth of a valuable staple food.

Cupa was the closest big village to Aguanga. They were usually the first to know when the acorns were ripe. The whole village, men, women, children, dogs and horses, deserted their homes for that week. It was an easy morning's ride back, if someone wanted to return, or something came up that required attention at the hot springs. Only the old, the sick, the heavily pregnant like Melones or the stick-in-the-muds stayed at home.

Fall was the perfect time to go. It was not yet too cold, warm enough at night under the oak canopy. The late summer thundershowers had greened the grass and tempered the heat; the river flowed sweet and cool; acorns lay thick upon the ground and bowed the heavily laden branches overhead.

They set out early on a hazy October morning. The coastal fog had stacked against the western bluff of Mount Palomar, to creep around and settle as dewy mist in the valleys to the north and south. Everyone rode: Big Bear, Stomping Deer and the young men went first, led by No'ka and Antonio Garra, to hunt along the way and scout for other People who might already have arrived. Bill followed with White Fox, Pablo and Falling Star, trailing six pack mules to haul the heavy baskets of nuts back to Cupa. Shadow, now about seven months old, trotted alongside. They were elated. Behind them, the villagers stretched out along the path for a mile.

The trail was empty, the game gone to the brush, run off by the caravan leaders. Birds were their watchful companions, singing and chattering at the column's passage, swooping overhead or circling high in the light blue sky on invisible winds. If a rabbit did jump, Shadow would take off after it with a gangly burst of speed, ears and jowls flapping, his big paws pounding the earth.

He was always outmaneuvered and would return in a minute panting, his wide red tongue hanging down, ready to go again. Shadow was filling out, his muscles strong and defined: catlike. He would stalk game or other dogs like a mountain lion, creeping along on his belly until he was close enough to pounce, or just lying low, his head on the ground, thinking he was invisible, frozen in place until the prey came near. But his leap was a puppy leap. All he caught were nips from unimpressed dogs.

He liked to tease the horses by running at them, bouncing in the air on his four legs to make himself seem bigger, ruff, ruffing in his deep voice. The equines were unimpressed, and would charge him with head down and neck arched. When they were grazing, he would sneak up behind them and grab their tail, hanging on as they trotted away, to be kicked off with a quick hoof. Shadow would slink away yelping, feelings hurt as much as body-bruised.

Falling Star hounded Bill to keep her puppy away from the horses; afraid he would be injured by a kick or stomped to death. They kept Shadow in constant sight. He did the same with them.

Shadow was a menace in the village because of his size, awkwardness and boisterous personality. He chased and ran into things, sending them tumbling. He knocked kids down with his wagging head and tail. But when he tired, he would curl up at their feet, bent paws in the air, snoring like a baby, all mischief forgiven. Falling Star came to count on Shadow's snore as a signal that all was well. If she awoke from a dream, disoriented, that homey drone would send her right back to sleep.

Shadow's hearing was acute; his sense of smell, delicate and unerring. As they rode up to the grove at Aguanga, the hair at his shoulders and rump bristled. Bull Bear emerged from the brush along the river. Shadow charged, a silent hunter's attack.

The Bear saw him coming and called out, "Sombra. I'm your friend. You know me. Shadow! Cuidado, loco." Shadow kept coming, swerving at the last second to miss, passing at top speed to turn and come back with a drooling grin. Bull Bear gave him a cuff and Shadow's thick tail beat the warm air, thrashing tufts of paper-dry wild oats that carpeted the valley, knee high and golden.

"Over here," Bull Bear entreated. "We have the perfect campsite. No one else is here, come."

They followed him upstream to the shade of a monster oak. No'ka and Stomping Deer lay supine on the thick leafbed. Their heads rested on the base of the rough-barked trunk that formed the single support column for a great, sparkling, green-domed cathedral of leaves.

No'ka greeted them with a grin. Stomping Deer spread his arms and bowed slightly, presenting and paying homage to the grandeur of their guest home.

"You have chosen well," White Fox said, appraising the level site, with its good visibility in all directions and stream bubbling just outside the fifty-foot circle of shade. Brush and grazing were within shouting distance; the oak grove lay at hand on three sides.

She took charge. "Falling Star, you and the younger women can gather the fallen nuts, here first. Bull Bear can lead the diggers to make sanitarios there in the brush. Stomping Deer, we need a corral for a few horses. Hobble all of the others. Pablo and Bi', up the tree to shake out any ripe acorns, so we don't get stung by them when the wind blows." She looked at her husband and Bill thought she might assign him a task too.

"And you, Capitán Flojo, you just lie there pretending to be the very god that made this tree and the stream and the valley . . ." She gave No'ka a playful kick in the hip. He didn't budge.

Bill gave Pablo a boost up to the first branch, then Pablo pulled him up to climb into the canopy. Big Bear unpacked two short shovels that Bill had bought from Warner. Shovels and axes and guns were the Spanish hardware that most impressed the Indians. Sugar, coffee and tea were the Spanish foods of choice.

Falling Star arranged baskets to collect and store the acorns. Stomping Deer took all of the horses to drink, then pasture. White Fox piled the supplies and sleeping rugs temporarily outside the shade line.

Pablo and Bill clambered upward, until they clung to branches about the size of an arm. They shook them hard. Acorns rained down, bouncing off their heads and backs and peppering the chief, who jumped up to run after Stomping Deer. Shadow leapt at the falling nuts, growling and spinning if they hit him. He rooted his nose in the collecting baskets and batted the rolling acorns with his big paws. The climbers swung from branch to branch, growing bolder as they got used to the height.

White Fox was a good camp mistress. As tribesmen rode up, she would send them to help one of the four work groups. Young boys were sent up the tree. Women and children gathered the fallen acorns. A few men helped with the horses and latrines.

There were soon fifteen kids in the tree and fifty people below, collecting nuts to clear the way to set up camp. When the tree was shaken clean, Pablo and Bill found themselves sitting way out on a limb ten feet off the ground, watching the women fill small flexible carrying baskets, then dump them into the big, stiff storage baskets.

Pablo began bouncing hard, up and down, the branch flexing three or four feet on each push. Higher and lower they flew. On a downswing, the branch broke about six feet behind them, with a sharp crack. They hit the ground hard; no time to even put their feet out. Bill felt a sickening jolt to his spine, then nothing.

He awoke in a haze, cold water splashing his face. Falling Star, White Fox, Shadow and a gasping Pablo were all peering down at him. A soft bed of oak leaves cushioned his shocked back. Blinding lights twinkled in the shifting canopy. Shadow wagged his tail and gave Bill a lick on the cheek.

"I'm okay," he said, blinking and pressing his eyes. The faces relaxed. "Really, I'm fine."

He sat up, feeling a twinge in the tailbone, but that was all. He was fine.

"It knocked the wind out of me." Pablo was still sucking air. "You were out for a few seconds. You had us scared."

Falling Star's color was returning. She gave Bill a kiss and went back to work.

When all of the acorns were picked up and stashed in the big pack baskets, White Fox showed each family where to camp. She had the boys remove any loose sticks and deadwood that sullied the soft bed of oak leaves. These were broken to usable size and stacked by fire sites she had chosen, downwind along the tree's shadow line. Men and women were hauling stones from the riverbed to make the fire rings. One fire pit was dug deep enough to roast a steer or deer. Orcones, or forked limbs, were buried at each end of this pit, to hold a thick green sapling of willow on which to impale and rotate the roasting animal.

White Fox was hoping the men could find antelope, which were numerous in this long valley they called Temecula. They were shy creatures. At the slightest alarm they would leap to the brush and disappear on tiny trails too small for man or horse. No'ka and Stomping Deer led the hunting party, joined by Pablo. Bill was happy to nurse his sore tailbone on a fur rug, and watch the camp unfold.

The tribe had become one big family. At Cupa they lived in separate houses and saw each other regularly, but casually. Here, all camped beneath this one tree, more than a hundred people, laughing and gossiping, working and playing, doing everything together, under the watchful eye of White Fox and the elder women.

A group of women began to grind acorns at a humped field of black granite boulders. Hundreds of years of grinding with the mano, a round hard stone, had left a dozen depressions six inches deep in the hard granite. A handful of acorns were thrown in the hole, ground to paste, then removed and placed in a basket. Any shells or caps were winnowed out, the paste was washed in the river, then soaked overnight to leach out the tannic acid. The next day it would be washed and soaked again.

Other women gathered wild onions and greens by the riverbank; picked sage, rosemary and lemongrass. Boys collected firewood and dead logs, hunted frogs and squirrels with their miniature bows and arrows, and caught snakes and earthworms with which to scare their sisters.

Bill watched his wife and mother-in-law direct these activities with appreciation. They were thorough, organized and tireless. White Fox commanded without being bossy. Falling Star personally pitched in to keep everyone moving toward the various goals. She still found time to come to lie with him; to rub his bruised back and kiss his neck and ears. Then she would jump up to finish a task, breasts bouncing like ripe unpicked fruit.

SHADOW came to flop by Bill's side in exhausted sleep. Bill dozed with him and woke to the smell of antelope turning on the spit. They had been

skinned, gutted and rubbed with salt, sage and rosemary. Droplets of fat siz-
zled on the coals, emitting a mouthwatering smoky aroma. The sun was sinking low, the air cooling down. Everyone gathered under the tree, famished
from the day's excitement. All eyes were on the browning antelope flesh,
slowly turning over the fires.

Bill sat up stiffly. Pablo knelt to tell him how the hunters had split into two
groups as soon as they spotted the herd of antelope. One line crept on foot to
the right, one to the left, stringing men along the way until the herd was surrounded. Then No'ka stood up and loosed an arrow, sending the agile creatures bounding toward the opposite hunters. They shot their arrows, turning
the wounded herd back to the center.

The herd bounced from one side of the circle to the other, losing a couple
of animals each run, until finally they broke through to freedom, disregard-
ing the shouts and missiles hurtled at them as they leapt past, close enough to
be touched by hand. Twenty had been killed.

The hungry tribe devoured a sumptuous feast of seasoned antelope roast
with acorn dumplings, onions, dandelion and mustard greens. The fires were
fed, and they sang and danced till late into the starlit night. Bill fell asleep
snuggled with Falling Star under rabbit skin robes. They were head to head,
feet to head, side to side with No'ka and White Fox, Pablo, Stomping Deer,
Shadow, Big Bull Bear, the Garra clan and all the extended families, blanketing the oak leaf mattress that had become their communal bed.

Bill felt the strength of their togetherness, of ultimate safety, of harmony,
purpose and love, lying there side by side under the living halo of oak leaves.
Heaven must be like this, he thought. He hugged Falling Star close. He
kissed the base of her neck and told her so.

"We are *Kupa-ngakitom*," she murmured, "we who sleep here." Thus did
they make Bill one of them and bind him unto them: Kuupiaxchem.

29

THE CAHUILLA

ILL awoke early, disentangling himself from his protesting wife, nudged Pablo, wrapped in his robe, and carefully stepped over recumbent bodies until he reached open ground. There was a dramatic drop in temperature and cold dew as soon as they left the oak's shelter. The big trees create their own mild climate. No grass or bushes grow under them due to the thick layer of leaves and lack of direct sunlight. Like a well-built house they stay cool in the day and warm at night. Only a heavy rain could ruin a stay under an oak's protective roof.

No'ka had posted four guards around the great tree, two with the horses. Pablo and Bill were to relieve the horse keepers. They found the camp guards asleep. Each received a kick, but only groaned and fell back to slumber. At the brush and rope corral they saw no one. Shadow found the two men bundled together under a small oak, snoring peacefully. They left them adream, took a couple of horses from the corral, and rode out to find the loosely hobbled main herd.

Pablo was an excellent tracker. The horses were peacefully grazing along the river, about a mile from camp. They returned to the corral and let the other horses out for the day, herding them down to their companions. They left two good horses in the corral, for those who would come at noon to relieve them.

Shadow and Bill spent the morning hunting rabbits while Pablo watched the herd. Bill managed to kill four with his throwing stick before Shadow scared them out of range. Shadow was determined, stalking them like a cat, belly to the ground, but he was too big and dark to be invisible. Inevitably the rabbit would dart off and he would have to pursue. If he ran one down, the rabbit would simply change direction and Shadow would lumber past, raising dust as he braked with his big paws. By the time he turned, the rabbit would be fifty yards away. Only if Bill knocked one down, did Shadow get the chance to grab it in his toothy jaws, shake it violently to kill it and bring it proudly to his master.

Pablo had shot a fat deer with his bow and arrow, by sitting still against a tree and letting him graze to within ten feet of the arrow tip.

"When you're an Indian, the animals will offer themselves to you," he said with a smile. "You simply say thank you and take them. No chasing across the plain like a mad dog."

Shadow's tongue hung to the ground as he sniffed the buck.

"It helps if you're sitting on a pile of acorns, the favorite food of deer."

"Who but a native knows that? Help me with this gift from the gods."

They strung the deer from a branch, gutted him and roasted the liver and heart over a smokeless fire. Shadow ate the guts with relish and fell immediately to snoring.

Over breakfast, Bill recounted Warner's latest Californio gossip:

Mexico had appointed Governor Micheltorena over the protests of the Californios. He had been unpopular since the day he landed in San Diego with an escort army of cholos—convicts and ruffians—and his mistress, irritating everyone with his pompous orders. In Monterey, public opinion had forced the governor to marry his dusky girl, but he remained extremely unpopular. The Californios could not believe that Mexico had the nerve to send an army of Indios—which is what the cholos were—to police them. Even Micheltorena's mistress was some kind of an Indian. It was an insult.

The governor had taken it upon himself to bring the rebellious state of California to heel. He called in Señor Vallejo of San Francisco, the leader of pro-American Californios in the north, and made him swear allegiance to Mexico. Micheltorena demanded that Vallejo supply one thousand horses for the army he was raising to march south to subdue any rebels.

The southerners, under Pío Pico and Alvarado, with their rebel capital at Los Angeles, had refused to recognize Micheltorena. He had been a general under Santa Anna. He was a career military man, out of sympathy with the loose and easy Californio style. They would oust him. The governor of California should be a Californio, not an appointee from Mexico. Pico had raised his own army to oppose the cholos.

Micheltorena gathered his ragtag troops and marched south, following El Camino Real. Shocked by the conditions he found at the looted missions—all but Santa Barbara had suffered secular administrators—and among the Christian natives, living in misery on reduced and unproductive lands,

Micheltorena had ordered most of the missions returned to the friars, with all of their property. In the north, there was some grudging compliance.

In the south, Pico had simply ignored this order. He carried on as though Micheltorena didn't exist. He doubted the governor's ability to take Los Angeles. As Micheltorena drew near, Pico was gathering every weapon and able-bodied man he could muster for the defense of his capital.

Pablo had been listening passively, his face a mask.

"Are you sure of this story?" he demanded.

"Warner just returned from Los Angeles. Pico is his brother-in-law and friend. I'd say it's all true."

Pablo exploded. "Pico, ha," he spit and Shadow twitched. "As foul a piece of Spanish shit as ever fell from the fat ass of Señora Spain. Mierda! Spain sent its shit to Mexico. We had a revolution to throw them out and they changed sides like that." Pablo snapped his fingers. "They declared allegiance to Mexico and now we'll never be rid of them. And you'll see how quickly they'll drop Mexico if the Americans come.

"The padres told me about Pico's type in Spain: Cortés, Pizarro, all the lowest peasants; banditry from Extremadura; penniless, landless, illiterate. They came to Mexico to be princes. Did you know that every one of Cortés's men personally slaughtered at least twenty-five hundred Aztecas? Pizarro killed even more Incas. They were butchers without conscience, scrambling for bloody riches over mountains of dying People.

"Greed and gold. Land and slaves . . . Pío Puerco's cut from the same mold. We People don't forget. We'll send him straight to hell!"

Shadow growled threateningly. Pablo was cheered by his sympathy.

"You'll tear his throat out, won't you, big boy?" Pablo patted the alert pup.

Shadow growled again, looking west. The hairs on his back bristled. The horses pricked their ears; the herd swung to the west, like a weathervane.

Pablo put his ear to the ground. "Riders," he said. "Lots of them."

They were expecting Ignacio from Santa Ysabel and Manuelito's Pauma, from the south. The Los Coyotes under Chapuli would come from the east and the Cahuilla of the mountains would come straight down the hill from the north. No one was expected from the west. The riders were coming up the valley fast, through empty land.

Pablo and Bill caught their ponies, mounted to see better, and prepared to move the herd to the brush if necessary. There were no hostilities among the tribes, nor with the Mexicans, as far as they knew, but a herd of horses, mounted or not, could stampede their own, or lead them off, or mingle with them and be impossible to separate. The nature of horses was to join together. And horse thieves liked to mix herds and drive them away, claiming confusion if discovered.

Around a bend and behind a clump of oaks, they saw a huge dust cloud. Horsemen emerged in a ragged column, two or three abreast. Bill's eyesight was good. "Indians," he told Pablo. Shadow growled and crouched low.

"Let's ride out to meet them. I don't want them near our horses."

Pablo raced off at a gallop. Bill followed at a slow trot, a pace Shadow could keep.

Pablo reached the column a mile ahead of Bill. Two or three hundred riders, with twice as many horses, spread across the valley. The men were fiercely painted from head to toe in black and white and red patterns; stripes, spots, circles and swirls. They were all armed with lance, bow and arrows, knife and tomahawk. There were a few guns. There were no women. It was a war party.

Pablo's horse laid back his ears. He snorted and whirled. Pablo was about to let him have his head and run, when he recognized Juan Antonio and Baupista, the Cahuilla capitánes, at the head of the column. He waved and turned toward the river, where they seemed to be headed.

Bill found Pablo squatted with the two men at the foot of an oak. Hundreds of painted men lay wearily in the dirt. They seemed to have dropped wherever they had slipped from their mounts. Horses dotted the river and its banks, heads down, drinking, tearing at clumps of grass. Bill dismounted, tied his pony to a branch in plain sight, and entered the shade zone. Shadow walked at his heel, hackles up, tongue out.

Pablo stood to make introductions. The others did not rise, but looked at the white Indian curiously, raising a hand.

"You met the Cahuilla chiefs, Juan Antonio and Baupista, at your wedding," Pablo reminded in English.

They motioned Bill to sit. Juan Antonio continued his conversation with Pablo in Cahuilla, a dialect full of clicks and squeaks delivered at a breathtaking pace. Pablo would reply; Antonio would rattle off again for five minutes.

Bill studied the men. Both chiefs cradled shotguns that seemed new. They were dressed in native fashion with random additions. Antonio wore a military jacket of Spanish design, with no pants, and Baupista an armless ruffled shirt, unbuttoned and cut short, with leather chaps tied over his apron, open at the back. They looked ludicrous and fierce, with dusted jet-black hair and pink slashes of mouth in wildly painted faces, darkened and cracked by the sun. It was easy to see why the other tribes feared them—and the padres and Spanish had left them alone.

After half an hour of parley, they remounted. Pablo and Bill led them toward the camp at Aguanga, riding a little to the side of the chiefs. It would not be polite to have them eat their dust.

"Antonio wants to buy Shadow," was the first thing Pablo said.

"I hope you told him no."

"I told him I'd ask you."

"The answer is no. I'd sooner sell you." Bill laughed. "Tell him I'll give him a pup, when they come. What's with all the armament. Is this a war party?"

"They're returning from helping Pico drive Micheltorena's army out of Los Angeles. Apparently Micheltorena and his cholos took the pueblo with the help of some American riflemen from Sacramento. When the Americans and their rifles went home, Andrés Pico attacked with a force of Californios and these Cahuilla. Micheltorena surrendered and agreed to return to Mexico.

"It was a typically Mexican encounter. Cannon shots were exchanged followed by two days of negotiation. No one really got to fight. The Cahuilla were disappointed by the lack of action. Pico couldn't wait to dismiss them. He gave Juan Antonio some worthless broncos and mules, stolen from San Gabriel Mission, and five English shotguns he had ordered from Hawaii. He forgot to supply ammunition of course," Pablo grunted.

"The Cahuilla are on their way home. They say they came this way to hunt in the valley before entering the desert. I think they were looking for better horses to steal. We must make sure they leave with only those animals they brought."

"They look dangerous," Bill said apprehensively.

"They once were warlike. We were traditional enemies, before the padres banned intertribal warfare. The Pauma were just as fierce," Pablo said with passion.

"But the Cahuilla were never conquered, or Christianized."

Pablo looked pained. "They were not worth conquering. If you ever visit their rocky and barren lands you'll understand why. They live on lizards and snakes and eat the flesh of birds of prey and buzzards."

This was the rankest bird flesh on earth, worse than seagull.

"Maybe that is what makes them so tough."

"For want of food, they are tiny men. Big Bear could crush four of them at once. Don't be fooled by their scowls. White Fox will have them eating out of her hand. Just watch your dog and possessions. They are clever thieves and eat anything."

Shadow instinctively shrank from the Cahuilla.

/ / /

W H E N the visitors arrived at camp, most of the tribe was spread out through the grove, gathering acorns. No'ka and White Fox greeted the chiefs warmly. Both spoke Cahuilla fluently. They reclined under the oak, gossiping and eating the leftovers from supper. Antonio Garra joined them.

Pablo and Bill lounged in the shade, after sending Bull Bear and Stomping Deer to guard the herd and fetch the buck Pablo had hung. They stayed alert for any thievery in the camp, but the Cahuilla rested gratefully under the oaks, while their large herd of horses grazed with four watchful riders in the nearby valley.

Mesmerized by shimmering leaves and the murmuring of the chiefs' voices, Bill daydreamed. Shadow growled and started up. One of the painted Cahuilla came trotting up from the river, probably to speak to a chief. Shadow flew to meet him. The warrior kept trotting, oblivious to danger. Shadow launched his hundred and twenty pounds of bone, muscle, tooth and claw, striking at shoulder level. His long fangs sank into the poor man's ribs, just under the arm. Shadow's momentum carried the terrified Cahuilla with him. There was a scream and a heavy thump as they hit the ground. Shadow kept going and turned to growl at the downed man.

"Sombra," yelled No'ka and Pablo together. "No."

"Shadow," Bill called. "No. Bad dog. Leave him alone. Come here."

Antonio and Baupista were laughing. Shadow trotted obliquely toward them, slinking, trying to decide whether to come or run.

Bill ran to see how badly the man was hurt. There were three ugly puncture wounds and a scratch. He was out of breath and frightened, but the bite was not serious. White Fox led him away, to clean and pack the holes with herbs.

"Bad dog," Bill said to Shadow, as he cringed.

"Good dog," said Juan Antonio. "You sell, I buy."

"He is a gift we cannot sell," said No'ka, stroking Shadow's silky ears.

A F T E R about an hour of eating and talking, Antonio dozed a bit. Baupista and No'ka continued to debate, both getting excited and gesticulating to amplify their points. Then they too dozed. People began to return to the campsite at midday, with their pack baskets full of acorns. In the commotion, the Cahuilla chiefs roused themselves, thanked White Fox for the meal, called their sleeping men to horse, and departed for their home villages — the first of which were only a two-hour ride north, up the canyon at Aguanga, over the hills and into Anza Valley.

No'ka was glad to see the Cahuilla file out of the grove. It was the only war party he had ever seen. Their numbers, thrice his own, all men, heavily armed, made him feel vulnerable.

"They talk big, but they never even got to fight," Pablo scoffed

No'ka shook his head. "Such feats improve with age. The forced march to Los Angeles alone is worthy of a victory dance. Most war songs are made from lesser deeds."

White Fox nodded in agreement. "It has been many, many years since any of the People have danced the war dance. For the Cahuilla, the year will be marked by this event. Do not underestimate what they have done."

"War is not only about killing enemies," No'ka explained. "It is also about making friends. Those men have bonded with the Californios, with Andrés Pico, Alvarado, the Osunas, their comrades at arms."

Bill hadn't thought of the Osunas in months. He touched the scar where Leandro's whip tip had raked his ear. No'ka leaned forward.

"My argument with Baupista had to do with this bond. He says the Cahuilla will support the Mexicans in any war with the United States. I protested. I listed for him all the grievances we People have had with the Spanish-Mexicans: the lands taken, people forced to work under the lash, religion and customs banished, villages burned and women defiled.

"The Spanish never harmed the Cahuilla, was Baupista's reply."

"They never harmed the Cahuilla because those desert reptiles have nothing the Mexicans want," Pablo interrupted.

No'ka held up his hand. "I said, but what of the harm they have done to us, to your brothers?

"That is not our concern, he said. You must settle your own quarrels.

"So if we were to support the Americans, then you would fight against us? Against your own brothers? I looked into his heart.

"We hope that this will not come to pass, Baupista replied, looking away.

"Baupista evaded the answer that was pounding in his breast." No'ka faced his wife. "He would love to seize our lands. Never again can we trust that man, so long as the Mexicans rule us."

"Are these the thoughts of Juan Antonio too?" asked White Fox.

"Baupista does not have his own thoughts, my dear. You know him better than I," No'ka snapped.

He sprang with youthful agility to stalk off toward the river. White Fox flushed in embarrassment.

/ / /

T H A T evening, tucked in with Falling Star, her cool naked plumpness melting against his hot angularity, sinking into warm equilibrium and delicious slumber, Bill received this soft-spoken explanation:

"My mother once had an affair with Baupista, on a camp trip just such as this. She was very young. No'ka was very jealous. It meant nothing, then or now. It was the news from Antonio and Baupista that barbed my father's words. He has already apologized."

"Mmmm . . ." was all Bill could manage in reply.

30

A DANCE PARTY

IN THE afternoon Manuelito arrived with about sixty-five Pauma. All work stopped while they set up camp. Pablo's mother had come, and 'Zul, who had begged a vacation from the Osunas.

When Pablo saw 'Zul, he lit up like a peacock, eyes ablaze, chest puffed out, step springy, arms in motion, teeth flashing, muscles flexed, strutting, posing. He introduced everyone of the Pauma to all of the Cupeño with a double-circle dance, the two concentric circles revolving slowly in oppposite directions. He shouted out jokes, making them comfortable.

"Look, my fellows, here we are at camp. There are no priests to scold us, or Spaniards to tut-tut. It's hot. Why are you dressed like scarecrows? Come on, you're making us look like savages."

They had to laugh. The Pauma were dressed in mission shifts or work clothes, with a few caballero outfits and a couple of tatty cast-off Mexican gowns. Only Ladislaya really looked good, in a fitted gingham dress she had made. The Cupeño were nearly naked in the fall heat.

"Look at me. We are brothers and sisters. Discard your tired rags. Dress as we once dressed, when we were men and women, and our own masters."

Pablo did a cartwheel, took 'Zul's hand, knelt and pleaded, "Please . . ."

She lifted her dress over her head and threw it to her father. With a sheepish grin, she took Pablo's hand and they ran off to splash in the river. The Cupeño clapped and cheered. A few others from Pauma followed 'Zul's lead. Then everyone settled in to organize the camp, the ice truly broken.

There was no time to hunt for dinner. White Fox sent the young men out to kill a couple of fat calves. A butchering party of twenty boys whooped off at a gallop.

White Fox looked to Bill as she gave this order, and he shrugged in ignorance.

"They are your calves," she said when the boys had charged off.

"Do you really think so?"

"No, Bi', you belong to us, and they do too," she retorted. "You can organize a firewood-gathering expedition among the children, if you have nothing better to do."

"Si, señora." Bill bowed low and she tapped his crown in benediction.

THE beeves were roasting on the spit, juices popping and spitting on the red-hot rocks below, oak coals aglow like chunks of lava, smells of burnt fat and meat and spices mesmerizing the assembled men and dogs. The sky was afire with orange light; topped by puffy pink clouds and pale blues so deep they looked fake. At that pregnant moment, Ignacio and his tribe from Santa Ysabel filed into camp.

Ignacio had come with only a few families. Santa Ysabel was far from Aguanga and had its own fine oak groves to harvest. They had not ridden fifty miles to load down their horses with heavy baskets of acorns. They had come to dance.

The revelers ate, sang, pounded on drums, danced, smoked wild tobacco, played reed flutes, gossiped, kissed, held hands and watched the stars rise and fall until dawn's greater glow obscured them. They collapsed into a deep and peaceful sleep, safe from the sun's rousing rays, cool in the circle of shade drawn round by a million oak leaves.

By the time Bill awoke, some time after noon, everyone had left the camp except the three chiefs. Even Shadow was gone.

Ignacio was standing, waving his arms, exclaiming, "Let those dried-up raisins of men puff and brag and strut around their rock-pile lands like lords of war. We know the truth. They do not live like lizards among the boulders and sand by choice, but because our ancestors drove them back to their hiding places every time they tried to move into our lush valleys."

He squatted to face No'ka and Manuelito, who were reclined on the leaf-bed. "The Cahuilla are tough, yes, because you must be tough to live as they live. But they are not fearless. They are as all the desert creatures, who only survive by running and hiding. They are born with the fear of Kumeyaay and Kuupiaxchem arrows in their backsides."

"But many generations have passed since last we flew our arrows in their direction," No'ka warned. "A man who thinks he is tougher than he is, is a dangerous man, for he may do a foolish thing."

"I don't see how they could think they were tough," said Manuelito. "I have the story of Los Angeles from 'Zul, who heard it from the Osunas. By the time the brave army of the south arrived, the Yankee riflemen had gone back to Sacramento. Micheltorena withdrew to Cahuenga Pass, and invited Pico to talk. They ate lunch in the general's tent, drinking red wine served by Micheltorena's whore-wife. Pico stumbled back down the hill and everybody rode home."

No'ka and Ignacio laughed.

"If they had seen the American riflemen in action, they would think twice about supporting the Mexicans," said Manuelito. "I hear they have a new gun that is accurate at two hundred paces, and can be reloaded and fired in seconds."

No'ka grunted.

"Micheltorena and Santa Anna were driven from Texas by less than five hundred American settlers," said Ignacio. "The Mexicans had an army of five thousand. They don't have a chance."

The chiefs were silent for a few minutes. Bill sat up and said, "I have seen the new guns. Warner brought a repeating rifle and a pistol back from Connecticut. They have a revolving chamber to hold powder, cap and ball."

The chiefs looked at him sharply, startled. They switched from Spanish to Cupeño and went on talking, ignoring his contribution.

Later, No'ka was reproachful. "Bi', it is not polite to interrupt."

"I was sleeping, I awoke," he protested.

"Then you should have pretended to hear nothing. Like we pretend to hear nothing when you and my daughter are working so hard at making our grandchild."

"She's pregnant," Bill said to cover his embarrassment.

"Then you must be trying for twins." No'ka slapped his shoulder. "I will like being a grandfather. Thank you."

T H E pack baskets were full of acorns by the end of the day. The tribe would straggle back to Cupa by twos and threes and families, some remaining until the last campers left Aguanga. Falling Star wanted to rush home to be with Melones for her child's imminent birth. Bill had to get back to work. Pablo would stay with 'Zul and Ladislaya until they went back to Pauma, where his mother had decided to live.

Manuelito had asked Ladislaya to marry him, shortly after Francisco's death. It was known by all that Manuelito had loved Ladislaya since they were children at the mission. His wife had graciously agreed that he could take her best friend as a second wife. They already lived together. Ladislaya had married in the time-honored fashion: Manuelito offered her a gift, the seeds of a watermelon, her favorite fruit. She accepted. Ladislaya hoped that Pablo would come to live at Pauma too, and eventually marry 'Zul.

When Bill and Falling Star were all packed, Chapuli, chief of the Los Coyotes band of Cahuilla, slipped into camp with forty of his people. He was a jolly, tubby man, and No'ka's closest ally in the mountains. There was no question of leaving. The four capitánes were rarely together. They shared friends and family among the Los Coyotes, who were a hybrid of Cahuilla and Kuupiaxchem. The feasting, singing, dancing and visiting went on into the night again, the oak-roofed village reverberating to drums and rattles, flutes, shouts and laughter.

The People could dance. They danced for hours, the men and women each in their own separate dances. Sometimes the dancing was relaxing: so languid, they rested in motion. Then the music would speed up and they would burn every ounce of energy they possessed, each person gyrating alone, wiping off sweat with a small wooden scraper. Then everyone slept for twelve hours. One of the purposes of dancing was to wear yourself out—to ensure a good dreaming communion with the spirits.

Falling Star was blooming with her pregnancy, filling every curve with a ripeness that rivaled Melones. She was proud of her blossoming body. She strutted around the camp, head held high, her chest jutting, ample bottom swishing her tule skirt. There were other women to look at, but Falling Star simply glowed.

Since their marriage, Bill had become accustomed to the luxury of sex. But the acorn camp activities had left little opportunity for intimacy. They made up for the intermission that last night, slipping off with blankets to an unused oak, slithering together like love-sick salamanders, lost in the throbbing and singing, and the pounding of their own hearts.

31

A GIRL
AND HER DOG

T H E Y departed in the morning, No'ka and White Fox remaining to supervise the breakup of camp and roundup of horses. The Cahuilla had left a large herd to graze in the valley, the broncos and mules that were their war spoils, all too wild to ride. The chiefs didn't want any of them to follow, "by mistake." They could allow no excuse for a Cahuilla raid.

The minute Shadow saw Falling Star loading the packs, he whined and wagged his tail, then gave a couple of deep barks. He led down the trail at a trot, big paws raising little puffs of dust, glancing over his shoulder to make sure they were following.

The camp had been a good lesson in socializing for Shadow. He had made a dozen new friends at the camp, dogs and people. He had bitten only the one Cahuilla, and avoided fighting the older dogs. He was still too much of a puppy to challenge the canine pecking order. If a dog would not play with him, he left it alone, although he did love to charge at man or beast to see if he could make it run.

Shadow knew basic verbal commands, although he would guiltily ignore them at times. Bill had taught him to take offered food daintily, picking it from an outstretched hand with his purple lips and small front teeth. This skill earned him numerous treats and saved offering hands from a mangling.

The big puppy had been praised and admired and adored. Falling Star proudly followed Shadow's swaying rump home.

32

A BIRTH

ELONES'S child was born on the twenty-ninth of October 1845. She went into labor about eight in the evening, on a moonlit night, clear and warm. The sun was just setting. There had been a thunder shower in the afternoon. The ground and carpet of oak leaves smelled fresh and fecund. The moon had risen while the sun set, as though pulled up by some invisible string, to light the darkening sky.

Melones was in the pool, floating her big belly to ease the strain on her back; Falling Star and Bill were entwined like seahorses; Stomping Deer was talking insurrection with Big Bull Bear.

Melones gave a groan, stood up and said, "Ya, ya."

The baby's head was sticking out between her legs. She squatted down, and stood up quickly. The baby plopped into the pool. She picked him up, for it was a boy, and held him.

"Ayúdenme," she pleaded.

Falling Star leapt to take the child. "Bring me a knife," she shouted.

Big Bear was the first to reach her with his knife. Falling Star cut the umbilical cord and tied it expertly. She threw the placenta onto the rocks.

"Help her home," she ordered. She was patting the boy on the back to start his breathing.

The Bear picked Melones up like a child. He followed Falling Star and the newborn baby up the bank to the village.

MELONES had so much milk that she wet-nursed another child whose mother was dry. As promised, the few times they were alone together, what was left went to Bill.

"Please, Bi'," she would say, touching her breasts tenderly. "Help me." The corners of her mouth would turn up; she would inhale and bat her eyelashes.

Her milk was sweet and thick. Bill watched it dribble down her breast and licked it off. He would chew on her nipples, suck, bury his nose in her cleavage—it's impossible to describe such a foolish pleasure. They were innocent, chaste, frolicking like a mare and foal. Bill belonged to Falling Star, but he could give something to Melones, and she to him; something of value; a lightness of being. Her spirit was as delicate and free as her body was voluptuous and earthbound. They communed in giggles. Giggles were their password; giggles their vocabulary. Giggles were the sounds they first heard from the two babies.

33

PABLO'S CURE

PABLO couldn't sit still. The more content Bill became, the more he was possessed by restlessness. He had found a place for Bill to thrive, but he himself remained adrift.

He returned to Pauma with his mother and 'Zul, hoping to forge a new life there, but after two days, 'Zul had insisted on going back to the Osunas. 'Zul's continuing loyalty to Lugarda was a mystery Pablo could not understand or accept. Ladislaya tried to help her son see 'Zul's viewpoint.

"It is a brave thing she has done. The Osunas are a difficult family and cannot get help from the local People, who curse Juan María Osuna for stealing their land. She and Lugarda have been together all of their lives. They love each other and need each other. Lugarda is lost without 'Zul."

"But we too love and need each other."

"Lugarda accepts her, she dresses her beautifully, she protects her and gives her an exciting modern life in San Diego that she cannot have with you. That is the truth. What have you to offer? Only a return to the old ways she does not value."

While Pablo was staying with his mother, Pauma Valley had been deeded to Juan Antonio Serrano, a friend of the Picos who lived in San Diego. Governor Pío Pico owed Serrano a large gambling debt, now repaid by confirming ex-Governor Micheltorena's provisional grant of the year before.

Juan Serrano arrived at Pauma ranchería with his son, Jesús, his brother, Manuel, and two brothers-in-law, José and Ramón Aguilar. The men drove a hundred head of cattle. They had come to take possession of their valley.

Juan Serrano was polite, showing Manuelito his approved application for the Pauma grant, asking Manuelito to respect his cattle's grazing rights. Serrano proposed giving Manuelito five calves per year, as payment for watching over the herd.

Manuelito read the deed and passed it to Pablo. Pablo read it carefully in silence. When he looked up, his face was dark, and stone hard. He stabbed at the parchment with his forefinger.

"Your grant is for unoccupied lands, Señor Serrano. They could not be here, for it is obvious that the Pauma have possession of this place—where we have lived since before your great-great-grandfather was born." Pablo shook the deed, biting his tongue.

Serrano looked away and said to Manuelito, "There is room for everyone and all of our cattle. I live in San Diego. If I do build a house, it will be on unoccupied land. I do not claim your village or ask anyone to leave it. You have my word."

Most Mexican and Spanish land grants said "unoccupied," unless the grant was to the natives themselves. By Mexican law, Christian Indians were citizens with possessory rights. Their land could not be granted to others. But the question of how much land around a village belonged to the villagers had never been answered—to the satisfaction of the natives or colonists. The usual solution was to pretend there was no village at all and let the grantee make arrangements with the natives.

Manuelito was acquainted with the Serranos and Aguilars. He knew they had the backing of Governor Pico and his military commander. He could not say no to Serrano. He could only negotiate. He did not want to debate with Pablo in front of these men, to weaken his authority to bargain. He held up a hand to stay any protest.

"You may leave the cattle so long as you do not bring other men to work them. We Pauma must do all of the vaquero tasks, including the hide harvest, for which we will receive the customary fifty percent. As well, we must receive ten percent of the calves.

"You may construct a home for your family at an agreed upon location, at least one mile from any village. Again we must be the builders of the house and paid one head of cattle per month per builder. In this manner we may live in harmony on our lands."

Juan Serrano was quick to agree. He knew how easily his cattle could disappear into the wilderness. This was a good first step. He could exercise his full rights of ownership bit by bit, in the future. Poco a poco, mañana.

"I am in accord, Manuelito. In return, you must respect the rights of my family and in-laws to come and go as they please, to inspect the cattle, count the harvest and supervise construction of the house we will build." He indicated those present with a wave of his hand. "We will likewise respect your rights. We enjoy our life in San Diego. We only want pasture for our cattle, and shelter for the cold nights when we visit."

Manuelito agreed. The men shook hands. Pablo was outraged.

"It may mean slavery and serfdom, like the Kumeyaay at the Osunas'; or a partnership such as Ignacio has with Edward Stokes at Santa Ysabel; or you may ignore each other, as the Cupeño and Warner do. But in each case the choice is not for the People to make. It is the landlord who decides."

"No, Pablo," said Ladislaya. "You heard Manuelito. It is both sides who make the relationship."

"And what happens when Serrano sells his lands to someone else?" Pablo shouted. "Do the Pauma go with the land like the trees and bear and deer? Have our lives been granted to Serrano too? Are we to be some kind of feudal tenants, in a medieval system where every leaf belongs to the landlord? Or will we have to flee, as we fled Las Flores?"

When they were silent, he said, "I cannot stay here, Mother. It is too piti- ful an existence."

W H E N Pablo told this story on his return to Cupa, Stomping Deer and the other young men set up a howl. Even No'ka angrily pounded a fist into his palm.

When the yelling stopped, Antonio Garra said, "Perhaps Bill could ask Warner to show him the deed to our valley. We should see if it too claims unoccupied lands."

"It doesn't sound like it makes a bit of difference," No'ka said.

"You are probably right. Whether it says we are here or not, either way the deeds should be invalid. But it would be good to know whether we are rec- ognized to be here, or invisible; legally invisible." Garra's hands danced in desperate sign.

When they were still, Bill said, "Yes, I will try."

I T would rain some hot fall days, huge thunderheads gathering over Eagle's Nest, lightning striking out with its random arrows to split rock and rend trees, thunder rolling across the dry plain, stampeding deer and cattle and sending the dogs whimpering for shelter. Big drops would hit the dust, throw- ing out tiny puffs, until the surface saturated. Sometimes even hail pelted down, stinging cold, bouncing off man and beast, rock and leaf, to melt on the hot ground. A good rain would cool the whole atmosphere, then stop as suddenly as it began, evaporating in the heat, to rise and fall again the next afternoon.

Other days were just hot, cloudless and bright blue, only good for swimming and sleeping. Pablo paced, rain or shine. Or he sat around in the pools sighing. He felt he did not belong anywhere; not with Father Ibarra at San Luis Rey; not with 'Zul at the Osunas'; not with his mother in Pauma nor with Bill at Cupa. A part of him longed for each home but nowhere could he be content. It was sad. Only for Shadow, did he so much as crack a smile.

White Fox finally grew disgusted with Pablo's moping. She begged No'ka to send him on a mission.

"High Cloud, I need a favor, if you will do it for me," No'ka said, one sweltering dry afternoon.

"At Palomar there is a meadow, surrounded by pines, where cattle and horses often go to escape the heat. It is twice as high as we are, cool and green even now. There, I hope you will find my big black stallion. I have not seen him since we returned from Aguanga. I would not like to lose him. We were at the meadow together last summer. He knows the place. It is a fine summer pasture, accessible from all sides of the mountain. You may find him with other good horses or cattle you can bring back."

"I will go with you," Stomping Deer said, jumping up, trotting in place.

No'ka cut his son off. "I need you here with me. Pablo should go alone."

Pablo said, "Yes, maybe I need to be alone. I will do this task for my capitán."

"The air is thin at Palomar," said No'ka with a smile. "Thin and light. It may relieve the heaviness your soul feels. You will be closer to the heavens than you have ever been, on land that belongs to no one but the gods and the great grizzlies; land as it was before even we came here. It is good for a man to know the existence of such a place."

"When shall I leave?" asked Pablo.

"Now," said the chief. "White Fox has a basket of acorn flour for you. You'll need bow, arrows, knife, lance, rope, a fur for the night and one strong horse. The tools of a man."

"It's hot," Bill said. "Why not wait till morning."

"It's no hotter on the trail than here," No'ka shot him a glance of disapproval, "and without the pleasure of movement."

"I'm on my way," Pablo said, with more energy than he had shown in weeks. He gathered his few things and dissolved into the waves of heat.

"How nice it feels without him here," said White Fox softly. "When a man is not happy where he is, he should not stay in that place. It is bad for him and infects the rest of us. There is nothing wrong with Cupa."

"Even I was beginning to feel nervous, walking on this ground that he keeps reminding me belongs to Warner," said No'ka.

"He's right," said Stomping Deer, stalking off. "We should be nervous. And Warner should be nervous too."

"Maybe," said No'ka with a shrug, "But here we all are, enjoying our land as ever."

"Pablo is an unusual man," said White Fox. "He needs to know the meaning of his life at all times. He can't do things by halves. It will do him good to be alone, to feel who he really is, or might be. I'm sure he's never been alone for one day in his life."

"Pablo seems always alone," Falling Star said.

"I don't know if we can truly know the meaning of life, or our part in it," said White Fox. "But we can know the joy of living. Joy gives life meaning. Pablo has none. I hope he will find it at Palomar."

She rumpled No'ka's shaggy head.

Falling Star nodded in agreement, "You should have made him marry in the village, as you did Bi'. Then he would be content."

"Pablo wants to serve his people. Somehow the priests instilled this idea of service into his being. That is the heart I see in him. We can help him by giving him tasks of service." White Fox was now sitting in No'ka's lap, her arm around his shoulders.

"He would make a good spy." The words spilled from Bill's mouth.

DURING his stay at Pauma, Pablo had reluctantly agreed to gather information about Lugarda. But he didn't approve of Bill's interest and had slanted all news to discourage, though he swore that he only repeated 'Zul's words, verbatim:

"Lugarda is happy with José María. He does her every bidding, and she asks for many things. She does not like living at Rancho San Marcos. It is too far from the sea, too hot in summer, too cold in winter, and too lonely. A ring of hills surrounds the ranch on all sides, making her feel trapped. She far prefers Rancho San Dieguito where the whole valley opens to the sea. She misses her family, especially her mother."

And, "San Marcos was too far from San Diego. Lugarda has moved to the Alvarado home in the pueblo. José María stays at the ranch much of the time. She only goes there for a fiesta. Lugarda sees her own family more. She dances at all of the bailes. She is making little clothes for her child, due in January or February. She is more beautiful than ever, in the early glow of pregnancy. She has cramps at times and nausea. She never mentions Bill."

That was all Pablo would say. Bill supposed he could see her himself, after the next hide harvest, after her child was born, and his. That would give them something to talk about. He found it hard to recall the joyous feelings they had shared. He thought, how frail the lovers' knot, unraveling so willingly to the tug of time.

W H E N E V E R Warner was gone for a few days, Bill slept in the barn with Luna, no matter how icy the night. Luna's silence was welcome, after Anita's nonstop chattering. He was silent, but he was there, just like Shadow.

They had become inseparable in a strange way: They always knew exactly where the other could be found. Bill attributed this to Luna's uncanny ability to communicate without speech. In time, it must have rubbed off on Bill, because he too understood Luna, without words or gestures.

Anita was exactly the opposite. She had a keen eye and sharp wit; she was entertaining and lively; she was energetic and willing to partake in any venture; she was shrewd—but she was no mind reader. Whether you were tired or sad, lonely or hurt, depressed or moody, or just wanted to be alone, she carried on as she always did, bubbly and enthusiastic, blithely cheerful. This was her charm. By sheer ebullience and lack of awareness of any mood but her own, she could lift you out from under the darkest cloud. Anita levitated the lonely Warner homestead above the dust and mud, and made time fly.

One day Bill asked her to show him Warner's deed. He saw the dread word, "unoccupied," at the head of his petition—"The place known as Valle de San José, which is unoccupied," were the exact words—and thus had the petition been approved. Bill's heart raced and the hair on his arms stood up. He put the paper down and stared at it.

"It says, unoccupied." He couldn't look at Anita.

"Of course it does. Look around us, There's nobody here. Our closest neighbor is Edward Stokes, at least fifteen miles away." She put the deed in a wooden box and put the box back in a trunk, which she locked.

"What about the Cupeño?"

"What about them?" She looked puzzled.

"They're occupying your land. Or you are theirs."

"Oh Bill, there's plenty of room, what would we do with forty-eight thousand acres anyway? And where are the fences or boundaries? All the land around us, hundreds of thousands of acres, can be theirs. It's just a piece of paper. John loves No'ka and would never kick him out, even if he could. He says we'll work it out in time, and I'm sure we will."

When Warner returned, his mules laden with supplies, Bill asked him about the wording. He was just as blunt.

"If I had said: 'Occupied by a tribe of Cupeño Indians, under their Capitán No'ka,' I would never have gotten approval. I told No'ka to put a stone fence around whatever land he thought was his. I said this when first we came. I keep saying it. He still has not done so."

"Who could build enough fence for what they own?" Bill protested.

"'None of the land is mine. All you claim is ours.' That was No'ka's answer to me. And that's how we've left it." Warner shook his head as though to clear it.

"I mean the Cupeño no harm. I wanted to have a store at the desert frontier; to sell goods to the immigrants who are sure to come. Portilla and Pico had already tried to claim this valley. I just took over their grants because they contained this location, on the Santa Fe Trail. Sometimes I wonder myself what I'm doing here."

"So do we," Bill muttered.

Warner looked at him sharply.

"The Cupeño are better off with me than with Pico or Portilla. That's a fact no one can dispute. Now let's get these things unloaded. These mules are pack-sore and hungry."

As the grateful mules rolled in the dust, Warner became jolly and excited, "Texas has annexed to the U.S. I just heard the news from Stokes. Now all we have to do is wait for Santa Anna to declare war. When the Americans win, all these deeds will be scraps of paper. I'll probably move back to Los Angeles, after I've made my killing selling goods to the settlers who pass this way. Then the Indians can have it all to themselves. It's too lonely here for Anita—we've got another child coming—for me too, and I get out a lot more."

"I'm exactly the opposite of lonely," Bill said.

" F R I A R Ibarra told me Texas has been ratified by the U.S. Congress as a slave state," Pablo said.

He was relaxed, thinner, smiling and confident, on his return to Cupa from Palomar. He had descended the mountain's steep west side for a short visit to the priest at San Luis Rey.

"That's a shame," Bill said.

"Will California be slave or free?" Pablo's smile twisted a bit.

"Free," No'ka and Bill spoke together.

"We are a free people." No'ka sighed. "Mexico does not allow slavery. I cannot imagine otherwise . . ."

"And your friend John Warner, the slave-owning Mexican citizen, what will he choose?" Pablo asked, his smile gone awry.

"Free," Bill said. "Warner is anti-slavery. He doesn't consider Fanny and Luna to be slaves. He bought their freedom."

"But they can't leave, they work for him and they do not get paid. They are slaves," Pablo insisted.

"Warner is as complicated a man as you are, Pablo," No'ka spoke up. "Connecticut Yankee and Mexican citizen. A friend of Pico, and working with Thomas O. Larkin to help the U.S. defeat Pico; a friend of the Kuupi-axchem, who claims he owns our land, but says it is ours; a man against slavery who has slaves; a shopkeeper who lives in the wilds. If the Americans come, he will have as many problems as any of us."

No'ka sank into the cold pool, until they could just see the top of his head and a few bubbles.

"I'm not that complicated," said Pablo to the bubbles.

At Mount Palomar, Pablo had found no horses or cattle, only untouched wilderness. For three weeks he lived with the animals, eating and lounging in the day, gazing at the almost touchable stars at night. The creatures had been so tame that he found it impossible to kill them. He subsisted on a diet of roots, greens, herbs, berries, acorn flour and pine nuts.

"I would stare into the heavens for hours," Pablo recounted, "waiting for a sign from God or the Great Spirit. But nothing ever happened. Nothing. No one spoke to me but the birds and chipmunks, squirrels and bear.

"It was very peaceful. I was content for about two weeks, but then grew restless. I had thought I might be able to live there forever, alone with the animals, a pure native life. I was annoyed by my inability to be happy in such an ideal place.

"I examined my entire self, to the darkest corners, seeking the source of my restlessness. I had no luck. I just found a lot of separate pieces that didn't seem to be connected. And then I knew that was it: I cannot live contentedly as one part of me, to the exclusion of my own knowledge and desires in other worlds. Altar boy, scholar, Spanish caballero, rancher, native hunter, lover, loner, all of these are me.

"Therefore my restlessness, therefore my need to move. I must be free to wander: to stay here, to visit 'Zul, see my friends at La Playa, stay with Father Ibarra at San Luis Rey, and return to Palomar when I need the wilderness. I must nourish all of my parts, in this fragmented life that has been given to me. Then I will be content."

Pablos's face shone with inspiration. There were tears in his eyes. White Fox gave him a long hug, and said, "You are so thin. You could use a good meal, Pablito."

"I would like for you to be my eyes and ears in these worlds you will visit," No'ka said seriously. "We need to learn about the coming storm."

"A spy, a spy, an Ipai spy," Bill sang. "I told you, didn't I."

"It will be a pleasure, Capitán," Pablo said. "It is good to know thy enemy, and greater still to have a friend whom you can love and serve."

34

WILI

ON THE eleventh of December Bill's son was born. Falling Star did not allow him to be present.

"I don't want you to know my sex as a bloody, gaping wound. You'll never want to kiss me there again. The women will take care of me," she reassured him. "If I need you I'll call."

Bill waited with No'ka and Pablo, up to their necks in the hot spring, protected from the cold clear night by steaming vapors. He tried to ignore his wife's bloodcurdling screams, as No'ka explained why he had never converted to Christianity.

"It came down to work. Work is an invention of the Christian God. The padres and their king work for their God. The neophytes had to work for the padres and the king. I did not want to work for anyone.

"We Kuupiaxchem do not even have a word for work. Our gods do not ask us to work. They do the work for us. We have only to enjoy the bounty that they provide. I could not abandon such benevolent and generous gods, to work for a lesser god, or for men acting in his name."

"But you will work for a woman," said White Fox, who had slipped unnoticed down to the stream, veiled by steam. "Bi', you have a son. A beautiful boy with green eyes and hair as black as night." She glanced at her husband.

"Come see him," she said, excited. "Our first grandson."

She led them back to the house. Falling Star, pale but smiling with the pride of creation, lay on her bed, half propped up by pillows.

"It's a little man," she said weakly. "Look how he sucks at his milk, strong as a calf."

Bill gazed in wonder at the tiny wrinkly body, pink and splotchy, with clumps of matted black hair. She tried to turn him over. His baby mouth came off her breast with a slurping sound. He began to wail and wave his arms.

"His eyes are green and brown." She stuck him back on the other nipple. "You will see when he has finished nursing."

Bill gave both of them a kiss. Falling Star closed her eyes contentedly.

"She needs to rest," said White Fox. "I will stay with them."

Back they went to the hot pools, No'ka announcing, "I have a grandson!" and, "Bi' ya es papá."

"Blessings; felicidades; what good luck," the people replied.

Bill glowed.

"You have made a good beginning to your family," Pablo said with pride. "Can you imagine what we would have thought a year ago—of everything that has transpired? We were going to be caballeros, riding out in shiny-buttoned suits, with señoritas fluttering their fans our way."

No'ka laughed.

"I far prefer a society with no word for work," said Bill.

35

THE ART
OF LEAVING

P A B L O stayed with his godchild for a week, then left one morning to visit San Luis Rey. He had become obsessed with the impending war, and Friar Ibarra would be the best source of up-to-date news—with his church's wide network of contacts in both California and Mexico. "I just can't sit here waiting for something to happen," he said to Bill. "I have to be out in the world, stirring the pot and licking the spoons."

"I'll come to San Diego with more hides, maybe in February," Bill told him. "We can meet then."

"Yes, that would be amusing. I will have to be there to keep you out of trouble."

They embraced, Bill holding on too long. He couldn't get a word out. The departure felt permanent.

Pablo patted his back. "I'm leaving you in good hands," he said. He gave Shadow a nudge with his knee. Shadow pushed back, wagging his tail.

When Pablo was mounted, Bill managed a smile. "Don't forget to write."

"I'll see you." Pablo touched his sombrero.

"Que te vaya bien."

" T H E art of living is the art of leaving. That's what Tío Pablo says," Falling Star crooned to little Wili, as Bill snuggled into her unoccupied side. "You have to learn to leave happy. If you wait till you're sad, things go bad."

"I'm not going anywhere," Bill mumbled into her shoulder blade.

"He's right," she said. "But if you ever do leave me, don't bother coming back. There is no artful way to leave a woman."

The coming of Wili had been rough on their marriage. Falling Star was always tired. Wili woke her to nurse at any hour he chose, usually when she had just fallen asleep. She wanted Bill to wait on her, to cook for her, to hold Wili while she slept during the day. She resented the time he spent working at Warner's. They had no sex life. When they tried to resume, it hurt her, or she was too tired, or Wili got in the way. She thought his birth had ruined her for lovemaking.

Among the Kuupiaxchem, it was the custom for the husband to fast when his child is born. For about two weeks he eats no meat or fat. This guarantees that the child will live and grow strong, gaining the flesh saved by the father's fast. The logic was tenuous, but Bill had fasted, felt no worse for it, and Wili had thrived.

It was also the Indians' belief that the husband should not bed his wife until the child can walk—or they will conceive no other child. The day a child walked was celebrated, with a naming feast and dancing.

The village reaped a lot of laughter at the expense of sex-deprived husbands—holding their toddlers by both hands, dragging them along, tiny turned-in feet barely brushing the earth, exclaiming, "Look, she's walking, my niña is walking!"

This was too much. Bill knew that a woman usually could not conceive while she was nursing—normally at least until the child walked. On this unrealized fact the native superstition must have been based.

Bill argued the point with Falling Star and her parents, but they insisted there were other good reasons to wait: For one, it guaranteed that the father paid attention to the child, and taught it to walk. The sooner the baby walked, the less the burden on the mother and the better the chance of survival. The ban also gave the wife a much needed rest, after her nine months carrying the child, allowing her to recover her strength and devote full time to the infant. And the day a man came home to find his child taking her first steps toward him, alone, was a double joy, worth waiting for.

But that day might be a year or more away. It was too long.

"This custom goes hand in hand with polygamy," Bill told them. "It drives the men to take a second wife, or a lover."

No'ka laughed. Falling Star glared. Her mother scowled.

Bill hadn't meant it as a threat. It was logical to connect the two practices. He didn't want a new wife. It was Falling Star he desired.

Bill resented the attention Wili received. It was hard for him to relate to children at that stage, so tiny, frail and demanding, their heads rolling around on wobbly necks, dribble and drool oozing from mouths and bottoms. It took a mother to love these little creatures.

Seeing Falling Star with child at breast only stimulated a primitive urge in

Bill—to be sucking the life-giving milk from the other, while at the same time joined as her lover—to celebrate in ecstasy the whole glorious cycle of birth and creation.

But Bill's mate did not share in this rapturous vision. Radiant in nascent motherhood, she was content to be with Wili, nursing and napping, humming strange lullabies and chatting to Him. Melones was her soul-mate for this phase of child worship. Bill was irrelevant, having fulfilled his indispensable role ten months ago.

THREE

THE

WARPATH

36

RUSTLING

T H E Californians nervously awaited Mexico's declaration of war, especially the pro-U.S. contingent. There was no Mexican army to speak of within fifteen hundred miles, and they were prepared to move fast on first word. In the north, where there were more American settlers, they grew impatient.

"Things are starting to heat up," said Fitch to Captain Stokes. "A couple of hundred American settlers seized Rancho Sacramento, up-river from San Francisco, placing Don Mariano Vallejo under house arrest. They tore down the Mexican flag and raised their own banner, a white cloth with a bear sewn on, one red star and 'Bear Flag Republic' written across the bottom. The fools celebrated the new republic by consuming Vallejo's store of wine and brandy. When the grog was gone, they released Vallejo, took their flag and went home."

"I heard some of that from Padre Ibarra," said Pablo, banging the shop door behind him. "Speaking of brandy . . . I brought your order."

He set two flagons on the counter.

"They say the banner was so crudely drawn, the bear looked like a pig," said Fitch, whisking the flagons out of sight.

Captain Stokes grunted. "No matter. When the time comes, the navy'll do the job. Commodore Sloat's sailed his squadron to Mazatlán, to await the official declaration of war. Then he'll bloody well sail right back to Monterey and take it for good."

"I can't believe he would wait in Mexico for the war with Mexico to begin," said Pablo.

"Mazatlán's close," Fitch said, splashing some of the fiery liquor into a mug and pushing it at Pablo, "with plenty of food, cheap whores and leaky canoes for a navy. By now Sloat'll have the whole village in his pocket. If the alcalde don't warn him, he'll hear the good news right from the whores's mouth." Fitch wheezed at his own joke. "With plenty o' time for them poxy-pricked sailors to yank clear o' the cathouses, load up on rum and cruise north, before the Mexis here even know a war's on.

"Drink up, choirboy, you're way behind us."

"A N D   that's exactly what happened," said Ibarra, that evening. "I just received the news that Commodore Sloat raised the American flag at Monterey on July 7, entering the bay and landing to a gracious surrender, not one shot having been fired. He claims that war was declared May 13. The commodore has three battleships in his fleet, and plans to send one to Santa Barbara and one to San Diego."

"There's a hide ship loading at La Playa in a few days," Pablo said, counting out the coins for the brandy. "We'd better get your skins down there quick. I'll send word to Manuelito and No'ka. It may be the last chance for a while. Stokes and Fitch swear the U.S. Navy's going to shut California tighter than a strapped and nailed keg of whale oil."

"I strongly doubt there's even a single whorehouse in Mazatlán," sniffed Friar Ibarra, sliding the silver across the dining table and into his purse.

B I L L   slipped out at dawn with Bull Bear and Stomping Deer to take their hides to La Playa. They had received Pablo's message. They could be paid on delivery if they hurried to meet the ship. It would be a fast trip, four days, traveling by the full moon when necessary.

Falling Star hated to see him go. She fretted about the impending war, and jealously wondered if he would be seeing his novia, Lugarda.

"I have to go, and I will see her if I see her. She has a new daughter. Lugarda will be in the same unromantic mood you were in, your first month with Wili. It is you I love. She I have forgotten."

This was the truth, but Falling Star couldn't accept it. It was his mood that had been miserable. She had been loving her child, being a mother. Wili had not yet learned to crawl, much less walk. She felt estranged from her husband.

"Go then, go," she had shouted. Shadow cringed, and didn't even try to follow.

The Cupeño trailed eight mules piled high with hides, two for the Warners and six of their own. They each had two horses. They kept a brisk pace in order to reach the ranchería of San Pasqual the first night. There, about a hundred Kumeyaay Indians lived, many of them refugees from San Dieguito, whose land had been taken over by the Osunas.

The People lived in poorly built grass and brush huts, drafty, smoky and cold. They dressed in cast-off rags of the Californios. There were no fur animals left in the area, so they wrapped in sheepskins at night and made crude sheepskin coats sewn together with cowhide thongs for day.

'Zul's auntie, the one who had arranged the meeting at Box Canyon, emerged from a hut to greet them. She invited the visitors to eat with her. She told Bill, Pablo had promised her a fat calf. He had not returned.

Bill assured her that he would talk to Pablo and bring her the gift.

"We need sugar, tea or coffee, and clothing," she replied.

He promised to see what could be had in San Diego.

In the morning, as they rode out of San Pasqual, Stomping Deer was fuming.

"I don't know why they have not put a lance through each of the Osunas. Can you imagine what we would do to Warner if he drove us from our lands?"

"Eat him," grunted Bull Bear.

"If you want to kill you must be prepared to die," Bill said. He had heard No'ka utter those very words, arguing with his son.

"I am not afraid to die," spit out Stomping Deer. "What I fear is a life that is dead." He gave his horse a savage kick and raced ahead. Bull Bear galloped after him.

O N the approach to San Diego they skirted the pueblo and went directly to La Playa to unload the hides. Bill sent one of the Hawaiians to find Pablo in town. While he concluded their business, Bull Bear and Stomping Deer explored La Playa. The *Saratoga* was at anchor, unloading ballast to make room for a cargo of skins. They were dumping the ballast into the harbor, which was illegal. They were supposed to carry it to a designated dumping area called Ballast Point. It was too shallow there to approach with a ship, so this meant double handling, unloading first into a small boat, then unloading again on the point. The hide buyer told Bill that ten boatloads of ballast went into the harbor for every one that reached the land. It was silly of the lazy captains, for soon the harbor would be too shallow for their ships to enter.

Pablo arrived, dressed in his dandy caballero's suit, carrying a cane similar to Alcalde Juan María Osuna's. His hair was carefully cut clean around his ears; he wore a very thin mustache. He had rented a one-room house in San Diego, and was making a living with his language skills and by his connection to the friars at San Diego and San Luis Rey. Fitch, and Don Juan Bandini, who had problems with the resident Indians at his big ranch at Tecate, found his services especially useful.

In Pablo's first weeks as a resident, many San Diegans had taken affront at the handsome Indian's nerve. The alcalde was still irritated by Pablo's fancy suit and cane. Pablo could imitate Juan María Osuna perfectly. When he transformed himself into the pompous little mayor, with his ever-present silver-knobbed staff of office, no one in the pueblo could keep from laughing. Even the Osunas had to bite their lips to hide their grins.

Pablo had quickly insinuated himself into the tiny town's company-starved society. He was witty and sharp, quick with a riposte in every language. He was also perceptive and useful, helping the Californios with their Indian workers and servants, recovering "lost" or stolen items, providing information at crucial moments and passing lovers' messages discreetly.

Pablo had taken to social drinking, a habit he had first acquired sipping wine with the friars. At Ybarra's dram shop in La Playa, he treated the visitors to a drink of mescal, a golden liquor made from agave cactus.

"Just one," he laughed. "Firewater bad for natives."

It went down like a wet mouthful of chiles and settled like molten lava in Bill's stomach. The glow spread to his limbs, then up his spine, raising the hairs on the back of his neck.

Bull Bear's grin widened. "Es bueno," he laughed nervously. "Now I am drunk." It was the Bear's first taste of alcohol.

Pablo laughed. "It warms you up on a cold and dreary day. Come outside and you'll see you're fine. It takes a few of those to get you drunk."

They went out into a chill afternoon. The sun shone pale as a moon, through thick overcast. The northwest breeze swept cool across False Bay, fluttering the many-colored flags on the hide warehouses of La Playa.

On its barren hill three miles east, San Diego looked like a toy town. They could almost see tiny figures moving in the streets. A horse and wagon, the size of an ant, passed through the plaza.

Pablo led the way to a round house, marked by the smell of pork roasting over an open fire. The Hawaiians lived in an abandoned brick oven, built by Russian sailors who had passed a season hunting the otter in San Diego Bay. The oven was dome-shaped, with a hole on top and one arched door in front. It easily slept a dozen men.

A few of the islanders were sitting outside, around a pit lined with rocks, where a small pig dripped lard onto hot coals with a steady crackle. The piglet was brown as leather and crisp-skinned. Two of the big men played tiny ukuleles, singing a pretty song in their language. The voices were deep and melodious, the tune familiar.

"Pablo," they cried. "Where you been, brudda?" They motioned for the guests to sit down on driftwood logs that served as benches.

A man named Makua said, "You like kau kau, we eat. Da pig stay big."

"My friends are hungry," Pablo said. "It smells so good."

"Amigos," another Kanaka named Blah said with a smile.

Makua had a huge knife, almost a machete. He felt the edge and fine-sharpened it with a flat stone. The others continued their singing, while he sliced a big piece of skin off the pork shoulder, laid it on a clean earthen bowl, took a thick corn tortilla from a basket and sliced a chunk of pork onto it. He folded the tortilla over the pork and handed it to Pablo.

Pablo gave it to Bull Bear, who bit noisily, taking half in one mouthful.

"Big bite," said Makua, approvingly.

They all ate four or five of these tasty morsels in quick succession. The pork had been washed in the bay, then rubbed with sea salt. It was tender and delicious.

"We're looking for a shirt and jacket for my friend," said Pablo.

There was to be the customary fiesta at Bandini's for the *Saratoga's* captain and officers. Bull Bear needed clothes if he wanted to attend. The Hawaiians were about Bear's size.

"Mahanna, you like sell da extra shirt you wen' bring wit' you?" Makua called to one of the singers.

Mahanna answered in Hawaiian.

"No like sell. He lend 'em," translated Makua.

"Thank you," Pablo replied. "We only need it for tonight."

Pablo supervised the bathing and dressing, trimming their hair with scissors borrowed from Ybarra. He shaved Bill's wild beard and mustache, and splashed them all with rosewater from a stoppered blue bottle. Brushed up, they were a dashing trio, passable for caballeros, as long as the lighting was dim and no one spoke.

They rode the few miles to the pueblo quickly, in the cool glow of cloud-shrouded sun. The mules stepped lightly, heads high, frisky without their heavy packs.

Behind Pablo's small house were Bandini's corrals. They watered the horses and mules. Big Bear and Stomping Deer went to the riverbank to cut some grass. Horses always come first in California. They were lucky at Cupa to be able to simply turn the animals loose to graze on the lush plain.

Bill entered Pablo's adobe. It was dark, cool and neat, with a bed, a chair and a small table, all from San Diego Mission, and a rack made of sticks tied with rawhide thongs that held his clothes, neatly folded.

Pablo lit a fire and sat on the bed. Bill took the chair. They watched the flames take hold in silence.

"I suppose you want to know all about Lugarda."

"Uh huh," Bill said. "Every little thing."

He could feel her closeness. Her house could be viewed from Pablo's door.

"I've seen her a few times. She looked grotesque before she had her baby. She was slim as ever, with a watermelon bulge at the waist. She complained of backaches, her breasts hurt, she couldn't sleep. The baby kicked her at all hours. She couldn't wait to get him out.

"Lugarda screamed like a madwoman during the birth. The whole town suffered with her cries. Now she is depressed. The girl child is very demanding. She chews on her, kicks and pulls and screams bitterly if removed from a teat. She wishes 'Zul had a baby too, so she could wet nurse."

For a moment, Pablo was silent.

"How is 'Zul?"

"She is fine; happy to have me near. She would like to have a baby." High Cloud looked at Bill closely. "But I refuse to have a child of mine born to servitude in the Osuna household."

He sighed, then smiled.

"I'll go see 'Zul and Lugarda, to tell them you're here and find out whether her brothers or husband are in town. Maybe Lugarda will dance tonight." Pablo turned toward the door.

Stomping Deer and Bull Bear tapped and slipped in, in the graceful way the People have of moving in small spaces, hardly disturbing the air.

"Not much grass near this town," pronounced Stomping Deer.

"Big feast being prepared, smells good." Bull Bear rubbed his belly and grinned.

"I'll meet you at supper," Pablo threw the words over his shoulder. "Mind your manners."

T H E Y were seated on a shadowed bench, at the edge of the crowd of San Diegans and Yankees from the *Saratoga*, their plates piled high with tamales, chiles relleno, steak, roast corn and tortillas, devouring the delicious delicacies, deliberately, ravenously . . . when Pablo emerged from the Alvarado adobe with 'Zul and Lugarda on either arm.

Whale oil lamps hung on verandas and from the rafter ends along the front of Bandini's house. In the warm, mobile light, Lugarda glowed, her hair held high by a huge tortoiseshell comb, her face a sculpture of light and shadow, serene, watchful, proud and classically beautiful. Her eyes had been darkened and outlined, her lips a rosebud red.

Pablo was as handsome, immaculate in his short dark blue jacket, silver-studded, with tight blue pants, silver-buttons in front and down the legs, matched by a silver-studded belt and long dark boots. He wore his flat-topped, stiff felt hat at a rakish angle and carried the knobbed cane in his left hand.

'Zul was coiffed exactly as Lugarda, hair piled and held by a tall comb. Her beauty was more exotic and less aggressive. Her dress was a twin to Lugarda's: low squared bodice, long-sleeved, full skirt almost touching the ground. They both wore long sea otter shawls draped over arms and shoulders.

They seemed to float toward the diners. Pablo spotted Bill and steered the women to him. They curtsied; Pablo bowed low.

Bill stood up, carefully placing his plate on the bench. Pablo made the introductions as though they were not acquainted. "Mucho gusto," they all said. The hubbub of other diners died.

Bill's tongue was tied. He locked eyes with Lugarda. Up close, the dark circles under hers were real. She looked fragile.

'Zul giggled at the way Bull Bear and Stomping Deer looked.

"The last time I saw you, you were naked in the creek at Aguanga," Stomping Deer teased her. He spoke in his language. "Now you look like a queen."

"You too were naked, my friend," she replied with another giggle. "Now— I think he looked better naked," she said to Pablo in Cupeño.

"So did you," said Bull Bear, getting a laugh.

Pablo ushered his escorts toward the buffet table. Bill's eye contact with Lugarda finally broke with an unsettling jolt. The connection between them was so engaging, so utterly exclusive of time or place, he marveled that he could have forgotten its bewitching power. He wondered whether Lugarda's gaze snake-charmed every man upon whom she cast her lovely eyes. The thought of being with her for a couple of hours made him giddy. He picked at his food until the trio returned to the bench with their plates.

The band in Bandini's house warmed up and began to play. People wandered in to listen and dance and to escape the chill. Stomping Deer and Big

Bear went to stand outside Bandini's door watching, too shy to go in. When Pablo took 'Zul's hand and excused himself to go dancing, Bill was left with Lugarda. It was very dark, the full moon not yet risen. Nothing but blackness could be seen outside the glow of lamplight. They scooted down the bench into deeper shadow. Lugarda took Bill's right hand with her left, and clasped her fingers between his, so that they were joined as in prayer, palm to palm, thumb to thumb.

"I missed you," she said.

"I missed you too," Bill lied.

They were silent for a long time, just holding hands in the dark.

"How have you been?" Bill finally asked.

"Well," she said.

"And your family?"

"They are fine. Please, let us not talk about my family. They have nothing to do with us," Lugarda whispered. Bill was quiet.

"I belong to my family," she said matter-of-factly. "But the part of me that misses you cannot belong to anyone."

They settled against the wall, pressing each other from knee to shoulder.

"Will you dance?"

"Perhaps. I haven't danced in months. Maybe it is time, but not yet."

She nestled closer. He inhaled her fragrance. He felt her chest expanding against his arm with each breath and her light heartbeat. He closed his eyes.

"We could talk about Pablo," she interrupted his swoon.

"What about Pablo?" Bill asked, on guard.

"He is very entertaining. He brought some life to our town and laughter to my confinement. Now he has told me everything about your coming, and how you have found a place among the Kuupiaxchem."

She said the Indian word perfectly.

"My life with them has nothing to do with us." Bill squeezed her hand.

"No, it doesn't, but it is interesting." She gave him a curious look. "I like to know what you are doing."

"I like to know what you are doing too."

"No you don't. What I do is of little interest to anyone but me, and often barely that." She made a wry face. "You are the only interesting thing about me." She kissed his cheek.

When Bill turned—he was thinking of kissing her back—Pablo and 'Zul were standing at Lugarda's side, breathless from dancing.

"Come on, 'mano. We've got to ride." Pablo pulled Bill off the bench by his free hand. "Leandro and Ramón just showed up."

Bill stumbled as he turned to say goodbye, but Lugarda had been swallowed by darkness.

"Where are we going?" Pablo had not mentioned coming with them.

"We will take some calves to the ranchería at San Pasqual."

"I don't understand Lugarda," Bill said, thinking aloud.

"I once asked her why she didn't marry you. She said she wanted to remain a stranger, an intimate stranger, to the one she loved the most . . ."

"That doesn't help."

Pablo put a hand on Bill's shoulder. "Don't think you're the only one who balks at the logic of women. I will never fathom 'Zul's devotion to that family. It is beyond comprehension."

"I can understand her devotion to Lugarda."

"And what of her devotion to me?" Pablo's voice twisted. "Lugarda has you and José María and a dozen other devotees."

At his house, Pablo carefully removed and folded his clothes. He put on riding pants, chaps and a warm sheepskin jacket.

"Vámonos. We can gather calves at San Dieguito while the brothers dance, and herd them to San Pasqual for the ranchería. The moon will light our way."

"They wanted sugar, coffee, tea and clothes," said Stomping Deer.

"Yes, yes," snapped Pablo. "Sugar to pacify the tongue. Coffee and tea so they can keep working without food. Clothes to hide their starved and bony bodies. These are the conqueror's devices to enslave the natives; worthless addictions; nothing we can make or raise ourselves; all imports we have to buy with labor or hard-earned coin. Buy from the invaders, of course.

"Think about what you have said, Stomping Deer. Fifty years ago we did not even have the words for those items, nor for the work required to get them. Now they are all our poor people want. We will take them meat on the hoof, to feed them for the years to come."

"They'll sell the hides to buy sugar and coffee themselves," Bill said.

"Perhaps. But we will not. We know better. Leave the shirt, Bear. I have to return it."

They hustled into the night like rangers, trusting their leader completely. When Pablo pointed out calves, They rounded them up, wherever he found them. They went north at first, then east to the edges of the Osuna ranch, up the San Dieguito River to the Alvarados', and on to San Pasqual at dawn, gathering fifty calves of various ages. When the light was sufficient to see, they cut out all of those that were branded. Stomping Deer, Bull Bear and Bill held them. Pablo drove the rest to the ranchería, where they were gratefully received.

The branded calves were led back toward the Osuna ranch and scattered in the hills. Pablo was pleased with the night's work.

"If anyone looks for their calves, the trail will lead to the Osunas, where they will be found. Of the rest, nothing could ever be proved, even if tracks were followed to San Pasqual."

"This is a deed worthy of Leatherstocking," he said to Bill with a wink.

Bill had loaned Pablo John Warner's copy of Cooper's *The Last of the Mohicans.*

"How did you like the book?"

"I still haven't finished. Did the Mohicans really do such cruel things to the colonists? Stealing women was common among the San Diego tribes before the padres came. But they only did it once to the Spanish colony. Yumans stole two of Pico's cousins from Jacumba. The army searched for the girls for months, and never found them."

"Maybe that's why he hates us," said Bull Bear.

"Perhaps. But that was a long time ago. I think greed explains everything about the Picos." Pablo turned back toward San Diego. "I must return to the pueblo. Please tell No'ka there is little to report. So far the war is all rumors, except for a little rustling."

37

WAR

H E N war did come, it came quick and hard. Pío Pico had long been poised to pounce on the missions and their remaining riches. As wartime governor, he immediately sold Mission San Luis Rey to his older brother, José Antonio, for six hundred dollars, "to finance the war effort." A fair value might have been sixty thousand.

Pablo sent No'ka this note: "Andrés Pico and José Antonio Pico arrived with their soldiers to evict Father González de Ibarra and they are still there, looting and despoiling like the Vandals in Rome, eight hundred years ago. We only hope the library will survive until the Americans can restore order. (We assume they will win.) The good friar, my surviving father, has gone to Santa Barbara to wait out the war. I will stay with Father Oliva at Mission San Diego. We fear for Pico's next move . . ."

The man who brought the letter, a Pauman from Las Flores named Juan One Ear, said that Pablo had been out among the Indians on Pico's ranch, asking them to refrain from fighting for the Mexicans. Pico was desperate for men, and needed their help. To withhold it would cripple his chances. The People at Las Flores had agreed to aid the Americans by staying peacefully at home.

Then, from San Diego, Pablo wrote: "Today was a sad day in this sorriest of pueblos. Pico *gave* San Diego Mission and all of its assets to Santiago Arguëllo 'for payment of past services.' In other words, Pico's gambling debts!

"This morning Father Oliva left for Santa Barbara, evicted by the Arguëllos. He could not walk because he had driven nails into his feet. We carried him to his favorite mule, Ambrosia, the only piece of property he was allowed to take, and watched him ride off alone to report to his superior. It was heart-breaking. The Kumeyaay People from the mission wailed so mournfully, I had to cover my ears. The San Diegans were outraged at losing their only priest. Half the town threatens to support the Yankees.

"Pico will certainly find no soldiers among the Kumeyaay. Without the Indians, there are too few Californios to field any kind of army. With a little luck the *momnawechom* will kill every one of these bastard Spaniards. I will stay in San Diego to be near the action. Ever your servant, High Cloud."

No'ka's brow creased in a frown.

Ironically, with a war on and the country in an uproar, both the Warners' and Bill's lives became calmer, more family-centered and stable than ever. They stuck to the valley, tending crops and cattle. Every day stood out in crystalline perfection during this lull before the storm—for they feared that the gods of war would descend eventually upon them.

ON the thirtieth of July came good news: The ailing Commodore Sloat had been replaced by another high-ranking naval officer, Captain Robert F. Stockton. Commodore Stockton had immediately departed Monterey for San Diego, aboard his flagship, the USS *Cyanne*. Under full sail before a stiff nor'wester, he had flown south to arrive at Point Loma in three days. On the twenty-ninth of July, he had planted the American flag at La Playa.

With the commodore was Lieutenant Colonel John C. Frémont, U.S. Army, who had arrived from Utah and Oregon with fourteen army regulars, accompanied by Kit Carson, forty heavily armed mountain men and Frémont's personal bodyguard of five Delaware Indians. In northern California, Frémont had raised a militia brigade of another hundred American riflemen, wild and hardy as the Indians. Captain Archibald Gillespie, a U.S. Marine who had traveled overland with President James K. Polk's war orders, plus the fleet's contingent of two hundred marines, rounded out the U.S. forces. Frémont's brigade had marched on foot from La Playa to San Diego, and occupied the pueblo without resistance.

The Americans' first objective was to obtain horses. After thoroughly pacifying San Diego, Colonel Frémont planned to lead his brigade overland to Los Angeles, showing force and fight where necessary, and on to Santa Barbara, while Stockton sailed up the coast providing support. General Andrés Pico had driven off all of the horses in the pueblo, escaping to the north upon learning of the *Cyanne*'s arrival. Frémont was now scouting the surrounding ranches for mounts.

This information came from Cockney Bill Williams, who had galloped over from Santa Ysabel to tell Warner that every sympathetic rancher was being asked to donate horses and pack mules to the dismounted cavalry.

Warner was jubilant. He immediately left for San Diego to visit Carson and Frémont, whom he knew slightly, to see if they had instructions for him from Thomas Larkin. He didn't take any extra horses.

"They can requisition them from the Mexicans. There are enough horses on the coast for five such armies," he told Bill excitedly.

For once Falling Star was happy to see Warner leave and ask Bill to stay at his ranch. Bill too had wanted to ride to San Diego the minute he heard the news. She didn't want to lose him to his countrymen, or to their war.

When he had returned from the La Playa hide delivery, Falling Star had rushed to welcome Bill with a long hug and kiss. Wili was then almost six months old. He had developed a more regular nursing schedule; she could get some sleep. White Fox had stepped in to help, and Melones, who was still a milk cow in full production, could take Wili if Falling Star and Bill wanted to spend a few hours together.

Falling Star would ride to Warner's with Bill and accompany him on his rounds of the ranch. They swam in the hot pools and walked the hills behind the village with Shadow. Exercise brought her back to life. Her paunch retracted, the tone returned to her legs and hips. She paced again with the prancing spring that was her trademark.

She confessed to Bill that White Fox had ordered her to get up, snap out of her lethargy and start riding. She had to bind her breasts with a sash while mounted, otherwise she was her old light and sassy self, racing across the plain or walking her horse for miles, matching Bill step for step.

The renewed pleasure of returning urges excited her. When they stopped to rest they often ended up in a bucking tangle. It then became Bill's duty to support her breasts, his big hands accepting their weight, milk dribbling between his fingers where her nipples nestled.

They had only drawn closer in the ensuing weeks. Turmoil swirled around them, but they were content.

38

FRIENDS

AND ENEMIES

N O W war news flew through the gossip channels.
From the moment Stockton sailed into San Diego Bay, on the twenty-ninth, the war had turned the pueblo upside down. All of the tough-talking Mexicans fled to their ranches: The Picos, Carillos, Aguilars, Serranos, Alvarados and Juan María Osuna, staff of office clutched in hand, were gone before the longboats hit the beach at La Playa, their homes shut tight and doors locked.

The pro-Americans, Bandini, Jesús Machado, whose application for a land grant had been consistently denied by alcalde Osuna, Fitch, Stokes, the Ortega's and for some reason, Santiago Arguëllo, the new mission owner, cleaned house and prepared to welcome their American rulers.

Some families were split. Josefa Carillo Fitch sided with her husband, to his delight. When they had fallen in love, her family had refused Captain Henry Delano Fitch's marriage proposal. The defiant lovers had embarrassed and infuriated the Carillos by eloping on the next ship to Chile. They had been forcibly separated on their return, though they had a marriage certificate signed by the bishop of Santiago. Fitch was held prisoner at San Gabriel by Josefa's powerful uncle, until the governor intervened and declared them legally married. Fifteen years later, Fitch was still only grudgingly accepted by the family.

"I hope I've seen the last of you inbred bastards," he shouted, as the Carillos rode away.

After greeting Commodore Stockton, Bandini immediately offered to organize a ball. Stockton had a thirty-seven-piece orchestra on board the *Cyanne*, at his own expense. They were all Italians, to Bandini's joy, and knew all of the popular songs—as well as Italian opera, French and German symphonies, and the great Catholic madrigals and hymns.

The band was too big to fit in Bandini's house, but they had enough volume to fill every home in town with music. Each night they would set up in the plaza and play into the wee hours. The melodies could be heard for a couple of miles downwind. Stockton and Bandini became fast friends, drawn close by their mutual love of music. They inspired a glorious week of song and dance in San Diego, as far from war as a mind could stretch.

B Y the end of their rough voyage down the coast, Commodore Stockton and Colonel Frémont had seen enough of each other. They were natural rivals: educated individualists, Army and Navy Academy–trained, proud, and well connected. Stockton had the President's blessing and Frémont was married to the daughter of Thomas Hart Benton, Missouri's influential senator. Each expected to be named California's first governor.

"The Colonel's French," complained Stockton to Captain Gillespie, his highest-ranking marine. "We got stuck with the Frémont family when we made the Louisiana Purchase."

Archibald Gillespie was a beefy man. He had never met a marine, or any other man for that matter, tougher than himself.

"He acts like he's already been promoted to general," Gillespie growled, "ever since President Polk authorized his command of the California militia. And he's got those filthy redskins in his troop. I'd like to see you take the Colonel down a peg or two, sir."

"It will be amusing to see Frémont's face when a real general arrives to take his place." Stockton looked sharply at Gillespie.

"Yes, sir, it will." Gillespie looked away from his superior.

"I'd like you to accompany Colonel Frémont's ragtag army; to keep an eye on them for me, Captain."

"Yes, sir."

Stockton and Frémont had already agreed to leave Gillespie as commandant in Los Angeles, the largest center of Mexican population in the south, but a dusty, out-of-the-way post.

Neither of the commanders could abide the bristly marine. He had guarded his dispatches from Washington as though they were personal property, only revealing the president's orders to Stockton or Frémont individually, not allowing one to see those of the other. The Captain hinted that there was more, to be unveiled at the proper moment, on order of his commander-in-chief, President Polk. Gillespie was a stickler for rules, letting both commanders know he disapproved of their free-spirited ways.

Colonel Frémont asked Pablo to join his brigade as a scout for their march north. Pablo had loved Frémont and the Delaware Indians on sight. He was thrilled to meet the natives he had read about in *The Last of the Mohicans*. The fact that they were looking forward to scalping Mexicans added to their allure. They became friends and introduced Pablo to their commander. Pablo's wealth of knowledge of southern California and his language skills had impressed Frémont.

Gillespie disagreed. "We've already got Carson, sir. He knows the way."

"But he doesn't know the ways, like High Cloud does."

"His name's Pablo Verdi, and he's a Mexican, sir. The enemy, sir."

"He's not Mexican. He's a local native of the Luiseño tribe."

"What do you think the Mexicans are? They're all Indians, so far as I can tell. Or half-breeds," Gillespie said in disgust. "Sir."

When Warner arrived in San Diego, Gillespie refused to give him any information, and instructed Frémont and Carson not to either. He knew that Larkin and Warner were large landholders, with close business and personal ties to the Californio leaders. He called Warner a Mexican. He told Juan José that he and Señor Larkin were under suspicion for playing both sides of the war. They could not be trusted and were possibly traitors.

"And where are the horses we asked you to bring?" Gillespie had demanded. "Don't tell me you don't have any."

"Nobody likes him," Warner told Bill on his return to the ranch. "They plan to park Gillespie in Los Angeles for the duration of the war, while Frémont rules from Monterey, and Stockton headquarters in San Diego."

"What about the Californios, what will they do?" Anita asked. She rocked her new son Andrés, named after his uncle, the Mexican Commander.

"With your brave brothers Pico on the run, and Frémont's wild rifle brigade to terrorize them, nothing. Not a thing. This war is over."

O N August 12, Chapuli rode into Cupa yelling with excitement. Pío and Andrés Pico had fled California via Temecula, Anza and Coyote Canyon, down the Sonora Trail to Mexico, escaping the advance of Frémont's fearsome army. Chapuli had seen them pass through his village.

"Pablo must be celebrating," No'ka said.

"He's probably already moved back into his old house," said Bill. "We should ride to Las Flores to help him hold it."

"Best wait till we hear from him," said White Fox.

Antonio Garra brought word that Pablo was with Frémont's brigade, on their way to Los Angeles and Santa Barbara. Garra and his son, Tonio, Stomping Deer and Big Bear had followed after Pablo and Frémont, into Pico's ranch, north as far as San Clemente, rounding up unbranded cattle to herd back to Cupa. He told No'ka not to slaughter any more steers. The army and navy ate a huge amount of beef and paid cash for it, live on the hoof. When Stockton returned to San Diego with his fleet, they would need fresh meat, all they could supply.

A T Mission Santa Barbara, Pablo reunited with Friar Ibarra. They embraced and rushed to tell each other the latest news.

"Los Angeles capitulated without a shot," Pablo crowed, "I have been acting as guide and interpreter for Frémont, who is an interesting man; well bred, well read, Catholic and liked by everyone, even the Californios."

"Frémont has promised to give San Luis Rey and San Diego missions back to the church," gushed Ibarra, "which is joyful news. He only wishes to use them for a while, as barracks for his garrison troop."

"You can imagine my pleasure at riding through Las Flores and Santa Margarita ranches, with the Picos in exile, deep in Mexico. We commandeered the best horses we could catch, until each man had two good mounts. We feasted on fresh Pío Puerco beef and drove the rest of his herd with us to Los Angeles." Pablo smiled. "Revenge is sweet, a satisfying pleasure, not to be discounted. I may yet regain our land."

"I don't think that revenge would be the correct word. It is plainly God's justice. Will you continue north with Frémont?"

"I was planning to ask the colonel if I may return with you to San Diego." Pablo paced the wide-arched corridor.

"I shall not be going for a while." Ibarra shook his head. "It won't be safe for me at the mission until troops are installed."

"Then I'll send word when it is safe. I miss the pueblo. It has been so much fun, with Stockton's orchestra playing late every balmy night. The Californio ladies all came back to town, loath to miss the dancing. They charmed the soldiers, who were very gallant. There is a high level of discipline in both the army and navy. There were no fights, drunkenness or looting; they slept in their own tents by the river, cleaned the riverbank, and dug new wells. They made being conquered pleasant. If all Americans are as civilized as Stockton and Frémont, we will be well governed by them.

"By the way, the marines' uniforms are brilliant."

///

C O L O N E L Frémont stayed two days in Santa Barbara, then continued north on El Camino Real toward Monterey. Pablo set out to return to San Diego. When he reached Los Angeles, rebellious Californios were celebrating a great victory. They had raised an army and driven the Yankees out of the pueblo, down to the harbor at San Pedro.

Frémont had made a grave mistake, appointing Captain Archibald Gillespie as both alcalde and military commander. As soon as Frémont's army marched north, Gillespie had instituted a harsh martial law. No public assemblies were allowed of any kind. There was a seven P.M. curfew, in summer, when daylight held until nine. This meant no dances, no evening promenades, no social cups of coffee or hard liquor at the cantina. To those who had welcomed him, Gillespie showed the ugly face of a conqueror.

The Californios had met in private and grumbled. They had worked their macho up until they were ready to fight. Then, led by José María Flores, a patriot Mexican who had come in '42 as secretary to Governor Micheltorena, they attacked the Americans. Captain Gillespie and his men were still pinned down at San Pedro, backs to the sea. Their only hope was for a rescue by the navy, sailing away to the north, oblivious to their plight.

Made bold by victory, with Frémont as yet unaware of any problem, the revolt spread south. "General" Flores marched to San Diego, gathering Mexican supporters, including those patriot ranchers who had first fled Stockton's arrival. They chased the tiny garrison of Americans left at the pueblo onto a ship at La Playa. The *Stonnington* weighed anchor and sailed north.

The pueblo was occupied and sacked. Flores called for all Californios to rise up and chase the Yankees from the land. Andrés Pico had already returned from Sonora. The anti-American ranchers of San Diego, including the Osunas, Alvarados, Serranos and Carillos were organized into a brigade of rangers under Pico. Los Galgos they called themselves: the Hounds.

Los Galgos raided the ranchos of those who had supported the Americans, stealing stock, looting the houses and driving off all horses. They were ruthless. They were rangers in a civil war, not an army.

Pablo was in danger. He couldn't return to San Diego until the Americans retook it. He retreated to Pauma. He wanted to be close to the action and make sure his mother was safe until the Mexican uprising had been squashed.

Frémont, unaware of any problems, blithely marched north. He had sent Kit Carson and a small party to Washington, with dispatches from Stockton and himself, reporting a war well won, and California firmly in U.S. hands.

/ / /

WARNER kept to his ranch, nervous and irritable, angry that the well-prepared peaceful conquest had turned violent. He had fruitlessly revealed his allegiance to the Americans by meeting with Frémont and Gillespie in San Diego. Now he feared reprisal from the Californio rangers.

Warner insisted that his choice of sides was no secret to any of his friends, including the Picos. But now the hot-tempered were in control, armed and dangerous, with newfound courage based on the defeats of Gillespie and the San Diego garrison. Warner grumped around his ranch house, growling at Anita and abusing Luna, frustrated at having no choice of action but to lie low.

Bill kept out of his way and watched the stock graze, always with an eye to the east, where the trail came from Yuma and Sonora. They were more worried about a real army that Pío Pico might raise in Mexico, and march up the Sonora Trail, than any damage the rangers could do.

News came slower with Flores in control of San Diego, and the pro-U.S. Californios hiding out. There were no Americans to fight, so the Mexicans and Californios continued to harass each other, raiding each other's houses, stripping the countryside of stock, and making travel dangerous.

Pablo had remained at Pauma with Manuelito, guarding the village. They sent Ladislaya and a few other women and children to stay at Cupa. Ladislaya brought the welcome news that Americans had retaken San Diego with a small force, the same thirty men that had fled on the *Stonnington*.

"The Yankees unloaded three cannon from their ship at La Playa, then marched on foot to the pueblo pulling the big guns by hand, firing them alternately. Every horse went berserk. General Flores's rangers, married as they are to their mounts, had to flee with them to safety. They went north, to Los Angeles, taking with them all food and livestock. They left the local Mexicans in control of the countryside, with two small armies of rangers under José Carillo and Andrés Pico." Ladislaya nodded her head.

"We learned of this when the rangers came to Pauma, to steal cattle to feed their men. They talk tough of killing traitors, but have friends or relatives at all of the ranchos and have harmed no People so far. Manuelito asks that we stay at Cupa until it is safe to return."

"And Pablo?" No'ka asked.

"Pablo has gone to San Diego to help the besieged Americans. There is nothing to eat, they have no horses and do not dare venture from the pueblo.

Pico and Carillo are so bold, they occupy the hill above the town and fire on anyone who moves in the plaza."

It was eerily silent in the valley. The war seemed so remote from this corner of the world. It was hard to imagine that Pablo was right in the thick of it—only a day's ride away.

39

A BATTLE
OF BELLES

WH E N Flores had occupied San Diego in September, he literally occupied the place, moving his men into the homes of the traitors who had sided with the Yankees. The owners had fled, leaving behind their women, children and possessions, as had the pro-Mexicans when the Americans first came.

When Flores and his army retreated north, the Yankees once again in control, the pro-American Californios had crept back to the pueblo one by one, to find their family homes, their very hearths and beds, defiled. Property had been looted, females compromised, messes made and filth laid. Respect for the rebel Mexicans, once an honorable foe, had turned to anger and hatred.

By the time Pablo sneaked back to San Diego, the raiding of ranches had driven everyone but the rebel-rangers into town—even the womenfolk of the rebels, who were afraid to be alone at their own ranchos while their men were off looting.

The uncivil war had infested the ranks of women in the pueblo. Patriot-rebel and traitor-collaborator ladies staged well-planned raids on each other's homes, to recover stolen or suspected stolen items and heirlooms. There were pitched battles between screaming housewives over carpets, chairs, teacups and brooms—removed from one house and installed in another during the occupations.

Fitch's store had been cleaned out by rebel looters—not unexpected, being pro-American and his store such a treasure trove. Fitch threw a fit. He directed most of his anger at his wife, Josefa Carillo, sister of José Carillo, rebel leader, whose men, if not he, had looted their well-stocked shop. As it had been her brother's thievery, it was Josefa's responsibility to recover what goods she could from the homes of her neighbors.

She took to this duty like a bulldog, concentrating on houses belonging to families of the rebel looters, attempting to identify and repossess any item once belonging to the shop. But every good was in short supply, and Flores's men had taken most of the valuables with them. No one willingly offered to give her a single thing.

Josefa knew in her bones that the rebel Osuna boys, Leandro, Ramón and Santiago, had stashed Fitch's goods in the family home. She said as much, loudly and publicly. Señora Osuna would not allow Josefa to enter her one-room house. Josefa would lurk outside the door trying to get a glimpse of something she could claim.

She also dogged Lugarda, wife of "that rebel José María Alvarado," who had once been her friend. Lugarda just as vehemently denied Josefa entry to the Alvarado home. She closely guarded the door against Josefa's prying eyes.

Lugarda was standing in the plaza, sheltered from snipers by her own house, enjoying the weak fall sunshine and the warmer attentions of Pablo and a group of American officers, when Josefa spotted a new tortoiseshell comb securing Lugarda's carefully piled coif. She was certain the comb had come from Fitch's collection of South Sea Island craftwork.

Marching up to Lugarda with a determined scowl, stopping her forward progress only when their petticoat-filled skirts were pressed hard against each other, Josefa glared rudely, interrupting the lively flow of conversation.

"Where did you get that comb, Lugarda," demanded Josefa, without offering a greeting.

"Excuse me?" replied Lugarda, raising an eyebrow. "Lieutenant Edward Beale, I would like you to meet Josefa Carillo de Fitch. You know Pablo," she said, nodding at him.

"That comb. Where did you get it?" Josefa ignored the pleasantries.

"My husband gave it to me," purred Lugarda, turning back to the lieutenant with a smile.

The reply infuriated Josefa, both confirming her suspicion about the source of the comb, and blocking any possible action to recover it. A gift from a husband is sacred among women.

Josefa was a striking woman. She had once been a great beauty. After her dramatic elopement with Fitch, she had reigned as San Diego's romantic heroine for a generation. But time and tortillas, gambling and brandy, had taken a toll that dress and makeup could not repair. Lugarda was everything Josefa once had been. The disrespect of her rival's turned back was more than the aging beauty could bear.

Her face splotched bright red. Tears of rage pooled in her heavily lined eyes. She sucked in a gasped breath. She leaned across the barrier of skirts, grasped Lugarda's half-bare shoulder with one ringed hand, snatched the comb down with a wrench, and stalked across the plaza toward home.

Lugarda uttered one "Ooh." She touched her loosened hair and sprinted after Josefa with the agility and acceleration of a startled antelope. Josefa heard her coming and broke into a wobbly trot, but Lugarda was upon her. She rode the bigger woman for a few steps at mid-plaza, trying to grab the comb. They toppled over in a heap of petticoats, flailing arms and legs, dust and curses.

The onlookers were too startled to move. They could only watch the struggle in open-mouthed amazement. Two dogs stood at the wrestlers' side barking. People spilled from doorways; the shadows of three high-circling buzzards flitted across the square.

Pablo looked at the officers. Lieutenant Beale held up his hands, palms out. His expression said, "I can do nothing." The Americans were under strict orders not to touch a Mexican woman, dancing with permission being the only exception. This was not that kind of dance.

Pablo saw Fitch cursing his way across the plaza and yelled at him to grab his wife. He caught Lugarda's arm but she scratched and bit his wrist, drawing blood. Pablo couldn't see a polite way to hold her, so he gripped one pantalooned leg and walked backward, dragging her from Josefa, who was now held by Fitch. Pablo kept pulling Lugarda across the plaza, while she kicked and clawed, trying to get back to her antagonist.

Fitch lifted Josefa up. Her face was scratched, oozing blood from the nose, and coated with dust. She spit sand from her mouth and wrapped one arm across a tear in her dress; the disputed comb still embedded in her other clenched fist. Fitch threw a hateful glare in Lugarda's direction. Then they were gone.

Lugarda quit cursing. She said, "Let me go," without looking up. She arranged her dress around her legs, sat for a moment breathing hard, then got shakily to her feet, ignoring Pablo's proffered hand. She seemed unsure what to do next; got her bearings; finally turned on Pablo angrily.

"A gentleman does not touch a lady without her permission," she said, steely-eyed. She slapped him sharply on the cheek, spun on her toes and stalked off to her house, slamming the heavy oak door with a force born of fury.

Lugarda stormed into the kitchen screaming at 'Zul, "You are forbidden to see that ill-mannered Indian. He will be hearing from my husband." She then locked herself in her room.

The silent square exploded in mirth. The tale grew in retelling, until Bandini heard that they had fought for fifteen minutes, ripping each other's clothes off, and had to be carried, naked and bleeding, from the plaza.

Neither woman appeared publicly the next day. Bets were two to one that Josefa would emerge first, as she did win possession of the comb; a small victory to balance against the much greater loss of dignity they both had suffered.

PABLO slipped out of town, dressed as an Indian, and used his ties to the People at Tecate and Ti Juan to arrange a sheep drive for the pueblo's relief. One of the chiefs accepted a payment of six hundred dollars to herd the same number of sheep up the Coronado Peninsula, to a point where they could be safely loaded onto boats to cross the bay.

The sheep arrived safely, two days after Commodore Stockton sailed back into the harbor aboard the *Congress*, his new flagship. On board was a full brigade of marines, as well as Captain Archibald Gillespie, late military commander of Los Angeles, and forty of his newly humbled men.

When the rebel-rangers saw the big battleships, they made one last desperate attack before reinforcements could debark. Eighty Californios charged the pueblo at a gallop, but were repulsed. There were no injuries on either side. The rangers disappeared into the hills. Once again San Diego fell under the spell of Stockton's version of war. The sheep were slaughtered and roasted. Stockton had two ships full of stores, including fine wines from Monterey. His big band of Italian musicians livened up the plaza in the evenings. There was nice weather for a change; Indian summer the Americans called it, and everyone but Gillespie enjoyed the break.

Captain Gillespie and his men roamed the countryside like an angry swarm of hornets, seeking horses, determined to avenge themselves for their disgraceful eviction from Los Angeles. With their superior mobility, Andrés Pico's rangers avoided the flat-footed Gillespie. But Pico and Carillo were forced to keep well away from the pueblo.

Bandini insisted that Stockton should occupy his big house, and this was once again the nightly dance hall. Lugarda Osuna reasserted her place as belle of the ball. She was so constantly surrounded by seamen, that Fitch called her the SS *Lugarda*. "Because so many sailors wish to come aboard." Bandini's floors would not survive Stockton's stay, according to the majority of bets placed.

Stockton had decided to make San Diego his fleet headquarters. He liked the harbor, the warmer weather and the hospitality. "Monterey is a dour and boring town," he told Bandini. "There is not one building big enough to hold a good dance, and if there were, I doubt the people would come. The harbor, if you can call it that, is just as inhospitable, exposed to every winter storm."

His military strategy was not to pursue, but to wait. Let Frémont return order to the countryside. He was so confident that control of the seaports would bring inevitable surrender, he wouldn't risk a marine in battle. "Victory is measured not by the number of enemy dead, but by the territory occupied," he insisted.

40

THE ARMY
OF THE WEST

ARNER rode into Cupa at sunrise, mounted on a black mule. He was in a foul mood, cursing and spitting, jerking the mule's head around.

"I've been summoned to San Diego by order of Captain Gillespie—and Stockton, I presume. He sent Ed Stokes to give me the letter. I'm on my way now. Please stay at my ranch with a few men until I return. Three or four days at most."

"What do they want?" Bill asked.

"The Picos, I'm sure. And maybe to give me instructions for dealing with any force that might come this way. I'm not certain but I sure as hell don't like it." He patted his mule.

"They still need horses. I'm taking this old brute to show them what I've got," Warner said with a sour grin. "If you see either army approach, drive all of the stock to the hills. Pico could come from Sonora, Flores might appear, Gillespie may return with me, or a new American army could come from the Colorado River. That's four ways to watch; hell's fire."

"I'll keep everyone on alert."

"I'm sorry to leave you with the responsibility, but there's no one else. I can't leave Anita and the kids alone," Warner said with a shrug.

"Never mind. I'll go right over and stay till you reappear."

"Good, thank you, Bill." Warner turned and trotted down the trail, his half-wild mule kicking and taking little jarring hops.

Pablo had sent a note to Bill: "I trust that you are well, far from this madness, which I must admit I enjoy. War throws every convention to the winds, pits friend against friend, makes allies of enemies, clears the air and reduces life to its most basic essence: to live, to fight; to eat, to laugh; to love, to hate;

to procreate. I have been doing all of these with extreme gusto. I have yet to kill or be killed, though I am prepared for both events."

S I X days later, Anita received a letter from John, again delivered by Captain Stokes:

My dearest family and friends,

I have been arrested by Captain Gillespie. He accuses me of consorting with the enemy. He believes I know the whereabouts of all the Picos, Flores, Carillo and God knows who else. So I am held in the guardhouse like a common criminal. I am trying to get a message to Thomas Larkin, in Monterey. He can clear me. Until then, I miss you all, and most of all, my lovely wife, Anita.

He had signed his American name, John Trumbull Warner.

Anita collapsed in a flood of tears. Mary Ann whined, "When's Daddy coming home?" She sniffled and curled in her mother's lap.

Stokes motioned Bill outside. In the bright cold light of the yard, Luna watched them with a questioning expression.

"John's been on the fence too long. Now he's going to see out the war from inside the guardhouse. Gillespie told me Juan Largo was insolent and laconic in answering questions. That's about all I know."

"Thanks." Bill's brow furrowed. "How is it in San Diego?"

"Quiet, except for Stockton's balls at Bandini's." Stokes chuckled. He looked for the sun. "I'd best get back to Santa Ysabel. Let me know immediately if you see or hear anything. I'll do the same. My regards to Missus Warner."

Stokes tipped his top hat, mounted his chestnut stallion, and trotted toward home, where a warm fire and a bottle of wine awaited.

"Warner's in jail," Bill said to Luna with a sigh.

It was only the end of November, and the winter had already turned gloomy and cold. It was weather to be cozy in a fur-lined cocoon, not sleeping in the drafty barn with Luna. Bill wearily returned to the big house to see how the family was doing.

Anita did not rebound from her initial shock at Warner's arrest, remaining morose and withdrawn. Little Andrés, who was less than a year old, had a fever, and Mary Ann took on her mother's depressed mood, hardly speaking at all. They sat around the fire, wrapped in quilts like mummies, bundled for the bitter cold, contemplating the loneliness and impossibility of their continued existence without Papa John.

Bill spent as much time as he could out of the house, with the livestock. The snow on the mountains and continuing cold had driven all mobile animals down onto the plain. Horses, cattle, sheep, deer, antelope and rabbits grazed on the yellow grass, tails turned into the chill wind. Great numbers of coyotes lurked at the edge of the fields, others lay boldly in the open, waiting for a weak animal to falter, or a careless mother to allow her offspring to stray. Carrion birds swooped and soared. They huddled against the sleet in the tops of trees, anticipating the next warm meal to be served up by the coyotes — on a bloody plate of kill-trampled grass.

O N December 2 the weather cleared. A weak sun warmed the downwind side of Warner's adobe. The air was crisp and bright, the swirling clouds' gray replaced by white. Dew on grass gathered in droplets to slip down the stems, instead of freezing in place as it had been all week.

The Warner family emerged to partake in the joyful sunlight. Anita and Fanny leaned against the adobe wall of the house and basked like heat-deprived reptiles; the children played in the yard at their feet. Luna and Bill cleaned moldy bridles and other tack in an equally sunny spot beside the barn; the two sheepdogs dozed nearby.

A soft growl, almost a sigh, came from Zippy, the younger of the two males, and aptly named. He repeated the grumble, then lifted his head to face east and really growled. Luna put his ear to the ground and said, "Many men walking," without lifting his head. "Many men and horses marching." He jumped up and tromped his feet to show.

"Vámonos." Bill dropped his leatherwork to the ground. Two crows took flight from the ridge of the barn.

Luna put a noose around his pony's nose and leapt on bareback, kicking him into a gallop. Stomping Deer's scouts were already stampeding the horses and cattle toward the mountains, yelling and flapping their hats and riatas like demented men attacked by wasps.

Bill ran around the corner of the house.

"Inside," he said, "and bolt the door."

Anita was slow to react. Bill scooped up Andrés and thrust him into her arms.

"Inside, they're coming."

Now she moved. He sprinted to his horse, kept tacked up and ready to go. Luna had shouted at the scouts and was riding back at a gallop. They swung east, toward the sound, wanting to meet whoever it might be away from the ranch; to give the men time to hide the stock.

The hoofbeats rumbled close. Over a rise, a ragged column appeared at a walk. It seemed not to end. As it snaked toward them, Bill saw a tattered flag of red, white and blue. He galloped the quarter mile to the head of the troop in half a minute. Luna hung back. Bill stopped and let the leaders approach the last hundred yards.

Only about fifteen of the men were mounted, all on emaciated mules. The rest walked, leading more painfully thin mules and a few skeletal horses. Their dress was as ragged as the animals, uniforms torn, tattered and patched, trousers worn out at the seat. Many of the men had no shoes. There were about a hundred of them.

The motley company halted twenty feet from Bill, and two riders, with the look of mountain men, rode forward another few paces.

"William Marshall, foreman for John Warner, at your service," Bill said.

"Kit Carson, and this desert-dried mountain man is Antoine Robidoux. I'm glad you speak English 'cause Robidoux's our interpreter and he's too worn out to talk." Robidoux smiled weakly.

"We're scouts for the First U.S. Dragoons, under General Stephen Watts Kearny." Carson waved and Kearny rode forward, his uniform faded but relatively intact. He sat very erect, his feet almost touching the ground beneath his dusty black mule.

"General Stephen Kearny," he said. "Commander, Army of the West. We're on our way to see John Warner. My men are in pretty poor shape. Need food, water, fresh horses. I've been told he will help us."

"Warner's in San Diego. I'm the foreman in his absence. William Marshall, of Providence, Rhode Island."

Bill saluted and Kearny saluted back.

"Follow me to the ranch and we can see about putting together some food for your men and beasts," Bill said. "They look starved."

"Thank you," said the general. "You can't imagine how good it feels to see an American out here." He waved, more at the sky than the earth.

Bill fell in with Carson and Robidoux; Luna galloped ahead. They proceeded at a brisk walk to the house, excitement banishing weariness.

Carson questioned Bill on the state of affairs in California. Bill recounted the events of the last two months as best he could. Carson cursed for a couple of minutes, finally calmed himself and dropped back to talk to Kearny.

By the time the column reached the ranch house, thick cloud cover had returned. The south wind kicked in, clawing over the snow-covered slopes of the Cuyamaca Mountains, sliding down to chill the threadbare soldiers.

Luna said but one word to Anita, "Americanos."

She rushed out of the house to greet them, flushed and excited. She ran from man to man saying, "I'm so glad to see you, we're Americans. Come in. You must be hungry, please, get down, we'll see to the horses." She was delirious. She seemed to have no idea of the size of the army she invited to her table.

Kearny was genuinely grateful. He gave orders for camp to be made, a half mile down the road toward Cupa, within sight. He, Carson and a Lieutenant Emory, who was in charge of his Corps of Engineers, came into the house to sit before the fire.

Bill gave Luna instructions to ask the men to round up fifteen or twenty sheep for the soldiers to slaughter. He should then to ride to Cupa, tell No'ka what had happened, and return with as much food as could be spared.

When Bill joined the group by the fire, they were discussing the Californio fighting spirit, or lack thereof. Carson and Anita both insisted that the rangers would melt into the hills at the first sign of a real army. Kearny asked if Bill agreed.

"Yes. They'll fire a few shots, wave a white flag and then negotiate over lunch. That is their idea of a fight."

Carson nodded. He still didn't quite believe that Mexicans could have driven Gillespie from Los Angeles. He told Bill that he had met General Kearny and his battalion of three hundred dragoons in New Mexico. When Kearny learned that the war was won, Stockton and Frémont in firm control, he had sent two hundred of his dragoons back to Santa Fe, giving them Carson's dispatches to forward to Washington. He had pressed the trail-weary mountain man to turn on his heel and guide the column back across the deserts. The worried general now had less than one hundred and twenty men at his disposal, in no condition to fight.

Kearny was shaking his head. "When were you last in San Diego?"

"Months ago."

"Is there anyone nearby who can give us more up-to-date information?"

"There is an Englishman, Edward Stokes, who lives fifteen miles distant. He's sympathetic. He just came from San Diego with a letter from Warner."

"I showed it to them," Anita said. "The general is going to set him free."

"Yes, as soon as I get to San Diego. I have a letter from our consul in Monterey, detailing Warner's part in the political lead-up to the war. Captain Gillespie has made a mistake, not his first from the sound of it." Kearny shook his head. "Warner was to provide us with fresh mounts . . ."

"I'll do what I can." Bill was careful with his wording. Warner had left no instructions, except to drive off the horses. "Most of the horses have scattered to the mountains. Some can be caught, surely."

"We are a cavalry battalion. Without horses we're helpless. You saw the pitiful creatures we're left with. This is my primary concern. We will pay well for any useful mounts." He paused, then looked Bill in the eye. "Any help you can give us will not be forgotten, by me or my men."

"I'm happy to be of service," Bill said truthfully. But he couldn't give up Warner's best horses. Warner would provide healthy serviceable mounts.

"Would you be willing to ride over to Stokes's place and try to bring him here to see me?" Kearny asked. "You've got the only horse that looks like it could get there and back in under a day." He gave Bill an Irish grin. Bill knew Kearny would leave the ranch riding his big bay gelding.

Bill cantered most of the way, walking only to catch his breath. He returned in three hours, with Stokes galloping alongside. Kearny was at his camp. They dismounted at the command tent.

Captain Stokes had worn his signature uniform of velvet English hunting coat, ruffled white shirt, velvet trousers cut off at the knee and open on the outside to the hip, drawers of spotless white, leggings of black buckskin, and black boots with six-inch spurs. He doffed his beaver top hat, greeting the general with a merry grin.

Kearny dismissed Bill, wishing to query Stokes in private. It was after dark when he sent Lieutenant Emory to call Bill back.

Kearny's tent was spacious. It held a collapsible desk, four chairs and an army cot, all the worse for wear, dimly lit by an oil lamp. The general motioned wearily for Bill to sit down.

"Stokes has confirmed your account of the situation. It seems that Admiral Stockton only controls San Diego itself. I have given Master Stokes a letter for the admiral, asking that an escort of marines be sent out to meet me at Santa Ysabel, to guide us back to San Diego. I would like you to take us as far as Santa Ysabel, as soon as we are able to travel."

"Of course," Bill said. "I have an idea where you can get some horses that belonged to the enemy. They are pastured nearby at a place called Aguanga. I doubt they are guarded."

He was referring to the broncos that had been given to the Cahuilla for their service with the Picos against Micheltorena. He was sure they were still there at the edge of Cupeño territory, unused and unwatched.

Kearny brightened at this news. "Your men have brought in less than a dozen good horses. I'll send a party of dragoons now to capture this herd and bring them back in the morning."

"Davidson," he yelled out the tent door.

Within the hour, Lieutenant John Davidson led twenty-five already exhausted men down the trail past Cupa to Aguanga. A stone-faced Carson was their guide. The night was absolutely freezing, thirty degrees, according to Lieutenant Emory's thermometer. Bill was glad he hadn't been asked to go.

It was a little warmer in Kearny's tent. The general offered Bill a glass of wine from a bottle supplied by Anita. They sipped it and discussed the Indians. Stokes had told the general that Bill was married to the daughter of a chief and had connections with most of the local tribesmen. Kearny had been in charge of training horse soldiers on the frontier, at Fort Leavenworth in the Missouri plains, deep in Indian Territory. As commander of the First Dragoons, he had ten years experience fighting and keeping peace with the Plains Indians.

Bill relayed a message from No'ka offering his help. "Most Indians hate the Californios, and will support the U.S. in ousting them. No'ka, the local chief and my father-in-law, would like to meet with you."

"It sounds as though we won't be needing any help from the natives. But I do appreciate the fact that they don't support our foes. How many Indians do you estimate live in the San Diego area?"

"About five or six thousand," Bill guessed.

Kearny whistled in surprise. "And the Mexicans?"

"Three hundred fifty. They're easier to count."

"Best we keep the Indians peaceful. My experience on the Plains is that the warriors of fighting tribes will fight anyone, the other tribes, each other, or us. The peaceful tribes tend to stay that way. If these people are peaceful, we must do our best to keep them so."

"You are more experienced than I in these matters. But you should meet the chiefs out of courtesy. They value personal contact."

"Of course, of course," Kearny exclaimed, equally tactful.

"Most of the Indians don't want to fight any more than the Californios do," Bill said. "They'll be happy to let you do the shooting."

"Let us meet the chiefs together, at Stokes's ranch. He says there is a large tribe living there, who would also like to see the Mexicans sent packing." The general stood and rubbed his muttonchop whiskers, graying at the jawline. Kearny was a man of action, decisive and sure of himself. "It is a better idea, more respectful and definitive, to meet them all at once."

"Ignacio is the chief at Santa Ysabel. With your permission, General Kearny, I will invite the other capitánes who live near, No'ka, Garra and Mocate of the Cupeño, Manuelito of Pauma, and Chapuli of Los Coyotes." Bill left out the Cahuilla, who had declared for the Californios, and whose horses were being stolen this very night.

H E quit the general's tent and rode through the chill to Cupa. It would be good to spend a night at home. He found Falling Star with her parents, Wili asleep on a pile of furs by the fire. They wanted to know everything about the Army of the West.

"I will tell you all I can, as soon as I am immersed to my neck in a hot pool." Shadow wedged his cold nose between Bill's legs and pumped his tail in greeting, ready to go.

Bill took Falling Star's hand and pulled her out the door. No'ka and White Fox followed quietly. "I'll ask Melones to watch Wili," said White Fox. "I'll be right there."

Bill had his arm around Falling Star's waist as they walked. Her skin was warm under her rabbit coat.

"Did you miss me?"

"We were talking about you when you arrived," she said.

"What were you saying?"

"Papi was telling us how lucky it has been to have you in the family." She squeezed his arm. "We agreed. We were laughing about my angry tantrum, when first he offered me to you."

"You weren't angry. You were happy. It was me who was reluctant."

"He ordered me to marry you; I had to obey, even though I had every right to choose my own husband. White Fox told me to give you a chance; that I would learn to love you, if you were worthy. If not, we could always poison you. On those terms, I consented."

"You could poison me?"

"Not now. Never." She kissed his cheek. "Now I love you."

"But you didn't always love me?"

"Not to begin with. It took a little getting used to you."

Bill thought back. He couldn't imagine a time when she didn't love him.

"It was difficult," Falling Star said. "You were hairy. You smelled funny. We never talked. All you wanted to do was maul me and have sex."

"We were supposed to be making a baby. What was there to talk about. Your English was as bad as my Cupeño." Bill was indignant. "You were enjoying the sex as much as I."

"I enjoyed it when I enjoyed it. Otherwise I pretended. I didn't want you to complain to my father."

Bill thought about this as they descended into the streambed. He still had his arm around her. He supported her breast with his hand and stroked her nipple with a thumb. It stiffened.

"Your nipples have always loved me," he teased tentatively, unsure.

"Not as much as you love them," she said.

He pulled his hand away. "What are you trying to say?"

"No, keep it there, it feels nice right now." She put his hand back. "It is just that whenever I see you, the first thing you want to do is touch my breasts."

"They feel good," Bill protested. "I like to touch them."

"I know. My friends say I'm lucky you always want me. At first I thought that was all you cared about. That and the cattle Papi gave you. I thought you might be like the *sosabitom,* who love their virgin señoritas and only want to use the native girls for sex." She took his hand in hers as they walked across the rocks.

"Now I know you love me. I'm used to having your hands on me. I don't want them on anyone else."

They slid into the scalding liquid, to find their places where the water mixture was tolerable. Breath steamed in the cold air and joined the shroud of mist over the pools. Bill recounted the dragoons' story, realizing in the telling that a lot had happened in one day. No'ka's men had heard and seen Davidson's patrol pass toward Aguanga. They had not yet returned. All agreed that it was poetic justice for those Cahuilla horses to end up in the U.S. Army.

No'ka grunted when he heard Kearny's idea for a group meeting with the chiefs.

The hot water relaxed Bill's tense neck and shoulders and unkinked his ride-compressed spine. He couldn't hold his eyes open. He was melting into the molten pool, about to lose consciousness. Falling Star slipped onto his lap. "I'll drown if we don't get to bed," he said.

And sleep came, blessed sleep.

When Bill awoke he had a question. "Would you really have poisoned me?"

"If you had used me as Leandro Osuna uses the Indian girls, and loved only Lugarda. Yes."

"How come no one's poisoned him?"

"His time will come. When he is older. When he has inherited the ranch and is content to watch his children grow. Just when a man has everything he wants, when his life is most precious, that is the time to kill him."

B I L L was back at the Warners' by seven the next morning, the hour of dawn in December. Kearny's men had passed a miserably cold night. They were huddled around campfires, wrapped in ragged blue blankets, speaking wistfully of the hot desert days of the past weeks. They needed food.

Warner's larder held potatoes, onions, acorn flour, corn flour, dried chiles, beans, some eggs and milk—and plenty of sheep. Anita, Fanny, Luna and Bill loaded the food in a wagon and delivered it to the camp cooks. They fed the entire troop, who couldn't seem to get enough. Starved men usually only eat a little at first. The dragoons ate until stuffed, slept and woke to eat again. Somehow the hundred and twenty men managed to eat thirty-seven fat sheep in two days.

The Davidson patrol rode in at midday, driving over a hundred horses and mules, a scrawny and wild-looking bunch. The Californios had given the Cahuilla the most worthless animals in Los Angeles. Kearny had expected to find the powerful, well-trained steeds of California legend, not these scraggly mustangs and unbroken mules. Still he was grateful. Bad as they were, they were better than any of his desert-starved mounts.

By evening, Kearny was determined to proceed the following morning to Santa Ysabel. A day of food, rest and taming new mounts had renewed his dragoons. They were still as ragged and thin as on the morning of their arrival, but their spirits were up. They joked about the unruly horses and looked forward to a mounted march on the morrow.

41

POWWOW
AT SANTA YSABEL

BILL'S pleasureful sleep at home was interrupted well before daylight by the dull thud of raindrops on the thatched roof. A persistent waterfall on the ground below the eaves spoke of volume. Bill dozed again to the drum of steady rain.

The showers continued to gust and run into the dull dawn. Falling Star refused to get out of bed. Bill ran up to No'ka's, to find White Fox also buried under robes, her husband feigning disgust at her lack of toughness. When they were outside, No'ka grinned.

"It is good they stay at home, warm and dry in our beds. That is where they should be. War is the work of men." Water streamed down his face.

They donned hooded ponchos of beaver, warm and water-repellent, and sprinted to the corrals. The horses whinnied and stomped and threw their heads, anxious to be out running on the wet plain. Stung by driving droplets, the two riders pressed cold faces to their outstretched necks, and let them gallop into the wind.

Kearny's camp had been stricken and packed by the time Bill and No'ka pulled their snorting horses to a halt. Kearny gave the miserable men a curt "Mount up," nodded to Carson and Robidoux, and they set off in a long column for Santa Ysabel.

No'ka and Bill broke trail, then Carson and Robidoux. The tattered battalion followed their muddy track, pack animals to the rear. Capitán Chapuli, who caught up before they reached the forest, tailed unnoticed in the downpour. All of the beasts of burden behaved, happy to be moving at a walk together, their herd instincts overriding any will to revolt against unfamiliar loads, their show of docility further abetted by the half-blinding rain.

At Santa Ysabel the dragoons set up camp by the chapel, trying to ignore the storm. The men were provided with a few sheep and some tortillas, which they cooked under a large oak and ate in the shelter of the chapel. The officers repaired to Stokes's adobe house where he served them a meal of mutton, tortillas and wine.

No'ka, Chapuli and Bill lunched with Ignacio, joined by Manuelito and Antonio Garra. Mocate had declined to come. They were served chicken tamales, spicy beans and fresh corn tortillas, prepared by Ignacio's wife and daughters, who ran up to his door with the cooked food and handed it in to the relatively dry men. The chiefs ate standing, warming their steaming clothing by turning in front of a big blaze in the riverstone fireplace.

Only Manuelito had much to say. The others chewed, and listened to him complain about Andrés Pico's raids on Pauma livestock. No'ka, who seemed short-tempered, finally said, "Save it for Kearny, so that we can hear the story fresh. Once."

Bill escorted the chiefs to Stokes's house, presenting them one by one as they shook the water off at the door. The officers and Indians arranged themselves in a circle. Stokes and Bill Williams remained at the dining table with their bottle of wine.

The chiefs had come bearing gifts. This was a protocol they never ignored. No'ka gave Kearny a coyote jacket lined with rabbit, beautiful and warm. Ignacio presented finely woven baskets that stacked inside each other. Manuelito had a strong white horse tied in the rain, and Chapuli had done likewise, bringing a sturdy paint from his desert valley.

Kearny was grateful, especially for the horses. He asked Captain Moore to bring a cavalry saber for each visitor. The sabers were rusty, and only by two men yanking hard, would they come unstuck from their scabbards. Cleaned up, they would be beautiful weapons. The chiefs accepted them politely. The discussion began.

Kearny spoke first in English. Robidoux then translated to Spanish. Ignacio or No'ka would explain to Chapuli, whose Spanish was limited. If Bill had any doubt about the English-Spanish translation, he would catch No'ka's eye and the chiefs would ask Bill to explain. When the Indians spoke, the whole long process was reversed.

Kearny made a brief speech about the mission assigned to him by President Polk—to win the war and set up a military government. He did not request any aid from the chiefs. The general did ask for their opinions of the situation and whether they had any requests of him.

They agreed that they had had enough of Spanish-Mexican rule and welcomed the Americans. They hoped that the Californios would be defeated and sent back to Mexico. They offered to help, in any way they could. Kearny advised them to keep the peace and take no part in the war, on either side. That was all the help he needed.

Manuelito began a detailed account of the recent raid by Andrés Pico's men on Pauma's horses and cattle.

The soldiers looked at each other and settled in for a long story.

" . . . the Mexicans proceeded to drive every animal with four hooves down the valley toward the coast. It took them some time to round up the horses. They caught our chickens and tied them in bundles. They loaded baskets of corn and acorns, and the chickens, onto our horses. They followed the cattle and sheep down the trail. This was the last we have seen of these creatures, our livelihood and our food supply. Now we must face this harsh winter with little to eat." Manuelito gestured toward the pounding rain outside.

"In that case . . ." said Kearny slowly, thinking of his own need for horses and food, "well, if they will do such a thing to you, you must try to defend yourselves."

This statement was translated, to Manuelito's evident satisfaction, as granting permission to fight back.

"What will happen to our lands?" asked No'ka.

"All land in California, providing we are successful in our war with Mexico, will henceforth belong to the U.S. government. Lands will be deeded back to the people who have legitimate proven claims. The remainder will be government land, to be distributed to deserving settlers in limited amounts, usually no more than one hundred sixty acres per family, and to the Indian nations according to their needs. All Indians will have an appointed government agent to represent them before the governor, the courts and the U.S. Congress."

No'ka, Ignacio and Manuelito pressed for a commitment on stolen land. "What of the grants of Indian lands Pico has given to his friends, as he did at Pauma; what of his sale of the missions to his brother and to Santiago Arguëllo?"

When Kearny was slow to reply, Bill said, "Colonel Frémont has promised to return the missions to the church."

"I am only now becoming aware of these abuses," replied Kearny. "I have not yet heard the colonel's views on the missions. But the United States will not recognize any illegal grants of land. You may count on that."

With that statement the interview ended.

Kearny had decided to stay that night at Stokes's rancho, to await the requested escort from San Diego. Stokes had delivered Kearny's note to Admiral Stockton. Captain Gillespie would leave immediately with a small party of mounted marines for a rendezvous at Santa Ysabel. Stokes reckoned they would arrive the next day, the fifth of December.

Chapuli, No'ka and Bill departed for home. Cold and damp would be their companions all this stormy day. But every minute in the saddle brought them closer to fire, fur and family, making the icy ride tolerable.

Manuelito and Antonio Garra stayed with Ignacio. They would follow the dragoons, their unseen eyes on General Kearny and Kit Carson—El Lobo, the most famous scout, rifleman and mountain man on the continent. Manuelito and Garra hoped to observe them in action. To witness a battle between the Americans and Californios would be the thrill of a lifetime. They looked forward to seeing their tormentors punished.

42

A BATTLE
IN THE RAIN

ECEMBER 6. General Kearny had barely slept. His command tent leaked and he was so thin that damp cold penetrated to his bones, and could only be driven away by close proximity to a raging fire. But there was no fire to stand by, just the steady drip that seemed to find him no matter where he placed his tattered cot.

They were camped in the rain, by the head of the long narrow valley leading to San Pasqual. He had met Gillespie the previous morning, on the trail from Santa Ysabel. The marine had immediately presented a plan to surprise Pico's Mexican rangers, said to be occupying the native village of San Pasqual. At dark, Kearny had sent a patrol guided by Jesús Machado, to learn if the enemy was still there.

Shortly after midnight, the patrol returned. The Mexicans were sleeping in the huts of San Pasqual; about seventy-five men and even more beautiful horses. The patrol had gotten so close that the village dogs had begun to bark. They had escaped. They didn't think they had been seen.

Kearny gave the order to break camp and prepare for battle. As long as it rained, it was less miserable to be moving than still. They would leave in an hour and attack before dawn. "That's what we're here for," he told his men. They gave him a great cheer and set to work.

They proceeded in single file down a well-worn trail, clinging to the side of the narrow valley. Kearny rode about a dozen men back from the leaders: Captain Moore, the scouts and Gillespie's patrol. Lieutenant Davidson followed, with the cannon and the remainder of the brigade strung out for a mile behind. The excited soldiers slouched in their saddles, braced against the downhill jog of their half-wild mounts, caps pulled low, rain dripping from the brims.

Kearny was not happy. He was riding Bill Marshall's nice horse, but the army of tattered scarecrows he led was in bad shape. Their loaded rifles had not been fired in months. The caps and powder were wet and would probably never fire in this rain. Most of the sabers were rusted in their scabbards. Fixed bayonets were their only sure weapons. The men were spoiling for a fight, egged on by Gillespie, and the drudgery of the desert crossing, and terrible California weather, but they were in no condition for battle. And their mounts were incapable of cavalry maneuvers, much less a charge in the face of gunfire.

They needed horses above all else. With good horses, Kearny would have an army, even if their uniforms were held together by stitches and patchwork. Even if their weapons were useless. Gillespie and Carson had sworn that Pico's militia of ranchers would run at first sight of American soldiers, no matter how sorry the troops looked to their commander. The dragoons could capture some fine horses, and ride into San Diego as heroes, to face Stockton's spit-and-polish navy with pride and some style.

But Kearny didn't feel right. He was governor of California, but Colonel Frémont was acting like the governor, giving missions back to the Catholic Church, while Stockton was living it up in San Diego, waiting for Frémont to win the war. He was commander general of the thousand-strong Army of the West, but ninety percent of them had been left in New Mexico. He was following Captain Gillespie, a navy marine who had just lost Los Angeles, into uncertain battle. The careless night patrol had probably alerted the rangers. Even the weather was wrong. He was cold and wet and worried and risking his life.

Just as Kearny emerged from the canyon trail into the broadening valley of San Pasqual, and there was finally light enough to see through the mist to the men in front, a shout came from the head of the column.

"There they are. The Mexicans!"

"Pull up. Mass for a charge," shouted General Kearny to the men ahead.

"Move up, mass for a charge," shouted Lieutenant Davidson, to the men behind.

"Charge!" bellowed Captain Gillespie.

"Charge!" yelled Captain Moore.

The Army of the West charged. The ready rangers fired a single volley from their ancient muskets. Captain Moore fell dead with a ball in the forehead. Carson's horse went down. Lieutenant Beale's horse went down. The rest of the crazed steeds ran every which way. On Pico's command, the rangers lowered their lances and charged, slicing their way through a confu-

sion of riders and thrown men. Gillespie took a savage cut to the mouth and
cheek, a stab in the lung, another in the buttocks. He fell heavily to the
ground and fainted.

Kearny felt a searing pain in his left hip. A warm red stain spread to his
trousers. He wheeled his horse to see his wildly charging troop entering the
plain one by one, to be cut to pieces by Pico's lancers. Men on foot were run
down and skewered. The riders swirled in hand-to-hand combat, bayonet or
rifle butt against lance. More and more dragoons spilled from the canyon
into the milling throng.

Andrés Pico regrouped his men for a second charge, lances lowered to the
level of enemy waists, the least mobile part of a rider. A dozen more dragoons
were struck to the ground. The wounded were mercilessly stuck again. A cannon was roped and dragged off. Gillespie had come to. He staggered to his
feet. Someone from Los Angeles yelled, "Ya, el Capitán Gillespie," and
charged. The undaunted marine ducked behind an abandoned cannon and
lit the fuse with his glowing cigar, miraclously still clenched between his
teeth. It went off with a thunderous roar, shooting at nothing, spooking every
horse in the valley into terrified flight. Gillespie swooned. The Californios
galloped off into the hills—the last of Kearny's men straggled onto the battlefield.

It had been five, ten, fifteen minutes? A third of Kearny's dragoons were
dead or horribly wounded, leaking precious blood onto the wet plain. The
Mexicans and their horses were gone. All of them. The general held his
slashed side and rode among his moaning men. As the last of the showers
cleared, tears of pain and sorrow and frustration washed his cheeks. With the
sun peeking weakly through swirling mist, he led his army to the shelter of a
grove of oaks. He slid from his blood-soaked saddle to earth. He gave the
orders: Establish a defensive perimeter; attend the wounded; bury the dead.
He pressed his cold canteen hard against the burning hole in his side, and
slumped to the soft wet bed of crinkly leaves.

O N the seventh, a dry day, Antonio Garra trotted into Warner's yard at mid-
afternoon. He had been to see No'ka and was on his way to Pauma Valley. He
looked tired, but rode a fresh horse loaned to him at Cupa.

He quickly told Bill the tale of Kearny's progress: "Americans were lying
all over the bleeding grass, their guts spilling out. The Californios were
yelling, galloping, dipping their flags in American blood; sticking their lances
in dying men."

The sign language Garra used for this description made Bill feel every cold, steel thrust.

"Kearny and Carson?"

"No one knew. Manuelito and I parted. I to take the long way back to Cupa. He would follow the action and return to Pauma through Rincón del Diablo. I carried word of the fighting to Ignacio and Stokes, then on to No'ka at Cupa. He asked me to tell you the same story. He said, You tell Bi' just as you told me." Garra smiled. "That is all, I have told you."

Bill was obliged to give this discouraging information to Anita. Before he had finished, she burst into tears. Little Andrés howled with her.

"What if Kearny was killed, or they are defeated? What will happen to John?" She dabbed at her eyes with a sleeve.

"I'm sure Kearny will win. We must wait, Anita. John is safe in San Diego and we are safe here." Bill patted her on the shoulder. "It's just a matter of time."

43
WAITING

B UT time has a way of lengthening and shortening all of its own: One minute of waiting can equal hours, even days of happy activity. Bill tried to keep busy and keep the Warners occupied. He took them to the hot springs one day. Another, they rode east to the edge of the mountains, to look into the desert and feel a rising blast of warm air. Bill and Anita organized a birthday party for Wili they could look forward to, on the eleventh.

KEARNY was waiting too, becoming more and more desperate with each passing hour, sinking into depression. He had sent a note to Stockton, telling of the battle and asking for wagons to transport the wounded. But he had neglected to say just how bad the situation was. He had insisted they could make it alone, if necessary.

Stockton had neither good wagons nor the horses to pull them. Gillespie had taken all of the available horses. He sent a note to that effect back to Kearny.

The rangers harassed Kearny's camp from just out of rifle range and eventually drove the soldiers to the top of a rocky hill, which the dragoons fortified. For two days they lay on the hill with no food or fresh water, forced to eat their starving mules. The wounded were in agonizing pain, including their general. Under the circumstances, they could not be moved. Kearny swallowed his pride and sent Kit Carson, Marine Lieutenant Beale and a Delaware Indian to San Diego, to ask Stockton again for help.

They removed their shoes to travel silently, slinking from the hill after dark. Each messenger took a different route, to assure that at least one would get through the Californio lines. That sleepless night, Kearny heard every tick of his nervously wound watch.

/ / /

W I L I ' S party was at lunchtime, on a warmer sunny day. Ladislaya came
with Melones and her child, Primo. Falling Star brought Wili and his grandparents. Anita, Mary Ann and Andrés completed the group. Anita played
hostess, with Fanny and Luna serving.

They gathered at a table placed in the sun between the barn and house.
Children dominated the conversation, the games and eating. It was a joy to
watch the three boys together, Mary Ann as their shepherd. Anita had baked
a cake. Luna and Bill made ice cream with milk, sugar and blackberry pre-
serves, swirled with ice in a device Warner kept stored in his blacksmith
shop. No'ka made the wish and Falling Star blew out a single big candle.

The sweet dessert made the day memorable. Anita and Bill were the only
ones who had ever eaten ice cream. Bill demonstrated the mechanism, making a jarful for No'ka to take home. In the shade it was cold enough to stay
frozen.

Bill wished that he could have made a daguerrotype of the birthday party;
his happy family dressed so beautifully, all the people he loved together; all
but Lugarda and Pablo.

How seldom he thought of Lugarda Osuna de Alvarado. Still, whenever
he did, he felt a strong connection. He didn't miss her in any normal sense,
she was more like the ice cream they had eaten, a treat to be partaken with
joy, but not a daily fare, or even something you remembered you liked, until
it was right there in front of you.

Pablo was different. Bill thought of him all the time, either trying to imagine what he was doing, or wishing they were together. Pablo should have
been at the meeting with Kearny. He would have informed and challenged
the general in ways the chiefs could not. Kearny may well have conceded no
more than he had, but he would have left the meeting with certain knowledge that the Indians of California had the education and intelligence to
demand a fair share of the territory he planned to conquer and govern.

Pablo Verdi would be a model new American Indian citizen.

The party broke up when a black cloud billowed over Mount Palomar,
covering the sun. The temperature dropped in seconds; a south wind sprang
to life. Crows cawed in irritation, flying deeper into the woods for shelter.
There was another storm on its way, coming in fast.

Falling Star hurried home, carrying Wili inside her jacket. Bill rode a
way with them. She trotted as a few big drops splattered across the plain,
one striking her nose so hard it hurt. It began to hail, not dangerously—the
icy balls were only raindrop-sized—but big enough to sting. The wind

lifted her long skirt. Bill laughed at her attempts to keep it down. She let it flap.

"I'm freezing," she shouted, and kicked her horse into a gallop.

The hail pelted Bill at double force as he turned back to face the wind. He closed his eyes, lowered his head into his horse's flying mane and let him run. Just before they reached Warner's barn, a final flash of sun lit the glowering sky and washed the yard in yellow-orange light. Then darkness closed in.

44

A THOUSAND CUTS

I T S N O W E D gently during the night, leaving about two fluffy inches of white to crunch underfoot during the morning tasks. The clouds kept coming, bringing other flurries to cover their tracks, but the storm was soft, the winds light, the snow a welcome change from rain.

Mid-morning, when the chores were done and breakfast eaten, Luna and Bill tucked under the shed roof of the blacksmith shop to pound straight a box of bent horseshoes. A rider galloped hard up the trail toward them, veiled by fluttering snowflakes.

Horse and rider flew into the yard without slowing and slid to a stop, spraying muddy snow against the half-wall of the shed. Falling Star threw back her hood. She was wearing a pair of Bill's work pants long enough to entirely cover her feet. She did not dismount.

"Come quickly," she panted. "The Pauma have captured eleven Californios. They brought them to Cupa to decide their fate. Pablo, Manuelito and the Garras are all there. Chapuli too. They asked me to fetch you." She spun her horse around in a full circle.

"Come now," she demanded, lowering her hood.

Bill went directly to his horse, he said "Voy a Cupa," to Luna, mounted bareback and galloped after Falling Star. He didn't dare speak to Anita.

At the village the snow had stopped. They trotted up between the houses to the big oak, where a crowd had gathered. Bill dismounted and his wife led the horses away.

A large bonfire warmed the area. Around the fire lay the eleven Mexicans, naked, bound hand and foot, facing away from the flames. At the tree trunk, a conference was in progress. Pablo saw Bill and leapt to his feet. He was dressed in his best Indian attire.

He ran around the prostrate captives to embrace Bill, throwing his coyote robe aside. His eyes were wide dark pools.

"What's going on?" Bill asked in English, sliding his eyes around the circle of naked men.

"We are deciding what to do with these cabrones," he laughed. "How funny they look naked. Their pricks are the size of a child's."

Indeed, their sex organs were hardly there; shriveled by cold and fear.

"And what a gift we have delivered to you for Christmas." Pablo pointed to one of the men, whose skin was very pale, hair trimmed neatly, with a thin mustache that had grown out. Bill couldn't tell his age. He shrugged. He did not recognize him.

Pablo said, "Oh?" He tapped the man with the toe of his knee-high moccasin.

"José María Alvarado," Pablo said. "I would like to present William Marshall, the lover of your wife, Lugarda." The frightened man grunted.

Pablo kicked the next man ungently in the ribs, just under the arm. "And this is Santiago Osuna, Lugarda's brother."

Bill said, "Mucho gusto." He couldn't think of anything else to say.

The two men swore in Spanish. Pablo answered them in rapid-fire phrases. They both looked at Bill. Pablo was watching him too.

"Ayúdenos. Help us," Santiago pleaded.

"Only God can help you now," answered Pablo. "This is Manuel Serrano, who claims Pauma as his own," he said, kicking another man hard.

He led Bill to the tree trunk where No'ka, Chapuli, Manuelito, Antonio Garra and his son, Tonio, were sitting on cowhides piled with furs and sheepskins.

"What are you going to do with them?" Bill asked Pablo, in English.

"Kill them slowly if I have my way," said Pablo matter-of-factly. "But you are here to help us decide."

Bill said, "Buenos días," to all of the assembly. He sat down. He was trying to discern what he felt, if anything, about Lugarda's husband. He felt nothing. His brain was numb.

In the background hovered a group of fifteen or twenty men who had come from Pauma. They were shuffling and chanting a war song, a good way to stay warm.

No'ka cleared his throat. "Pablo has been relating to us the events of the last few days—of Kearny's march to San Diego. You know that Kearny attacked the Mexicans on the sixth of this month. Antonio Garra brought us that news. Now Pablo and Manuelito have nearly finished the story for us, as they were witnesses."

Manuelito nodded to Pablo, who took up the tale.

"I had come from San Diego as a guide for Stockton's relief force. No one knew the way as well as I." He looked at Bill.

"We found Kearny's army in terrible condition. They were in rags, half starved, and mostly without horses or even mules. Twenty men had been killed at San Pasqual. Another eighteen were badly wounded, including Gillespie and Kearny. The injured were in great pain, with horrible slices to the stomach, kidneys, liver and other vital organs. The doctor said most of the dead had bled to death; that lance stabs had severed their arteries.

"There was no choice for Kearny and his rescuers but to limp back to the Pueblo to recuperate. Later the marines and dragoons could set out again, to chase Pico and Flores to Los Angeles and beyond if necessary. That was the plan.

"I left the Americans when they broke camp. To my surprise, Manuelito emerged from the brush. The Californios had fled and we saw by their tracks that they had split up. We followed one group, heading toward Pauma. We thought they might be going there to raid, as they did last month. But they all went to Serrano's newly built adobe and locked themselves inside. We decided to capture them.

"We waited until nightfall. Crouching low, about twenty of us sneaked up to the house. Manuelito strode upright to the door and knocked hard. 'Quién es?' someone asked. 'Es Manuelito,' he replied.

"Serrano opened the door. We rushed in, overpowered them, took their weapons, stripped them of their clothing, and led them to a secluded house about a mile east.

"All night we danced to celebrate our success. Today we brought those eleven men here, so that the capitánes may help to decide their fate."

No one uttered a word.

"This we must do quickly," Pablo said. "Juan Antonio Serrano, José Aguilar, and Serrano's son, Jesús, were the only ones from this group we did not capture. They had ridden to Pala. Now they have followed us here. No doubt they will try to rescue the others."

There was general silence, a thoughtful expression on every face. The situation was shocking.

No'ka turned Bill's way. "We called you here to receive your advice as an American. Will General Kearny, who will be our new governor, be pleased if we kill these men? Or would he have us turn them over to him? Or should we set them free?"

They all looked at the American, Pablo very intently. Bill took a deep breath and let it out.

"I cannot speak for the general. But he has lost many men—and these are the enemies who so cruelly killed them. We definitely should not set them free to fight again. That is not a course of action he would appreciate."

All of the chiefs nodded in agreement.

No'ka looked worried. "We cannot keep them here," he said. "They are a danger to our village. We must take them to San Diego, or kill them as Pablo would have us do."

"They are dangerous no matter where we take them," Pablo said. "We could be attacked at any time by their rescuers. Even if we were to give them to Kearny, he would only keep them till the war is over. Then they will be released to torment our lives as they have in the past.

"These men are our enemies as well as Kearny's. The Osunas are those who looted the mission at San Diego. They drove the Indians of San Dieguito out of their valley. The Alvarados have taken some of our best land for themselves. They have given even more land to their friends. And here is Manuel Serrano, who claims Pauma Valley, our homeland, as his own. These men are a plague on our lives." Pablo took a breath.

"Now that I have seen how easily men die in war; how easy it is to kill a man. I can feel how good it must be to bury your enemies. How nice to wake up to this beautiful world, without the ugly presence of these men."

The Pauma war dancers let out a "Huh!" and stood still.

"I saw how bravely the Americans took their horrible wounds and death. These Mexicans have a debt to pay to those soldiers. The surest way to collect that debt is to kill them as painfully. Let their blood fertilize the good earth they have stolen from us People and the other creatures. Let them not live to call themselves Americans and drive us to servitude and extinction."

There was a general nodding of heads. The Pauma cheered. They resumed their chanting and stomping. Someone was shaking a rattle.

An Indian rode into the village accompanied by Stomping Deer. He was one of Ignacio's men from Santa Ysabel, dressed in pants and shirt and a wool jacket. He looked quickly at the pale men lying naked on the cold ground.

"Bill Williams offers ten head of cattle for each of these men," he said. "Juan Serrano came to Santa Ysabel to ask for help in saving his friends. They will pay ten cattle for each man."

Antonio Garra jumped up. "Tell them they cannot buy their friends with cattle that were raised on stolen land." He was wearing the dragoon's saber given to him by Kearny. So were Manuelito and Chapuli.

Holding the men for ransom had not occurred to the chiefs. The concept interested them. They debated the value of a man in cattle, then reverted to silence.

The man from Santa Ysabel said, "Twenty cattle, they will pay up to twenty cattle per man."

"Then why did you say ten?" demanded Garra.

"Do they think we would give a man his life for ten cattle?" asked Chapuli.

"Ten or twenty, what is the difference?" said Manuelito. "If we accept the cattle, how will we stop them from taking them back?"

"Dead they can take nothing," pointed out Stomping Deer. "Then we can seize their cattle as we like."

"Tell Bill Williams and Serrano we do not accept this offer," said Pablo, dismissing the messenger. "The judgment we will make has not to do with the value of a man, to be bought or sold. The choice is whether they deserve to live or die, no more, no less. Tell him that."

After the messenger had left there was another silence. The men on the ground asked for water. Each was given a ball of snow to suck.

"Enough talk," said Pablo. "Let each capitán state his choice."

"Who but you is talking?" said Chapuli. "These men have done nothing to me personally. Their crimes are universal to the sosabitom who came to conquer us. If they are to die for the sins of their race, then let them die, for those sins are worth far more than their eleven lives."

"They will have to die a thousand deaths, just to begin to pay that debt," said Pablo.

The dancers cheered and began to chant, "A thousand deaths, a thousand deaths, a thousand deaths."

Bull Bear, Stomping Deer and other Cupeños had joined the dancers. Bill wondered where the women were. Cowering in their homes, the givers of life, protecting their children from the madness of men.

Cockney Bill Williams rode into the village yelling. He had been drinking. He could barely stay on his horse. Bill went quickly to him.

"It's too late," he said. "Don't even go near. Blood will be spilling soon. Don't let it be your own."

Williams wheeled his horse with a vicious jerk of the reins.

"I'll be back with Ignacio and his men," he slurred. "Then we'll see whose blood spills."

As the drunken hoofbeats faded, Pablo took up a lance. He placed the point on a glowing coal at the edge of the fire.

"What do you say, No'ka?" he asked.

"I am too old for killing," No'ka answered, without hesitation. "In my entire life, not one person has been slain at Cupa." He eyed the growing throng of dancers. "I say take the cattle, turn the men free. We can slaughter the steers immediately and sell the hides later. Hides cannot be driven off, or easily stolen. The coyotes need to be fed."

"I agree," said Manuelito. "My heart is too soft to turn to killing."

"Bah," exclaimed Pablo. His eyes were wild. "What do you say, Duck Bill Marshall?"

"It is not for me to be their judge, but we cannot turn them free, not now, while they may return to fight General Kearny. Of that I am certain."

Killing them terrified Bill, and yet he couldn't think of a good alternative. When he thought of Lugarda's husband, it was even more confusing. Did she love this man? When had she last seen him? Would she hate him if they killed José María? Could he save this one man?

Pablo never took his eyes from Bill's.

There were no answers. The lives of these men did not matter to Bill. The things that did matter had little to do with them. He wanted to help Pablo do what he had to do. That was his only clear line of thought.

"Kill them," he said forcefully, startling himself and everyone else.

"Kill them," echoed Tonio Garra and Stomping Deer.

Antonio Garra lifted his hands and shrugged.

"You should have killed them at Pauma," he said to Manuelito. "Why else did you capture them?" Garra furiously worked his hands. "Let us see if they are as gracious in receiving the lance as they have been generous in giving it."

No'ka frowned. Manuelito shook his head.

"Kill them," shouted the dancers. "A thousand deaths."

Their stomping increased in force. Now the ground shook with pounding feet. Flutes joined the drumming.

Pablo pulled his red-hot spear point from the coals. He held it over the heart of Manuel Serrano, turned the blade so it would slip between the ribs, and said, "This is for taking our ancestral land at Pauma." He slid the point gently in, up to the shaft. The surprised man did not even move. He opened his mouth as though to speak, watched a fountain of blood climb the spear, and lay back dead.

There was bedlam in the camp. The dancers whooped and cheered, chanted and stomped. The prisoners all tried to rise. They got to their knees and pleaded, they cried and screamed for mercy. The chiefs leapt to their feet. Bill did too. No one was sure what to do next.

A young man, the youngest of the prisoners, a boy called Alipas, tried to comfort his companions.

"What is the use of crying, compañeros," he said softly. "We can only die once; let us die like brave men."

"Well said," Pablo told him. "And how would a brave man wish to die?"

"With a bullet in the forehead," Alipas replied. "Looking in the eyes of my assassin."

Pablo took a horse pistol from the pile of confiscated weapons, checked it to be sure it would fire, cocked the hammer, placed the barrel about a foot from Alipas's forehead and pulled the heavy trigger. The gun went off like a cannon.

The boy went down soundlessly, gore dripping from the back of his shattered skull. Everyone jumped as the shot rattled through the rocks. No'ka looked sick. He took a few steps away from the ring of prisoners, who now wailed twice as loudly as before. The dancers resumed their wild stomping.

Pablo put the smoking pistol back in the gun pile. He returned to address the cowered and praying Mexicans.

"The priests say, 'In suffering we may experience a thousand deaths.' You *sosabitom* have caused us much suffering these seventy-seven years that you have been among us. You have made us to suffer many small deaths during our lifetimes. You have denied us the right to lead happy, peaceful lives, dying only once at the very end."

He looked at Alipas, lying still, brains leaking into the damp oak mulch.

"Now you too will understand what it is like to suffer. You too shall experience a thousand little deaths. Then you may die knowing just how we have felt."

He took up the lance and placed the steel on a crackling coal. The captives cringed and Santiago Osuna shrank in terror.

"Fear not. You are all Christians. You shall die the martyr's death, as Christ did, bleeding for the sins of others. May He greet you in heaven."

Pablo handed the hot spear to one of the dancers. The man gently took a nick out of Santiago Osuna, who screamed in pain and clutched his bleeding leg. The spear was handed to the next dancer, who cut another man, a relative of the Picos, on the arm. Pablo was heating three more lances, which he distributed as the circle of dancers passed. The prisoners screamed and moaned as they were carefully poked, sliced and stabbed, no cut intended to cause death alone, but all cuts together sure to kill.

As each man thrust a heated lance he would chant, "For stealing our lands; for Pauma, for Las Flores, for San Dieguito; for the floggings; for rape, for robbery, for murder; for killing our cattle, for General Kearny." The other dancers would shout out after him in response; the blade was passed to the next man in line.

The flesh-burning spears cut and seared at the same time, leaving little bleeding from the wounds, ensuring a slow agonizing death: the death of a thousand cuts. Thus did these eleven men pay in pain for all the suffering caused by their race in California.

B I L L walked away from the screams and flames, shouts and stomping, down the street toward his house. There were women and children in doorways, looking in wonder at the spectacle at the end of their avenue. Near home, Shadow ran out to greet him, whining and growling at the bedlam that reflected off the low clouds and echoed off the cobbles.

A man ran down the street and up to Bill. It was Stomping Deer. He held out his hand, blood dripping between the fingers. He opened it.

"Alvarado's manhood," he said, giggling. He poked at it with a finger to show the separate parts.

Bill shrank back. Stomping Deer flipped the gory blob to Shadow, who let it fall to the ground and licked it tentatively.

"No, Shadow," Bill shouted. "Leave it alone." Snow began again to fall.

He pulled Shadow by the ear but the big dog held back, curious. Bill yanked him bodily into the house and shut the door.

Falling Star was sitting on the bed, rocking and nursing Wili. Bill stood there, holding on to Shadow's ear, staring at her.

"They're killing them." She said it as a statement, not a question.

"Yes. Slowly and painfully."

"Come, sit here by me." She patted the bed.

Bill sat, stroking Shadow's face, then lay back. He closed his eyes for a long time, until the screaming stopped. When he opened them Falling Star was watching him.

"Something finally made you forget the Warners," she said.

Bill sat up. He struggled to his feet. Anita would be beside herself.

"I'll be back tomorrow, I'm certain. Kearny will be in San Diego by now. Warner should be home by tomorrow evening."

He kissed his wife and child and Shadow goodbye. Outside, the gory lump was gone. Another dog must have eaten it. At the end of the street he could make out a pile of bodies and the dancers around them. The snow was whitening the rooftops, thickly blanketing the ground.

On the way to Warner's, he met Ignacio, riding hard with about fifty of his men. Bill held up a hand and they stopped en masse, horses stomping and snorting. The trail behind them was a wide dark mark, fading fast under the falling snow.

"The Mexicans have been killed," Bill told them.

Ignacio did not react, but his men shifted in their seats. Some crossed themselves.

"When?" asked Ignacio.

"More than an hour ago."

"We will see for ourselves, and hear No'ka's story," said Ignacio, looking up into drifting snowflakes.

"He will be pleased you have come. He was not happy." Bill raised both shoulders high and dropped them. "It happened," he added. There was no other explanation.

When they had passed, Bill trotted on to Warner's barnyard. Luna emerged, a question in his eyes.

"The Mexicans were killed."

"Bueno." Luna grinned.

Bill knocked on the door of the house. Anita answered.

"What happened, where did you have to go in such a rush?"

"To Cupa. I will tell you in the morning. Kearny is in San Diego. John should be back tomorrow." He hung his head wearily.

"Oh good," she exclaimed. "What good news. Mary Ann. Fanny. Daddy is coming home," she shouted into the house.

WARNER arrived the next day, just before noon. The snow had stopped. The sun blazed between tall clouds, threatening to melt the clean white blanket deposited the night before.

John was riding a small dark brown mule, his feet almost touching the ground, only the saddle thickness giving him some clearance. He stepped off cursing, stomped around the yard cursing, greeted his family and kept cursing.

"That son of a bitch Gillespie should be drawn and quartered," he ranted. "This whole goddamned war was his fault. Then he misled Kearny into an ambush, hoping to come out a hero. Got a lance in his ass, one in the lung and one in the teeth for his troubles. Serves him goddamn right.

"'Course he had to get twenty-one good boys killed in the process. A fifth of Kearny's army dead, another fifth badly wounded for nothing." He sucked his teeth.

"Then there's Kearny, that pompous, prideful Irish goat, who didn't want his ragtag battalion to ride into San Diego on broke-down mules and donkeys. He couldn't stomach the idea of Commodore Stockton, with his drill-parade marines in their fancy sailor suits, laughing at his bare-assed dragoons. So he sent those boys straight to hell, all in the hope of capturing a few good California horses."

Warner had worked himself into a fury.

"We heard about the fight," Anita told him.

"That was no fight. It was a slaughter." Warner rubbed his eyes. He focused on Bill. "Where the hell did you get that mangy, cockeyed bunch of four-legged sacks of caca you gave to Kearny?"

"At Aguanga. They were mostly the animals given to the Cahuilla by Pico." Bill was unable to meet Warner's eye.

"Never mind, weren't your fault. They would have got him safe to San Diego, if it weren't for that ass Gillespie. Goddamned son of a bitch.

"I heard the whole sorry tale from Lieutenant Ed Beale, who was in the ship's hospital. He walked all night barefoot, across all that prickly pear cactus and chaparral between Rancho Bernardo and San Diego, to deliver Kearny's SOS."

The storytelling was cheering Warner up.

"Bandini and Stockton were throwing another ball at the plaza. Goddamn band near drove me crazy, tooting and scratching all night long, every night. Onto the dance floor staggers a half-dressed Indian, then Kit Carson and Ed Beale, as poorly clothed and in even worse shape, talking to themselves and yelling about Kearny's plight. Stockton took two nights off to rescue the wounded general, then up starts the band again."

Warner shook his full-bearded head of filthy locks.

"No one's ever left San Diego as fast as I quit that flea-bitten town. Rode a burro to Santa Ysabel, then borrowed this mule. There's not a horse left within a day's ride of the coast."

"We've got horses," Anita cut in.

"Damn right we do," he shouted, clapping Bill on the back. "Damn right we do," he repeated, looking around his well-ordered stockyards. "Don't mind me. I've just spent two weeks in a box—an ice-cold box. Tell me what's been going on at the ranch? How's No'ka? I see the coyotes are still waiting for their Christmas dinner."

Bill took a gulp of air.

"The Pauma killed eleven Californios at Cupa yesterday. Andrés Pico's rangers."

"The hell you say," he exclaimed, staring in amazement. "Who, who'd they kill?"

"Santiago Osuna, Manuel Serrano, a boy named Alipas, one of the Aguilars, José María Alvarado . . ."

"Alvarado, they killed Alvarado? We'll I'll be damned. That evens the score a bit. I heard the Osunas, Alvarado and the other Serrano killed some of the dragoons. I can't believe the Pauma could get that riled up. They're not even wild Indians. They've been with the mission for years."

"They were riled up all right," Bill said.

"Were you there?" Warner's eyes bored into Bill's.

"Not for the killing," he half-lied. "I was there early but came back to watch the ranch." He explained a little of what had taken place, leaving out the "thousand deaths."

Warner kept shaking his head saying, "Well I'll be; well I never; who would've thought . . ."

"Do you mind if I go home?" Bill asked.

"Are you sure it's safe?" Anita looked horrified.

"Of course it's safe. The Cupeño did not harm anyone. I believe everyone else has returned home. I saw two big groups of men pass by this morning, riding south."

"Okay, Bill," Warner said, shaking his head. "Thanks for holding the fort. Anita and I are forever grateful. Let me know if you need anything. You can take off till after Christmas. We'll manage fine. I'm even looking forward to ranch work for a change."

Luna watched Bill pack in silence. When Bill was ready, he asked if he might ride along to the village for a look. Warner was inside, out of sight.

"Yes, let's go, quickly. Venga."

They rode up the street of Cupa to the oak, then back down. There was no sign of yesterday's drama. The bonfire had burned to a pile of gray ash. Fresh snow covered everything else. There were no people to be seen; it was like a ghost town.

Luna shrugged and trotted away. Falling Star, Wili and Shadow were waiting for Bill.

"Where is everyone?" he asked.

"Hiding in shame or fear. Anger, in the case of my father."

"The Pauma? Ignacio? Pablo?"

"Ignacio came with his men. They spent the night in dancing and endless talk. By morning all were in the hot pools. When dawn broke, Ignacio's group, the Pauma and some Kuupiaxchem took the dead bodies to bury across the valley, near Mount Palomar. Pablo went with them.

"They wanted to put the bodies where their families could find them, far from both Cupa and Pauma. Osuna and Alvarado were buried separately, out of respect, and for fear of retaliation against 'Zul. After the burial, Ladislaya went to San Diego, to take word of the deaths. She took a serape belonging to Osuna and Alvarado's rosary as proof. Ladislaya wishes to bring the news directly to their families, to save them the pain of learning such sadness by rumor. Manuelito hopes that with these kind acts, it will be known that he opposed the killings. Thus will 'Zul be spared."

Bill waited for her to continue, but she was silent, thinking.

"Pablo?"

"His mother told him to go to Padre Ibarra; to beg forgiveness."

"No'ka?"

"He is angry with himself for allowing such a thing to happen in our village. He saw Stomping Deer dance the death dance. They argued as they always do. This time No'ka said, 'You are no son of mine, you son of a Cahuilla.' Stomping Deer left with the Pauma and has not returned."

She looked at Bill closely.

"I told you at Aguanga . . . about my mother and Baupista . . ."

"Oh, yes." Bill could not look at her.

"Mother was furious. She has gone to Wilakalpa to visit her sister." Falling Star watched him again. "How are the boss-Warners?"

"Fine. Warner has given me time off, till after Christmas."

"Did you tell them?"

"Yes. Not every detail."

"Their reaction?"

"Surprise, absolute disbelief. Warner said, this will help to even the score for Kearny." Bill felt hot.

"Did you wish to see Alvarado dead because of his wife, your novia, Lugarda?" Her voice had a bright brittleness.

"No," Bill said truthfully. He met her eyes. "No, I never once thought there could be any advantage for me with him dead. Nor did I wish to save him. He meant nothing."

"And she? Does she also mean nothing?" Her voice was softer, with a tinge of hurt. Bill took both of her hands.

"She does mean something. I do not know exactly what. I do know that she is as a single snowflake in a snowstorm, compared to what you mean to me."

She looked carefully at him, searching for signs of weakness.

"I believe you," she said, squeezing his hands. "I am glad that she should suffer, for turning you down and marrying another."

Falling Star's logic eluded him, but Bill kissed her forehead in gratitude.

45

TALK HELPS

EAD?" cried Lugarda, dropping her screaming daughter to the bed.

"Dead," said 'Zul tearfully. "Your brother Santiago and nine others. Ladislaya said the Pauma killed them at Cupa."

"Your father is dead," wailed Lugarda. She threw herself on the bed and clutched her daughter, racked by sobs.

By the time 'Zul returned with Señora Osuna, Lugarda had composed herself. Her mother was dressed all in black, with a black lace head shawl. She wrapped her black-gloved arms around her daughter and they cried together.

"Papi?" Lugarda asked when her mother had wiped her face with a black handkerchief.

"He doesn't believe the Indios would do such a thing, especially the Pauma. He knows Manuelito Cota and Antonio Garra. They would never kill anyone, much less a white."

"What about my brothers, his sons. You saw how easily they learned to kill."

"I told them not to join the rebels," Señora Osuna whimpered. "They killed those American boys and now Santiago is dead. All for nothing. Por nada." She began to weep.

"Maybe they're not dead. Maybe they're hiding, pretending."

"Pablo's mother would never lie about something like this. What to gain by lying? She was very sad. She told your father where to find the bodies. When it is safe, he will go with your father-in-law to bring them for a proper funeral."

"Oh, Mami . . ." Lugarda burried her head in her mother's bosom.

"If only you'd had a son." Señora Osuna held her trembling daughter. "With no heir, San Marcos will go back to the Alvarados. You'll have to come home."

Lugarda just cried harder. When she calmed, she sniffled, "I should have married Bill Marshall."

"No. That boy got the heathen he deserves. You will marry another rancher with land and cattle and a house in the pueblo. There are many who would have you."

"But I won't have any of them," Lugarda shrieked. "Not a single one of them."

"Then you should have danced less and loved your husband more." Lugarda pushed away, as her mother shook a black-gloved finger at her. "Don't think I don't know how you shirked your conjugal duties. You could have had a son by now, and be a wealthy widow."

"No, Mami, no." Lugarda lifted little Juliana to her breast. "She hurt me so much, I couldn't think of doing it again."

"You don't think. You just do it. For your own good. You have to give your husband a son. Nothing else is necessary."

" T A L K   helps," Commodore Stockton said, as General Kearny lowered himself carefully onto the edge of a wooden stool. Kearny grunted and swirled his brandy, staring into the amber whirlpool.

"It can either be a defeat or a victory, depending on how you look at it," Stockton consoled the gaunt and wounded general.

"Doesn't feel like a victory. A third of my men dead or wounded—none of theirs even scratched . . ."

"We don't just count the dead, General. It's who controls the battlefield that counts."

"In my army the dead count," Kearny shouted. "Every dead man is a defeat." He took a fierce gulp of fiery liquid. His eyes watered.

"Yes, of course. But let's put a brave face on it. You can blame the untimely charge on Captain Moore."

"Which is what that bastard marine, Gillespie, has done," Kearny swore under his breath.

"Exactly. Moore is a dead hero. We bury the blame with him. You are the courageous general, who personally came to the rescue of his ambushed troops, and in the process sustained a glorious wound."

Kearny shifted uncomfortably. He still couldn't sit properly on his stitched-up breech. He felt no glory, there or anywhere.

"And when we've won the war, no one will ever remember your little skirmish at San Pasqual." Stockton sniffed his brandy and finished it with a satisfied flourish. The general closed his eyes and sighed.

"You know Polk's named me commaander of combined forces and military governor of California," Kearny muttered, watching with one weary eye as Stockton's smugness disintegrated in a series of tiny twitches.

"What? What news . . . congratulations, General. Well, well, well. I can't wait to tell Colonel Frémont. He's already strutting the territory as though he's governor, and president is next." Stockton forced a laugh and slopped brandy into his glass with a trembling fist.

Kearny let his open eye fall shut.

46

FALLEN ACORNS

T CUPA, the snow kept coming every few days. In between was bright sunshine. Falling Star, Melones, the two children, Bill and Shadow did everything together: cooking, eating, walking in the woods, soaking in the hot springs, sewing saddlebags and blankets, making baskets and riding out in fine weather. They hunted with Shadow in the meadows, watching him slink low and stalk and bound across the snow like a gray puma. He finally caught his first rabbit, slowed by the drifts, and brought it to drop proudly at Bill's feet.

White Fox returned from Wilakalpa and No'ka sheepishly begged her forgiveness.

He said, "We all wanted, in our hearts, to see them die, even I. I just did not want to kill them here, that night, in our village. I was afraid of the consequences. In a hundred years, no such thing has happened at Cupa."

Stomping Deer, Bull Bear, Pablo and their faction had remained at Pauma to celebrate their victory, ready to repulse any retaliation the rangers might attempt.

"See how nice it is in the village without the young and restless men?" White Fox observed. "Do you notice the change? The minds of men that age are too much ruled by their testicles. They have more energy than places to put it. I am glad to have a break from their rough play."

Bill's part in the killings was never mentioned. Whether to protect him or because he was irrelevant, he wasn't sure. Either way, he was grateful.

Fear of reprisal had abated in this peaceful atmosphere. All of the Californio lancers had gone north to defend Los Angeles, where they had their hands full, with Kearny advancing from San Diego, Stockton sailing alongside and Frémont approaching with a new brigade of volunteers, double-timing south from Santa Barbara.

/ / /

N E A R the end of the second week of January, the Pauma came again to Cupa. This time it was the entire tribe, on their way to Aguanga to collect acorns. They had only been able to recover a few stray cattle and even fewer of their stolen horses. They suffered from the cold winter and lack of food. They needed acorn flour to survive.

Manuelito wanted No'ka to accompany him, for safety in numbers, but they were cozy at Cupa. No'ka was nervous about leaving home, still rattled by the sacrificial killings under his great oak. Pablo and Ladislaya begged Bill to come, but he had to work at Warner's after his long vacation. Falling Star did not want to camp in the cold with Wili. The Cupeño had plenty of food and offered to share it, but the Pauma only accepted a few sheep to drive with them in case game was scarce. Antonio Garra loaned them some mules and a few horses to help carry the nuts home.

The Pauma proceeded to Aguanga that same day, leaving behind Stomping Deer, reconciled with his father, and a few sick women and children who wanted to pass a couple of days in the healing spring. Bull Bear and ten or twelve of the young men from Cupa, who had been staying at Pauma Valley since the killings, joined the camp train. Bull Bear had a new Pauma girlfriend and wished to be with her. •

"Thinking with his balls, like I told you," laughed White Fox.

As he mounted, Pablo had leaned over and whispered to Bill, "Lugarda looks good in black. I'll tell you on our way back." He had a mischievous smile Bill was pleased to see. Pablo had been right, Bill had to admit. It did feel good to have José María Alvarado gone.

T W O mornings later, Pablo was scratching at the door, shaking and crying, screaming and wailing, bleeding and naked as the Californios had been, the afternoon of their sacrifice.

Bill dragged Pablo in and sat him by the fire, still keening at the top of his lungs. Shadow lifted his head and began to howl. Falling Star sat up, spilling Wili from her breast. Wili joined the bedlam.

"What happened?" she shouted, leaping from the cot.

Pablo couldn't speak. Wili kept whimpering. They wrapped Pablo in a double layer of fur and tried to get him to drink some water. He didn't seem to understand what they wanted him to do.

Bill poured the icy water on a shirt and squeezed it into Pablo's mouth, then lay the shirt on his face. He kept screaming. After a minute he pushed the shirt away, looked at Falling Star in recognition, and started blubbering and moaning again. He was saying something in an Indian language. She bent close to listen.

When she looked up, tears flowed from her eyes, ran down her cheeks, fell from her chin and splashed on her breast.

"All dead," she translated. "Mexicans and Cahuilla came at dawn. Just like antelope in a hunting circle—all the People slaughtered in their sleep, men, women, children."

"Ladislaya?"

Pablo looked up and screamed. Falling Star began to sob, rocking, gripping her shoulders, her face a grimace of grief.

Bill ran out the door, calling for No'ka. Dogs were barking, roused by Shadow's hellhound wail. People appeared in doorways, then in the street, shouting, running toward the house. Melones came out sleepily from her parents'. She took a look at Bill's face and ran yelling toward his open door.

The entire town erupted in screams and shouting. All the dogs set to howling bloody murder. The cacophony spread from house to house, fearful, anguished, terrifying. It rose in a powerful wave, heaving against the earth's rotation, struggling to turn back time; to push back the sun, to shove it back down below the horizon, to unhappen what had happened.

Bill could barely see. He wiped his eyes on a naked arm; no sleeve to dry his tears.

Somehow he found his horse, slumped onto his back and rode from that grief-stricken bedlam. He rode like a madman until the sound faded to nothing. Then he rode until he was too cold to stay on. He slid to the ground in Warner's yard.

Luna had to pry Bill's hands out of the horse's mane, where they clung like icy claws. He dragged his friend into the barn, dressed him in some work clothes Bill kept there, rolled him in blankets and built a little fire. He curled the trembling body around it.

Later he fetched Warner, who poured hot coffee down Bill's throat. Bill sputtered out the few words he knew, crawled into the loft and fell into an exhausted coma.

W H E N he awoke, Luna was still there. Sunlight. It was still daytime. Luna wordlessly handed him a bowl of stew. When he had eaten all of it, Luna said, "Bueno, traigo más."

Bill dozed until Luna returned with another full bowl and some biscuits. He ate those too.

"You slept a day, a night and a day." Luna said. "We went to Cupa. No'ka told us of the slaughter at Aguanga." When Bill didn't reply, he said, "The same thing happened to my people when I was ten years old."

"I thought you were Yuman." Bill was puzzled. The Yumans were a large and active tribe of warriors.

"Not Yuman. A Yuman slave. They captured me after the killing." He used the word matanza. "Only four of our people lived to be sold as slaves."

Bill lay back and closed his eyes. He didn't ever want to get up.

Luna woke him in the cold gray of evening.

"You have visitors."

Over his shoulder Bill saw Pablo, No'ka, White Fox and Falling Star.

"We've come to take you home."

White Fox spoke softly, but with authority. Pablo and Falling Star were tearful. No'ka tipped his head toward Cupa.

Like a runaway child, Bill dressed, thanked Luna and the Warners, and meekly followed them home.

Shadow gave him a full-bodied welcome, his thick tail sweeping the air, his whole frame undulating. His broad head swayed with pleasure as Bill stroked his silky ears and rumpled around his eyes.

Wili said, "Daa, daa!" when Melones handed him over. Bill squeezed him; held him so tight he squealed and Falling Star had to take him. Bill gave Melones a hug and let her voluptuousness envelop him.

And so it was in the village. The mood was somber, but there was no more crying or wailing, children played in the snow, life went on, almost as before.

The night Bill returned home, No'ka called a meeting at the hot pools. Every person in Cupa was there, immersed or standing on the banks of the stream.

"The war is over," No'ka announced. "General José Flores surrendered to Colonel Frémont at Cahuenga, near Los Angeles, on the twelfth of this month. The Mexican soldiers have agreed to hand over their weapons and return peacefully to their homes. The Americans have won."

The People stirred and whispered. There were a few cheers.

"I only want to say this," he said, when all were silent. "We are alive, and in living there is joy. If we do not feel it now, surely it will soon return, for life brings joy in as many ways as there are creatures to experience it."

"For those of us who are still angry, angry enough to kill, think of this: We were driven to slaughter the sosabitom by their cruelties. They were angered enough to kill, by our cruelty. Now some of us are ready to kill again. The end to this cycle is death for us all. There will be no more killing. Let that be understood. I have seen enough death for a lifetime. If you wish to kill someone, then take up your weapons and leave this place at once. Go do your killing elsewhere."

He looked from face to face. No one moved.

"Would that I had said that a month ago. We all feel guilty—no one more than myself. Each man knows what he could have done to alter the course of events."

Manuelito, Pablo and twenty others who had fought their way to freedom were the sole survivors of the bloodbath at Aguanga. The Garra clan had lost many, including Bull Bear. All of the Pauma still alive had come to Cupa for safety. No'ka stared at each in turn.

"But we did not. What has happened happened. No one man is to blame. No one man is without his share of responsibility. We must make peace with ourselves, with our families, with our friends, with our lives. In peace we will be receptive to the joy we forever seek."

Manuelito said, "We must also bring peace to those who died so frightfully. Our only concern is to recover and bury the bodies of our relatives and loved ones. We will need the help of the American soldiers. We cannot risk going to Aguanga alone." There were murmurs of assent.

"Kearny told Warner, that another much larger army followed his, about thirty days march in the rear. That army should be here soon. We shall ask them to escort us to Aguanga. Until then, we must be patient. There is no other force in San Diego to help us. That is all."

"Huh!" Everyone melted into the darkness.

"The Mexicans would have already known the war was lost when they attacked Aguanga—it was on the sixteenth," White Fox said to No'ka, having counted back the days.

"It matters not. The details make no difference: when or why, who did what. What matters is that we go forward, we escape from the cycle of revenge and death." No'ka crossed his arms.

"And the Cahuilla? They do not have revenge as their excuse for killing. They have no excuse. Does that not matter?" demanded White Fox. Her voice had a dangerous edge.

"Yes. Of course it does," said No'ka. "But still, we have but two choices: Go to war or let it be. We must let it be. But I will not forget."

"Nor I." She had lowered her head and covered her face with her hands. She exhaled noisily into her palms.

Falling Star caught Bill's eye. She knew her mother was thinking of Baupista. She had a vision of White Fox luring her ex-lover to a rendezvous, and slicing out his heart.

47

BURY THE HATCHET

WEEK later, the Mormon battalion dragged itself wearily out of the harshness of the desert, cut a wagon trail through the rocks of Box Canyon and entered Valle de San José. They pulled up at Warner's ranch house, fell to their knees en masse, and kissed the earth of California. There were three hundred sixty of them, as dehydrated and starved as Kearny's men had been.

This time Warner was prepared. While the battalion labored in Box Canyon moving stones to make way for the wagons, three mountain men, the advance scouts, had arrived at the ranch to announce their coming. Warner asked Bill to round up all the horses and mules he owned and bring them in to hold for sale or barter. He also cut out a hundred sheep and twenty cattle to feed the men.

The battalion arrived on the twenty-first of January 1847, hungry, thirsty, sunburned and weary but proud of their achievements. They had marched all the way from Illinois, and pulled the first wagons ever to reach California in one piece, over the southern trail from Santa Fe.

Their commander was Lieutenant Colonel Philip St. George Cooke, a Virginian and West Pointer who had been an officer in Kearny's First Dragoons. He led an all-volunteer army made up entirely of Mormons, who had been driven from their settlements in Illinois by murderous mobs, and forced to relocate further west, in Indian Territory.

President Polk, in negotiation with their leader, Brigham Young, had offered to pay the Mormons to form a battalion of five hundred men under Kearny's command. At the end of the war they would be released from service, to settle somewhere in the new territory they would conquer.

This arrangement bolstered the Army of the West and removed an embarrassing religious colony from close contact with other Americans, who resented their practices, among them multiple wives. Brigham Young used the enlisted men's advance pay to finance the trek west for the remainder of the church membership. He planned to establish a Mormon empire somewhere on the new frontier.

Colonel Cooke had taken command of the battalion at Santa Fe. He had not been pleased by the sorry state of this army. The men were trailworn from travel on foot, undisciplined, their mules broken-down. Their families, including ninety-nine women, children and feeble grandparents, had been allowed to accompany them.

Cooke was a professional soldier, with thirteen years of service on the frontier. He undertook to whip them into fighting shape. He detached the sick, the women and the children from the battalion at Santa Fe. He established discipline and chain of command, purchased new mules and marched the grumbling Mormon battalion along the grueling eleven-hundred-mile trail to California.

Now they had arrived, grateful to be alive, grudgingly respectful of their commander. Those who had cried and cursed when their families had been left behind were now praising Colonel Cooke for his foresight, and the wisdom of that decision.

They had suffered the entire way: from shortages of food and water, Indian attacks, the deaths of their animals and a bizarre charge of the wagon train by a herd of wild bulls. At the Colorado River, the ford was a mile wide and up to four feet deep. It took the men four days, working night and day, to cross it. From the crossing at Yuma to Warner's, a distance of one hundred thirty miles that took ten days, they found not one thing to eat. Only dried-up wells that required time-consuming redigging and yielded poisonous-tasting water.

At Box Canyon the scouts had declared the way impassable with wagons. By the time the Mormons had finished, the road was wide and level enough for the last wagons to be pulled through by their mules unaided, the loads undisturbed.

Warner was pleased by this breakthrough of the wagon trail. Now his ranch was truly the immigrant gateway to California. He traded horses and mules generously, mostly taking two skeletal creatures for one of his fat strong animals. He gave the soldiers all of the sheep they could eat, only asking that they save him the hides. Cattle he sold to Cooke for ten dollars each. There was a shortage and the price was going up. Cooke bought a herd to drive with his army to San Diego.

The news that the war was over in California was greeted with cheers and celebration. Cooke informed the men that they had to remain in service until the official end of the war, which was still raging in central Mexico. This did not dampen the spirits of the Mormons, happy to have avoided a fight. The unknown fate of the women and children was their big concern, but they were confident that they would soon be reunited, in Brigham Young's new Mormon state.

At the earliest opportunity, Bill asked Colonel Cooke to meet with the chiefs. He outlined briefly the situation at Aguanga. Cooke agreed to talk to them the following day.

Manuelito and Garra roused themselves from their grief sufficiently to make a dignified appearance to press their petition, accompanied by No'ka and Chapuli, with Pablo as translator. They met in Cooke's command tent— a four-sided white canvas campaign quarters, with a wooden floor in sections, a folding metal bed, a desk, chairs and a bookcase. Colonel Cooke had two sides rolled high to take in the morning sun. He sat behind his desk. The chiefs sat on folding canvas stools; Bill and Pablo stood. The Indians all wore Western dress except Chapuli. Warner had absented himself, saying he had work to do. He wanted no connection to either of the massacres or their aftermath.

When he had heard the story, Colonel Cooke slowly shook his large bearded head.

"You have suffered a terrible vengeance," he said to Manuelito. "I will be glad to help you locate and bury your dead. My scouts say the only road to San Diego passable by wagon goes through Aguanga. When the battalion has rested, you may accompany us to this place, which is along our line of march."

Manuelito thanked him.

"As to this other tribe, the Cahuilla, I would like to speak to their chief before we break camp. You say he may have prisoners. If so we must ask him to release them." Cooke looked at the men's faces while Pablo translated. They were masks of grief and concern.

The chiefs spoke quickly to Chapuli in his language. He shrugged his shoulders and said, "Yes."

"They have asked Chapuli to summon Baupista, the closest Cahuilla chief, from Anza. Chapuli has good relations with Baupista," Pablo said to Cooke in English.

"Very well," Cooke replied. "You may all be present at our meeting if you like. I would appreciate having Mister Verdi translate again."

Pablo agreed, but added, "I am not sure that we can look on this man without harming him."

Colonel Cooke stood up and slapped his desk. "You had best get used to it. The war is over here. Any killing from now on will be considered murder, and punishable as such by me."

CHAPULI rode immediately to visit Baupista, returning with him the following day. Baupista had come alone.

When they were reassembled at the tent, only Manuelito declining to attend, Colonel Cooke addressed the Cahuilla capitán.

"You have done a terrible thing to these people, who say they did you no harm," he began. Baupista was silent.

"War is war, and perhaps that may be your justification. However, the war is over. Henceforth there will be no more killing. We have won the war. I issue this order as commander of the new military government.

"You must also release any prisoners you may have taken, at Aguanga or in any other action." Cooke stared at Baupista.

Baupista looked uncomfortably around the tent as Pablo translated.

Cooke made a motion with his hands, opening them over his desk as though to say, "Well, speak up, man."

Baupista chirped quickly in his language. Pablo replied and he repeated himself. Pablo's face froze. He turned stiffly, like a statue on a pedestal—he turned toward Colonel Cooke and croaked out the cruel words: "No captives. All were killed."

Cooke looked down at his desk. Antonio Garra leapt to his feet and lunged at Baupista, who skittered out of the tent. No'ka and Chapuli wrestled Garra back to his chair. Garra was shouting unintelligibly.

"Bring him back in," Cooke said to two of his men, who held Baupista.

They pulled Baupista into the tent. Garra spit at the Cahuilla chief. No'ka and Chapuli dragged Antonio out onto the grass.

Cooke shook his finger at Baupista. "Where are the bodies of the dead?"

"We left them as they lay, at Aguanga and along the trail north toward Anza," he replied.

"These people wish to bury their dead. My army will escort them to do so tomorrow. Do not try to impede them, do not go near the dead, do not go near Aguanga," said Cooke sternly.

Baupista's expression was defiant. Cooke rose and approached the chief. The colonel was a very tall man with a large straight nose, huge black beard and a fierce expression. He was a foot and a half taller than Baupista.

"To defy my orders would be very, very foolish, Mister Baupista," said

Cooke. "I have a large and well-armed force who have not yet had a chance to fight. If I were to give the order, they would chase you to the end of this land, killing your people as they went, to finally catch you, to return you to my presence for execution by hanging.

"That is the order I will give, if you so much as harm a single soul. Bury the hatchet, or I will bury you with it. That is my promise to you."

Pablo translated this warning, making it more terrible in the translation. Baupista became nervous and glanced fearfully at the soldiers.

"If you keep the peace, so shall I," said Cooke, sitting back down. He appeared to be satisfied. "Do you understand?" he asked.

Pablo translated quickly. Baupista nodded his head. "Sí," he said in Spanish.

"Very well, thank you for your cooperation." Cooke walked over to shake Baupista's hand. He also shook the hands of the rest of the natives. Baupista left the tent and immediately rode off with Chapuli.

"We will strike camp at seven tomorrow morning. You may ride with us. My men will help you to collect and bury the dead," the colonel said to Pablo, in a kindly voice. "We would appreciate some guidance on the road to San Diego if it can be arranged."

"Of course, sir," Pablo replied humbly. "I will be honored to show you the way myself."

V U L T U R E S circled overhead as the escort battalion approached Aguanga. Fifty coyotes slunk away to watch, when the column drew to a halt. Bodies were spread over a couple of acres of ground, around their last campsite under a great oak. They were in varying states of decomposition, from perfectly preserved and clothed, as though killed yesterday, to torn to pieces and eaten to the bone by coyotes. It had been two weeks since they died.

All of the surviving Pauma had come, and about half the village of Cupa. People ran here and there trying to find their loved ones, tears staining their faces. When found, the bones, or parts, would be cradled and carried to a place where the Mormons began to dig a long trench. There they were laid tenderly to rest while the search continued for a brother or sister, mother, husband or lover.

Big Bull Bear and his new girlfriend were lying together on their robes under the oak. They had not even risen to defend themselves. Bull Bear's stomach had been eaten by coyotes and one arm chewed to the bone. Ants crawled from his eyes.

The woman was missing her guts and most of both legs. Her family had all been killed. Stomping Deer and Bill carried their remains to the common grave and gently laid them on the dark brown, almost black earth.

No one dared look at anyone else for fear of breaking down. People quietly sobbed, sitting on the ground, invisible, withdrawn into an inner world of grief. The Mormon shovelers were crying, the men holding the nervous mules were crying. Colonel Cooke sat against the oak's trunk with his head bowed. Pablo was talking to his mother as though she were still alive. Manuelito lay beside his wife until it seemed he too might be dead. Stomping Deer walked in circles, muttering prayers and singing to himself. Everywhere, the tears flowed.

There was little noise, almost none of the keening and wailing that was the norm in the case of death. That had been done. The Christians prayed, crossed themselves and fingered their rosaries. The sympathetic presence of hundreds of soldiers helped to calm the natural tendency to hysteria.

Antonio Garra and his son had ridden up the trail toward Anza to look for more bodies. About a half mile from the campsite they found another twenty dead, close together, some piled on top of each other. These were the captives, the old men, women and children that the Cahuilla had slain—for want of a better plan for their future. Colonel Cooke dispatched a wagon and a detail of men to bring them back.

The Garras rode with the corpses, Antonio's hands speaking to their spirits. On the mesa, those bodies had been exposed to the full sun. They smelled so foul that they were hastily dumped in the trench and covered with earth. The soldiers drove the sullied wagon into the creek to scrub it with wet brooms and buckets of water.

At the grave, no one could speak a word of ceremony. Even No'ka shook his head. Manuelito had to be forcibly separated from his dead wife. He was raving. He couldn't even look at Ladislaya. Someone put him on a horse and took him to Cupa. Pablo knelt in the trench, whispering to his mother as spades of earth thudded into the grave. All else was silence, but for the cawing crows.

White Fox finally roused herself. She picked up two handfuls of acorns and threw them into the trench.

"This grove has been sacred to the People since time began," she said in clear ringing tones. "It has provided the food that nourished us, generation after generation. I wondered how so many could die at once here, in a place so beloved, so much a part of us. I wondered how we could ever return to this place, that we must return to, if we are to live. I wondered what kind of God would do such a thing to his people.

"The gods used to demand sacrifices: blood in return for their favor. For a long time they have forgotten the taste of blood, and declined to ask for it. Now, with all the killing in our land, the appetite for blood has returned. The gods demand their share. And we have given it to them. We have paid for all we have taken from these great oaks, over the years, and years, with the blood of our loved ones.

"Let us ask that a new grove of oaks grow here, where we have buried our friends; a grove nourished by their very flesh and blood and bone; a grove that will give food and shelter to us for generations to come; a grove where we may commune with the spirits of those who gave their lives; a peaceful, life-giving grove; a grove of beauty and enchantment; a sacred grove.

"Let us sow the seeds of this new life—seeds of life to be nourished by death."

White Fox threw in another handful of acorns. Everyone solemnly followed her example. The long trench was filled. The Mormons tromped the earth hard with their boots. They planted a cross they had fashioned from two oars they carried with them.

White Fox's speech had rallied the People. They left the grove as clean as they always left it after a camp. All the Paumans' belongings had been buried with them, furs, shoes, bows and arrows, lances, baskets, tools, clothing, bridles. Every last scrap of human detritus was under the neat mound with the oar cross.

Colonel Cooke said goodbye. He saluted the chiefs. The kind army marched west, Pablo at its head, his face a blank mask of despair.

48

CATTLE BARONS

EVERYBODY was weeping.

Lugarda wept for her dead husband and for herself.

'Zul wept for her mother and Ladislaya. She wept for Pablo and cursed him through her tears.

The Osunas wept for their son and brother Santiago.

Leandro wept when he rode into San Diego to turn in his lance, with its Yankee-blood-stained pennant; to surrender it to Captain Gillespie; to salute his new ruler.

Captain Archibald Gillespie wept in anger and frustration at the sight of his own blood displayed so brazenly. He tongued the hole in his jaw. He fingered the disfiguring scar on his cheek. He jerked the lance from Leandro's hand and he cursed it and broke it over his knee. He made a bonfire of broken lances in the plaza.

General Stephen Watts Kearny wept because General José Flores had surrendered to Colonel John C. Frémont—instead of giving the honor to him, the supreme commander of the Army of the West.

Colonel John C. Frémont wept because President Polk had named Kearny governor—instead of awarding him, the conqueror of California.

Admiral Stockton wept because he had been trumped by the French colonel and the Irish governor—army men.

The Picos wept because they had lost everything: the war, the governorship and possibly their land.

Stomping Deer wept for his friend and brother, Big Bull Bear.

Falling Star too wept for Bull Bear. The village felt empty without him.

Manuelito wept for his wives and his people and the land and his own trembling.

Pablo wept until there was nothing left of him. He was a hollow man, an empty shell, washed up on the beach with nobody inside—washed clean by salty tears, beautiful and dead.

White Fox had had enough of weeping. "Eventually death must lead to life. Seeing friends and family die, horrible as it is, only makes me feel more strongly how good it is to be alive."

"How good it is to be alive," she said to anyone who came to her to cry.

And soon it was so.

M A N U E L I T O was the exception. He insisted on returning alone to Pauma Valley. He cared not whether he lived or died. The others took up life where they had left off, the day Kearny and his skeletal army had appeared, like tattered ghosts rising on heat waves from the desert, only two short months ago.

California had changed as radically as a world could change in a few months. The armies of Kearny, Frémont and Cooke totaled more than a thousand men. The navy had another thousand. Two thousand men doubled the nonnative population of southern California. More men arrived every day, all hungry. Coupled with the disruption of production by the war, there was a desperate shortage of all food and an insatiable demand for beef. In the same moment, the hide trade resumed, under the naval protection of Commodore Stockton. The price of cattle soon jumped to fifty dollars a head.

Warner and the Cupeño organized a drive of steers to San Diego, to capitalize on the high prices before the coastal herds could be replenished. A trip to La Playa would have to be much slower now, to match the pace of grazing cattle. They couldn't be pushed. They would lose too much weight.

The route they chose was exactly the same as Kearny's march: through Santa Ysabel to Santa María, down by San Pasqual to Rancho Bernardo, then to Sorrento Valley and on through Rose Canyon to False Bay and the pueblo of San Diego. There was good pasture along the way and only one short passage with a steep narrow trail, on the descent to San Pasqual.

After Pablo had led Cooke's Mormon battalion to San Diego, he had returned to San Luis Rey, to the care of Father Ibarra. Bill sent Pablo a letter asking him to join the drive or meet them at La Playa, to help with the selling. Pablo did not reply.

Falling Star wanted to come, or she didn't want Bill to go. The war had made her insecure. Having so many Americans around, seeing him chatting happily in English, too rapidly for her to understand, made her nervous. She wanted to keep him at home, with her, away from the corrupting influences she imagined lurked in San Diego, including the widow Lugarda.

But Bill had to go. No one else could deal with the Americans. Warner didn't dare show his face in San Diego just yet—even if Anita had been willing to release the chain with which she had John securely linked to home. And this was man's work in a man's world, potentially rough and dangerous. Bill wanted his wife safe in Cupa with her family.

He appealed to No'ka and White Fox. Eventually Falling Star relented, after eliciting a promise from Stomping Deer to watch her husband, and from Antonio Garra and Tonio to watch over both of them.

In the middle of March the men departed, driving eighty head of cattle. The first day was spent crossing the great valley. It was spring: the grass green and tender, the air crisp in morning, warm at noon and chill again at night. The steers grazed all through the midday, walking morning and evening. It was a lazy way to travel, with lots of slouching in the saddle, or lying in the sun watching the animals chew. They saw very few cattle at any of the ranches, and watched theirs closely to make sure none strayed.

Bill had worried about taking the herd on the narrow trail to San Pasqual, but it proved to be the easiest part of the drive. With nothing to chew on and nowhere to stray, the cattle filed placidly down the valley to San Pasqual one by one—just as Kearny's men had galloped into battle, to be cut down before their trailing comrades even knew a fight was in progress.

Pablo was waiting at the ranchería of San Pasqual. He looked thin but rested, recovered from his ordeal. When Garra told him this, he laughed.

"Thank you for saying so. When I confessed to Father Ibarra, he emerged from the booth with a worried expression. He said, 'My son, I cannot absolve you of sins such as those you have committed. Only our Lord Jesus Christ or God himself may do so. Nor shall I assign you penance, for you have paid threefold in sorrow for each and every sin. Do not expect to recover in this lifetime from the blows you have given and received.'

"That was the low point of my life. Strangely, it was also a beginning. Somehow . . . the conviction that I would never recover allowed me to accept these few horrible months as part of my life; a permanent part of my life, but in the past. I sensed that the joys of living were still there to be tasted."

Pablo chuckled. A little gray showed in his whiskers where they met his hairline.

"The father's good wines are one of those pleasures. His library is another. Tormenting the Mexicans is a third. The company of the widow Lugarda shall be a fourth. We will see her soon, I hope," he said cheerily.

"How does 'Zul take it all?" Bill gestured widely.

Every pretense of happiness vanished from Pablo's face.

"Badly," he said, hanging his head. "'Zul blames me for the deaths of her master, her mother and my mother. She is correct in doing so. I cannot defend myself. She has refused to see me." Pablo seemed to shrink, the weight of guilt bending him like an old man.

"Thank you for meeting us," Bill said quickly. "We need your help. I so wanted to see you." He hugged Pablo. Stomping Deer also embraced him.

"We needn't be long in San Diego," Garra told him as they mounted. "We will ride with you back to the mission when we have sold the cattle."

They left two fat beeves with the Kumeyaay at San Pasqual and drove the herd west toward San Dieguito. Pablo insisted this way was easier, with better pasture.

"And we can infuriate the Osunas by passing through their land. It is perfectly safe. When I rode into San Diego at the head of the Mormon battalion, there were twenty men who would have killed me, the friends and relatives of those we slew. At that time I would have been happy to kill them too. Colonel Cooke protected me from this madness. As we are now protected. Cooke gave them the same lecture he gave to Baupista. To touch us is the surest way I know to get hanged."

Pablo turned to Bill.

"The Americans would love to have an excuse to execute the Osunas. Leandro brags of the three dragoons they killed at San Pasqual. When he surrendered his bloody pennant, only an order from Kearny prevented Gillespie and his marines from slaying Leandro on the spot."

"Are the Mormons still here?"

"Yes. They have taken over the pueblo. They've cleaned it up, buried the trash, redug the wells by the river, repaired all the fences, built corrals to keep the bulls from meandering through the plaza, set up a sawmill and brick factory and are building the first brick buildings. These men are like the padres, true Christians. As long as they are here, we are safe."

They traversed the Osuna ranch without incident, stopping for half a day to allow the cattle to graze. There were riders in the distance, but they never challenged. The herd reached San Diego the next evening.

A cool March wind blew in from the west. Only a few clouds hugged the horizon, waiting for the sun to set them ablaze as it sank into the blue-tinged sea.

The Garras and Stomping Deer, who wished to be called Jacobo while in town, went to La Playa, where they would wait. They were nervous about the Californios connecting them with the killing of the eleven at Cupa.

Bill and Pablo led the cattle to the mission, where the padre set them to graze in a fenced field. They bathed, donned clean clothes and rode to the pueblo. Bill wore a short leather jacket of thick cow skin with rawhide thong stitching. White Fox and Falling Star had sewn it together. It was warm and very flexible. The hair had been scraped off and many applications of sage-scented tallow applied, to soften and waterproof it. He felt protected in this jacket. It was like an extra layer of tough flexible skin. Wool jackets did not impart the same secure feeling.

They first visited the neatly ordered rows of tents that comprised the Mormon battalion's camp, in a sandy area between the pueblo and the river, running high and muddy from melted snow and rain. The quartermaster quickly bought forty cattle for forty dollars each. When the money was counted, sixteen hundred silver dollars, Pablo and Bill could barely keep from jumping for joy. They lugged the heavy saddlebag to the horses.

They rode directly to Fitch's store. Bill and Pablo both ignored the Alvarado adobe. They did not see Lugarda or her brothers. Everyone they did meet was polite and friendly. There were no murderous looks.

"They're thinkin' about food," Fitch said. "And half the people here are glad you killed those rebel Mexicans. Everyone knows about Aguanga. There is no reason not to be friendly." He motioned toward the American camp. "The rulers of California are there in those tents. Every goddamned Mexican in California is on his best behavior. But don't go mistakin' manners for affection."

Henry Fitch was a large man, heavy of head, gruff and vulgar. He had come to San Diego as a ship's captain, and he carried that same blustering authority on land, in his store. But no one feared Fitch, for his imposing persona was somehow tinged with tenderness. You could see it in his delicate handling and display of South Sea Island craftwork, collected on his trading voyages; in the way he entered his accounts in fine clear flourishes of an ink-dipped quill; in his continuing affection for his wife, Josefa, an incorrigible gambler, whose debts he always paid in full, with an embarrassed oath.

Bill paid Fitch eight hundred dollars on Warner's account. Fitch took ten cattle for himself, for four hundred dollars, and the other four hundred in silver. Pablo bought sugar, coffee, tea and some Spanish port for Father Ibarra.

At La Playa, they planned to sell the last of the cattle to the navy. Pablo looked to find Lieutenant Edward Beale, but Beale had been rewarded for his bravery at San Pasqual with the honor of riding to Washington, D.C., with Kit Carson, carrying dispatches that announced the successful conquest of California.

The navy wanted all the beef they had. "Can't tell you how sick we are of stringy mutton," the purveyor told Pablo. "Those sheep you brought must have walked all the way from La Paz. When we took the filthy wool off'a them, there was nothing left for the cooks but gristle and bone."

"Let's hold back two steers for the girls," Bill said to Pablo.

"What girls?" Pablo shot back. But he sold all but two.

That night was spent with the Kanakas, who had taken in the Garras and Jacobo. These jolly men always had the best supper in San Diego. They produced a half-eaten piglet, put it back on the spit, and served up succulent pork with beans and tortillas. The little guitars came out to serenade the visitors to sleep.

B I L L had seen a tin bathtub at Fitch's store that he wanted to buy for Falling Star. The Garras were anxious to spend some of their silver dollars too, so they returned to the pueblo in the morning. Bill got the tub, a sharp hatchet for No'ka and a bolt of red and white checked flannel for White Fox. For Melones he bought a deep purple silk scarf from China. A set of tin buckets that fit inside each other was for Shadow's water, so he didn't have to go to the stream all the time. Shadow drank a lot, his big shovel of a tongue curling under to slurp the water down his throat.

While they were in Fitch's store, Pablo stood outside, talking to some of the Mormon soldiers, keeping an eye on the Alvarado and Osuna houses, hoping for a glimpse of 'Zul or Lugarda. But it was Leandro Osuna who emerged from his father's house and crossed the square toward Fitch's.

"Here we go," Fitch said to Bill. "This should be fun."

When Leandro drew near, Pablo called out to him.

"Leandro," he said, loudly enough to be heard inside the store. "Leandro Osuna, I'd like you to meet some of the men from Cooke's battalion." To the men he said, "Leandro was one of Pico's lancers at San Pasqual. He claims he killed three dragoons himself that morning."

In the awkwardness that followed, the dragoons touched their hats. Leandro touched his. He opened his mouth to speak but no words issued forth. The soldiers looked at the ground. Leandro turned. With a "Con permiso," and another touch to his hat, he began to retrace his steps.

"Cuidado, pendejo," said Pablo softly.

"Careful, asshole," was as close as Fitch could get in translation.

Leandro's right foot paused in midair as he absorbed this insult, but he put it down and kept moving, stiff as a dog before a fight.

"Fuckin' hell, Le can strut that rooster strut." Fitch flapped his elbows and did a fat man's imitation of Leandro.

Leandro kept walking, disappearing around the side of his house.

Bill nervously paid and they lugged their goods out to the horses. But no horse would carry the tub and buckets. At the mission he borrowed a pack mule to load with all of the purchases. Pablo instructed the padre as to the disposal of the cattle. They rode north immediately, wishing to be at San Luis Rey before dark.

They were traveling light now, and light of heart, swiftly up El Camino Real, retracing the route of Bill's initial trip with Pablo three years ago. At midday he was telling the story of their feast of seafood at Encinitas. It made the Garras and Stomping Deer ravenous, so they detoured to the coast on a trail that ran along the side of San Elijo Lagoon.

Just as the horses entered the beach and turned north to hug the narrow shore, a small flock of gulls rose to wheel low over their heads, crying distressfully. They kept circling, only a few feet above. Antonio Garra said, "Aca," and pointed to where a seagull lay, too sick or wounded to rise. The bird was well hidden, its gray and white color blending perfectly with the sand.

"Pobrecito," Pablo muttered. They looked at each other in sympathy. The cries of the dying gull's fluttering companions pierced their ears, with the same mournful and inconsolable tones the men themselves had so recently uttered. And forgotten. In the happiness of a good sale, presents bought, a fine ride and the thought of a great meal, they had forgotten. The sun was still out, the way still beautifully lit by reflections on the water, on the flecks of fool's gold that glinted in moist sand, and on the pale pink cliffs. But now they rode in somber silence, hunger forgotten, enveloped in their own dark cloud of remembrance, oblivious to the joy and beauty of their surroundings, that knew not the measure of mortality.

At the mission, their spirits revived. The Garras, like Pablo, had been educated there. Father Ibarra was so excited to see them, to find them alive and well, that all were soon laughing and exclaiming, infected by his delight. Jacobo shyly watched the friar's every move.

Father Ibarra took the Garras to the confessional, while Jacobo, Pablo and Bill relaxed in the corridor with a glass of pink wine. They sipped in silent communion until the confessees returned, visibly cheered by their absolvement and the kindness of the padre.

Pablo stayed at San Luis Rey, where he felt he could be of most use, and keep out of mischief. He refused any money from the cattle sale. At the mission they led a simple life and had no need to buy anything. He wished his share to go to the Pauma who had remained at Cupa.

Manuelito expressed a similar wish, when they visited him in the otherwise deserted village at Pauma Valley. He had been able to recover the nucleus of a cattle herd, visiting neighboring ranches to locate Pauma-branded stock, and beating the brush for strays. He had even climbed the slopes of Palomar to search the meadows of that high country. There he had found few cattle, but did observe some game waiting out the war. The more easily accessible countryside, which had teemed with animals only a year ago, was now barren.

Manuelito gave the Garras a fine bull and five pregnant cows to drive to Cupa. The bull was huge and unruly, requiring constant vigilance to keep him moving on the trail, and to avoid a goring by his sweeping horns. Garra named him Pico, after the reckless ex-governor.

The rest of 1847 passed in peace and the pastoral pursuit of animal husbandry. Cattle were king in California. Land ownership questions were postponed until the end of the war in Mexico and establishment of a civil government—so whoever owned cattle grazed them where the grass was best—and the prices kept climbing. Pico the bull proved to be a greedy and prolific sire for the herds of Valle de San José, once he had established his dominance. Everyone grew fat and happy.

General Kearny deserved credit for this good year—a year that had begun with so much violence. His military governorship began with the court-martial of Colonel John C. Frémont, for mutiny and insubordination, establishing the tone of impartial discipline that he demanded of his troops. The conduct of civilians was expected to be equally obedient and corruption-free.

Kearny named Fitch as alcalde in San Diego and appointed Antonio Garra to be commander in chief of the various Luiseño tribes. The mostly ceremonius honor went to Garra because of his mission education, because he had impressed Kearny at the Santa Ysabel powwow, and for his leadership in killing the Mexicans at Cupa—which Garra was bold enough to claim credit for, and Kearny too discreet to mention. It was more enemy dead than the general could claim for his entire campaign. The deliberateness of that act, and the fact that a number of tribes were involved in the decision, had demoralized the Californios, outnumbered as they were by natives they now knew would not hesitate to slaughter them, if given half the chance.

At Aguanga, the tribes had paid in blood for this crucial pledge of allegiance. Governor Kearny was grateful, and he treated his wartime allies accordingly. When Alcalde Fitch decided against Warner, in a dispute with the Cupeño over some horses, and Warner refused to comply, Kearny was quick to back Fitch's decision with his military muscle. After the chaos of war and the last years of haphazard Mexican government, these were welcome changes, even for those more naturally partial to lawless ways.

Four

VANDALS IN

PARADISE

49

THE GOLD RUSH

COLONEL Frémont's been convicted," Commodore Stockton told Juan Bandini. "That'll be the end of Kearny's career. Frémont's father-in-law is on the Senate's most powerful committees—with President Polk in the palm of his hand. Kearny will be punished. He'll be gone before they sign the treaty with Mexico. You can bet on it."

"That would be a shame. Kearny's done a good job here. Great job if you ask me. Frémont disobeyed his commanding general. He had to be disciplined. What can the president do?"

"Whatever he is forced to do—by gold and politics."

"Do you mean the gold they found at Sacramento?"

"Washington politics, California gold. The gold is reason enough to remove Kearny. Can't have him governor of all those promising riches. That was to be Frémont's reward . . . or mine."

Gold was discovered on the twenty-fourth of January 1848, Frémont convicted on the thirty-first of the same month. The verdict was upheld by President Polk; sentence commuted. Polk signed the treaty with Mexico at Guadalupe Hidalgo on the twenty-first of February 1848. The next week, Kearny was transferred from California to Veracruz, Mexico, where he contacted yellow fever. Polk appointed him military governor of Mexico City in May. Kearny withdrew from Mexico in July with the last of the U.S. troops, ordered to return to his old command, the Sixth Military Department, Fort Leavenworth, Kansas—a demotion. Exiled to the prairie dog plains, Kearny was finished.

NEWS of the treaty with Mexico and the discovery of gold had come to Cupa together, engendering great celebration. All of Alta California was ceded to the United States. The new border ran from the bottom of Texas to the Pacific Ocean at the mouth of the Ti Juan River, about forty miles south of San Diego.

"We're just inside, and we'll be rich," predicted John Trumbull Warner, happy to be American again. He still planned to make his pile selling goods to the immigrants. No one knew how big the gold strike would be, but every treasure seeker and settler who arrived by the southern trail would have to pass by Warner's well-stocked trading post. Bill Marshall would be the store-keeper who collected their money.

Inspired by Antonio Garra and Manuelito, the Cupeño and Pauma strat-egy for prosperity was to raise more cattle. They had the pastureland, they had Pico, the huge and insatiable bull. Demand for his progeny could only grow.

While Kearny was dying of yellow fever, the gold rush roared into south-ern California with the sudden force of a flash flood. The Cupeño dream that the Spanish/Mexican *sosabitom* would disappear with the U.S. conquest, drowned in the first great wave of miners. As news of extravagant gold discov-eries in California spread south, the Mexicans of Sonora and other nearby states began to flow north, up the old Anza Trail that led right by Warner's and Cupa. Four or five thousand Mexicans passed through before the sum-mer of 1848. Pío Pico hadn't been able to raise a single company of patriots to defend his territory during the war. In July he swept back to California in an unending river of gold-crazed Mexicans.

Pico's return was an ill omen. He symbolized everything despicable about the Spanish colonial: ruthless ambition and greed; exploitation and intoler-ance of the natives; corruption; the crookedness and penury of the habitual gambler. But the sheer numbers and poverty of the few thousand other Mex-icans that passed through the valley reduced Pico's impact to that of a pin-prick.

Arriving poor and hungry, thirsty and exhausted, they stole every horse, mule or donkey they could catch, ate cattle and sheep without bothering to ask, drove off or killed any game that they sighted, carelessly lit the grass with their camp fires, and bought nothing from Warner's store. These weren't the immigrants John had envisioned.

Thankfully, in their haste to make it to the riches of northern California, no one stayed long. But groups of ten or twenty men passed by every day in the first Mexican wave of 1848. Bill was forced to keep a twenty-four-hour watch on John's cattle, sheep and horses—the Cupeño did the same.

Parties of curious and desperate men endlessly trooped through the village—there were almost no women among the Mexican miners. All men came armed, so the villagers were constantly ready with guns, bows and spears. Most visitors simply looked and rode on. Many stopped to pray in the chapel, which was well maintained by the Christians. Others lingered, a threat in their manner. They stared rudely at young girls and muttered murderously when confronted by a naked man. Nudity to the Mexicans was the height of ill manners and whoredom. A naked Indio was a savage to be used or killed. To these men, No'ka showed the readiness of his force, deterring even the bandits and escaped convicts among the miners—who were only in California to prey on the natives and those lucky souls who struck it rich.

The Cupeño had no rest in the summer and fall of '48. In November came the disheartening news of Kearny's death from yellow fever. California was desperately in need of a strong military leader. No one of equal talent had replaced him. Frémont, the only other competent officer, had resigned from the army. After Kearny's departure, most of his soldiers had deserted to the gold fields. There was virtually no one to enforce military law, the only law they had.

As the year progressed, California descended into chaos, anarchy and madness. Lawlessness spread south from the gold fields like a plague. Murderous greed superseded all other emotions. Men fought for claims, the tools to dig them, the gold they found, food and supplies, space to put their tents, and for the few women who followed the mining camps. There were gangs of robbers who never even bothered to dig. Vigilante mobs of miners hunted down and hanged the robbers.

By the end of 1848, in a country of thirty-five hundred non-Indian Californios, thirty-five thousand migrant men searched madly for the golden nuggets. By the end of 1849, two hundred thousand were at the gold fields. It was impossible for any Californian to imagine such an invasion. One year it was a peaceful, pastoral, sparsely populated country with a couple of ships visiting each month. The next year miners were elbow to elbow for hundreds of miles, half of them drunk with joy and riches, the other half desperately digging, bitterly jealous, or broke and starving, freezing through a snowbound winter. And nine of ten were men, many of whom didn't speak English or Spanish.

The few Americans the Cupeño had met before '48 were mainly mountain men, adventurers and explorers, accustomed to living among Indians, and even married to them. Warner and Bill were not atypical. At the very least there was tolerance of the People among the frontiersmen; some understanding and never any fear.

When the armies had come, they were under such strict discipline that even if there had been rougher elements, who may have hated and feared the natives, the Cupeño and other tribes were never molested. On the contrary, they had been aided by the soldiers and had good relations with their commanders. Kearny, Cooke and Frémont were always mentioned with affection and respect in every Indian ranchería.

Now they met another breed of American. As the desert had cooled down in the fall of '48, trains of Americans began to arrive at the valley, by way of the Santa Fe Trail. They were tough, poor and uneducated; either pioneers, used to killing and being killed by the warlike frontier Indians, or city folks, whose only knowledge of Indians came from novellas and wild newspaper accounts of massacres and scalpings. Loutish gangs of city boys joined mongrel hayseed packs, to pool their savings—coins stolen from a mother's pin-money jar or grandma's mattress—to finance the trek west. And among them came outright outlaws, thugs and convicts with many names and many schemes of greed and mayhem.

Every man carried a rifle or pistol. Some told stories of fights with the Indians along the trail. The Apaches, Comanches, Pawnee and Yumans especially delighted in picking off stragglers, stealing horses and livestock and frightening the invaders. The migrants had come prepared to defend the golden treasure they were certain would soon be theirs. In the meantime the guns were used for hunting, settling disputes and shooting Indians.

BILL'S days of riding the range, watching the cattle and sheep graze, overseeing the planting of corn and wheat, were over. There were so many people arriving daily that the store needed a permanent man, and Warner was always busy, or gone on his frequent buying trips.

Bill was usually first to greet the thirsty, half-starved and sunburnt men as they dragged themselves into the ranch yard and wearily dropped their reins, packs, rifles and all else they carried to embrace the good California soil.

Bill had a pat speech about the friendly local Indians. He would offer them native guides to show them through the valley to Temecula and the road to Los Angeles.

"If I collected a dollar for every time I heard someone say, 'I'll shoot any Injun comes near me or my horse,' I could buy a chunk of Warner's ranch and built a ten-foot-high stone fence around Cupa," he told his wife. "That is what it would take to protect us from the menace of these ruffians."

There were constant confrontations in the valley over livestock. Most commonly the starved and wasted stock of the immigrants would mix with the local herds and then have to be separated on departure. This was hard work, required cooperation, and disturbed the feeding animals. Often Warner had traded good horses or mules for two exhausted counterparts. It was up to the Indians of Cupa, who did all of his range work, to make sure that the right horses and cattle—as well as the correct numbers—went north with the proper owner.

On the fenceless range, with a daily stream of men arriving and departing, this was impossible. The sight of an armed and half-naked group of Indians galloping up to check their mules and horses set the southerners on edge. There were arguments in broken English or Spanish. There was gunfire. There was spontaneous unprovoked gunfire.

By December of '48, seven Indians had been killed on the range. They didn't dare retaliate. The wartime killings at Cupa and Aguanga were one thing. This was another. It was peacetime, but an increasingly lawless peace. The valley desperately needed a military garrison to police the migrants.

O N E very chilly December afternoon three men, brothers from Missouri, dirty and bearded, dressed in ragged farm clothes and beat-up boots, bought a bottle of brandy and sat on Warner's stoop, passing the jug and talking about the ranch they would buy when they struck it rich.

When the liquor was gone the men wandered off toward their tent, presumably to sleep off the drunk, sheltered from the cold. Before they had time to pass out, someone mentioned the hot springs, and off they rode for a visit to the baths.

When they arrived at the spring, White Fox and Falling Star were lying in the pools with Wili. No one else was with them, but many were near. The village dogs snarled and barked at the men and Shadow growled, but White Fox called them off. She and Falling Star ignored the intruders.

One of the brothers said, "That's for me, boys." He tied his horse to a branch, stripped naked and went to one of the pools. It was scalding hot. The next one he tried was freezing. While the others laughed he went from pool to pool and finally plopped with a big splash into White Fox and Falling Star's shallow sandy pond.

"This one's just right, I reckon," he said. "And the company's purty good too."

He winked at White Fox and called to his brothers, "Come on in, boys, there's beaver in this 'ere pond. An' I got just the bait they can't resist."

He stood up and waved his penis, which hung limp, at the women. The brothers laughed and began to strip.

Falling Star grabbed Wili and headed for the bank. White Fox dodged the man in the pool and followed, picking up a bucket she had brought to take water back to the house. The man grabbed the bucket handle and held it. "Wait a minute," he said. "We gon' have some fun." White Fox pulled, but couldn't get the bucket away.

Shadow had been watching, growling deep in his throat. He launched himself from the bank, taking the wet man by the shoulder without touching down, driving him across some rocks with his momentum, to smash him into one of the ice-cold pools. He held the man underwater, shaking his big head to drive his teeth deeper, ripping flesh and cartilage.

Falling Star yelled, "Shadow, Shadow, leave him alone."

The brother closest to Falling Star called out, "Get the rifles." The third sibling, who was nearest the horses, ran back, chased by White Fox's little pack of dogs, led by Casimiro, a compact, black and white beagle type with brown eyebrows.

"Get him, Casi," screamed White Fox. "Sombra!"

Shadow let go and left his man bleeding in the pool.

The running man still had his pants on. With Casimiro pulling at his leg he leaped on a horse, reaching for a rifle kept in a scabbard tied to the saddle. Shadow came bounding across the gravel bank, taking seven or eight feet with every stride. Six feet from the horse, he rose like a demon-dog from hell, his powerful hind legs thrusting his hundred and forty pounds skyward with no pause in forward motion. He hit the rider chest high, carrying him across the second horse, and plowing him into the third. All three equines screamed and bucked in panic.

Shadow let go and ran from the churning hooves. The yelling and barking and howls of pain had alerted the village. A group of boys tackled the second brother, before the dogs could get to him. Women pulled the mangled man from the icy pool. Falling Star collected the guns; someone caught the horses. The men were stripped, tied, hands behind their back, and led from the village.

Stomping Deer, who had come late to the ruckus, helped the terrified Missourians to mount. Blood dripped from the arm of one man and stained the chest of another. No'ka stood silently as riders led the three now sober men back down the trail toward Warner's. Not one word had been said. When they were out of hearing, Shadow accepted praise and thumps on the shoulder, his golden eyes and cocked ears still following the enemy riders.

Standing orders from No'ka and Warner were to remove any men involved in incidents immediately, either sending them on their way north to Los Angeles, or back to the trading post. They didn't want other trigger-happy migrants thinking they needed to rescue a fellow traveler from the hands of the savages at Cupa.

When the dejected trio arrived back at the store, there were a few minutes of commotion as explanations were heard and weighed by Warner. Then he passed judgment.

"You're lucky they didn't feed you to the dogs then and there," he told them. "Get some sleep and hit the trail in the morning. Don't stop anywhere near the hot springs. Keep your pants on. All of you," he said to the little crowd that had gathered. There were a few chuckles.

Warner gave their rifles to another group of miners that would be following the brothers north, with instructions to return them when they reached Los Angeles. He poured brandy on the two bitten men's wounds and gave them some clean cotton cloth for bandages. In Valle de San José, in the absence of the army, justice had gone to the dogs.

THAT evening, after dinner, No'ka sat on his front porch and beat his drum until all of his tribesmen were assembled, shuffling in the cold air.

"These cabrones are going to kill us all unless we take immediate measures. We cannot fight hordes of treasure-crazed men. There are too many of them to count and more arrive every day. We must take action to protect ourselves.

"From now on, until the immigration ends, we must dress as the Americans do. That will protect us from random shootings. We will take the example of Pablo Verdi, who uses costume as armor against his enemies. If he can be accepted as an American, so may we be.

"The price of cattle has risen to nearly two hundred dollars in gold per head. We can afford to dress as we please. Bi' will go with Stomping Deer and the Garras to San Diego to buy the clothing we need. We will ask Pablo to help."

There were murmurs of approval. In the middle of winter, clothing sounded like a good idea.

"The second thing we must do is learn English. The many men who pass us by, fortunately, do not tarry. But neither do they have time to learn our words. Spanish will not do. English is the language of America. Tonight we will all learn four important words. Most of you know them."

He paused and looked at Falling Star, who nodded.

"My daughter will teach us. Everyone must learn."

Falling Star stepped forward. "Good morning," she said, pointing to the east. "Good morning," echoed the crowd. "Good afternoon," she said arcing her arm across the sky to the west. "Good afternoon," they repeated. "Goodbye," she said, waving. "Goodbye," they said, waving. She said firmly, "No thank you." She wagged her finger. They all mimicked her, "No thank you."

"We must build a bathhouse for visitors," said No'ka. "It will be screened from view. We will charge one dollar to use the bath. This will keep most men out, but in a very American way. This is the idea of Bi', who says Warner recommended it. I am willing to try this plan.

"The bathhouse will be for the privacy of visitors. When visitors are here, we will refrain from bathing in the nude so as not to offend or excite them. There will be no consorting with the miners."

The crowd joked and grumbled.

"We will try to live with these barbarians—common American folk—as Warner calls them. We must adopt their ways, at least outwardly, if we are to have any peace. Otherwise they will bury us."

"We should drive them from our lands," Stomping Deer shouted angrily.

"How do you propose to do that?" asked No'ka. "And where are our lands? That is a question only the American president can answer."

"Our lands are here, where we sleep. We are Kuupiaxchem. We know our home," Stomping Deer cried, with the crowd's support.

"Yes, we do, and in time we will claim this land." No'ka stomped on the ground hard, one foot at a time. The tromping must have echoed to the core of the planet and stirred the gods who dwelt there, for they seemed to answer with a tremble of the earth. Everyone felt it.

"Until that day we must survive, so that we will still be strong enough to claim what is ours. Now it is cold. Let us go to our warm beds. Those who wish to further discuss these matters will find me in our blessed hot pools."

With that speech, Cupa became an American town. At least the villagers thought of it that way. The Kuupiaxchem still had their customs, but they would have them as Americans first.

50

THE SHOPPING TRIP

F ALLING Star wanted to go with Bill to San Diego to choose the women's clothing. She would bring her mother and leave Wili with Melones. There was no dissuading her.

Warner didn't want to let Bill go. The endless train of gold seekers now averaged one hundred men a day, a number almost impossible to deal with. Anita had a new baby, Isabelle, less than a month old. There was a solid foot and a half of snow on the ground, the most Warner had ever seen. An army was stuck in the desert about thirty miles east of the ranch, unable to move through the heavy drifts with its starving horses and mules. It was General Joseph Lane's command of four companies of dragoons, on their way to California to restore order in the gold fields.

General Lane had walked to the ranch with an escort in mid-December, desperate to escape his miserable frozen camp and get help for his troops. He arrived during a severe snowstorm, leading sixteen broken and starved army mules. Lane's escort spent the night and rode out the next morning for Los Angeles, on eight fresh horses Warner had reluctantly traded for the mules.

Bill agreed to stay at the ranch until the bulk of the army had passed.

On the twenty-ninth of December Major Lawrence P. Graham led most of the weary troops over the rocky pass to Warner's and on to San Diego. He traveled with a sumptuous tent, a mistress and several cases of whiskey, his medicine for the cold. The only benefit from his passing was a beautiful stallion that became enchanted with one of Warner's mares. He followed her into the hills and stayed.

Warner would not trade any livestock with Graham's command. He had done his patriotic duty for the general. There was no feed on the ranch for starving animals. The grass was still frozen under a foot of snow. Graham was annoyed, but Bill assured him that there was plenty of good pasture for his stock at the coast, where rainfall had been heavy all winter.

Only a small contingent of soldiers, commanded by a Lieutenant Givens, still remained at Graham's camp in the desert. They were cleaning up, bringing in stray animals, and salvaging broken wagons and supplies. They would follow at their own pace.

Now was Bill's chance to leave, but Warner decided he should go himself, to buy supplies for the trading post. Bill threatened to quit. He was not bluffing. The strain of dealing with the store, the Warners and the migrants was making him edgy. The severity of the winter had not helped. Everyone had chills and fevers, aches and pains, and a housebound pallor and sourness. There was no longer any pleasure in the job.

White Fox and Falling Star were excited about their first trip to San Diego, looking forward to the relative warmth of the coast. They pressured Bill and he refused to give in to Warner. Falling Star had never liked Bill working for Warner, and with the price of cattle so high, they didn't need the tiny salary he was paid. The idea of quitting, once uttered, became real.

Warner made peace with Bill—if Bill would do his buying, loading four pack mules with goods for the store and hauling them back. Bill agreed.

Next morning, the party of fur-bundled Cupeño rode gaily across the snow-white plain, following the San Luis Rey River from source to mouth, where they would join Pablo at the mission. They drove fifteen cattle to sell and led eight pack mules to freight their purchases. The Garras and Stomping Deer escorted them, heavily armed.

Wili and Shadow had been left in the capable care of Melones and No'ka. Wili was almost four, walking like a little man and talking in three languages. The travelers said, "We'll be right back." The big dog and tiny man accepted this statement, romping in fresh snow as Falling Star rode out of the village. She hoped their sense of time was as flexible as it needed to be.

The day had dawned clear and cold, but as soon as the sun rose above the Cuyamacas they were shedding furs and wraps to bask in its welcome warmth. The only breeze was the air stirred in passing; the sole sounds were horses' hooves, crows cawing, and the lowing of cattle. Stomping Deer (now usually called Jacobo), and White Fox were as excited as Falling Star to be on the trail together.

Rabbits in their winter coats scurried from the path, quail ruffled their feathers and hid in snowbanks, a bobcat slunk low, his white and tan color rendering him almost invisible. They saw no deer or antelope. The valley had been stripped bare by migrants.

First stop was Pauma, where they stayed the night, snug in Manuelito's adobe and stone house, an oak fire roaring in the fireplace, tangy stringy venison stew and hot tortillas rounding their bellies. Everyone camped on the floor, sleeping packed like cigars in a box, talking and giggling until the coals ceased to glow.

Falling Star had never been farther than Pauma, so every turn of the following day's journey brought surprise and delight. The migrant road to San Diego went through Santa Ysabel, far to the south. This lesser canyon trail remained untouched by the thousands of men passing to and from the gold fields. The deer, trout and bear were shy, but still visible, as they had been the first time Bill passed this way. The river flowed unmolested, through live oaks and leafless sycamores, tules and willows.

At first sight of San Luis Rey, they stopped on a rolling hill to rest a minute and allow the animals to graze. The distant mission lay magnificent in its valley of tilled fields and vineyards, wooden fenced pastures and fruit orchards. When it had snowed at Cupa, rain had fallen on the coastal hills. The earth and leaves smelled freshly washed, the grass newly grown, tender and moist. There were huge shady oaks, but they chose to loll in tall grass, letting the welcome sun bake winter-pale bodies. The distant mission floated on green, like a dream.

They would don clean clothing here. Everyone stripped to spend their last naked hour warming in the flattened oats. Bill studied his five companions, dozing peacefully in the sea of grass, surrounded by dark green mushrooming oaks, and back-dropped by a sky of brightest blue, dotted with stationary puffed, white clouds reflecting the winter sun. He looked upon them and saw nothing but innocence; the innocence of nature and wild creatures; the innocence of men as part of nature, before Adam and Eve, before the Bible, before even the idea of innocence. They were just there, like the grass or trees, sky or sun, just as graceful, and equally eternal.

He fell asleep and dreamed of Lugarda. She was standing over him. He could smell her perfume and hear the ruffle of her skirts. He reached to tickle her ankle, and awoke, blinking into the light. Falling Star was laughing down at him.

"Wake up, naked husband. You slept like a dreaming boy and now it is time to dress you and take you to the mission."

She was clothed in an emerald green dress, a present from Bill, and dainty black low boots. Falling Star and White Fox had brushed their hair, long and straight down their backs, with bright scarves to hold it in place. The Garras and Jacobo were dapper in short blue jackets, tan trousers and white shirts.

They wore hard felt hats with silver ringed bands and gold braid on the brims. Their boots were blue-black and polished.

Bill scrambled to his feet. They laughed and helped him to dress.

"We thought we should let you rest," said the elder Garra. "You were sleeping like a baby. A big pink baby," he gestured for length.

"I saw one of the People," Jacobo told him. "He says Pablo is at the mission. The horses are ready, though the cattle could graze here for a week, never lifting their heads."

Bill splashed water on his face and plastered down his rumpled hair.

They rode slowly, to keep the cooled horses from breaking sweat, preserving the freshness of their only clean change of clothing. The cattle snatched at tufts of grass; the Garras barely kept them moving.

The women gazed in wonder, as they approached the great Franciscan mission. It dominated the landscape like a beautiful angular mountain, declaiming to all who beheld it the majesty of the God who dwelt within — and the intelligence and skill of those who had built it.

When they drew nearer, San Luis Rey looked run-down. The cobblestoned coachway that led to the mission was full of weeds. Plaster had fallen. Heavy rain had caused the exposed adobe to run brown down the whitewashed walls. A shout arose from the gate. Pablo was in the entry, Padre Ibarra at his side. They kicked their horses to a trot and entered to the cadence of hooves on cobblestone.

After they had been shown to their rooms, the horses, mules and cattle led to pasture and water, Pablo met them in the patio for a tour of the mission. It was beat-up and decrepit, still used as an army barracks, though presently deserted, all the men gone to dig for gold.

To the women it was marvelous.

"Now I understand your parents' pride in having helped to build this house of God," Falling Star told Pablo as they entered the church. "I had no idea so grand a place existed."

Pablo pointed out the two-story domed ceiling, the intricate designs painted on tall walls, the fine woodwork, colored images of saints and carved gilded statuary.

White Fox admired the big courtyard, completely enclosed by connecting rooms. "It would look perfect at Cupa, with the oak meeting tree in the middle," she remarked, wistfully.

As they strolled the long corridors, peeking into doorways, Pablo fell behind to walk by Bill's side.

"So now the Serpent has entered the Garden," Pablo said, using the intonation of a preacher, "and the People must cover their private parts, and conceal themselves from unclean thoughts."

"When I see the ragged line of migrants, snaking across the valley toward Cupa, I do sometimes think of the Serpent."

"And evil may be warded off with pretty dresses and new trousers? That has not worked in San Diego or San Francisco."

"It will help; it will give them one less reason to tarry, one less excuse for abuse."

"You are probably right. One lust breeds another. Never have I seen anything like this lust for gold."

"Fortunes are made overnight."

"And lost the next." Pablo sighed. "We will stick to cattle. They are hard to lose and their prices rise and rise."

Padre Ibarra led the way to a long narrow storeroom, lined with folded clothing, and rolls of homespun cotton and wool cloth, remnants from the mission's active days. There was enough to clothe the whole tribe.

"Take whatever you need. The neophyte's clothing is about the only thing the Picos didn't steal."

The materials were roughly woven, but soft to the touch. Falling Star pulled a dress out and made a face.

"No one will wear these," she whispered. The dress was like a flour sack with holes for arms and head. "No wonder the Picos left them."

White Fox took it and held it to her chest. She gathered it at the waist. "They will be nice with a wide shell belt," she said. "We can alter them, drop the neckline. You will see, daughter, how lovely you will look."

"The idea is to conceal your beauty, ladies," said Pablo.

"That is a man's idea, that will not find success among women," said White Fox. "We will dress, but in a way that pleases us."

Father Ibarra wisely said nothing, though words formed on his lips, begging for release.

T H E visitors enjoyed a deep sleep in the thick-walled silence of their spartanly furnished guest rooms. Falling Star and Bill had fallen asleep in separate narrow beds, but during the night she climbed into his cot and made love gleefully, hoping to start a baby in these celibate quarters.

When Bill awoke, her eyes were already open. "I want you to introduce me to Lugarda," she said.

"Why? Get up. We're leaving. I can hear the others ready."

"I would like to meet this woman who shadows my life."

"For what purpose? Come on, get up." Bill stripped her covers. "You look good." He bent to kiss her.

"I want to know if she is a threat, or just the friendly ghost you make her out to be."

"And if she is a threat?"

"Then you and I will have to destroy her. Or we cannot go on."

"What if you see that she isn't a threat?" Bill got her clothes.

"Then I will know that you are the foolish man that I love, and I will forget about her." She raised her arms and he slipped a warm underdress over them. "Though you will not."

When he had dressed her, Bill said, "We may not see Lugarda. She is engaged to Jesús Machado. I myself have not seen her since . . ."

"Since you watched her husband killed?"

"A lot of people were dying. I wasn't watching him."

"We will visit her together. If not, I'll go by myself to see 'Zul. We three can have a nice talk without you ruining the fun."

A T San Diego there was incredible bustle. Tents, hide houses, wooden houses, brick and adobe houses had sprung up—at La Playa, around the pueblo, on the hillside and by the bay. The plaza was jammed with activity. Men bought and sold every conceivable item, showed off big gnarled nuggets of pure gold, and spun tales of greed and hard work, generosity and robbery, heat and blizzards, intelligence, stupidity, and always luck, luck—good or bad. Hundreds of hard-bitten, trail-weary men waited to catch a ship north to San Francisco, unable to face another six hundred miles on horseback or by foot. They saw themselves lying in a hammock watching the sea slip by, awaking to dock at fortune's door—never imagining how rough or long that upwind passage could be.

Lugarda was crossing the busy square alone. Bill made the introductions. All eyes were on Lugarda Dionicia. She colored slightly.

"Mucho gusto," Lugarda said. "I have heard so much about you."

"Mucho gusto." Falling Star took a good look as she dropped her eyes. The magnitude of San Diego's foreignness had shaken her confidence.

"I'm sorry I don't speak your language—just a bit of Kumeyaay and Luiseño." Lugarda studied Falling Star's flawless face.

"We can speak English. Bi' has been teaching me." She met her rival's probing gaze.

"You are a fortunate woman."

"Yes, I believe I am." She looked at her husband and darted her eyes toward Fitch's store. She had seen enough.

As Bill steered his wife to the shop, Lugarda admired Falling Star's springy step. She swished her own skirts and threw her hips as she crossed the plaza to the Alvarado house. White Fox watched her intently until the door closed.

Pablo had auctioned the skinny cattle for an average of two hundred forty dollars each. Fattened, they were worth four hundred. The women quickly made their purchases, taking all the dresses Fitch had in stock. Trousers were sold out. Bill paid for Warner's order and listened to Fitch gripe about Juan Largo's defiance of the shopkeeper's pronouncement against selling liquor. Fitch was still the alcalde and fond of issuing orders. Drunken brawls were his biggest problem. He only sold alcohol to a select clientele, behind closed doors.

The Cupeño left town immediately. The women were curious, but frightened by the chaotic boomtown, choked with boisterous, armed foreigners. The Garras and Jacobo were extremely nervous. Only Antonio could stand still. There were rumors of coughs and mysterious fevers, carried from Panama or Guatemala. There was no place to stay and sanitation was bad. Major Graham had gone to Los Angeles; his battalion melted into the stream of miners flowing north. There was scarcely a half platoon of dragoons to maintain order. The pueblo they had known, had been buried under a human wave. Mean, dusty, sleepy and flea-bitten as it had been, they missed the San Diego of old.

W H E N he had seen them off, Pablo went back to Fitch's. Bandini was at the counter.

"Your sailor-boy friend runs with a motley crew," Fitch said, handing Pablo a tumbler of brandy.

"I thought they looked pretty good," Bandini said.

"Under them fancy clothes, is what I'm talkin' about. The two young bucks, all stringy muscle and sinew and bone, nervous as penned deer, tight-wound and set to spring at anything says 'boo.' Antonio Garra, as stone-faced and thick as a boulder, counting out his cattle coins like beads on a rosary."

"An' what's her name, Foxy, No'ka's wife?" Fitch asked Pablo.

"Fox Who Protects Her Kits In Their Den," said Pablo.

"Exactly. But built like a bobcat, with claws and teeth to match. Her daughter all dolled up like an expensive San Francisco whore, prancing like a puma, plump and smooth, rump-round and hard as a horse."

Bandini caught Pablo's eye. Both were grinning.

"Sailor-Bill coiled and sleepy, burnt dark as an Indian, silent and strong as a python—did you see how he slung those hundred-pound sacks of flour?—just itching to coil an arm around something and squeeze it to death . . ."

"It's the squeeze of a pretty woman he likes," said Bandini. "From what I've seen and heard."

"Yeah. I'd sure like to get a squeeze o' that squaw o' his. Bet she's got the cunt-grip of a smithy's vice."

"Dios mío, you've got a foul mouth, Fitch. Put this stuff in your little ledger. I'll square up at the end of the month. Hasta luego."

Bandini saluted Pablo and left the store, banging the door behind.

"Sure you will, and you'll go back to goddamn Peru next week too," said Fitch, writing in his thick, greasy, leather-bound account book.

"How about me," Pablo said, sipping his brandy. "You left me out."

"You're the choirboy assassin. And I for one am glad you finally got up the nerve to give them *sosabitch* Mexicans some of their own medicine."

"Are we speaking about the operating end of a lance?"

"Sure as hell are. You never fooled me. I could always see that you hated those cabróns—wished you could kill and eat the lot of 'em."

Fitch chortled as Pablo blushed.

"Fitch," he said, "you always delight in peeling back the polite layers to expose a rotten core. But you're easy to fool. You're so busy looking for the dirt you miss a lot of good things."

"What the fuck you talkin' about?"

"Your own case for example. Look beyond the meanness and bluster and foul mouth, you find a kindhearted man. I watch you curse and shout and complain, and then grant credit to even your poorest customers. Half the People in town would be dead without that dog-eared notebook you keep your accounts in. And every new year you cross out dozens of pages of unpaid debts. Let me see that book."

Pablo reached for the ledger.

"Get away, choirboy. This is my private business," Fitch slid the book into a drawer. "Don't go thinkin' I've a bleedin' heart o' gold. Those poor bastards always repay me, even if they have to steal to do it."

"The People repay kindness with kindness: a tidbit of useful gossip, a dirty joke on their masters, a tip on the location of some stolen item. I know how you keep your accounts."

"So I barter, so goddamn what. Your sweet-mouthed Father Ibarra is the only one always asks cash for the poison he brews." Fitch took a huge swallow of brandy and banged his mug on the counter. "And don't give me no more o' your 'the People' bullshit. The People this, the People that—as though you're the only pissant people on earth. What does that make me?"

"You're an American. *Momnawechom.*"

"And you're Indios, Indians, Natives, Kumeyaay, Cahuilla, whatever."

"The People."

"You're a fuckin' smart-ass, clothes-horse, Mexican-killer Injun. That's what you are, choirboy." Fitch slapped Pablo hard on his slight shoulder. "Just keep the padre's booze comin'. These miners is thirsty and they pay cash, unlike some people we both seem to know."

" W E L L ? " Bill said, when they had settled into the homeward trail.

Falling Star pulled alongside.

"I am happy that you chose such a beautiful woman. She loves you because you are exciting to her, not because she wants to keep you. And you make her more interesting in the pueblo."

"How do you know all this? You hardly spoke four words."

"Women talk without speaking. She is marrying a man she does not love. She told me you belong to me. I am happy. I need never return to that place again." She shuddered and waved toward San Diego.

After a night at Santa Ysabel with Ignacio, they trotted across their snow-covered valley to the welcome of home.

Bill hardly had time to kiss his son before No'ka pulled him into a corner to say that Warner had been arrested, by Lieutenant Givens, commander of the Graham battalion's mop-up detail. The charge was stealing U.S. Army mules—that Warner had in fact traded two for one for fresh horses, with General Lane's escort. Warner and the evidence mules had been removed to Los Angeles, for trial.

"Anita has been alone with Fanny and her sick children for three days," No'ka said. "She is starving herself with worry. We posted guards at the ranch but she has not calmed down. Luna comes every day to see if you have returned."

Bill looked at Falling Star, who was rocking Wili in her arms and telling him about the trip. She nodded. The honeymoon was over. He took a few things and went dejectedly to his tired horse, to ask the favor of a few more miles. The horse didn't seem to mind. Shadow bounded in the air and raced down the trail. He had had enough of playing with children.

"Did you meet the Mexicana?" Melones asked, when Bill had gone.

"Yes, we did, in the plaza at San Diego," Falling Star told her, taking Wili in her arms.

Melones waved her hands in little circles, asking for more.

"She is very slender, graceful, beautiful . . ."

"She walks funny," said White Fox. She imitated Lugarda's walk, crossing her legs in front of each other. Melones tried it, bouncing and jiggling.

No'ka said, "Tell me about the pueblo."

"Scary," said White Fox.

"Awful, frightening." Falling Star opened her eyes wide. "Strange men making big houses everywhere, speaking in ten tongues, all with guns."

"The Mexicans?" No'ka asked.

White Fox shook her head and shrugged. Falling Star said, "Most of them are at the gold fields."

"What did the Osuna woman say to you?" Melones asked.

"She said I was a lucky woman. Bill is mine. They are friends."

"What kind of friends?"

"I don't care. Like you and my brother, or Bull Bear and I were."

"Or your mother and Baupista," said No'ka, grinning.

Falling Star looked at her mother, who made a face.

"Stomping Deer and I are more than friends," said Melones.

"It is good to be home," said White Fox, sinking back onto her bed with a moan.

51

UNHAPPY

SHOPKEEPERS

NITA was hysterical, unbathed and disheveled. She had a fever. She raved about her husband, berated Bill for leaving them, and cursed the weather, the U.S. Army, Americans in general and the gold rush.

Warner had resisted arrest physically and verbally, swearing that he had traded for the mules with General Lane. He hadn't wanted the worthless creatures to begin with. Only compassion for the general's plight had compelled him to make the trade. Lieutenant Givens had lost his temper. "If the mules you stole are that worthless, you can walk to Los Angeles," he shouted. He had tied Warner and led the cursing frontiersman off through the snow by a rope.

Bill stayed at the ranch that night and brought the new trade goods to the store the next day. Migrants were still straggling in. Few were prepared for the bitter cold and snow of that winter. Bill quickly sold out the wool coats he had bought. To one and all he said, "It's warm and sunny on the coast." The best way for them to survive in the cold was to keep moving.

Warner arrived that night, cursing and stomping through the house like a madman. He was out on one thousand dollars bail and had to return directly for trial. He had only come to make sure Anita was all right and take her to a safer location. Now that Bill was back, he could return to Los Angeles with a clear conscience.

It began to snow about four in the morning and continued for three days, bringing all movement at the ranch to a halt. Warner raged at his bad luck, worried about losing the bond money and cursed the army: Major Graham and Lieutenant Givens were the devil and his disciple; Los Angeles a hellhole of military corruption and senseless murder. The ranch was a frozen wasteland; the store a burden; the gold rush a black plague.

Bill hid in the barn with Luna and watched the snow fall softly, steadily, silently, whiting out the ceaseless progress of men.

THE storm finally passed, Warner was acquitted, rejailed by Major Graham, reluctantly released to return home, after two more torturous weeks in Los Angeles.

The immigrants kept coming in greater and greater numbers. The entire state of California groaned to accommodate them. There was no law, there was no order, only chaos, as feverish men elbowed their way into the gold diggings.

The U.S. Army finally saw fit to establish a garrison at the Colorado River where it met the mouth of the Gila River, one hundred thirty miles east of the ranch. It was to be called Fort Yuma.

This was a flash point on the trail. The Yuman Indians, who charged travelers a toll for their passage, had traditionally controlled the crossing. There were frequent disputes over the toll fees. There were robberies and horse stealings by the Yumans and retaliatory attacks by the migrants.

For a while, a gang of scalp hunters from Texas, who had been exterminating Apaches on behalf of the Mexican government, took over the crossing. Their leader was a joyful killer named Glanton. They murdered the Yuman chiefs, built a ferry and charged five dollars a person for the short trip across the Colorado.

The Glanton gang soon amassed a treasure chest of gold, coins and jewelry. The drunken outlaws lived in squalid splendor with a dozen Indian mistresses and two white concubines.

One night, alerted by an unwilling native girl that the entire gang had passed out after a three-day binge, the Yumans took revenge. Sneaking into Glanton's camp undetected, they killed each snoring man with a crushing tomahawk blow. The white women were also slain. The gang's treasure was dispersed among the jubilant tribesmen.

The Yumans retained control of the crossing until the arrival of Major Samuel P. Heintzelman. With him was Lieutenant Colonel John B. Magruder, second in command, leading a company of dragoons. They established a military garrison and began to build a fort.

The soldiers arrived at Warner's ranch in May of 1849. Major Heintzelman announced his appointment as commander of U.S. Army forces in San Diego. He would be in charge of twenty thousand square miles of territory, from the Colorado River to the Pacific and north to Los Angeles.

Heintzelman and Magruder, like Kearny, were West Pointers and dedicated officers, determined to do their duty. Warner related the problems he was having with the unruly gold seekers. He asked them to leave a garrison at the ranch, or nearby. They promised to do what they could, spent one night feasting on beef provided by Warner, then rode on to San Diego.

J O H N Warner grew progressively disenchanted with the stream of his countrymen through the ranch. Once the migrants bought what they could afford, he wanted them out of his sight. They naturally wished to camp as near as possible to the store. They were worried and afraid. They wanted to visit his blacksmith shop; to talk horses, cattle, gold, the relative merits of trails north, politics and Indians.

Warner loved to talk, but even he could only say the same thing so many times. He was grouchy, curt with questioners and cryptic in answer.

Anita too was transformed by the hordes: from a gay and exuberant girl who begged for company, to a bitchy mother of three wild children, who dreaded the next knock at her kitchen door. Luna and Fanny spent half of their time shooing the curious away, trying to keep the barnyard clear of loiterers and potential looters.

Thankful as the travelers were to be in a green valley, with trees and clean water, and a store conveniently full of every possible need for their comfort, they resented the high prices that Warner asked for every item. They saw him as an opportunist, preying on their great need. They were in no mood for meanness, having just traversed the grueling wastelands of the desert.

They did not yet understand that everything was expensive in California. They were incredulous when Bill told them, "Prices only go up from here." They only saw the shopkeepers as fat and sassy, living high off the captive market of their misery, extracting the last of their pitiful savings.

"If ya'all make it to Warner's 'thout gittin' scalped by Injuns, you're sure as hell gonna git scalped in that store o' his," was a standing joke.

Warner never denied food or water to any man who came to the ranch, whether paid for or not. He would take anything at all in trade, from a broken wagon to a rusty knife, a belt buckle to a rattlesnake skin, a half-dead donkey to a newborn puppy. He resented the ingratitude. He soured, and his reputation as a skinflint and grouch grew. Warner could only deal with the forty-niners by keeping them moving. There was nothing in the valley for them but water, a good meal, some supplies and a clear trail north to Los Angeles, or south to San Diego. On this, Warner and the Cupeño were in absolute agreement.

52

LUGARDA OSUNA

WARNER'S store needed restocking but Anita wouldn't let John travel—to San Diego or anywhere else.

"You're never leaving me here again," she said, stamping her feet.

He could only bow his head and ask Bill to go once more. The Garras rode guard. The previous excursion had cured Falling Star, White Fox and Jacobo of their big-city curiosity. Only Antonio and his son had the concern for their cattle, and the stomach to face the miner hordes. The value of a steer had risen to three hundred fifteen dollars.

Fortunately, Pablo was in town to help get this unheard of price. He settled the Garras in La Playa and took Bill to dinner at the Alvarado house, where Lugarda and 'Zul now lived alone. All the ranching families were permanently ensconced at their bovine gold mines, hand-feeding, breeding, counting and guarding the precious herds.

The four friends enjoyed a sociable meal at the usual late hour of nine, after Lugarda's daughter had been put to bed. Candles on the table and two matching whale oil lamps bathed the dining room in mobile yellow light. 'Zul and Lugarda had cooked a flounder from the bay, baking it in a pot with chiles, onions, potatoes, tomatoes and chayote squash. They sprinkled it with sea salt and served it with a white-grape wine that Pablo had brought from the mission.

For a side dish 'Zul had scraped hard goat cheese onto opened oysters and baked them too. The melted cheese and plump oysters, swimming in salty juice, were slurped from their shells like delectable spoonfuls of chowder. Dessert was a very American apple pie, whose recipe Lugarda had taken from the notebook of one of Admiral Stockton's cooks.

'Zul had finally forgiven Pablo, her anger softened by time and gifts, beginning with the two beeves he had sent, that dark hungry month just after the war. Lugarda was completely recovered from her husband's shocking death. Her mourning period was over. She was looking forward to her marriage to Jesús Machado in the spring, enjoying the excitement of San Diego's gold rush boom and Bandini's endless balls. Machado had recently bought a large ranch at Buena Vista, adjoining San Marcos. He rarely left his ranch, but was building her a house in the pueblo.

It felt good to be together. They spoke of nothing personal; there was so much news to tell; so much gossip to relate. By the time Pablo and 'Zul rose to say good night, evening had faded to morning.

When they were gone, Bill pushed back his chair. He thanked Lugarda for the supper, found his jacket and went to the door.

"Where are you going?" Lugarda asked, blowing out the candles. She walked over to him and took his hand.

"We sleep at La Playa, with our Kanaka friends."

"Girlfriends?" Lugarda raised her eyebrows.

"Not at all." Bill laughed. "Very big, very nice men."

"You could stay here," she said, looking at their hands. "You could stay here with me if you like." She looked up.

She read his confusion and immediately blurted, "I don't know why I said that, it just came out. It's not what I was thinking."

Bill was wary. They had not been intimate in any way for years, not even in conversation. Since her husband's death, he had tiptoed around her. It was impossible to see her without seeing him.

"Do you want me to stay?" he asked.

"Yes. Yes, please stay." She squeezed his hand.

Shivering a little, she pulled her shawl tighter and led Bill to her bedroom. He excused himself to go outside to pee. Standing in the cool fall air, he looked to the sky for a sign—found only a mute gray cloud bank, no star in sight, and no moon. He had wanted her for so long—it seemed so long ago—that he couldn't say no. There was nothing to do but go back to Lugarda's soft bed with its cool linens and fluffy down covers.

She was lying deep in folds of white, dark hair and eyes showing above the sheets. A candle on a nightstand gave mobile light.

"Get in here quickly, Bill. I'm freezing," she implored, submerging completely.

Bill did as he was asked, blowing out the candle on the way in.

She was wearing a long flannel nightdress. He hugged her from behind, wrapping himself around her. She was indeed cold, from the nape of her long neck where he breathed hot air into her hairline, to her slim feet, which he chafed when she brought them up to his hands. He was warm, as usual in the evening after a meal. The coolness of the bed felt good.

"You're hot-blooded," she commented after a few minutes, when the bed had heated up a bit. She snuggled closer and felt his softness. She put a hand behind her back to touch him to be sure. She took it away.

"I wanted to sleep with you just this once," she said matter-of-factly. "I've loved you for so long . . . we may not have another chance."

Bill pulled her nightdress up. Her legs and back were cold. Her breasts were cold, nipples wrinkled hard.

"How did you get so cold?" He rubbed his legs and hips against hers, hands kneading shoulders and breasts.

"I'm always cold at night, unless I dance."

When she warmed, he relaxed and nestled against her.

She turned around and wrapped a leg over him. He hugged her close and she found his lips. She kissed him tentatively. Her mouth tasted of wine and apple pie.

Lugarda felt his reluctance. She recalled the rapture and abandon of his kisses, in her parents' living room and at Box Canyon. She held his head gently in both hands. She pressed against him.

"Everyone already thinks we are lovers, so we might as well be," she told him. "The pleasure has already been accounted for."

Bill pulled her nightdress over her head. She was right. He wanted to be naked against her nakedness, to warm her cold hard nipples against his, to melt her, if he could.

S H E   lay against his chest to catch her breath. She was moist to her breasts. He pulled the blankets up to cover them.

"Oh, that feels like nothing I've ever felt before," she breathed into his ear. She kissed his cheeks, his eyes, his ears; his nose and mouth.

"How does it usually feel?" Bill asked. He was lifting her hair to cool the back of her neck.

She replied slowly. "Not like this. Never like this."

He couldn't believe it was true — but it was nice to hear.

"My husband stayed on top. Sometimes he turned me over," she told him, snuggling down, swaying her hips contentedly. "He was quick."

Bill saw the severed lump of José María's bloody organs, oozing in Stomping Deer's hand. He shriveled.

He rolled Lugarda to the side. He wanted to fall asleep and wake up somewhere else. He sighed and stayed still.

"Were you there when he died?" she asked, after a while.

"Yes, I was there, but I didn't see him die." It was true; it felt like a lie.

"I never could decide whether killing him, or saving him, would have meant you loved me more."

"I could do neither," Bill confessed. "I could only look away."

"I too have had to look away." She shuddered.

She hugged him and settled into the bed, but sleep refused to rescue him.

Lugarda's arm and leg, thrown possessively over him, were a deadweight. He listened to her slumberous breathing. He couldn't toss and turn for fear of waking her. It was all he could do to keep from jumping up, pulling on his pants and fleeing into the night.

He lay there, meditating on all of the linked events that had led up to this moment, starting at the beginning, at La Playa, Lugarda sitting in the carreta. He went back even further, to the first time Pablo had mentioned her, before they had left Hartford. He tried to remember every single time he had seen her, spoken to her, thought about her, or talked about her.

By the time he got to her husband's death, he was cramped. Her breath whispered in his ear. Her hair spilled soft and warm over his shoulder. He gently lifted her arm—light as a feather—that had so heavily pinned him to the bed. He slipped his leg from under hers. She nestled herself but did not awaken. In a tiny shaft of light he could see her face—just the white and dark of brows and lashes, nostrils and lips. He contemplated her beauty, the purity of her beauty. He knew that sex had not been his goal with her since way before her husband's death. Nor marriage. It was her friendship that he craved . . . and then forgiveness.

Her wanting sex had made him feel put upon. He didn't wish to know her in that way. Now he was glad that he had complied—and felt bad that he had been so grudging; so ungenerous. It was the only thing she had ever asked of him. Her friendship, her forgiveness and her strength as an ally against the unforgiving, all of these, she had granted him. She had given him her beauty and the wonder of her love.

He kissed her forehead tenderly and held her close. He resumed his meditation, beginning with Juan María's demise. He contemplated her sleeping beauty. He worshiped her.

/ / /

WHEN Bill awoke, Lugarda was gone; the house was quiet. A ray of light showed at the edge of the shutters. Bill dressed quickly and tiptoed down a hallway to the back door.

He carefully slid the wooden latch and opened it a crack. It creaked noisily. Bill saw no one. He backed out the door, pulling it gently closed. He heard a swish and a scuff above and looked up as a lasso settled over his shoulders, jerked tight by Ramón Osuna. The noose pinned both arms to his sides. Ramón strained to lift him off his feet.

A heavy blow glanced off Bill's skull and neck and slammed into his collarbone. He wrenched his head to see Leandro grinning, whip butt raised to strike again.

Letting the rope take his weight, Bill pushed off the door jamb with both feet and slammed into Leandro, throwing him back and deflecting the second blow.

Bill banged hard into the wall on the back swing, but managed to get his right hand into a moccasin, to yank his deckhand's dirk from its sheath. It was a stabbing knife, with both edges razor sharp, and a wooden grip with a metal stop, so you couldn't drive your hand down onto the blade.

Bill held the dirk in his right fist, low against his side, blade pointed back, and thrust off the wall again as he heard Leandro charge.

A crushing blow to the ear blinded Bill, but the knife made satisfying contact, the blade parting flesh, stopping against bone. He arced painfully back into the door frame, hitting with his left hip as Leandro screamed.

Bill kept his weight on the rope and sawed at it madly with the blade. It quickly gave way, dropping him to earth with a breathtaking thud, ribs crunching on the stone doorstep.

Bill gasped for air, scuttling back against the door with his feet to face any further attack. But Leandro limped off around the corner of the house, holding the bloody top of his thigh with both hands, cursing.

The whip lay in the yard. Ramón looked down at Bill for a few seconds, then scuffed away across the flat roof.

Bill pulled himself to his feet and stumbled toward Bandini's corrals. His head cleared enough to tell him to put the knife away and walk as nonchalantly as possible. It was early, but dawn had passed, and he smelled the smoke of many breakfasts cooking.

Fortunately, the Osunas had not thought to take his horse. Bill threw the saddle on, cinched it and slumped over the gelding's neck to ride off toward La Playa, holding the unused bridle in his hand.

Bill never told a soul about that incident, not even Pablo. To someone else it might have seemed obvious that he had fallen into a trap—Lugarda the irresistible bait—but Bill refused to think she had betrayed him. They had been in intimate communion the whole evening. She couldn't be that great an actress, or he that great a fool. She was his friend, if nothing else.

Anyone might have seen him enter the house—and waited for him to come out. He had been cocky and careless. That's all. The beating didn't matter. The evening with Lugarda did.

53
LUNA IS FREED

T THE end of November, California's Statehood Convention voted to enter the U.S. as a non–slave state. Their decision only remained to be ratified by Congress. Northerners, mountain men, ministers, priests and Californios had united to win this crucial vote. Mission bells were ringing and wine flowed in celebration.

Pablo rode into Cupa one morning with Manuelito and announced that they had come to free Warner's Indian slaves. Pablo had always spoken out against the purchase of Luna and Fanny. He enlisted the support of No'ka and Antonio Garra, Sr. They rode over to Warner's ranch to confront the slaver.

Bill was tending the store when they arrived. After the excited greetings and backslapping had subsided, he looked from face to face and asked, "Qué pasa, Capitánes?"

Pablo and Manuelito had not been to Cupa since the war. The four leaders hadn't been together since the Aguanga burial.

"We wish to speak to Juan Largo," said No'ka.

"Any particular topic of discussion?" Bill asked, looking at Pablo.

"Tell him it's about his slaves," said Antonio Garra.

"We've come to ask him to free Luna and Fanny," Pablo admitted.

Bill went to the barn and returned with John. There were warm greetings all around. Warner shook Pablo's hand and said, smiling, "Nice uniform. Did you scalp the dragoon or win it at poker?"

Pablo didn't laugh. He was wearing the dark blue wool overcoat of an army officer, minus the ranking stripes, and a captain's cavalry hat. A light blue wool shirt, and yellow scarf, navy pants with braid down the outside of the legs, and polished high black boots completed his military attire.

"The uniforms of deserters are piling up in San Diego and Los Angeles," Pablo explained, examining his sleeve for lint. "Every morning, commanders arise to find empty uniforms laid out on the cots, as though the bodies had dematerialized in their sleep, to be transported by dream directly to the gold fields." He shrugged. "They are cheap, well cut and impress the backcountry yokels."

Warner offered coffee and called Fanny to bring it.

When she arrived with the cups on a tray, Pablo said to her in Yuman, "You may stay. We discuss your future. You should listen."

Fanny blushed. She said, "No, no, perdóname," and retreated into the house.

"We have come to free your slaves, Juan José. We have come to tell them they are free men," announced Pablo.

"I have no slaves," Warner said, stiffening.

"Fanny and Luna," said Pablo, meeting John's gaze. "And Sally."

"They are here of their own free will. I rescued them from the Yumans," Warner retorted.

"Do they get paid for their labors?" Pablo looked at Bill.

"They get room and board and everything they need," said Warner.

"They are slaves, Juan Largo," said Antonio Garra.

"Or indentured servants, perhaps," said Pablo. "You have bragged about paying one bushel of corn for Luna. That is three or four dollars. A working man earns at least three dollars a month. He has paid for his freedom sixty times in five years. He is a free man either way."

Warner tried to laugh. "Luna is not a man, he is a boy—"

"Not according to the village women," cut in No'ka. Luna had a girl-friend, Narcissus, a cousin of Melones.

"He's still free, man or boy," snapped Warner.

"We will ask him," said Pablo. "Call him please," he said to Bill. Bill yelled out the door. Luna, who was always only a few steps behind Warner, scurried in. He looked from Bill to Warner to Pablo.

"Luna, Juan José Warner says you are a free man. You may come and go as you please, just as we do. Do you know this?" Pablo asked.

Luna shook his head and looked down. "No," he said softy.

Everyone looked at Warner.

"Tell him," said Pablo.

Warner hesitated, red in the face.

"Slavery has been abolished . . ." Pablo began for him.

Juan Largo took over angrily. "California is to be a free state when it is admitted to the United States of America, sometime next year," said Warner. "Slavery will not be allowed. You have always been free. I only bought you to save you from a worse fate."

"You are a free man, Luna," Pablo enthused. "You may ride out with us now, to live in Cupa or anywhere else you choose."

Luna looked at Warner.

"You may go with them or stay with me, as they say," said Warner flatly. "You are free to choose." His lips pressed to a thin line.

Luna looked from one to the other, then at the three chiefs and Bill. No one said a word.

He looked at his feet. "I will stay."

Warner's face relaxed. Pablo looked disgusted.

"That is your choice. You are a free man. But know that you must be paid to work. You may leave at any time. You are as free as I am," said Pablo.

"You're not free, Pablo." Warner gritted his teeth. "You're just an over-dressed Indian who's read too many books."

"And you're a Connecticut Yankee skinflint, far from where you belong. No one of us is truly free, but I can walk out that door and never have to come back, and so can he." Pablo pointed at Luna. "We are that free."

"Walk on then," said Warner. "It's fine by me. Excuse me," he said stiffly to the chiefs. "I've got work to do."

Warner stomped into the bowels of his house, slamming the door. "God-damn gall . . ." he shouted.

54

TIME TO QUIT

INTER was mild in '49–'50. It only snowed once, very lightly, in late January. The valley was lined with tall grass; the skies clear and filled with California sunshine. The wagon trains stayed longer at the ranch, letting their bony animals graze, resting in the balmy weather before going north. New people kept piling in.

Gold had been discovered at San Gabriel, near Los Angeles. In an instant, every immigrant heard the news and every stop of the wagon trains became an opportunity to prospect for gold. The amounts of gold in San Diego were minimal, but no one knew this at the time. Who would want to be known as the miner that walked right by a fortune?

The clink of picks and hammers on rock haunted the hills and gullies. Squatting miners lined the riverbanks like women doing laundry, swishing their pans of gravel for specks of golden glitter.

Game animals that had left the plains to shelter in the arroyos, gullies and hills were flushed out and slaughtered. Grizzly bear families were wiped out in a single morning: shot for their skins, or to drive them from a potential claim site. Deer became scarce and antelope virtually disappeared. Even bighorn sheep, living in the rockiest crags, were heavily depleted.

Cattle prices rose to a peak of five hundred dollars a head. A fat cow was worth more than a panful of gold. Guards were doubled on the valley herds to prevent rustling or butchering on the open range, which occurred right around the ranch and Cupa.

Major Heintzelman was forced to establish a garrison at Santa Ysabel, only fifteen miles from Warner's, in order to bring some order to the mountains. Fortunately, most of the gold prospecting took place south of Warner's ranch, in the territory of the Kumeyaay and the Cuyamaca. These Indians in their remote meadows and pine-tree-lined valleys suffered the brunt of the miner invasion. The situation was volatile. Colonel Magruder headed the garrison at Santa Ysabel, while Heintzelman remained at Fort Yuma, where he owned fifty percent of the new ferry business.

P A B L O continued to keep in touch by letter. He referred to the tribe as "Covered Cupa" when he sent news from the fast moving coast: The old-guard Californios were dying off: Juan María Osuna succumbed to a fever. Juan Ortega and José Carillo died of some plague, contracted from the miners. Fitch dropped dead in his store with a single curse, cradling a bottle of brandy to keep it from breaking as he went down. His ledger had disappeared in the confusion, to the joy of those with debts to pay. Fitch cast a large shadow. He had been a brilliant shopkeeper, always managing to have just what one needed, the goods beautifully kept, with credit for anyone he knew. His avaricious generosity, scathing tongue and blustery humor had touched every resident of the county. As acalde, he had kept the scales of justice in delicate balance. Henry Delano Fitch was sorely missed, the more as time went on, for there was no one to take his place.

On January 30, Lugarda married Jesús Machado. She spent part of her time at his new rancho, Buena Vista, twelve hundred acres purchased from an American named William B. Dunn. Dunn, an ex-dragoon in Kearny's army, had acquired Buena Vista by marrying the daughter of Felipe Subria, the local Luiseño chieftain. Felipe Subria gave the tribal land to his daughter and Dunn as a wedding present—in the same communal spirit that Bill had been given the Cupeño herd of cattle. But when Dunn abruptly left his wife and took up with a fourteen-year-old Luiseño girl, he didn't return the dowry, as was the custom. He sold it to Jesús Machado, including the site of Felipe Subria's village. The tribe was outraged.

Machado had placated the chief by promising never to sell Buena Vista, and by allowing the natives free range for their animals. If he should receive title from the U.S. land court, Machado promised to deed the village and its surrounds back to the tribe. When they shook hands on the promise, Felipe Subria had said, "On your life."

"On my life," Jesús Machado had replied, happy to have finally acquired a land grant.

The title was tenuous at best. The Machados raised and sold as many cattle as possible, unsure how long Buena Vista would be theirs. All of the Californio ranchers were worried about the outcome of their title claims in a future land court.

The new government was slowly taking shape. On February 18, 1850, the county of San Diego was created. It was huge, extending from the Colorado River to the Pacific Ocean and north to Los Angeles County. Election of officials came next. On April 1, Count Agoston Haraszthy won election as both county sheriff and city marshal of San Diego.

"The Count was truly an April Fool's joke. Harass Thee, is what we call him," Pablo wrote to Bill, "His aristocratic family was forced to flee Hungary when they supported a revolution that failed. Now he has landed among us to extract his fortune from San Diego.

"Given five thousand dollars to build a new jail, he spent five hundred and pocketed the change. The adobe walls are so sandy and weak that a man can dig his way out with a spoon. But why bother? It is much easier to wrench the bars from the windows with bare hands, or kick out the locked door. Each of these methods of escape has been proven in the first month.

"The only thing this sheriff does efficiently is collect taxes. All San Diego is complaining. He even wants to tithe the missions. God only knows what he does with the money he collects.

"You are lucky to be in a remote mountain corner where you don't have to deal with him. He takes his badge seriously, claiming authority above the army. Nobody likes the stiff Hungarian. But nobody wants his thankless tax-collector's assignment either."

L U N A   did stay with Warner. But he got paid a couple of dollars a week. He took Sundays off except in emergencies, and he spent more time at Cupa.

"I do the same things; I am still a slave to Warner's command," he told Bill, "but I feel free. The days are shorter and the weight is lighter."

The more Bill thought about it, the more he felt like a slave himself. He certainly wasn't free. He was mired in Warner's mudhole and the muck of migrants he served. He remembered how good it had felt to shout, "I'm free," at the top of his lungs. He recalled the thrill of learning that the Cupeño had no word for work. When Pablo had said to Warner, "I can walk out that door and never have to come back . . . we are that free," Bill had cringed under the weight of his own shackles.

He stewed on this topic and one morning when he trotted up to Warner's barn, to John's greeting of, "Good day Billy-boy. Can you turn out the milk cows before you open the store?," Bill said, "John, I don't want to open the store anymore. I quit."

He went to the barn to gather the few things he kept there, stuffing them into a saddlebag. John finished washing his hands and came to stand over him.

"You can't quit on me, Bill. We need you here. I can't run the store alone. You know that."

"Then close it. I've had enough of catering to your sorry customers and so have you."

"I can't close the store. The migrants would tear the ranch apart."

"You can close the store or leave it open, as you like, but I'm quitting right now, today." Bill looked at Warner, but John had stomped out into the yard. A door slammed.

When Bill dragged his belongings outside, the whole Warner family had assembled to plead with him. Even Fanny and Luna were looking at him as though he were deserting a sinking ship. But the more they pleaded, the more trapped he felt, the stubborner he got. Bill wished he could have left them in the night, as he had the *Hopewell*. He had been as fond of Captain Saxon and the crew as he was of the Warners, but he still had to quit, then and now.

When he went to get his horse, the family returned to the house. Warner admitted that he too was disenchanted with storekeeping. He wanted to run for state senator in the first election in November. If he won, he would need Bill more than ever. There was no one else he could trust with the ranch, for those times he would be away at San José, the temporary capital.

Bill was determined to quit. The Cupeño were making so much money with beef, he did not need the job. He wanted to be at home, with Wili, Shadow and his wife, who was pregnant with their second child.

Warner proposed that Bill leave now, while he was there to manage, and come back to help only if he were elected, and only during those times the Senate was in session. Bill agreed. He could always say no later, if and when he was asked to return. He tied on his saddlebags and rode home.

For a few days he did nothing but sleep late, loll in Falling Star's embrace, play with Shadow and Wili, eat leisurely meals, and saunter to the hot pools to soak and gossip. Melones was there to help cook, while her boy, Primo, wrestled with Wili. White Fox and No'ka stopped in every day, bearing gifts of corn or blackberries, quail or a rabbit. Bill felt like a prince returned from the wars. The cocoon of Cupa closed once more around him.

55

VILLAGE POLITICS

U T the turmoil of war and the gold rush had changed the village.

Jacobo Stomping Deer had begun to take more interest in women after Bull Bear's death. Eventually he had fallen in love with Melones. He was possessive and jealous and they all thought he would get hurt by Miss Flirt. But she withdrew from her other involvements and refrained from throwing her arms around everyone she knew, when Jacobo was around. She and Bill had to be especially careful about how they touched in front of him, and eventually never did so. Jacobo was aware of the consideration Melones showed him and loved her all the more.

The Pauma who had stayed at Cupa—under the protection of Antonio Garra, who had retained his post as Luiseño commander in chief—had not been successful in burying the nightmare of Aguanga. According to White Fox, there was widespread guilt among the survivors. Black Feather, a Cupeño of the Garra clan, a shaman whose family had been shamans from the time before Christianity, had, from the day of the massacre, blamed the demise of the Pauma on the influence of the Catholic priests. Black Feather condemned the tribe for having followed the false God. He said, over and over, that the wrath of the old gods residing at Aguanga had fallen on the faithless Pauma. Many believed the shaman.

Feelings of guilt and despair were so strong that two Paumans committed suicide by eating poison. In the early winter of 1850, a mysterious illness had infected the Pauma, but not the Cupeño. Black Feather claimed that he had cast a spell on the sick men and women, as punishment for praying in the chapel. When seven of the ill eventually died, a dark dread hung over the survivors, their guilt compounded by fear of the shaman. They believed that all were condemned; that they should have died with their brothers at Aguanga.

As chief of chiefs, Antonio Garra's prestige had grown, aided by his command of languages, including English, and his good relations with the various village captains.

After the war, the Garras had rounded up every stray unbranded cow, calf and steer within a day's ride of the valley. Their AG brand was carried by hundreds of cattle. Economically, Antonio Garra was the most important native chief. At Cupa, No'ka was the elder leader, but he deferred to Capitán Garra. No'ka had grown listless. He was uninterested in the new economy of cattle ranching and selling goods to the migrants.

When the seven accursed Pauma had perished, Garra and his son hanged Black Feather for practicing witchcraft. No'ka was not consulted. He was treated as a bystander. White Fox berated her husband and tried to goad him into reasserting his authority. No'ka ignored her.

It was the end of August when Bill came home to stay, seven months after the hanging of the shaman. Capitán No'ka had withdrawn more and more from Cupeño leadership. White Fox represented him on the council at most meetings. Antonio Garra was the obvious chief, controlling the votes as No'ka once had.

White Fox asked Bill to talk to his father-in-law. The Cupeño were drifting into the Garras' influence, but still loyal to No'ka. The women felt he should either retire, naming Antonio Garra as his successor, or get back on his horse and lead as he once had.

B I L L chose a scorching dry day in late September. The sun had cooked the sky white, the grass brittle brown, the soil baked to a dusty crust, too blistering hot for bare feet to touch. Even the dogs scurried from shade to shadow to keep from burning their paws. Every other animal lay immobile under a dark, oak-leafed canopy, which gave relief from the relentless cooking of the sun, but was still penetrated by the skin-cracking, moisture-sucking desert wind. The people were in cool pools and on the banks of the creek, dipping in and emerging to dry in a minute; or sitting with their feet in the water, soaking in the only humidity under the whole ovenly arc of sky.

Those who dunked fully clothed kept cool, long enough to allow for useful activity: arrow making, sewing a moccasin, soaking acorn flour or basket weaving.

No'ka wore a store-bought, blue long-sleeved shirt and khaki pants, wet. He sat on a rock, carefully chipping little arrowheads for bird hunting. The ducks and geese would be coming south soon. When waterfowl arrived, they blackened the sky and covered the lakes and estuaries.

Shadow lay in the shallows at No'ka's feet, eyes shut, flinching and twitching his ears every time a stray flint chip landed on him.

Bill splashed with Wili, in and out of the pools, searching for just the right temperature. He watched No'ka finish an arrowhead about an inch long, half an inch wide and a fourth of an inch thick at its center. It was perfect, delicate and sharp. As No'ka put in the notch for tying to the arrow, he pressed too hard with his antler-tool and broke the tiny point. Half of the arrowhead landed in the stream. He threw the other half after it with a grunt and took up his flint source to begin another.

"It will be nice to see the flocks of ducks again," Bill said. "They are one of the few things unchanged, since first I came."

No'ka looked at Bill intently. Bill checked on Wili. He was with some other children and Melones. When he looked back, No'ka was searching the flint source for a good spot to flake off a new point. He put the stone down and nudged Shadow with his bare foot. Shadow opened one eye. No'ka glanced at Bill. He looked back at Shadow and stroked his ear.

"The men who flock to California walk upon this earth, but they do not feel a part of it."

He was talking to Shadow, softly pulling his ear. Shadow closed his eye. He had heard No'ka's monologues before. They were good for a long nap.

"They think not of tomorrow, except that it may bring gold."

No'ka still spoke quietly to Shadow. Bill had to lean in to hear him above the creek noises.

"I do not understand the obsession of these men with the yellow metal, which is only good to adorn women. I do not understand their religion that puts them apart from all other men, and men apart from all other living things. I do not understand these men who do not see us."

He turned his head to Bill and raised his shoulders.

"They look at me, but they do not see me. They see right through me to the thing they want, whether it is a warm bath or a fat cow, a glinting rock or a running deer. I am only the unworthy keeper of those things they desire.

"They do not see us as we are: brother People, who love our world as much and more than they do."

No'ka splashed water onto his shirt, filled his hat and put it on, letting it stream down his face and hair. He watched the drops from his chin hit his lap.

"They put us apart. We are nothing of use; we are like the crows and eagles, coyote, bear and mountain lion. What they cannot eat, they therefore exterminate."

He looked sharply at Bill.

"Who are these men? Where do they come from? Do they not have homes and family and a land that they love so much that they can hardly leave?"

Bill opened his mouth, but no words issued forth. He had arrived as detached from home as any Forty-niner.

"More and more of them will come and more and more of us will die. That is what I see."

Bill nudged Shadow's back with a big toe. Everything No'ka said of his countrymen was true. He was only a little less guilty.

No'ka touched his hand, his face softened.

"I am sorry to tell you this. The world is changing too fast for me. In two years, all of the antelope have disappeared. The deer are hidden in the highest hills. The coyote must hunt the smallest game. The bear are dead. The cattle are too valuable to eat so we sell them and eat sheep.

"Remember the great matanzas, when we slaughtered four hundred steers for their skins, for two dollars? Remember the plain dotted with deer and antelope? Now what is there to hunt?

"One beef sold makes a man rich. We live off these migrants as Warner does, like coyote lying in wait along a rabbit trail. We even charge them to bathe," No'ka said disgustedly.

"We have always survived by eating many different things. If one runs out, you have the others. I fear the cattle will not live through the droughts that plague this land. If they die, then what? I am not comfortable putting all our dependence on them.

"I am capitán and it is my place to look ahead and behind, to lead and to protect my people from harm. I cannot see how to do so in this new world. I will pass leadership to Antonio Garra, who has more confidence, believes in cattle and recognizes the Christian God. He has a better chance to successfully guide the People on this path."

Bill opened his mouth to protest, but No'ka stilled him with a raised hand.

"I am too old-fashioned for this time. I was old-fashioned when you came to live with us." No'ka brightened.

"In those years, I knew exactly what we as a people should do. I was proud to be capitán. I pointed the way with joy in my heart. Now, the way that must be pointed brings me no joy. My heart will not allow the fingers of my hand to uncurl. Antonio Garra is a good man. The People like him. Let us see where he can take us.

"I am content to follow, grumbling to myself, playing with my grandchildren and their Shadow, who know not the past or future, and see the world as it most truly is: a joyful place to live and die."

Shadow stretched and rolled in the moist sand. He lay on his back and offered his tummy for a scratch, grinning and swishing his fat tail. Wili came running, shouting, "Daddy, tata." He had a tadpole in his hand that was almost a frog, with legs and arms fully formed.

"Let's release him in the cold pool, Wili," No'ka said, getting up.

"You should tell the whole tribe what you just told me," Bill said, standing up too. "You should lead, even in giving up leadership."

No'ka gave him a smile.

"I always practice my speeches on Shadow. He's a good listener. I will tell the People tonight, when it is cool and we have eaten."

Muffled shots came from from the direction of Warner's. No'ka froze. Every person at the creek went silent. There was another burst of gunfire and some whooping, then more scattered shots. Shadow jumped up. His ruff stood out all along his spine; his ears cocked toward the sound.

"Drunks probably," Bill said. "It's too hot to be anything else."

"Too hot to go see," No'ka replied.

Half an hour later, Luna galloped into Cupa on his sweat-lathered pony. He was breathing hard. "California was ratified by the U.S. Congress as a free state. It was the nineteenth of September," he yelled from the bank.

Bill cheered. Luna had a huge grin on his usually solemn face. He spun the excited pony and sped back down the trail.

No'ka looked as though he'd been slapped.

He shouted out the news in Cupeño to the questioning bathers. There was no response.

"It means that this land is now officially one of the United States of America," said No'ka loudly. "We no longer belong to Mexico." This brought murmurs.

"I guess that makes us all Americans," he said to Bill with a shrug.

"Damn right it does." Bill clasped his arm. "I'll go tell the women."

As Bill turned away, a frown creased No'ka's face. When Bill looked back, the chief had taken Wili's hand. He was smiling, but tears welled to spill down both cheeks. He jerked his head toward the houses, signing Bill to keep going. No'ka took his hat off, filled it with water and put it back on with a lopsided grin.

Wili squealed, "Let me do it, tata, let me do it."

Bill dunked his clothes in the stream and donned them as he went up the path. Shadow stayed in the cool sand, watching Wili, wary of mischief.

56

WILI'S SIBLING

N THE morning of the sixteenth of December, Falling Star's water broke. Bill helped her to her mother's house where she went straight into labor.

Wili was curious and afraid when he heard his mother moaning. He wanted to stay with her; Shadow too cocked his head in concern and didn't want to leave. White Fox shooed them away with a wave of her hand.

Bill took them for a walk up the trail to Eagle's Nest. The air was fresh-chilled and clear. Shadow sprang ahead, but Wili kept looking back.

"Why can't we stay?" he whined.

"She doesn't want us to see her like that."

"Like what?"

"In pain, the baby coming out."

"Does it hurt?"

"Yes, a lot." Bill took Wili's hand to keep him walking.

"Is that why she was crying?"

"Yes," Bill said.

"Is there blood?"

"A little, like when the lambs are born."

"What if the baby won't come out?"

"It has to. Otherwise it would grow too big and kill the mother."

Wili held his father's hand tighter.

"I hope it comes out," he said.

"It will."

They followed Shadow to the lookout. It presented a panoramic view, Cupa way below, as perfectly miniaturized as a ship in a bottle.

"It's all so far away," Wili offered.

Bill had a moment of panic. Everything seemed so fragile; as though they were barely there, barely touching the earth. An eagle circled beneath their feet. It made Bill dizzy. He took a step back.

"Let's go see whether you have a brother or sister." He felt the tremble in his voice. He clutched Wili's hand.

Shadow took off down the trail and they bounded after, Bill's heart pounding.

He breathed deeply. "Wait for me, Shadow," he called. Shadow came back. His tail wagged steadily, like a pump handle. He nudged Bill with his cool nose and took the lead again, powerful haunches swaggering from side to side.

"I like it when we do everything together," Wili said.

"I do too." Bill gave his hand a squeeze.

"Shadow worries when you're gone."

"How do you know?"

"He has a worried look when you leave. He stays right by Mommy and me till you come back."

"He's a good dog."

"He's the best dog. I hope he never dies."

"That's just what I was thinking."

"Will the baby be there when we get home?"

"Yes." Yes. He prayed for Falling Star to be all right.

They hustled down the trail and entered the village to cries of "It's a boy; a son; you have a brother."

Falling Star named him No'ka Soaring Eagle, after the eagle who had watched over his birth. For Wili, there could only be one No'ka. "Cano," he dubbed his little brother—and that is the name that stuck.

57

THE PROMISE

P A B L O came to Cupa on a tour of native villages to explain the confusing U.S. Indian policy. Antonio Garra called a public meeting of the tribal council. When everyone was settled around the great oak, Pablo stood and raised his hand.

"I have been talking to Major Heintzelman, our military commander, and to General Joshua Bean, the judge for San Diego County. I ask them two questions: Are we natives to be American citizens? And, what will happen to our land? This is what they have said:

"Anyone who is Mexican and resides in California has become a U.S. citizen. This includes Englishmen like Stokes, Italians like Bandini, mongrel Spanish like the Picos, all of the miner-Mexicans who came in '48 and Californios like the Osunas and Alvarados. Indians are only citizens if they were once Mexican: baptized Catholic, Spanish-speaking and living in towns. I am a good example. The rest of you who live in the 'hills,' in native villages, on your own land, non-Catholic, were never Mexican. You were always Indians and will not become U.S. citizens."

Every person had a question, or something to shout out. There were arguments over who could and could not be considered a U.S. citizen; who had been Mexican, or felt themselves so; and who were Christians or mission-educated, or baptized. The Garras and the baptized Cupeño and Pauma could possibly qualify, as mission-educated Christians, but none of them would admit to having been Mexican. Bill was obviously American, but even his children were a question mark.

"As Indians, you are members of a sovereign nation, the Kuupiaxchem, or Cupeño to the Americans," Pablo explained. "You have no rights or obligations to the United States. Your relationship to the United States will be governed by a treaty, to be prepared and signed by the president sometime in the future."

There was some cheering. A sovereign nation sounded good.

"As to land, the policy is clearer. All land granted by legitimate Spanish or Mexican governments will be given to the grant holder. A land court is being set up to examine each grant. All land not part of legitimate grants will belong to the U.S. government, to sell, to give to settlers, to assign to the sovereign tribes, or to keep. In your case, Cupa is part of Warner's grant, of Rancho San José del Valle, and will eventually belong to him, if he has not sold or mortgaged it to someone else by then."

The village rose in outrage. There were screams of death and warpath. It took both No'ka and Garra, flapping his arms like a rooster, to hush the tribe.

"When an Indian agent is appointed for San Diego, when a treaty is prepared, you may apply for other land nearby. Or you may appeal to Warner to give you part of his land, or buy Cupa from him. This you must do. It is in the future, but it will come to pass," said Pablo, sitting down.

The People broke into a hundred conversations. Over an hour, their response distilled to this: They would present a united front as tribal Indians. They would seek a treaty and sovereign lands, sanctioned by the president and Congress. But the only land the Kuupiaxchem wanted was Cupa and the big valley around them.

It seemed certain that Warner would gain title to Cupa. There was talk of murdering him and his family; of opposing his claim; of supporting his grant deeds in return for part of the land; or buying the land from him. It was decided that No'ka and Bill should appeal to Warner for a part of his land. He had once promised the land surrounding Cupa to No'ka. As a first step, they could find out if he would still honor this promise.

Bill agreed to tie this appeal to Warner's own request—that he run the ranch and store during the first session of the California State Senate, which began the twentieth of January. Warner had won the election. If Warner were positive about the land, Bill would work for him. If not, Bill would decline and the Cupeño would work against Warner and his store in every possible way.

The tribe was united in this plan. There was not one dissenter. Even those who had been plotting to kill Warner since before Bill's arrival agreed that this was a prudent first move.

ON December 25, Bill rode to the Warners to wish them a happy Christmas. Bill hadn't been in their house in months. It felt good to slouch in a leather chair sipping a rummed eggnog, watching the children play with their presents in the warmth of a cheery fire. Anita had erected a small pine tree, decorated with cutout cookies, dyed string and colored hollow eggs. It had a tin star at the top. Under it she had arranged a nativity scene of carved wooden figures. The flock of sheep was especially well done, with white-painted curly wool, and black hooves, horns and nose.

Warner eventually slumped his big frame into the chair next to Bill's with a groan, and sipped on his eggnog. After polite talk about their families, Warner said, "I'm counting on you to manage the ranch for me this first session of the Senate. I'm taking Anita and the children this time. Six months is too long for me to be away from them."

He looked at Bill expectantly. Bill looked at the fire. He was nervous about what he had to say.

"I'm enjoying my life at Cupa, John. With the second boy, I have to be at home more to help with Wili, who's old enough now to want to do man's work. He follows me around like Luna does you."

Bill looked up to meet Warner's eyes.

"You can bring him here. There'll only be Luna and the other hands. I'm taking Fanny and her sister with me. Bring the whole family. It'll be good for them to live in a real house for a while. And good for you too," Warner said with a glance at Bill's worn moccasins.

"I can't have my wife and kids in the store. These migrants aren't that tolerant. I'd have to be watching them every minute."

"Then you can bring one of the grandmothers to cook for you, and a couple of men to help out. You can go see your family sometime each day. I've got to have you here. There's no one else can do the job. I'll pay you double what you got last year. I'll pay for two store helpers."

Warner leaned toward Bill. His only other choice was to close the store and leave a small crew to maintain and guard the ranch.

"The Cupeño are worried about losing their ancestral lands," Bill said, looking at the fire. "No'ka wants to know if you will honor your pledge to give them the land around Cupa . . . if your own claim is recognized by the courts."

Warner leaned back in his chair. He took a slurp of eggnog without taking his eyes off Bill. He knew where the conversation was going.

"No'ka wants to know, or the Garras?"

"Both of them, all of us. We're all concerned."

"Well, I'm not giving any land to the Garras . . . or to any of the Pauma, or to you," Warner said irritably, then laughed.

Bill knew that he resented the way Antonio Garra had come back to Cupa when the mission was dissolved, bringing all of his cattle to run on what Warner considered to be his land. He was jealous of the money the Garras were making on his property.

When Bill didn't reply, Warner said, "Of course I'd never make the Cupeño leave the hot springs. That's been theirs forever and will always be theirs as far as I'm concerned." His tone was conciliatory. "And I'd give you a piece of land to build a house right here by mine, if you'll bring your family to stay."

Anita had been listening, sitting on the arm of John's chair. She nodded in agreement.

"But the Garras have no rights anywhere else on the ranch," he said stubbornly.

"They're part of the tribe," Bill said. "Antonio Garra is now capitán. And the tribe needs more land than the hot spring's to survive."

Warner choked on his eggnog, coughing and snorting. Anita patted him on the back.

"The tribe . . ." he sputtered. "I've got a tribe too," he shouted. "How would the tribe like it if I brought my tribe here to live: the whole Pico family and all of their cattle, my brothers and their families. How would No'ka like that?"

There was nothing Bill could say. No'ka would hate it.

"You don't see me filling the land with settlers, handing out mining claims, leasing it to cattlemen. It's just me and my family. No'ka should have kept it that way too."

"He had no choice. The Garras' clan has always been here. Antonio didn't choose to live at the mission. They dragged him there as a child. He made the most of it and now he is back."

"Yes, I know, but No'ka didn't have to make that cattle thief chief. He did that all on his own. And he'll live to regret it."

Bill let the tongue-tied insult pass. He didn't like Garra being chief any more than Warner did.

"Besides, if he's really a member of the tribe, why does Garra still burn an AG on his cattle instead of just a K for Kupa like the rest of you. Every time I see that AG brand, I think, 'What are this man's cattle doing on my land?'" Warner shook his head.

"He's proud of his herd. He shares the money."

"I'm sure he does. Anyway that's not my business. We've always gotten along well with the Cupeño. If I ever get the court to recognize my grants, I'll give the land around the hot springs to them. Any cattle with the K brand can graze anywhere else they like. If Antonio Garra wants to run his private herd on my land, when I have clear title, he'll have to pay me rent. If he wants any land of his own, he can buy it. The ranch isn't worth as much as his cattle anyway. If he drove them to San Francisco, he'd get five hundred dollars a head." Warner leaned back in his chair. He looked tired and disgusted.

Anita stroked John's neck, calming him. He closed his eyes.

"So you'd sell some of the land to the Cupeño at the time you get title?"

"Sure. We certainly don't need it all. Anita would like to spend more time in Los Angeles—with her tribe." He smiled at his wife. "We want the children to go to school. I'd like to do something else. I'll try this senator job and see how we fare in San José. We've been out here on our own for six years now. It will be nice to be in a town."

"Tell him about the railroad," Anita cajoled.

"Well, that's another thing. If the railroad goes north, through the Sierra Nevada to San Francisco, which is the route they're promoting, then the Santa Fe Trail will be as dead as it was before the gold rush. Deader even.

"Dead trail, dead store; the Warners packed up and gone. The Cupeño will have it all to themselves. Tell that little story to No'ka. You can buy the whole damn place if that happens," John Warner grumbled.

"Y O U   must relate this to the capitán, the alcalde, and the rest of the council. They should hear the story fresh," said No'ka that evening.

"All of it?" Bill was thinking of the digs at Antonio Garra.

"Yes, all of it. How else can they make a valid decision?"

The council listened carefully, mostly in silence. When Bill had finished, they all looked to Antonio Garra.

Garra stared at his lap for a couple of minutes. Finally he looked up. He was struggling to control his face, which twitched and trembled. He passed both hands over his forehead and down, over eyes, nose and mouth, brushing them off his chin. He sat on them. He closed his eyes and he kept them closed for another minute.

Antonio Garra was an expert at sign language. It was instinctual. His hands flew and fluttered like a hula dancer's, making pictures of his words as he spoke, mesmerizing an audience. When he sat on them, he was holding back his thoughts, stilling his willful hands. Finally he released them to speak.

"Warner is an intelligent man. He turns us against each other, so that we will be weak and he can do as he pleases. I cannot defend myself against his accusations, for they are true. I have never hidden anything that he finds offensive. The AG brand came with me on my cattle. My cattle have proliferated in this valley. I do not deny these facts." His right hand chopped twice.

"But it is also true that I belong to this place, unlike Warner, who arrived with a piece of paper that said the land was his. And now, maybe this mighty nation of United States will confirm that the land truly is his. But the land was stolen from the Kuupiaxchem. This too is true. And Warner is the thief, and married to the sister of Pico, another thief." He stealthily plucked an imaginary coin from the air and put it in his pocket.

"How can you compare the branding of a calf, who strayed with mine, to stealing this whole valley?" His hands thrust and soared.

"Warner does not have to give me land. I will buy land if I need or want it. He does have to give land to the tribe. This is only just, and as he has pledged. We will hold him to this pledge, at penalty of death."

Antonio looked at Bill defiantly and drew a finger across his neck.

"As to my brand, when Warner truly owns the land, I will put a K on all of my cattle. I would be a fool not to." He chuckled and the listeners joined him. "If the council so wishes, I will also brand all future calves with a K, from this day forth."

He looked out and everyone nodded assent except his son, who was perfectly still. Garra Senior's shoulders slumped dejectedly.

"If I do not do a good job, if I make mistakes, if you want me to retire as capitán, or leave to wander the unclaimed lands, you have only to tell me truly. I will go willingly, and still be grateful for the kindness you have shown to my clan; for the home we have shared; and for the mantle of chief that you have bestowed on me."

He looked down at his hands, which had been moving gently, making eloquent signs. They stroked his feather cape as he raised his eyes.

"I did not come home to be, and I will not be, a burden to the Kuupiaxchem. Huh."

They all applauded.

"Let us save our money to buy this land when we can. Let us pray for the northern railroad. Let us look to the day when the whole valley is ours again, forever. Huh."

The whole assembly cheered a mighty "Huh."

58

HARASS THEE

ILL watched the boys napping by the hearth, while Falling Star washed their clothes at the creek. He threw a log on the fire. Cano gurgled and waved his arms. He had inherited his father's eyes and Falling Star's straight black hair. His skin was still a bright pink. Bill felt an overwhelming tenderness. They were living bundles of sweetness and joy, which he wished to eternally protect. But who could possibly protect them?

He ached for them, for the teasing they would get as children, for the name calling, the cold shoulders and whispers as adults. Where could they truly belong? Who would accept them just as they were, neither Indian, nor Mexican nor American.

The remarks tossed around the store—"squaw man," "half-breed bastards," "bucks" and "does"—rolled off without penetrating. But they stung. He didn't want his boys to be stung. And they would be. The world was there, everywhere, to be feared, enjoyed . . . endured. He could only try to give them a chance, as Pablo, Falling Star, No'ka and even Warner had done for him.

Hooves clattered on cobblestone; he heard voices in English, bad English, and opened the door a crack. Two riders were dismounting at the big oak, peering curiously at the houses. Down the street, at the entrance to town, milled another dozen riders. The afternoon sun silhouetted them, but Bill could make out sombreros among caps and felt hats: a mixed group of Californios and Americans.

Falling Star was coming up from the creek with the laundry, in a hurry. Bill slipped out and walked toward the two men at the oak. He passed a few people in doorways, curious, but no one moved. Over his shoulder, he saw Falling Star enter their house. He kept on alone.

The two men were armed with horse pistols and new rifles. Both horses packed a second rifle. One man was small and dark, rodentlike. He was dressed in a caballero's tight pants and black high boots, with a blue shirt and a dragoon's coat with brass buttons up each side of the chest. He wore a dragoon's cap. There was a bowie knife strapped to the mousy man's hip. The other wore what looked like a Mexican general's uniform, with knee-high polished boots; lots of braid and frilly epaulets in gold tassel on his coat. His hat was an odd tricorner, but soft, with a pheasant feather. Bill saw a second smaller pistol in his belt.

The fancy uniform stepped forward and nervously offered a hand.

"Count Agoston Haraszthy, sheriff of San Diego County and San Diego city marshal," he said in a thick accent. He gave Bill's hand three quick pumps, dropping it on the third. "This is my deputy, Mister Cave J. Couts."

Bill touched the smaller man's stiff hand, saying, "William Marshall, pleased to meet you." Couts took his hand back without a word and rested it on his pistol butt.

"Villiam Marshall. Ze Injun lover," exclaimed the count. "I have heard much about you." He looked down the street. "But, where are your Injuns? That we would like to know. Ha!" He laughed and Couts grinned.

Bill had jumped at the "ha." He took a breath.

"They're pretty shy, and it's cold today. What brings you way out here?"

"Actually, Willy boy, we came to see a man who is living here, by the name of Antonio Garra," Deputy Couts drawled.

Bill looked at his ratface, then back to the sheriff. "Your deputy speaks," he said with a smile. "And which Antonio Garra would you like to talk to?"

"Both would be convenient," said Haraszthy.

"I'll see if I can find them. Are those your men at the other end of town?"

"Yes."

"They can relax. The people here are peaceful. I'll be right back."

Bill walked quickly to the Garras' cluster of houses, which was just off the main street, in a clearing surrounded by oaks. They were both at home, sitting around a fire pit in the center of the main house.

They pulled on boots and coats and followed Bill to the sheriff. Haraszthy was stomping to keep warm, or from nerves.

"Sheriff Haraszthy, this is Chief Antonio Garra and his son, Tonio," Bill said in English.

The count bowed stiffly to Garra Senior and said, "Good to meet you." The son was ignored.

"Mucho gusto," said Garra.

Haraszthy pulled a paper from his coat pocket and handed it to Garra. Garra opened it and read it, then handed it to Bill.

"He doesn't know much English," Bill told the sheriff.

"Well, he should learn, if he wants to be American. Tell him it is his tax bill for years 1849 and 1850, from our treasurer, County of San Diego."

Bill looked at the handwritten note. It read, *Antonio Garra, Mexican/U.S. Citizen, of San Luis Rey, Pauma Valley and Cupa, 300 head of cattle at $1 U.S. currency per head per year, $600 U.S. total.* The due date was December 31, 1850. At the bottom it said, *Fee for grazing rights on U.S. Government land in San Diego County.*

Garra had his hands clasped. He could read a bit of English. In Spanish Bill said, "Do you understand this bill, Antonio?"

"No," he spat, "but I read the numbers."

Haraszthy straightened at the "No." He touched his little pistol.

"He said he didn't understand," Bill explained, waving down the sheriff's gun hand.

"Very simple," said the sheriff. "He owes six hundred U.S. dollars. Is January now, tax is due and we come to collect. We take payment in gold or cattle."

"Wait a minute," Bill said. "Garra is an Indian. The Cupeño are a sovereign nation. The cattle are on private property. He can't be taxed or charged a grazing fee."

"Yes; yes he can. He was a Mexican citizen, now a U.S. citizen, as so are you. We know he was educated at Mission San Luis Rey. He lived there. He cannot pretend now to be a wild Indian, to avoid taxes."

Bill was astonished at this speech. He knew Garra understood the gist.

"All land is U.S. government land, until land courts say otherwise. Grazing fees must be paid. We are a new county, all must pay some share of our many expenses of government." Haraszthy shrugged.

Bill translated to Garra, who remained immobile. Tonio cursed in Cupeño and Couts tightened his grip on his pistol butt.

Bill gave the deputy a hard stare.

"Our orders are to seize the cattle and hold them in lieu of payment, unless you have cash or gold," Couts said with a smirk.

Bill translated this.

"No one has that much money," Garra said.

"He doesn't have the money, but I'm sure he could raise it," Bill offered, hoping for time.

"We will take some cattle," Haraszthy told Garra. "Your steers have AG brands?" He looked from Garra to Bill.

"Yes," Bill said. Garra nodded sickly.

"We hear you're running cattle too, Willy boy," said Couts. "You have to pay a grazing fee on government land."

"I don't have any cattle. I work for Warner."

"What about your dowry, squaw man. What happened to those four hundred head."

Bill looked from one to the other, trying not to flinch.

"You ever heard the term, Indian giver?" he asked. "Well that's what happened to my dowry. I had to give the cattle back."

"We know about you, Villiam," Haraszthy nearly shouted. He had read Bill's surprise like a book. "Do not suppose we are stupid like your Mexicans. We know all about you. You are famous: ze Injun lover!"

He clapped Bill on the shoulder and Bill jumped.

"We will round up our AG brands now."

The sheriff started toward his horse.

"Hold on," Bill said. "How many cattle do you think you're taking?"

"At forty dollars a head, that makes fifteen," Couts told them.

"They're worth five hundred. You know that. Two hundred minimum."

"Maybe in San Francisco; not here in the boondocks. Forty a head."

They led their horses down the street toward their waiting posse, who had dismounted. Bill followed, the Garras speechlessly behind. Leandro Osuna, Ramón and a couple of other Californios slouched with a rough-looking bunch of Americans—miners and ex-soldiers like Couts.

Bill and the Garras watched them mount. Bill's thoughts were tumbling like a rock slide down a canyon wall. What fools they were, dreaming away in their mountain valley, thinking themselves invisible. The sheriff's information had certainly come from the Osunas, who would be delighted to make trouble for the Cupeño and Bill. Now they had come to Cupa to steal away a good herd of their cattle, skinny, but worth way more than the tax bill. Those cattle would end up fattening on the Osuna and Couts ranches. The thieves would be laughing at the memory of the Garras' incredulous faces for months.

The mounted men quickly rode out of sight. The whole village emptied from their houses into the street. The Garras were shouting and cursing, blaming everything on Warner. No'ka held Antonio, while Stomping Deer and two others wrestled Tonio to the ground. White Fox was screaming at No'ka. Garra's wife was crying and holding on to his leg. It was pandemonium.

Bill told Falling Star to keep everyone at Cupa. He saddled his horse and took the back trail to Warner's ranch.

59

THE VALUE
OF SILENCE

WARNER talked too much, to too many people. He could tell the same story a thousand times. He would let two or three idle men occupy his whole day. Bill had learned from the Cupeño the value of silence: the silence of companions working together, the silence of the negotiator, the silence of trade and gambling, silence between enemies, the silence of rest with friends. Silence was a pleasure and a tool: a strategy. It framed the things you did say.

Warner rarely employed it, so when he was quiet, people noticed. They felt he was angry; or holding something back, as Gillespie had felt when he questioned Warner during the war. Warner's silences were framed by unsaid words. They made people uncomfortable.

When Bill arrived at Warner's, John said, "So that pompous Hungarian visited you too? He was here looking for a stallion, stolen from Deputy Cave Couts. Probably the one stayed behind when Graham came through." He chuckled. "Have a look around the ranch, I said. It's so big I haven't even been to the other side in two years. I pointed toward Palomar." Warner shrugged. "That was it. They rode off toward the mountain."

"You didn't discuss the Garras' cattle?" There was no way Warner had had a two-sentence conversation with such an interesting pair.

Juan Largo kept his eyes on Palomar. "Not a word. 'Course you can't ride fifty yards on this ranch 'thout that AG brand jumping out of the red shank and stamping itself on your horse's rump. Everyone knows about Antonio Garra and his cattle. He sells them in San Diego. What was there to say?"

Bill didn't comment. An uneasy silence settled uncomfortably. He got up to leave.

"We'll be pulling out for San José the eleventh," Warner said. "I'd like you to come the tenth, so we have a day to go over everything."

"Fine, I'll see you then."

Warner followed Bill to the door.

"I'm sorry about the cattle. I'll talk to Judge Joshua Bean and see if anything can be done."

BILL'S six months' sentence at Warner's store was an unexpected pleasure. The atmosphere was entirely different without Warner and Anita, the children and their keepers, with no threat of them returning unexpectedly. He had no boss. There was no tumultous family to tiptoe around, no cantankerous owner looking over his shoulder. He stayed in the big house with its modern kitchen stove and stone fireplace. Most of the tribe visited at least once, dressed in their best, coming to buy things, to bring items to sell, or just to visit. Falling Star and the boys often spent the night. Wili would stay a week at a time, following Luna, as Luna had once followed Bill.

The shop took most of his time, but it too ran more smoothly without Warner. Bill kept every transaction businesslike. He didn't trade for things he couldn't sell. He sold out the liquor and didn't restock it. The huge pile of goods and broken equipment that had been collected over the years was liquidated, turned to cash or gold.

As he watched the safe fill, Bill ticked off Warner's shortcomings as a businessman: John could never resist a sale or trade, even if it was obvious that he was losing. He didn't want a customer to slip by. He had a soft spot for the trail-weary immigrant. He had the New England Puritan's fear of throwing away anything that might possibly be useful, down to a bent horseshoe nail or scrap of worn-out leather. Consequently, he thought any item received in trade would be valuable to someone, sometime. He bought useless gadgets, obscure machinery, broken wagons, rotten wagon harnesses, guns without barrels, one-wheeled carts. The place was a junkyard.

Bill purchased very little except staples, which he sent for from San Diego. At No'ka's suggestion, he took the rough tables and benches from their shady ramada and put them in the sunny hitching area, by the water trough. This reduced the customer's loitering time, without being too rude.

As a warning to potential troublemakers, Bill kept two heavily armed young men at the corrals between the barn and house. Pablo dressed them in U.S. Army uniforms and the marines' wide-brimmed hats. They carried a horse pistol at each hip and two rifles apiece. They mounted a defunct field gun on a raised adobe platform that commanded the barnyard. The guards were on hand night and day. They were never challenged.

L U N A bloomed that spring. He didn't grow any bigger, but his presence and energy encompassed the ranch. Bill let his girlfriend, Narcissus, move into the barn. They ran the milk, butter and cheese factory, tended the animals and maintained the barnyard, wagons, tack and wells. Luna did all of the blacksmithing, stocked the store, locked up at night, paid the workers, stacked firewood at the hearth each evening and removed the ashes in the morning. He loved having the Cupeño at the ranch. A smile glued itself to his face at dawn and stayed there even in his sleep, according to Narci.

"I wish Luna lived with us all of the time," Bill said to Falling Star, one cold evening as they sipped a cup of tea before the fire.

"Of course you do," she snapped. "Everybody loves to have a slave."

"He seems to like it."

"What else does he know. I'm sure the Warners make him do twice as much."

O N a breezy March morning a decrepit mountain man named Jim trudged into the store looking for John Warner. Jim was dressed in buckskins, filthy and tattered, and a worn-down pair of knee-high laced moccasins with fancy beadwork in black, gold and red. He had some nice lynx pelts to trade, now unusual, and little else. He claimed to be an old friend of John's, who had been with him on the first trading trip to Santa Fe, in 1831. Jim was on his way to the gold fields, like everyone else.

Bill was generous with whatever Jim needed and invited him to sup and spend the night. The mountain man, who was not so old when he'd washed and shaved, was thrilled to be sitting at a table, eating a home-cooked meal. Bill asked him to recount that first trip from St. Louis with Warner, and to describe what John was like as a young man.

"Green," he said. "We were both green as blades of grass in March. Warner was educated and prim, but we toughened him up pretty quick.

"Our first brush with the Indians—who were pretty ignorant about Americans; had barely seen any at all—John got real shook up.

"Two men dropped behind the train to hunt antelope, a half hour after we passed a Paiute village. Six Paiutes surrounded them and started shooting arrows. Only one man made it back to the wagons. John and I and four others went out to look for the missing hunter. We found him scalped and gutted. I guess they'd taken his heart and liver. Warner took one look and puked his breakfast. We strapped the chopped body to a horse and hauled it back to the camp to bury. Warner looked pretty pale for a week."

Jim laughed and slapped his knee. "But boy did we get back at those murderin' Injuns. A wagon driver had died the day before of smallpox. We took all of his clothes and blankets and his pillow, and bundled them up real neat, like a big present. We tied them to a pack saddle on a broke-down horse. That night we led the horse close enough to the village that he could smell it, and gave him a smack on the rump.

"Next year, we came back the same way after trading out in Santa Fe. That Paiute village was like a ghost town. Them few that survived were pockmarked for life. But them Injuns are too dumb to learn their lesson. The Paiutes is still givin' the trains a hard time."

Bill had never heard this tale from Warner, which surprised him. Then again it didn't. He mentioned the story to Falling Star, who told her mother. She told No'ka, and Stomping Deer, who told Tonio Carra, who told his father. The whole village buzzed for a week with this gruesome tale of murder and revenge.

Epidemic disease was the greatest fear of the People: death by unseen infection intentionally spread. Disease had been a weapon of the Spanish conquest as surely as the musket. When half of the tribe could take sick and die in a month, and none of the Spanish were affected, it was too obviously witchcraft; black magic, which the invaders controlled.

In California, Indian knowledge of disease was limited to a very few complaints, mostly problems of the gut from eating the wrong things, and the physiological aches and pains of life. The Spanish ability to kill them with this new magic devastated their self-confidence. It discredited the helpless shamans and chiefs. It broke the collective spirit, making the padres' job of converting them to Christianity easy.

The missionaries' denials that they caused these magical deaths on purpose were impossible to believe. In Baja California, the location of first contact with Spanish diseases, by 1830 there was not a native ear to hear the priests' protests. All were dead, the missions closed, the adobe walls melted back into the desert, the padres sent north in search of living people to convert.

But these were legends, dark fables, nightmare myths that every child was told, about the evil *sosabitom*. No one had ever seen or heard direct proof like this. The story had a big impact. Warner was demonized. The Cupeño were careful not to cross him. They feared that he might do the same to them.

W H E N Warner returned to the ranch, Bill asked him about the incident. John wouldn't look at Anita's questioning face. He stared at Bill for a long time in silence, jaw working—a silence that rang with unuttered curses.

"I was there. It happened. It wasn't my idea. I don't think I could have stopped it, even if I'd wanted to. We had just buried a mutilated friend," he spoke slowly and defiantly.

"You never mentioned it . . ."

"No, I didn't. I'm not proud of it. I don't like to talk about it. Just like you never mention the night they carved up those eleven Californios in front of you at Cupa."

That silenced Bill.

"And I never asked you about that," Warner added. "Don't forget who you are, Bill."

60

A LIFE TAKEN

THAT was the best advice Bill ever got from Warner. The day John and Anita had returned from San José, July 15, 1851, Bill left his employ, as though released from a trap, never to go back. He vowed to live and work at home, at Cupa. That's who he was.

The village had been peaceful those six months. Antonio Garra had recuperated from the cattle seizure in stony silence. He appointed Jacobo Stomping Deer to be alcalde of Cupa, with the approval of the young men and No'ka's supporters. The Garras retreated to their compound. When summer came, Garra and his son drove their cattle and horses to Palomar, to commune with the Great Spirit and to consider their past and future.

It was a dry spring and hot dry summer, punctuated by the passage of ten thousand sheep, on their way north for slaughter in the gold fields. They had been driven from Tecate and Jacumba. The sheep devoured what little grass was left, down to the roots, leaving a barren dusty swath that endured into fall. The range was useless. White Fox joked that the Great Spirit would tell the Garras to come back when there was fresh pasture for their cattle.

The elder Garra reappeared in late September. He had left his son with the stock at the high meadows. He called a meeting of the council and told them that the taking of his steers had been wrong. Something must be done. He would visit the other tribes to discuss the sherrif's unjust taxes and report back his findings. That was all he wished to say.

No'ka told Antonio that Haraszthy had also tithed the Kumeyaay and the Luiseño, though not as heavily as the Garras. Bill reported on Warner's promised talk with Judge Joshua Bean: the judge had said that tribal Indians were not subject to taxes and that they should refuse to pay them. Armed with this information, Garra, who still considered himself commander-in-chief of all the Luiseño, left to canvass the tribes.

T H E following day, White Fox's horse El Rey, a twenty-five-year-old stallion whom she had raised from birth, took sick and quickly went down. He lay on his side, thrashing, semiparalyzed, choking on dust and sand.

White Fox stayed with him night and day, holding his head out of the dirt, giving him water and tender grasses, desperately trying to nurse him back. Everyone helped, but after two days No'ka concluded that El Rey should be shot. He was suffering too much.

Horses are different for men than for women. Men will ride a horse to one locale and leave it there in exchange for a fresh one. Men turn them out if they are lame; shoot them and eat them, if they are too old or wounded or weak to carry on. Horses have to be ridable, or else they are meat.

Women tend to keep a horse for life, dote on him, weep over him and never shoot a sick animal unless it is absolutely the only choice. White Fox cried for hours. She screamed at No'ka and begged for one more day. The next morning, exhausted, tears still rimming her eyes, she agreed.

"I think he's dying anyway," she sobbed. "You'd better shoot him."

"Are you sure?" asked No'ka.

"It was your idea," she sniffed. "If you still think you should, then shoot him."

No'ka looked at Bill and mouthed the word "You."

"I'll shoot him," Bill offered. "I know how to do it."

"And he won't suffer?" She was watching El Rey thrash, hooves furrowing the stall floor, head trenching, mouth filling again with sand.

"No, he'll die instantly."

"Yes, then. But do it quickly, before I change my mind."

"Will you make a ceremony?" she asked No'ka. "I want to tell him we're trying to help."

She started blubbering again and No'ka wrapped his big arms around her shoulders.

"I'll get my rifle," Bill said.

When he returned, the whole family had gathered at the stall. Luna had ridden over from the Warners' with some veterinary medicine.

White Fox looked at the gun apprehensively. Tears streaked her face.

No'ka steadied his voice, clearing his throat.

"I have said that death is the price of life . . . but it is more. Death and life are inseparable. There is no life without a death; there cannot be death without a life.

"Suffering too is a part of life. And an excess of suffering makes death welcome; a godsend."

No'ka looked into the sky. His voice boomed heavenward: "Let it be known to all who look upon us, that we believe El Rey's suffering to be too high a price, for whatever short term of life the stallion may gain by our inaction.

"Let it be known that we do not take lightly our role as gods in hastening this death, that we accept our part with heavy heart, only to bring an end to El Rey's suffering; to grant him final peace.

"Let it be known that we too would ask for the same swift death, if we suffered as El Rey suffers." No'ka looked at each person. He spoke softly.

"With this death, may suffering end for El Rey and for those of us who cherish him. Let this death restore joy to the living, and peace eternal to our beloved El Rey."

White Fox hugged No'ka. She closed her eyes. He nodded to Bill.

Bill knelt about five feet from El Rey's head, steadied the heavy rifle and sighted at a point on an imaginary cross drawn between opposite eyes and ears. He cocked the hammer, held his breath and pulled the trigger. El Rey twitched once. He was still before the echo of the explosion had subsided.

A gallon of crimson blood gushed from his mouth with the force of vomit. It spread in a pool on the sand. The heavy ball must have hit the jugular vein, passing through his throat.

White Fox rushed to dip her hands in the warm blood and printed them on the stone wall. She was sniffling and giggling, putting little crimson handprints all over the stall. The witnesses looked at each other in wonder and concern. Bill sat to clean his rifle. Shadow sidled up with his tail tucked in, sniffing at the dark blood.

They left White Fox alone with her horse the rest of the afternoon. At nightfall, No'ka came to tell Falling Star that White Fox wouldn't come in. She had taken a tallow candle, some sage, a blanket and pillow out to the stall, planning to spend the night with her dead friend. No'ka looked helpless.

Falling Star went out with Shadow to visit her mother. No'ka sat by the fire with his head down. "I didn't want to shoot El Rey myself. I don't want her to remember me that way, or to throw it in my face in an angry moment. She loved that horse."

"That was a nice thing you said."

No'ka stared at the coals. "I wanted her to feel better. She suffers so."

Falling Star came back. "It's freezing out there. She won't come in. Shadow stayed with her."

"Leave her alone," Bill told them. "She'll be fine."

"Let's bury him first light." No'ka said. "I don't want this to go on."

Bill awoke way before dawn. He walked in the cold to the stall. White Fox, Shadow, her faithful dog, Casimiro, and El Rey were all still as death. The tallow taper flickered eerily. He tiptoed back to bed.

In the morning they dug a hole eight feet long, four feet wide and six feet deep. A team of mules with blinders dragged El Rey into the hole. When he landed, his head turned under his neck.

White Fox yelled, "Don't leave him like that, straighten him out."

Bill and No'ka jumped in the hole and tugged and lifted until she was satisfied. By ten o'clock the dirt was packed over the horse. They covered the mound with river stones and built a fence to keep animals out. White Fox placed yellow daisies and purple desert blossoms on the stones. She spread fragrant sage around the perimeter and lit a tallow candle for each corner. Only then would she come in to breakfast.

White Fox stayed quiet, but her spirits were up. She was looking forward to raising one of El Rey's colts. Two of the mares were pregnant. She prayed that he would be the father.

61

A BIG BUCK

BILL went hunting with Wili and Shadow before sunrise on a cloudless and frosty morning. He wanted to get a deer for No'ka and White Fox, who were complaining about their diet of stringy mutton, stewed with acorn flour dumplings and a few vegetables. They couldn't afford to eat their high-priced cattle.

The hunters took a little used trail, northeast over a rocky ridge to the next valley, hidden well enough from migrants that deer dared to venture from the thick brush to graze, and near enough for Bill to arrive at the exact hour when the sun's first rays melt the frosted tips of fall's yellow grasses, rendering them soft, moist and appetizing.

They walked as fast as Wili could go, Shadow taking the lead. Wili carried a small bow and quiver of arrows No'ka had given him on his birthday. Bill had his powerful bow, the same one Pablo had taught him to hunt with, and new deer arrows with forged metal tips that Luna had pounded out in Warner's blacksmith shop. He was still a poor bowman, but with Shadow's help tracking, they had a good chance.

Silently they entered the hidden meadow, the first weak solar rays rendered visible by a fine mist clinging to the overhanging oak leaves. Bill motioned toward a rock, downwind from the probable approach of deer and large enough to conceal both men. At a hand signal, Shadow crouched behind the rock. Wili and Bill flattened themselves against its shaded side, standing with ready bows, one above the other. Wili braced against Bill's leg and hip, trembling.

The mist had evaporated by the time sunlight hit the grass. They were frozen in place, cold as their rock shelter, shivering after only five still minutes. A twig snapped and a stone rattled on gravel. Shadow tensed. Wili held his breath and quit shaking. Bill drew back his bowstring, breathing shallowly through the nose.

A buck emerged suspiciously from red shank and sumac. He sniffed and scanned the meadow. Four does and two young males followed him tentatively into the clearing. They began to graze, too far away for a clean shot. Father and son waited, arms vibrating with strain.

The big buck had not yet put his head down. He stared at them, walking slowly forward, never moving his gaze, nostrils flared, ears twitching. He kept coming steadily, curious. When the buck was ten feet from his arrow tip, Bill let it fly. So did Wili. Thunk and whap, the arrows entered chest and throat. The buck reared, twisting in the air. He ran a few paces toward his herd, then sank to his knees. Shadow was upon him, jaws clamped to the back of his neck. They toppled to the side as Wili and Bill ran up. The buck was dead.

Shadow bolted after the other deer, crashing through the underbrush. Wili's eyes opened round as teacups. He held the buck's head up by the antlers while Bill slipped his dirk into the exposed jugular vein. Blood flowed purple and Bill scuffed a drain for it in the sandy soil.

When the bleeding stopped, he told Wili to pull his arrow out. It had penetrated the neck about two inches and came out with a hard tug. Bill's steel point was broken off. "I think I hit the heart," he said. "He died so quickly."

"I aimed for the throat," Wili said proudly. "Grandpa says that's the only place a little arrow has a chance."

"It was a good shot."

"How come he walked right up to us?"

"I asked his permission to kill him. No'ka says a deer, if asked, will offer himself to be killed and eaten, so that we may have a good life. It is a gift."

"I think he saw us and wanted to find out what we were."

"Then he was doing his job, protecting his herd. It is still a gift."

"Thank you, deer, thank you," Wili said, patting its shoulder.

They hung the deer by his antlers from the nearest oak limb. He was way too heavy to carry back, even butchered. Bill gutted him. The broken arrow was lodged in the heart. Bill wrapped heart and liver in buckskin and put them in his pack. He tossed the guts in a deep gulch.

"I'll have to get some horses. Wili, you and Shadow can guard the deer. You stay in the tree. If a lion shows up, shoot him with your bow. Shadow can take care of a lion. I'll be right back."

Bill gave Shadow a lump of liver and boosted Wili into the tree. He trotted back up the trail, heart pounding. He had only killed three deer with his bow. The steel tips were a big improvement.

Bill sped up as he neared the village, beginning to worry about leaving Wili alone, and arrived at a dead run. When he quit gasping, he knocked on

No'ka's door. It was Wili's first deer. He imagined the three of them riding triumphantly back to the village, the ten-point buck draped over Wili's packhorse.

White Fox opened the door. She looked rattled.

"Oh, Bi'," she said, "How good you've come."

No'ka sat by the fire with the Garras, who had been gone at least a month. They all looked agitated.

"Wili and I killed a big buck on the trail to Wiliya." Bill took a couple of quick breaths. "I need to take a couple of horses to bring them back."

Everyone stood up.

"I'll go," said No'ka. "You shouldn't have left Wili."

"You left Wili?"

"Shadow's with him."

"I'll go too," White Fox said. "I need some air."

"Stay with Antonio." No'ka put his heavy hand on Bill's shoulder. "He wants to talk to you. We won't be long."

"Momentito," Bill signed to Antonio—thumb and forefinger a half inch apart—as he followed No'ka out. "What's happening?"

No'ka was moving fast toward his corral.

"The Garras want to lead us on a warpath."

"Against whom?"

"The Americans, who else? Talk to them."

He kept walking, muttering. White Fox ran by, buttoning her fur coat.

"Están locos," she twirled a finger around her ear, but didn't smile.

Bill saw blood, the blood of El Rey, the blood of the deer, Wili's blood, his own blood, flowing into the sand. He trudged back to No'ka's front door, angry by the time he got there. He jerked the door open and stormed in.

"Antonio! Antonio, have you gone mad. The warpath? You want to get us all killed?"

The Garras sat still.

"Buenos días, Bi'," Antonio said. "Sit down, sit down, calm yourself. Let us explain. There is much you must know. Then you can decide if we are mad or sane." Tonio patted a chair by the fire.

"Buenos días, I'm sorry. So tell me." Bill sat, clasping his hands. He stared into the coals—spear points danced, red- and white-hot—he closed his eyes and listened.

Antonio Garra spoke calmly and clearly.

"I have been to see the Luiseño at Pala, Las Flores, Temecula and San Luis Rey, the Kumeyaay at Santa Ysabel, and San Pasqual, the Cuyamaca in the Sierra Laguna, the Yumans, Cocopas and Cuchanos of the Colorado, the Cahuilla of the mountains and Chapuli at Coyote Canyon. I wanted to know their minds, and they to know mine. We are all of agreement on this point: The Americans have treated us cruelly and unfairly. All of us have been affected: killed, robbed, beaten, raped, starved, insulted or ignored. None have been treated as brothers." Garra's hands were flying.

"This is not new to me, or to you. What is new is that we are in agreement to rise up in revolt; to overthrow this American scourge." His voice rose to a powerful screech that stirred the hairs on Bill's arms.

"This year, the sheriff will again levy taxes on the native People, for their use of government lands to grow and graze the cattle that keep us alive. This is not legal according to General Joshua Bean, alcalde in Los Angeles, and the judge for our part of California. We will refuse to pay these unjust taxes. I have already told the sheriff so. If he tries to seize our cattle, we go to war. That is all. We will not give up one steer." He spread his arms, palms down, in a gesture of finality. Tonio nodded agreement.

"Have you spoken to Pablo?"

"Yes. It is he who talks to Bean."

"What does he say about this warpath?"

"That we are fools and will all be killed." Garra made a circle around his ear with a finger and drew it across his throat.

"He is right. The Americans will crush you. Do you know that Kearny marched all the way to Mexico City? Mexico gave up half its territory to get rid of him. You Indios couldn't even defeat the Mexicans. How can you defeat the U.S. Army?"

"If we cannot live at peace, then we shall live at war," said Antonio stubbornly. He crossed his arms.

"Suicide," Bill shook his head.

"What did you say?" Tonio was on his feet.

"It's suicide, Tonio. You know what killers they are."

"The Americans like to kill, yes. But do they like to die? That is what we shall find out," Tonio shouted in Bill's face.

"They have taken all of our land. They have not given any back," Antonio said. "Now they want to take our cattle. We are dead anyway." His hands and arms were flailing. "If so, then let them take our lives as men, at war, not as cowards, starving us to death, body and soul." Antonio's voice went soft and sad. He waved his arms in smooth circles to calm them.

Tonio took Bill's hands. His eyes were bright. "The first place we attack will be Warner's store. We'll need your help. We'll take the guns, money and supplies. With these, no one will be able to stop us."

"If war comes, yes, Warner must be the first to die," confirmed Antonio.

Hooves clattered. There were shouts. Bill opened the door to a street full of people. The big buck was tied across a packhorse led by No'ka. Wili strutted behind. Shadow walked stiffly alongside the prize, drool dripping from his pink and gray jowls, alert for any interference with his kill. The Garras slipped out the door to admire the stag.

Wili ceremoniously presented the deer to Alcalde Jacobo, who threw a rope over an oak limb, tied it to the antlers and hoisted the heavy carcass high to cure.

I N the evening, when they had roasted the liver and heart, No'ka cut a piece of each, first for Wili, then for Bill and finally for Shadow.

"We honor the courage of this brave buck, who gave his life so that his family might live. Partaking of his heart, we partake of the source of that courage. We thank him for feeding us, and ask that we ourselves shall grow as strong and die as bravely."

They ate, but with no pleasure. White Fox was sorry they'd killed the deer. She said, "I wish we were eating the Garras' cattle. All of them."

"I want to talk to Pablo," No'ka said. "I need to know who would join Antonio's warpath, and what the Americans might do to us."

"Can you stop the Garras?"

"I cannot stop a man from doing what he will do. But neither can he stop me."

"Then let's go see Pablo," Bill said, getting up.

62

TOUGH TALK

T H E Y took two horses apiece, some sleeping furs, a bundle of venison with acorn flour tamales and trotted down the darkened trail, into cool still night. The moon was new, invisible, stars and sky stretching from horizon to horizon like a glittering black bowl. The Garras' war drumming accompanied them halfway to Warner's; then only the night birds, hoofbeats and the creaking of leather.

They turned at the fork that led west along the southern rim of the plain and down the San Luis Rey River. The horses stuck close together. Bill could just barely see No'ka as a shape.

On the winding and steep descent to Pauma Valley, overhanging trees blocked even the starlight. The horses walked slowly, nervous, nickering to each other. The men jounced against the front of their saddles.

"This is the most fun I've had in a long time." There was nothing to attach the voice to, but it was No'ka's.

"It's good to be doing something. I can't stand to sit helpless, waiting . . . for God knows what."

No'ka grunted. This was the first time they'd ever done anything important together, just the two of them. It was also the first time Bill had seen No'ka leave the mountains.

"Do you want to stop at Manuelito's?"

"No," No'ka said. "We can see him on the way back. I want the mission to be the first thing I see."

They kept going in silence, stopping only once to drink and switch mounts, until a pale glow lit the forest. No'ka turned to Bill.

"Let us rest a bit and eat. I want to be fresh. We still have a long way to go. Here is grass for the horses."

He waved at a knee-high field of fresh shoots, slid off his horse and unrolled his furs. He wrapped himself in them and immediately fell asleep. Bill kept watch.

S E Ñ O R A Osuna opened her parasol. "We'll stop by Lieutenant Cave Couts's new house on our way to San Luis Rey."

"It's nowhere near finished and way out of our way," complained Lugarda. "And I can't abide that man."

"I know where Rancho Guahome is. My new buggy makes it easy. I want to see this grand palace he's supposedly building. Everything these Yankees do has to be big, just to make us look like peasants."

Whenever Lugarda was at her husband's Rancho Buena Vista, her mother would visit on the way to San Luis Rey's church, still the best in the county. 'Zul joined them for the outing. She wanted to see Pablo. The three women and Lugarda's daughter climbed into the lightweight, springed buggy. Ramón Osuna drove, and they bumped along the track toward Guahome.

Couts had married Juan Bandini's most attractive daughter and received Guahome, a twenty-two-hundred-acre grant of Luiseño land, as a wedding gift from his brother-in-law, Abel Stearns. With profits from supplying cattle to the same brother-in-law, the wealthiest merchant in Los Angeles, Couts had begun construction of his mansion.

"It's big all right," Couts said, pacing the new foundation, a horse whip folded under his arm. "None bigger in the county, save for the mission."

Señora Osuna counted the large spaces that would be rooms. It was ten times the size of her simple adobe.

"It will be expensive," she sniffed. Couts smelled of brandy.

"No problem, with the price o' cattle. I'm getting rafters and tiles cheap from the broke-down parts of the mission. An' these Injuns just about work for food." Couts unfurled his whip and gave it a playful crack over the ragged mob of Luiseño who labored at cementing adobe blocks and preparing wooden beams. There were more than a hundred men at the job. They ignored the whip.

"I bought your old ranch at San Marcos," he said to Lugarda. "It can feed another thousand cattle. If your husband ever gets back from the diggings, he says he'll sell me Buena Vista too." Couts twirled a curl of greasy black hair that sprung from his dragoon's cap. "You can keep the house, I just need the pasture."

"What on earth do you need pasture for? All of your cattle went north with my husband."

Jesús Machado had driven a collective herd of cattle, for Couts, the Osunas, himself and Abel Stearns, to Sacramento.

"Never you mind, Missus Machado. I'll get more of 'em." He turned to Señora Osuna. "Have you heard any more about this tax revolt that Injun chief Garra is trying to stir up?" Couts cocked his whip.

A boy had been talking to 'Zul. She gave him a coin from her pocket. "Gracias," the boy said—as Couts's lash snaked out to wrap around his arm. The coin dropped. Couts walked over to pick it up and handed it back to 'Zul.

"Can't have my Injuns begging. Makes me look bad," he said with a pointy-toothed leer. He cracked the whip again, this time across the boy's back, twice. The boy crumpled.

"What a horrible man," Señora Osuna whined as they drove off. "I wish Leandro would stay away from him—and that phony-count sheriff."

"They're perfect for each other," Lugarda said. "My husband too."

"Didn't Jesús promise Felipe Subria he would never sell Buena Vista?"

"Yes he did. He swore to it on his life." Lugarda glanced at 'Zul.

"That's not good," Señora Osuna fretted.

'Zul was watching Ramón, who tilted his head and perked an ear.

"You made me marry him," Lugarda reminded her mother.

"And you still haven't given him a son."

"You should have married him yourself, Mami. You're more his age and you make such nice sons." Lugarda put her arm around little Juliana.

"If the Indios kill Jesús, you'll be known as a Black Widow. You'll never find another husband."

"Mierda," said Ramón, under his breath.

"DARE I call Garra's bluff?" Sheriff Haraszthy asked Leandro Osuna and Major E. F. Fitzgerald, retired, First Dragoons. "Major Heintzelman's taken all of his soldiers north to Los Angeles."

"No matter," said Fitzgerald. "San Diego's nothin' but ex-army-navy-marines. I can raise a militia in four hours—tougher'n those green dragoons o' Heintzelman's."

"We Californios know how to deal with rebel Indios," Leandro told them. "Garra would never risk to attack us."

"If they do, we'll kick their asses clean back to the other side of the Colorado," boasted Fitzgerald.

/ / /

I N No'ka's absence, Antonio Garra had called a meeting of the tribe. He urged them to rise against the whites and slay them.

The Garras' plan of action was to attack Warner's store and Fort Yuma simultaneously. Then, with the guns captured from those armories, to hit San Diego and Los Angeles in force. The Cahuilla would take Los Angeles. Garra's men, the Yumans, Cuyamaca, Kumeyaay and Luiseño, would over-run San Diego. All non-Indians would be killed.

Antonio Garra had taken to wearing a grizzly bearskin. The robe was complete to the claws, with the intact skull for a headpiece. Garra was a fearsome sight and drew strength from the reactions he provoked. He had reached back into the darkest prehistory of the Kuupiaxchem, invoking the legend of Hoboyak, the common ancestor of all the tribe.

In some far-before time, the Kuupiaxchem had been slaughtered in a battle with their enemies. Hoboyak was the sole suvivor. He defeated his foes with the help of a magical bearskin—which became a real bear whenever he desired. The victorious Hoboyak had married two Luiseño girls. Every Kuupiaxchem descended directly from them.

Now Garra wore Hoboyak's invincible mantle. He confidently urged individual Cupeños to join him in certain victory. He read from a letter he had written to the Cahuilla capitán, Juan Antonio. "This war is for a whole life. If we lose, all is lost—the world if we win. Then it will be forever. Never will it stop."

Many young Kuupiaxchem, including Stomping Deer, had cheered and pledged to join Garra.

White Fox spoke for the majority: "You will lose this war. You cannot trust the Cahuilla and we would lose any war with the Americans. All will be lost. It is a fool's war, over cattle we care not for."

" I T ' S all a plot by Couts and Haraszthy and Abel Stearns to get more of the state's funds down to southern California," Pablo told No'ka. "The north is filthy rich and San Diego doesn't even have a penny to pay the troops. Heintzelman went to Los Angeles for the winter, just to be sure he has enough food for his men."

"An Indian uprising would get the attention of Sacramento," said Ibarra, "and convince them to regarrison the county and station a naval fleet in San Diego. Stockton moved his dance party to San Francisco and hasn't been back in three years. Sacramento has been ignoring her poor southern sister for far too long."

"War will be good for the local economy," Pablo said, "especially a frightful war, easily won. As a side effect, Indian land claims will be discredited before the courts. Nothing could be worse for us than this war."

"I'm sure they'd like to get a rope on Garra's cattle," Bill said.

"Even more than his neck," said Ibarra. "Couts needs cattle to fatten on his ranches. Haraszthy provides him with as many head as he can tax out of the people. Garra has more cattle left than anyone else in San Diego. If he revolts, they will take them all."

"Who would take part in a revolt?" No'ka asked, standing up, knocking over his chair. He put both hands on the table to steady himself.

"Not one native I have spoken to," said Pablo. "Of course, everyone is sympathetic. But the People on the coast have seen too much of the Americans to wish to fight them."

No'ka picked up his chair. "Gracias, Padre, thank you for your hospitality and information. I must go to my people now."

He touched Bill's shoulder and Bill stood.

"I'm coming with you," Pablo said.

"God bless you." Ibarra made the sign of the cross. "If the army or militia ever come, go to the chapel of Saint Francis. They will not dare to harm you there."

"Adios!"

"Adios!"

"I s that why you wore riding clothes to lunch?" Bill asked Pablo. "Had you already decided to come with us?"

"I'm on my way to see 'Zul at Buena Vista." Pablo whispered. "She's pregnant."

"Pregnant?" Bill twisted to face him. "Congratulations."

"The padre married us." Pablo smiled, young and shy again. "Lugarda wants to see you. She felt awkward after your last night together."

"She's been to the confessional?" Bill still hadn't told anyone about that night. He'd forgotten . . . there were no secrets in San Diego.

"No, she told me herself. 'Zul filled in the gaps."

"Tell her I'd like to see her too. After the revolution."

They laughed; it seemed so ridiculous.

Señora Osuna's buggy, coming fast down the San Luis Rey River Road, forced them into the brush. Ramón did not stop.

"Lugarda . . ." Bill waved.

Lugarda was only able to hold out her hand and smile in greeting.

With a salute to Bill, Pablo turned back after them.

"So that's the famous Lugarda," No'ka grunted, whacking his horse with both heels.

Bill watched the buggy until it disappeared, then galloped after No'ka.

63

THE GAUNTLET

HEN No'ka related what he had learned, the council meeting broke into excited argument. Some were in favor of Capitán Garra's plan for a widespread war to kill the whites and drive them from the land, or die trying. Jacobo and Tonio were among these. Some liked the idea of killing Warner and his family, so that there would be no one to claim their valley before the land court. This plan had more adherents. The majority didn't want a war at any cost. They were intent on outsmarting and adapting to any enemy that might arise. Bill's whole family was of this mind, although the women wished Warner and his kindred dead, somehow, without actually having to kill them. But not one of the Kuupiaxchem based his or her position on the fate of the Garras' cattle.

Antonio Garra listened, his arms crossed, hands tucked in, silent and defiant. He made no move to stop the debate. No'ka finally said, "Enough, enough. This is a grave matter. We must think on it and wait for the sheriff to make a move. If he tries to collect the taxes, then we can decide." Capitán Garra did not challenge this wisdom.

HARASZTHY appeared the next afternoon, a cloudless November day, warm and a little hazy from a coastal fog that had stalled at Mount Palomar. Haraszthy rode into Cupa with Cave Couts at his side, followed by Leandro Osuna. They were bristling with guns. At least a dozen more men blocked the entrance to the village.

The riders passed Bill's house and stopped at the end of the street. It was Bill's duty to talk to them. He walked up unarmed, hands out of his pockets.

The three did not dismount. They watched Bill come. With the sun behind him they couldn't be sure who he was. Couts had his right hand on a pistol butt. Leandro slouched in the background, rifle ready. When Haraszthy recognized Bill, he got down, handing his reins to Couts.

"Villiam Marshall, squaw man, so good to see you again. Always nice to see a familiar voice in the wilderness." He grinned and shook Bill's hand.

"Sheriff." Bill nodded at the others.

They peered down the empty street.

Haraszthy pulled out a sheet of paper with Antonio Garra's name on it. He handed it to Bill. It was an accounting of Garra's grazing fees for the year. The total was eight hundred dollars. Bill returned it to the sheriff.

"Is Señor Garra in?" Couts looked toward the Garras' house.

"No, he's gone hunting," Bill lied.

They all laughed.

"If only you knew how often we've heard that line," Couts said.

"You can give him this tax assessment." Haraszthy handed back the bill. "It must be paid by December 31. If not, we take more cattle—to sell for taxes."

"General Joshua Bean told him not to pay."

"Yes, yes, General Bean is a busybody. But attorney general overrules him." Haraszthy laughed. Bill looked at Couts.

"Sheriff's got it in writing," Couts said.

"Can I see it?"

"Sure, drop by my office anytime." Haraszthy showed his yellowed teeth in an insincere grin.

"You know this means war," Bill said. "Garra will never pay. He'd rather die fighting."

"Is that a threat, young man?" The sheriff drew himself up to his full five feet two.

"It's true."

"Very well. Let me tell you what else is true. Señor Garra was Mexican. All Mexicans in California are now U.S. citizens. So he's an American Mexican. They must pay property taxes. Only foreigners, or Indian nations with sovereign lands, are exempt. This is the law. He is as American as I am, or Couts or Osuna. Or you."

The sheriff tapped a forefinger lightly on Bill's chest.

"Señor Garra cannot declare war. He cannot hide here and pretend to be Indian. He can only break the law and become a criminal."

"Call it what you like, when the Garras get this tax bill, they will go on the warpath. Many will follow them." Bill folded the invoice.

"That would be a big mistake," Couts said. "But it will never happen. The Injuns here are soft. They know their place."

Haraszthy mounted. His horse spun once and stood.

"We need money, Villiam. In San Diego there is not even to pay for the soldiers' food. All must do their part. Life goes on. It will not kill Antonio Garra to pay. He is a rich man. You tell him, please."

They started down the street.

"I do not enjoy this," Haraszthy said over his shoulder. "But if he does not pay, we return to take cattle."

Bill watched them until they were dust, then walked to the Garras' compound and slipped the tax bill under Antonio's door. He shivered, walked to the hot pools and slid himself into the hottest water he could stand.

Within half an hour, the whole town was in an uproar. People shouted and talked, pounded on doors, ran up and down the street, argued, jumped on horses and galloped down the trail. War drums and war songs soared on the breeze.

The gauntlet had been thrown—and taken up. It seemed as though Haraszthy and Garra were scheming together to foment a war.

64

WARNING

ORNING found the village quiet, everything seeming normal. The Garras and ten others had gone to consult with Chapuli, Baupista and Juan Antonio, the Cahuilla chieftains.

Their plan had not changed. They would capture the armories at Warner's and Fort Yuma, then simultaneously hit Los Angeles and San Diego in force.

It was a bold and brilliant strategy, if you could count on all of the tribes, and discount the Americans' defense. But you couldn't sanely do either. They might possibly capture the armories. To attack the cities was suicide.

Those who opposed the Garras' plan gathered at the hot springs to discuss their next move. It was suggested that the Cupeño betray the Garras, and stop the war before it began, but No'ka said, "No, no. Let them do what they must do. We do not want the blood of our brothers staining our hands. If they must die, then let them die as they wish, at the hands of the Americans."

"We must work for a cooling, not a spilling, of the Garras' blood," White Fox said. "Perhaps we could just pay the cattle tax for them."

It was decided to make this offer to Antonio Garra, and to inform him that the Kuupiaxchem, as a tribe, would not partake in the revolt. Individuals could do so, if they so wished.

They worked out an evacuation plan. No'ka and White Fox would take most of the tribe to Mount Palomar at the outset of hostilities. A few would remain to keep the village, monitor the war and explain Cupeño neutrality to any avenging force.

GARRA came home triumphant. The Cahuilla had joined his warpath. They would attack Warner's and then Los Angeles. The Garras would go to the Colorado to lead the Yumans, Cocopas and Cuchanos, the river tribes, against Fort Yuma. Then they would march on San Diego. Antonio had learned that Heintzelman's garrison at the pueblo had withdrawn to the north on November 14. San Diego was defenseless.

No'ka politely told capitán Garra that his family and most of the tribe would not join in the rebellion. They would not try to stop those who did. That was all they could do. When No'ka offered to pay the grazing taxes, both Garras were offended.

"This war is not about a few cattle. It is a war to regain our pride and our land," Antonio shouted, his arms flailing in unintelligible signs.

"It is a war to defeat our lifelong enemies," Tonio interpreted.

Antonio warned his tribesmen not to aid the Americans or to alert the Warners. "If you do, you become my enemy, and will suffer accordingly."

The Garras repaired to their compound. Falling Star kept track of their plans through Stomping Deer, who prepared to take part in the coming battles. He was convinced of the rightness of the Garras' war, and wished to succeed or fail with them. His decision bore hard on No'ka and White Fox. To them, their only son was already dead. Melones wept when she heard them say this.

On the nineteenth of November, the Garras left for the Colorado River. They were jaunty and gracious.

Tonio said, "You will see what glory we will bring to Cupa. You will be envious, when we tell our war stories."

Antonio was conciliatory. "I do not hold it against you, No'ka. You are you and I am I. Each must follow his heart. You will be proud of me, no matter what the outcome." No'ka hugged him. They tapped each other on the back. Antonio mounted his decorated warhorse. His war party of fifteen slipped down the back trail through Wiliya and Coyote Canyon to the desert. Stomping Deer did not go. He would lead the attack on Warner's as a scout for the Cahuilla.

When the last of the warriors had vanished into the rocks, No'ka turned to go to his house. His face was grieved. He looked old. He put his hand on White Fox's shoulder as they walked. He shook his head slowly.

"Not a good day."

Bill tried to cheer him. "Let's see what happens. It may not be as bad as you think."

"We must warn Warner," White Fox said. "That will help our chances."

"I thought you wished him dead, my wife," No'ka accused gently.

"Yes, I do, but should he live, he must know that we tried to help him."

"I'll tell him," Bill offered. He had been avoiding the Warners. They were still miffed over his quitting. Falling Star grabbed his arm.

"No, it must be No'ka. He speaks for the Kuupiaxchem. You are American. That you should warn him would not absolve us as clearly."

"As capitán, and his oldest friend, I will alert him," No'ka agreed. "Now I am tired. Tomorrow it will be done."

Luna and Fanny rode over the following morning to buy some eggs. There was a big group of migrants at the ranch, hungry for a California breakfast. Falling Star took Fanny directly to see No'ka. This was their chance to help John and Anita without alerting the rebels.

No'ka told Fanny of the Garras' plan to attack the Warners. He emphasized his opposition to the war and hope that it would somehow fizzle out before it began. Fanny thanked him. She confessed that the Warners had asked her to come, to verify rumors of an Indian uprising. The store was open; migrants arrived as usual; all was normal, save for the rumors.

Falling Star gave Fanny fifty eggs.

"The Warners would like for Bi' to come by when he has a chance," Fanny said. Falling star nodded and touched Fanny's hand.

Luna carefully stored the eggs in his pack. They rode home. Warner had been warned.

B I L L was cleaning his horse's left front hoof, holding it up with one hand and scraping at it with a bent antelope horn. Cold turned their breaths to steam. The warmth of the pony's body heated a halo of air that Bill could partly enter by leaning against him. Melones padded up and said, so softly that he could barely hear her, "Bi', I'm pregnant."

She stroked the horse's neck, while Bill finished the hoof and placed it carefully on the ground. A shy smile tugged at the corners of her mouth. She had pulled a coyote robe snug around her, the collar above her ears.

"Are you sure?"

"Sí." She opened the robe and stuck her stomach out. It was hard to tell in all her roundness.

"Pull it in," Bill said, putting his hand on her belly.

She sucked it in, but it stayed round.

"Three months without blood," she said. She gave off warmth like the horse.

"Jacobo?"

"Sí."

"Good, that's good news." Bill hugged her. Melones's softness enveloped him. "Have you told his mother?" he asked. Cold air rushed between them as he let her go. Her eyes were dark pools.

"She knows," she answered, shivering, pulling her robe tight around her curves. "You are always the last in Cupa to know." She smiled.

"Are you happy?"

"Sí, very happy." She looked like she was about to cry.

Wili ran out from behind the house with Shadow, yelling, "We're ready, Papá."

"I'm almost ready. Bring me the saddle." Wili kept running.

"You're worried about Jacobo?"

Melones nodded tearfully. Her eyes followed Wili.

"We will have a beautiful child," she said in English, which surprised Bill.

"Yes, but not as beautiful as you." He wiped her tears with his thumbs and kissed her cheek.

She blushed and hunched her neck down into her fur. "Bueno," she said. "I'm going in. Hasta luego."

Wili came trotting up alongside Shadow, holding the saddle in place on Shadow's back. The stirrups bounced in the dirt.

"Don't drag the stirrups, Wili."

When Bill picked up the saddle, Melones was gone.

"Cano could ride Shadow with a small saddle," Wili said.

"His skin's too loose. Don't you remember when you were little, trying to hold on to him, and falling off the side?"

"No. Then he could pull a cart. With Cano in it."

"Yes, he probably could. But Cano likes to ride with your mother. When you have your own horse, he can ride with me. Shadow likes to run free."

"Where are we going today?"

"All the way around the edge of the plain. We're gathering cattle. Tomorrow we'll drive them to the far side by Palomar. Then, when you go camping with Grandpa, they'll be ready."

All the women and children, the nonrebel men, and the cattle would disappear into the forests of Palomar at the first sign of war. Only Falling Star, Cano and Bill would remain in the village. It would be Bill's duty to explain to the Americans—army, posse or militia—that the Cupeño were not in revolt, that they opposed Garra and only desired peace. A guard of five tribesmen would be hidden nearby to help, if necessary, and carry messages. When the war was over, the tribe would return.

Everyone had been busy, making sleeping bags, packing food, tools and weapons, and hiding what would be left behind. The horses were fattened and groomed, packs were repaired and warm clothes readied. The children were excited about seeing the frozen pond and camping in the snow. It would be cold at Palomar, but as No'ka said, "Warmer above ground than under."

T H E very day that Warner had received his warning from No'ka, he took Fanny, Sally, Anita and the children to Santa Ysabel to stay with Ed and Refugio Stokes. Stokes would remove them to San Diego in the event of trouble. Warner returned with one of Stokes's men. With Luna still helping, they continued to run the store and ranch as before. Passing migrants told Bill that Warner was unconcerned with Indian threats. He had scornfully advised them not to worry either.

"They've been threatening to drive me from the valley since the day I arrived," Warner told them. "It's all a lot of hot air. If they do try to take the store, they'll be sorry. The crack of a carbine will bring them back to earth."

Bill never did go to see John, partly because he was busy, but mainly for fear that he would be asked to defend the store, or to spy on the Garras, or some other impossibly twisted complication. He too carried on as though nothing was wrong. Most of the time, it felt that way.

T H E night before Thanksgiving, No'ka called the tribe together. They were all nervous. Tomorrow night was the planned attack but they had neither seen nor heard of any war parties. No'ka said this: "We will not move unless there is reason to. Then we move very fast for Palomar, driving all the horses and cattle we can find.

"If by tomorrow morning we have heard nothing, I shall ride to Wiliya to see Chapuli," No'ka said. "Bi', you should come with me . . . to paint a vivid picture for Chapuli, of the wrath of twenty million angry Yankees." He looked at Stomping Deer, who kept his head down. "We will try to stop this madness. I cannot think of anything else we can do."

Stomping Deer sprang up, shrieking, "You could help us. That is what you could do. Not oppose us. Join us in overthrowing this plague of *sos-abitom* and gringos."

No'ka stared his son down. Stomping Deer danced in fury. He shouted, "Putos." He spit. Then he stalked proudly from the meeting.

In the morning he and his cohorts were gone. Their tracks led down the trail to Wiliya. Bill and No'ka ate a quick breakfast and followed them.

The trail was little more than a path, with steep climbs and drops, winding northeast through rocky hills. It was more suited to foot traffic than horses and painfully slow. Wiliya, Chapuli's village in Coyote Canyon, lay about twelve miles down the torturous track. There was an easier access up Coyote Canyon from its mouth, on the parched desert floor, two thousand feet below Cupa, but that way was three times as far.

The day was clear and cool; a warm breeze brushing their faces; the scenery spectacular. No'ka picked his way among the rocks, mostly descending. Shy mountain sheep, deer, antelope, golden eagles and bobcat hunted and fed in lushness—made possible by an unseasonal tropical rain that had not made it across the mountains to Cupa.

The winter desert was in full bloom: every cactus pregnant with water and flowering, the normally dry sticks of ocotillo waving green with red blossoms. Yellow and purple and white flowers mingled with delicate grasses underfoot, and the sharp air reeked with sage, red shank, sumac, scrub oak and all of their fluorescence. Even the rocks smelled good as they warmed up. If you were still, you heard the sound of bees and other bustling insects, birds calling, lizards scurrying on the stones and a whisper of cool wind. Bill rode drunk on blossom-air, his spine rubbery and relaxed from the swaying of the saddle, drowsy from the cadent clip-clop of hooves on rocks.

No'ka held up his hand. They stopped, quieted the horses, sat stiff to prevent the saddles creaking, and listened.

In the stillness, over the sounds of birds and the whirl of the wind, drumbeats came clear, pounding at a furious pace. Chanting swelled and faded on the breeze. They hurried on, all else forgotten.

It took another anxious hour to reach Wiliya. By then the war dance had wound down. There was only desultory drumming. A few chanters sat around the remains of a bonfire, roasting hunks of meat on sticks over the coals. Dozens of men, faces and bodies painted grotesquely in red, black and white lines and patterns, lay in the shade of scrubby oak trees, or the ramadas of small, domed, stick-and-thatch huts that comprised the village. They looked exausted. More than a hundred horses were penned in brush corrals or tied to bushes.

Wiliya was scattered on a shallow rise in the floor of Coyote Canyon, where it met three rocky side canyons. A trickle of water flowed from one of the side canyons. It looked as though the whole arroyo filled with water at times, scoured by flash floods. This explained the poor nature of Chapuli's capital.

No'ka spoke to a warrior, who pointed to one of the huts. He dismounted and led his horse to its entrance. Two children playing with a marble scurried inside. There was no sign of Stomping Deer or his friends.

Chapuli emerged sleepily from the hut. His round face had red and white lines painted on the cheeks with a black dot on the forehead. He wore a worker's pants and shirt, dirty, and no shoes. He still managed to look jolly, and embraced No'ka, grinning grotesquely over his shoulder at Bill.

"So you've come to join us," he joked in his language.

Bill got off his horse and handed the reins to one of the warriors. No'ka tied his to a bush and told a boy to bring them water. The capitánes sat on a flat rock in the sun.

"What are your plans?" No'ka was unusually abrupt.

"We raid Warner's tonight."

"With just these men? What about Baupista and Juan Antonio?"

"We will do this alone, what sense to share the spoils." He grinned wickedly, stretching his warpaint. "Antonio and Baupista agree we do not need their help. Your son tells us Warner has only one other man with him."

"Yes, but a thousand to take his revenge and ten thousand to back them," No'ka argued. "This is not a wise thing to do."

"Wisdom does not send a man on the warpath. It is the heart and the spirit. We can take no more abuse. We are ready. We have danced and sung these weeks. Now we will fight. That is all." Chapuli smiled peacefully.

No'ka stared at him for a while. Then he looked at Bill. Bill had no idea what to say.

Chapuli looked at Bill too. "Ask him where Warner keeps his guns," he said to No'ka in Cupeño.

"In the room behind the store."

"The money?"

"In a chest in his bedroom closet. Most likely he took it away with his family."

"We shall see. The store is yet open?"

"So far as we know."

"Then there will be money."

"He does a lot of trading." Bill shrugged doubtfully.

"Then this will be his last trading day." Chapuli laughed heartily, his face-paint cracking like a clown at a second performance. "El último!"

He stood and clapped No'ka on the shoulder.

"Do not look so worried, my brother. Celebrate. It is a fine day to live or die. Now I must rest. Excuse me."

Bill shook Chapuli's hand and said, "Good luck."

No'ka hugged him. "May the Spirit guide you."

"Gracias," Chapuli said to both of them. "Que les vayan bien."

"Do you know where Stomping Deer is?" asked No'ka.

"He has gone ahead to watch Warner. He is a good man. Do not condemn him. Celebrate his bravery."

Chapuli ducked inside the low doorway of his hut. The two little boys scampered out and skittered around the corner.

No'ka and Bill retraced the path, a little easier riding uphill, reins loosed, letting the horses set their own pace. They were home by dusk.

65

ATTACK ON WARNER

ALLING Star met Bill with the news that Luna had come to invite them to a Thanksgiving lunch at Warner's. There were no migrants; Juan Largo was alone at the ranch with Stokes's man. She had declined, explaining that Bill had gone with No'ka to see Chapuli. She told him to take care. Cuidado! This was supposed to be the day of the attack. If she had any news, she would send it.

She looked from No'ka to Bill and back, questioning.

"Stomping Deer is watching the Warners' store," No'ka told her. "They will attack tonight."

He slid from his horse with a weary grunt and went toward the hot springs, limping on his right leg and rubbing his hip.

Bill unsaddled the horses, stalled them and followed to the pools. In the sulfurous waters the trail weariness and grime fell away. The cold pool refreshed for a minute, then back to the heat he went.

No'ka huddled with White Fox. Falling Star rubbed Bill's shoulders and back. He thought about Warner, at home with a stranger, preparing for an attack like a mountain man: saddling horses, cleaning his rifles, preparing powder and ball, filling water buckets, packing food, boarding the windows, clearing the yards of potential cover, hiding his valuables. He would not be easy to kill.

"Will you go to Warner?" Falling Star asked gently.

"No. He had his warning. He would only try to make me stay. And Stomping Deer would see me."

"Yes, better to do nothing. Let them do what they will." She sighed and kissed him on the cheek.

"I hate this," Bill said. "I hope they kill each other. All of them."

She wrapped her arms around his neck and shoulders, leaning her head around to kiss his lips. They toppled over with a splash. White Fox said "Aay!" as the tangle went under. They came up sputtering. They kissed for a long time. Falling Star sloshed water at her mother without breaking away. "Quit looking, Mami, we're married," she gulped quickly, and returned to Bill's mouth.

She was trying to cheer him up, to distract him from the feeling of dread that knotted his gut. If Warner died, the wrath of the white men would surely descend. If Warner lived . . .

Falling Star quit kissing Bill's stiff lips and put her mouth to his ear. "I love you, Bi' Marshall, more than anything in the world. You are mine and I am yours." That was the only thing he wanted to remember of that night.

T H E Y were awakened by gunfire. It crackled for about two hours at a comfortable distance, but perfectly clear. Then it reached a crescendo and stopped. Bill pulled on a robe and went out to look toward Warner's. No'ka was out too. It was still dark but there was a glow in the sky. They went into No'ka's house to make coffee and wait for daylight. Falling Star came over with the children, who fell back to sleep before the fire. The adults stared at the coals. Not a word was spoken.

In maybe an hour, they were roused by a thunder of hooves on the nearby plain. The ground vibrated as they walked out into a cold and misty dawn. Dew lay gleaming on every surface. Droplets joined to slide off the thatched roof ends and splatter to earth in ragged lines.

Riders charged up the street yelling, circled the oak and charged back. There were at least a hundred painted Cahuilla and Cupeño, shouting and singing, dressed in stiff new clothes, parts of suits, blankets, quilts, the curtains from Anita's dining room, her red-checked tablecloth—carrying every imaginable sort of goods from Warner's store. Children's clothes and toys, blacksmith tools, spare reins and coiled wagon traces were tied to or hung from saddles. Two wagons were laden with heavier goods: the stove and pipe, a mattress, a chair, some pillows, saddles, wood, sacks of grain, barrels and the grandfather clock. Everything possible to carry or cart or drag away had been removed from Warner's house. His milk cattle and horses were milling out in the fields at the end of the road. He had been cleaned out.

"Did you kill Warner?" White Fox shouted when she saw Stomping Deer. He just rode past screaming. Bill looked for Chapuli.

No one dismounted; it was absolute bedlam. Bill held Shadow to keep him from being trampled. Finally Chapuli came forward. He threw a new rifle down to No'ka. "Good hunting," he shouted. He held up a fresh scalp. His horse wheeled on its hind legs and came down in front of Bill. Chapuli waved the bloody trophy.

"Warner?" Bill yelled.

"No. Escapó!" he shouted back, and charged down the street, knocking horses and riders out of his path. White Fox put her hand to her mouth.

"Ooh," she moaned.

No'ka said, "We must move fast. Warner will be back soon with help."

If all had died it would have been a while before the news got out. Warner was probably already at Santa Ysabel, removing his family to San Diego, raising the alarm. No'ka gave the order to prepare for the evacuation to Palomar. Departure must be immediate.

Chapuli rode off with most of his men, taking the wagons and stock north to Anza, to get them safely into Cahuilla territory. The mountain trail to Wiliya was too difficult. About thirty warriors remained, occupying the Garras' compound.

As Bill started for the stable, planning to help with the horses, Stomping Deer strode down from the Garras'. His face was blackened with soot, his eyes red and wild, his shirt torn. A strip of flannel was tightly tied around his right shoulder. The inside was bloodstained. A trickle of blood ran down his arm to his elbow.

When he got to No'ka, he said, "Papi, we'll only be here a while to rest and patch our wounds." He glanced at his shoulder. "I know we are a danger to you." He turned to go.

White Fox said, "Let me fix your shoulder, hijito."

She reached toward him, but No'ka held her arm.

"The men will do it, Mami, thank you," Stomping Deer said.

Hooves clattered again from the valley. Four men rode up the main street. From the way they slouched in their saddles, they were migrants. Whites.

Stomping Deer took off with a leap, just like a startled buck.

The men rode up, two abreast. They had rifles and pistols, but did not hold them at ready. Bill stepped forward to greet them.

One of the first pair dismounted with a moan of pain. His legs almost buckled, asleep or cramped.

"Levi Slack," he said, sticking out his hand. "I'm looking for John Warner. We hear there's a hot spring on his ranch, that cures the fevers," He looked over Bill's shoulder, as Bill searched for the right words.

"The hot spring's here but it's not a good time. Warner lives a couple of miles south." Bill pointed toward the ranch house. Slack's eyes followed Bill's finger, and then he grunted. He lurched forward; his eyes bulged. He reached for his back and turned toward his companions. An arrow stuck out under his ribs, burried halfway to the feathers. In a shower of arrows, the rebels were upon them.

In ten seconds, all four were dead, stripped, lanced and stabbed repeatedly. The villagers roared, running out and gathering to witness the gore. Painted men lashed the legs of the unfortunate four together, tied a rope to the lashes, secured the other end to the ugliest of their horses' saddle, and sent the frightened beast galloping down the street with a whip on the rump, dragging the naked bodies like a human plow.

The three good horses were led up to the Garras' compound, the rebels dancing and singing their war chant, walking on air.

Heavy silence descended on the rest of the tribe. It was like a repeat of the ritual killing of the Californios, only there was no ritual, only killing. And no meaning, but the same danger. These four had simply been in the wrong place at the wrong time. And so had the Cupeño.

They packed for Palomar in a daze. In no time all were assembled and ready to go. There were no words of goodbye, no ceremony. Wili got on the horse with White Fox; Shadow followed Bill. Falling Star came too, carrying Cano in her pack, afraid to be in the village alone even for an hour. Out into the plain they rode. It couldn't have been later than nine in the morning.

A wisp of smoke marked Warner's ranch. Bill thought of all those mornings that welcome sight had called him to breakfast. He looked quickly away. The drag marks of the four bodies led toward Aguanga.

"That's the only bit of luck we've had all day," Bill said to No'ka as they drove the cattle, keeping them downwind from the people. No'ka didn't even grunt. He was eyeing the train of villagers, strung out over a quarter of a mile: dogs, ponies, colts and donkeys, mules, horses, sheep and pigs. It was an exodus.

When they reached the edge of the forest, No'ka said, "It is always good to see the People doing something together, united in purpose. I only wish you were coming with us."

"I have to stay. I'm the only one who can explain what happened . . ."

"I know, but it is not a good feeling I have."

"We'll be all right."

Falling Star came to say goodbye to her father. They didn't dismount, just leaned across their saddles and hugged. Bill went to Wili and White Fox and did the same.

"You help with the hunting, Wili, don't leave all the work to your grandpa."

"I will." He clutched White Fox tightly.

Bill got down to talk to Shadow.

"You have to go with Wili." Shadow shoved his nose in Bill's crotch and wagged his tail. Bill pulled his ears gently. He rubbed his flanks. "I'll come get you soon. I won't be long." He pulled Shadow's head up so he could look into his golden eyes. "You'll be good, won't you. You have to be good—stay with Wili—don't bite anyone." Shadow's body undulated with the swing of his tail. He pawed the air. Bill took his arm and rubbed it. He pawed again.

"All right, that's it, I have to go."

Bill looked up to find the whole tribe watching. He gave Shadow a hard hug and remounted. Everyone said "Goodbye, Bi', adiós, Falling Star, hasta luego, vaya con dios, que les vayan bien." They trotted off a little way until the caravan started up again. They stayed to watch the tribe vanish into the woodlands.

It was a silent and dreadful ride back to the village—their lovely valley seemed bleak and doomed. Halfway, Bill realized that he had not said good-bye to Melones. He had forgotten her in the confusion. He turned to look.

Falling Star said, "I forgot her too. I wish she had stayed . . . she and Shadow. It's hard to be afraid with them near." The wind moaned and ripped at her words.

When they reached home, Luna was sitting on their doorstep. He asked for Narci. When he learned that she was safely on her way to Palomar, he went silent. They took him to No'ka's, lit a fire, made him a warm stew and waited for him to tell his story.

He finally calmed enough to speak. He addressed his words to Bill, hunched before the blaze, ignoring Falling Star.

"They came in the night. I had seen men watching all day. Warner and the other white man slept by turn. They were ready. They shot many times. I loaded the rifles. When there was no more powder, we ran for the barn where the horses awaited. The other man fell and Warner stopped by him. He shot four attackers with his revolving Colt. At the barn one horse was dead. Another was crazy. We both mounted the third and burst from the door. Shots and arrows buzzed us like hornets. We did not stop until we reached the forest at the crossroad to Santa Ysabel." He took a breath.

"The horse was winded. Warner left me there to walk to Santa Ysabel. He was afraid the horse would not go well uphill with two of us. I waited awhile, then returned to the ranch, keeping to the edge of the woods. The house was burning. Everything was gone; the barn burned. I walked to Cupa and found no one. I was very tired and sad. It was a good house," he added wistfully.

Luna wanted to wait at Cupa to see if Warner would return. He was afraid to stay at what was left of the ranch. They all moved into No'ka's, with its stout walls and big fireplace. That first night everyone slept poorly, waking at all hours in cold panic. The house felt hollow without No'ka or White Fox, or Shadow's rumbling snore.

A chill storm blew in from the north Pacific, freezing the dew to frost and capping the surrounding peaks with a mantle of snow. Dark gray masses of cloud stretched from horizon to horizon. They hibernated. The snowfall barely stuck at Cupa but each day Palomar's growing white gleam reminded them of the tribe, huddled there under brush shelters, fires burning night and day.

66

NERVOUSLY WAITING

I N S E E K I N G recruits, the Garras had widely publicized their plan for a pan-Indian revolt. When Warner rode into San Diego with his family, screaming as though the Cahuilla were five minutes behind him, everyone prepared for the worst. When news came of the Levi Slack deaths, their fears were confirmed. They nervously awaited the impending full-scale attack of the united tribes, stocking food, cleaning weapons, forging lances, preparing ammunition and fortifying the plaza, which was jammed with refugees from the ranches and rancherías.

In Los Angeles, Major Heintzelman and his troop organized the town's defenses, digging in, preparing to repel the expected Cahuilla assault.

At San Luis Rey, Pablo and Padre Ibarra anxiously awaited news from Cupa or San Diego or Los Angeles. The mission was deserted, all mobile persons having fled to the pueblos or the hills. Ibarra was not feeling well enough to travel, and Pablo had remained with him.

No time travels slower than that spent waiting for something bad to happen. The minutes stretch to hours, the hours crawl through the day and the days seem like weeks. When ten long days had crept past with not one thing happening, and no news, people began to twitch and stir.

In San Diego, the braver Californios sallied forth on swift horses to check their ranches and cattle. 'Zul and Father Juan Holbein, the new American priest at Mission San Diego, detached themselves from the pueblo in the predawn hours to ride to San Luis Rey. They reasoned that an Indian woman and a priest, together, would be safe no matter whom they encountered. Holbein wanted to check on Ibarra and bring him back to San Diego, if he could. 'Zul had news to share with Pablo and hoped he too would return with them.

///

" L U G A R D A is worried about Bill," 'Zul fretted.

"I'm sure he's all right." Pablo looked worried too.

"There's talk in town that he's one of the rebel leaders."

"That's ridiculous. Is it Warner saying so?"

"Not directly. But he has everyone stirred up. He says the Indians turned against him after Bill quit as majordomo. Lugarda thinks you should talk Bill into coming to the pueblo until the revolt is over. She asked me to show you and Padre Ibarra this letter from her husband." She placed a thick envelope on the table. "I wish you would come to San Diego."

"I'm trying not to get involved . . ." Pablo frowned at 'Zul and her growing belly.

"You are involved," 'Zul said.

"We're all involved," said Padre Ibarra.

Friar Juan Holbein rushed into the dining room. He had been stabling the horses. His soft, unlined face, usually pale, flushed with excitement.

"Did you know that four more were killed at Warner's hot spring? Migrants found them on the road."

"Who were they?" Pablo asked.

"They didn't know. They had been dragged beyond recognition."

"Not good," Ibarra said, shaking his head. "Not good. Sit please, Friar Holbein. Have some soup. We will talk."

'Zul patted the letter. "Señor Machado says the army slaughtered a whole tribe of Pomo people at Clear Lake and another at the Russian River, as punishment for killing two ranchers who had enslaved and raped the wife of their chief." 'Zul was watching Pablo. Pablo looked at Ibarra, thinking of Aguanga.

"They also killed a white miner, who protested when the army tried to take his Indian wife away to a new tribal reservation."

"I'd better go to Cupa." Pablo sighed. He took 'Zul's hand.

"May I read the letter?" Ibarra asked.

"Thank you," 'Zul whispered, handing it to him, tears forming.

"I'll move to Pala," Ibarra said. "The People there may need me. Not a soul has been to this chapel since Warner was attacked."

"I could go with Pablo," Holbein suggested. "I may be able to help."

They all looked at him, considering.

"I've never seen the chapel of Saint Francis," Holbein explained, as though they were going on a picnic. "I could offer a service."

"You have the right spirit." Ibarra touched his hand. "But you are needed in San Diego. The frightened souls will want comforting, and you may be able to calm the more impetuous. You'll send me warning if there is trouble." He stood weakly. "Please, I must take my siesta. Then I will go with Pablo as far as Pala."

Pablo and Holbein helped the padre to his room.

"I am way too old a man for war," Ibarra told them wearily. "Wake me in two hours or I may dream right through it."

A t Cupa, the five guards lived in the remotest house and kept to the look-out points. The others rarely saw them.

At noon on the first sunny day one of the guards ran into the yard, breathing hard.

"Rider, coming from the south."

"Let him come," Bill said. "If you see more, let us know."

They were lounging in the sunlight on the south side of the house, soaking up its heat and cheery brightness.

When the rider came up the trail, Bill recognized Pablo immediately: erect, balanced, his horse dancing up the path. He wore a black priest's smock and the round hat of the Franciscan.

Bill and Luna took his tired horse as Pablo slid down. He took two steps and sagged to the ground.

"I'm okay," he said. "Just let me lie here a while." He stretched out flat on his back, the cassock spread like a black blanket, and sighed.

"It was a long ride. I'm so glad to find you here; where are the others?"

Luna pointed to the mountain.

"Up at Palomar," Falling Star told him. "Freezing under all that snow."

In the bright sunshine, the mountaintop sparkled so white, it seemed even the trees were buried.

"They're building snowmen and sliding down the slopes on frozen cow skins. The little ones are throwing snowballs at the dogs. They're having a ball," Pablo said with a relieved grin. "Shadow is trying to walk and goes nowhere. He has to leap and disappears completely in the drifts. When Wili calls, he stands on hind legs to see."

"Do you think it's that deep?" Falling Star worried.

"Of course not. Two feet at the most."

"Mother must be making snowshoes. Father would be grumbling about his cold bones."

Pablo was stretching by pulling his knees to his chest.

"You should soak your back in the hot pools," Bill said.

"I'll prepare lunch and call when it's ready," Falling Star told them. "You two take Cano."

"He looks just like you," said Pablo.

W H E N they had submerged, Bill told Pablo what had happened.

"We heard most of it," Pablo said. "Warner galloped into San Diego as though the rebel hordes were right behind him, ready to overrun the city. A militia was formed under Major E. F. Fitzgerald. You'll remember him. He retired in '48. Cave Couts has been made captain and Haraszthy first lieutenant. There are about seventy of them.

"They organized a twenty-four-hour guard, and prepared their defenses, but nothing happened," Pablo said with a smile. "Not a single shot fired. Just a lot of scared people, nervously waiting.

"There can be no general uprising," Pablo grumbled, "with the Cupeño hidden at Palomar and the rest of the tribes cowering in San Diego. The Cahuilla are the only possible force."

"They were supposed to attack Los Angeles," Bill said.

"We'll see. If there is no attack on Los Angeles, Heintzelman's army will eventually return to restore order and punish the insurrectionists. In the meantime, the militia is restless and dangerous." Pablo looked at Luna. "Any news from the Colorado?"

"Not a word," Bill said.

Luna stirred. "The Yuman are too cowardly to fight. They will murder the weak and unsuspecting. Not battle the army."

"The army there is less than thirty men," Pablo told him. "Captain John Davidson was on his way with sixteen men to relieve the guard of eleven stationed there. No word of them since."

Luna sneered but did not reply.

F A L L I N G Star was preparing a stew of rabbit with chiles, dried tomatoes and acorn flour dumplings. She whacked the rabbit into chunks on an oak stump her mother kept in the kitchen, crunching through flesh and bone with a sharp hatchet. It was not a nice sound. She rolled two scalped heads into the pot.

"It smells good." Pablo sniffed as he came to sit wearily on a stool by the fire.

"Bi' killed two rabbits with his throwing stick yesterday." Falling Star stirred the stew. "They will be a little chewy."

"Your English is much better."

Luna looked into the pot.

"We don't have many vegetables. The others took everything."

Bill said, "She's been practicing. Her father wanted her to be ready for the American invasion, remember?"

"And she was ready when you came," Pablo teased.

Falling Star blushed.

"I never considered myself part of the invasion. But you are right. I am one of them," Bill said dejectedly.

"No," Pablo said. "You were welcomed. You were invited."

Falling Star had begun to cry. Bill took her to sit on the bed.

"I invited him to come," Pablo told Luna. "It was I who brought Bill here, to this village, to marry and live among us."

Bill held Falling Star, gently rocking her, kissing her neck and shoulder. When she put her head up, he kissed the tears from her eyes, her cheeks and her mouth. For a few seconds they forgot the others.

"As soon as we heard about the murdered merchants, I hurried here as fast as I could ride," Pablo said gently.

"There was nothing we could do," Bill said. "They rode up just as the raiding party returned from Warner's."

"So they were killed here?"

"Yes, right in front of the door." Falling Star didn't seem to be breathing.

"They were found by another party of migrants, mutilated and dragged raw." Pablo sighed. "You can imagine the frenzy when the news reached San Diego."

"The Cahuilla did it, not us." Falling Star jumped up to move the pot away from the flame. "No one could have stopped them." She took out bowls and spoons and set them on the hearth.

They ate the stew, blowing on it to keep from burning their tongues. The meat was sucked off every little bone, the bones tossed into the fire.

"I think you should go to San Diego," Pablo said to Bill. "You will be safer there."

In the evening, they all, including the guards, retired to the spring. The night was crystal-clear. Crisp frigid air fell from the sky to chill the hollow. The stars felt low enough to touch, reflecting on the steaming-hot pools like dancing fireflies. The bathers were speechless, comatose, and would have fallen asleep in the soothing heat if it weren't for the fear of drowning.

///

I N   the morning, Falling Star warmed tortillas Pablo had brought from the mission with the leftover stew. The hearty breakfast cheered them.

"Sister." Stomping Deer was standing in the doorway. "Pablo, Luna, Bi'!" They embraced. Stomping Deer was alert and suspicious.

"I came to check on you, my sister." He relaxed a bit. "And to see little Cano." He peered at the sleeping child's wrinkled face.

"Come and eat, then we will talk, my brother."

"I miss the hot pools. I will bathe, then eat. Pablo, I must hear the news from San Diego."

"Yes, we'll bathe too. The news is not good."

Pablo outlined the situation in San Diego. When he got to word of the merchants' murder, he said, "That was a bad thing. It will bring the fury of every American upon you."

"I wish we had killed more. Their fury has long been upon us. Let them feel ours." Stomping Deer went stiff, defiant.

"What news from the Garras?" Stomping Deer just scowled. Pablo waited for the warm water to calm him.

After about ten minutes, he said, "They haven't returned yet. Two of the Cahuilla came back to Wiliya yesterday. They said that four shepherds were killed at Yuma. The fort was surrounded. The Yumans and Cocopas quarreled about the division of more than a thousand sheep. While they were fighting, the Americans marched from the fort toward Jacumba. They took the trail over the mountains to San Diego.

"The fort was looted and burned. Then the Garras and many Yumans followed the soldiers. They were afraid to attack. They sent runners to alert the Cuyamaca to help."

"How many soldiers?" Pablo looked at him sharply.

"A few less than thirty."

"Then Captain Davidson did reach Fort Yuma."

Stomping Deer looked disgusted. "There are hundreds of warriors at the Colorado."

"You see what cowards are the Yuman cabrones." Luna spat twice.

"Now I am ready to eat." Stomping Deer stood and brushed away the water.

W H E N the others returned to the house, Falling Star was alone. Stomping Deer had gone back to Wiliya.

"I asked him not to stay. I am nervous with him here. He can return when this is over." She was nursing Cano, who kneaded her breast with his tiny hands as he sucked. His hair was dark, but not as black as Wili's. His skin was still pink, but a little browner. He saw his father and pulled away with a plop. Bill took him to Pablo.

"This is Tío Pablo, a very learned man. Remember him?"

Cano looked up and waved his arms. Bill handed him over.

"He's getting big," Pablo said. "They grow fast."

"Too big," Falling Star said. "Now I appreciate the times my mother and Melones took him off my hands."

"I'll help," Pablo said. "I need to practice. 'Zul will have our baby in the spring."

Falling Star was staring out the door toward Mount Palomar.

"Where will you live?"

"That has yet to be decided." Pablo frowned. "I won't go to the Machados' and she won't leave Lugarda."

"You could come here," Bill said.

"Lugarda lives in San Diego?" Falling Star was watching Bill. He looked at Pablo.

"Yes, most of the time. She has not changed—still dancing till dawn at every ball in town."

"Could you live at the mission there?" Bill suggested. "Then 'Zul could be near enough to help Lugarda."

"That is what Father Ibarra suggests. Juan Holbein will be in charge for the next few years. He has invited me to help manage what is left of the mission. But Ibarra is old. I would hate to leave him now."

Cano was fretting. Falling Star took him to her other breast. He held it with both hands and latched on to the nipple. "Ouiee, not so hard, you beast," she winced. "He's worse than his father," she told Pablo with a sidelong glance, thinking of Lugarda's strange hold on both of their loved ones.

67

AN EVIL WIND

T H E weather turned hot, like it can at any time of year in San Diego. A hard dry wind blew from the desert, parching the landscape and sending dust into the atmosphere, to redden the sunsets and every teary eye that observed them. Fine dust filtered into the houses, beds, food and clothes. The world was coated in dust.

The wind did not let up at night. It made the stars twinkle madly. It made Bill and Cano nervous, sleepless and irritable. When Cano cried, or a shutter banged, Bill would sit up with a start, heart pounding, then lie back to toss until dawn. He had decided not to take his family to San Diego. It made no sense to Falling Star, or to him. But it didn't feel right here either. At daylight Bill would fall into an exhausted sleep, not to wake till noon. The others took the wind in stride, but he hated it.

By the third overheated day, the visible snowcap had melted on Mount Palomar. Luna stared at the gray-green mountain.

"We should go there, I do not like this waiting."

No one spoke. They looked at the mountain.

"I am a desert dweller. I do not like the snow. Now it is gone, I will go to Narci." Luna raised his arm to point at Palomar.

"We'll go with you," Falling Star said. "Tomorrow is Wili's birthday. We can surprise him."

"A ride would be good," said Bill. "This wind is foul. If we were sailing, we would put it at our backs and blow with it, wherever it took us."

"I have a theory," Pablo told them. He jumped to his feet. "It's part of the art of leaving. When it's time to go, you must just go. Let's us leave today, right now. Once we are gone we can decide when to return."

"Huh!" they shouted. They divided up the tasks to prepare and went to them, their mood lightened by action. The wind was blowing them somewhere—and motion was its own reward.

Bill rode with Luna to find the spare horses. In the dust storm, they had scattered and taken to the forest around the plain. They needed two riding horses each and four more to carry pack saddles: twelve in total.

They worked along the southwest edge of the grasslands, thinking the horses would have gone with the wind, but found no tracks until they neared Warner's burned-out ranch house. Two decomposed bodies lay in the yard. Animals had taken the others, or someone had come to claim them.

The wind had obliterated all but the freshest of tracks. Luna found hoofprints outside the yard, partly covered in fine sand, but clear enough to follow. It made sense that the horses would come to the ranch. They were used to finding food and water there. The tracks led south, toward Santa Ysabel.

They followed them at a walk. Bill's first look at the ruined house had made him nauseous. He had spent a quarter of his life there. No going back now.

"Look," Luna said. He stooped to examine some fresher tracks. "Riders." He pointed toward the Santa Ysabel trail. A dozen men had emerged from the trees, not three hundred yards away. They came forward at a trot. They were Americans, not Indians—maybe migrants.

Bill said. "We'll wait." It was too late to run.

At a hundred yards, he recognized the stiff bearing of Haraszthy. Beside him were Couts and Leandro Osuna. The other's he didn't know. The wind was blowing their hair around, flapping their shirts and jackets. Each man had two rifles and two pistols. One rifle was kept in a scabbard alongside the saddle. The other was held across the pommel, ready to use. As they drew near, all rifle barrels aimed their way, fingers on triggers.

"Don't shoot, we're friendly."

"Ah well, we meet again, Mister Marshall." Haraszthy's accent had not improved. "And who is this one?" He jerked his head at Luna. A hammer cocked.

"Warner's boy," Bill said. "He helped to defend the ranch."

"Yes, yes. Mister Warner would like to talk to him. And you too. You didn't help him, did you? What brings you here? Looting? Horse stealing? Hunting for travelers?" The wind whipped at his words.

"We're looking for our own horses. The wind scattered them to God knows where." Bill's horse stamped and spun in a gust.

Seven rifles followed him. Couts wiped hair from his eyes with a forearm.

"Who is at Cupa?" he asked. "Are there any hostiles in the area?"

"I don't think so. The Cupeño did not take part in the uprising. They are in hiding. They don't want to be shot for something they didn't do. Only a handful remained to watch the village. We have not seen any of the other tribes."

"You will take us to your hot springs, yes?" Haraszthy motioned with his gun barrel.

Bill didn't think he had a choice, so he led them at a trot. When they could see the town through the dust cloud, Couts said, "One wrong move and you're coyote bait, squaw man."

All guns trained on Bill's and Luna's backs as they rode up the street. Pablo and Falling Star came out to meet them. She held Cano in her arms; she looked scared. Pablo was acting the host, saying, "Sheriff Haraszthy, what good timing. We were just getting our horses to come see you. Mister Couts, Leandro, get down, put up your guns. Let's get out of this wind."

"It's the priest's boy," Leandro said and spit. They didn't dismount.

"I know him," Haraszthy said.

"Not as well as I do," said Leandro.

"Oh? Who else is here?" Haraszthy asked Pablo.

"No one." Pablo discounted the five who were hidden, watching.

"Take a look," said Couts to Leandro.

Leandro rode cautiously up the street to the Garras' and back. No one else moved.

"I see no one, but they could be in the rocks." Leandro eyed the boulders nervously.

"They all left as soon as we learned of the raid. The Cahuilla are as dangerous to them as they were to Warner," Bill told them.

"But they were no danger to you?" Haraszthy stared at him.

"There is always danger," Bill said.

"The Cahuilla didn't burn your houses," Leandro observed.

"Where were you, choirboy?" Couts asked Pablo.

"At San Luis Rey."

"Where are the Garras?" Haraszthy asked Bill.

"They've gone to the Colorado."

"The Cahuilla?"

"We don't know."

"You're sure?"

"Yes," Pablo insisted.

Leandro smiled thinly.

"Very good." Haraszthy was nervous. "Well then, get your horse. Better you come with us to San Diego. We can get to the bottom there. Him too." He nodded at Luna. "Warner wants to talk to this one."

"Now?" Bill turned to Falling Star, who shook her head once.

"Now," said the sheriff. "It's a long ride."

They eyed the rocks apprehensively. The horses champed at their bits and shifted their weight, making the saddles creak. The beasts looked tired and thirsty. The wind moaned in the oaks and blew crinkled leaves and fine sand down the street and around their feet. Pablo's horse danced in the dust. He took his place next to Bill, head cocked away, wordless.

Haraszthy looked at Couts, who shrugged. Leandro nodded yes.

"Vámonos." They wheeled their horses and set out at a trot.

Falling Star ran alongside as the group turned down the street. She touched Bill's hand; she cradled Cano in her other arm.

"Don't worry, we'll be back in at most five days, wait for me," he said.

"I will. I will. Adiós, my husband."

T H E Y rode into that dreadful wind, hunched down, necks pulled into coats like turtles, hatless (for what hat could possibly stay on), a bandanna tied snug over nose and mouth, hair whipping at slitted eyes; a tight and speechless party, each man alone in his thoughts.

At Santa Ysabel they stopped to water the horses. No one came out to greet them. They saw not a soul.

In the reddened dusk, the wind turned chill. Rushing down from the Cuyamacas, cooling itself on icy snowcap, it sought out the low valleys and hidden dales. It settled and swirled, frosting tender grasses, icing shallow ponds, causing creatures to bury their noses in fur or feathers, till the relief of dawn.

The silent men kept on, slowly in the dark, taking a trail Bill had never ridden, from Rancho Santa María through a narrow pass and steep canyon, eventually to the head of Mission Valley. A sliver of moon in a star-filled sky danced wildly on the wind, not bright enough to light the way. Horse followed horse, followed horse, until the glow of day and a widening trail allowed them to group.

With the light, the wind at their backs upped a notch, funneling down the long valley toward the mission and San Diego. When they were still a couple of miles from town, Haraszthy led down a sandy wash to the river. They dismounted wearily and lay on the bank while the horses drank their fill.

"Get a drink, top off your canteens and wash up here," Couts said, not unkindly. "It's pretty rugged in San Diego, what with all the extra people."

They hadn't seen a soul since leaving Cupa. The wind, the war or their fearsome appearance had denuded the country of human and animal life. There wasn't a cow in this lushest of winter grazing grounds.

When they were ready to leave, Haraszthy said casually, "We'll half to cuff you. We can't have you running off this close."

"What?" Bill snapped. "We've come willingly."

Three rifles raised to cover him.

"Really? Ze cuffs. Him first."

Couts strapped a pair of heavy cast iron cuffs, about two inches wide and joined by a chain, to Bill's wrists. They had no key, closed with a bolt.

Luna's wrists were too narrow; his slim hands pulled through. They tied his legs under his pony's belly.

When they came to Pablo, he said, "This really isn't necessary, Sheriff."

The sheriff nodded. Pablo's knife was taken. He was cuffed.

He didn't resist, only saying sarcastically, "You'll be quite the hero. I can see the headlines: Count Agoston Haraszthy Escorts Three Dangerous Criminals to San Diego—After Daring Arrest in Hostile Territory." Haraszthy grunted. Everyone else chuckled.

"It's for your own safety," Couts said. "The folks are pretty riled."

They tied ropes to their bridles and the three leaders hauled the prisoners behind. The other men rode at the rear, abreast, their guns ready. The weary horses trotted, sensing home.

Bill looked at Pablo and Luna. They wore dusty trail clothes with coyote and rabbit fur coats; on their feet, winter moccasins; hair hung stringy and wet from the river wash. He felt his scruffy beard. They weren't dressed for town. With the cuffs they did look bad, even dangerous.

S A N D I E G O had become a fortified camp. Wagons were drawn into the spaces between houses, logs and barrels piled beneath their beds. A cannon poked out between two wheels. The roads were similarly blocked. Horsemen patrolled the perimeter in pairs, armed with rifles and pistols. None were in uniform. The army had not yet returned.

Half a dozen men pulled a wagon to the side. As soon as they rode by, it was rolled back in place, an effective gate.

The plaza was full of men: miners, Indians, sailors, ranchers, Mexicans, immigrants, layabouts, all armed, not a familiar face. They jostled the horses and shouted at the sheriff:

"Who you got there, Sheriff? The Injuns gonna attack? It's the squaw man from Warner's. Them the ones murdered Slack? That's the Warners' boy, in'it? String 'em up, I say."

Haraszthy didn't answer. At the new jail, adobe walls crumbling and door sagging on its hinges, all dismounted except Luna, who had to be untied. Haraszthy's posse held the crowd at bay while the door was unlocked. Haraszthy went in. "Get out, out," he shouted.

Five men stumbled into the morning light. They were swallowed by the crowd.

"In you go," Haraszthy said.

"We don't need these, Sheriff." Pablo held up his cuffed hands.

"For your protection, get in. We'll talk after breakfast."

They went in, the door slammed shut.

F A L L I N G   Star jerked awake. Cano whimpered. The wind howled and tore at the roof thatch.

"Nasty *sosabitom* took your papi," she whispered. "And they'd better give him back." Cano mewled and thrashed. She took him up.

Outside it was still dim. Dusty swirls of wind whipped at her legs. She called for Quil-sil, leader of the guard.

"Please send a man to Palomar. Inform No'ka that the sheriff has taken Bi' and Pablo and Luna. Tell him I fear. He must come, if he does not see me in five more days."

"You should go now," Quil-sil said, looking toward the mountain.

"What if my husband should return, or send a message," she cried. "I must stay."

" W E caught your rebel sailor boy," said Leandro, as his mother pulled off his dusty boots.

Lugarda stared at him. She and 'Zul had come with a breakfast basket to the Osuna adobe on the plaza. Food was scarce in the beseiged pueblo.

"Your new husband too," Leandro told 'Zul, rubbing his rank feet.

"Where are they?" 'Zul asked.

"In the jail, but not for long."

"How long?" Lugarda fussed with the basket.

"Just long enough to build a gallows to hang them."

Leandro watched his sister flinch and smiled.

"I told you that deserter would come to no good." Señora Osuna stroked her own soft throat.

Lugarda was already out the door.

"Pablo hasn't done anything," 'Zul protested, gliding away.

"He killed my son, Lugarda's brother," Señora Osuna complained bitterly to their backs.

"And now you'll get to watch him strangle, Mami." Leandro sniffed at the covered basket. "Sailor boy too." He pulled at the cloth wrapping and took a long whiff. "Is that our breakfast? I'm starved."

68

THE INQUISITION

T H E jail was one room, about fifteen by twenty feet with small windows at both peaks of the sloped roof. They were barred. In one corner was a bucket of water; in another a half-full pail of excrement. Some blankets lay crumpled on the stone floor. The prisoners made a pile of them and sat down together. Luna unscrewed the bolts on their handcuffs with his teeth. Pablo threw them at the door with a clatter. Someone said "Hey," but the door didn't open.

When it did, it was Haraszthy. "Come," he said. He didn't notice or didn't care about the cuffs.

They got to Bandini's house without attracting a crowd, escorted by four new guards. They followed Haraszthy into the main room, scene of so many balls, and Bill's first dance with Lugarda. At one end, the big dining table was set for breakfast. The wood floor was new. Haraszthy's black boots echoed unpleasantly against the polished oak planks. Their winter moccasins swished gently.

At the table, Bandini, looking older and tired, but ever the host, pulled out chairs and said, "Eat, eat while the food is warm." The famished guests tucked in while he poured coffee. Haraszthy went into an adjoining room and returned in a few minutes with Warner and Couts. They sat down across the table. Bandini joined them, then another man who was introduced as Major E. F. Fitzgerald, commander of the militia.

Warner watched Bill chew and swallow his last mouthful of egg and tortilla. He looked haggard and angry.

"Thanks for the help on Thanksgiving," he said sourly. "After all we did for you."

"Good to see you too, John. I'm glad Anita and the kids got away safely. There was nothing I could do."

"You could have helped me. That's what you could have done. You could have picked up your rifle and ridden over to help me defend the ranch. I nearly got killed."

"They would have killed me too. I made sure you were warned."

"But not by you."

"By my family, what's the difference? You scoffed at the danger. You should have left the ranch with Anita and the children."

"Were you there with them, shooting at me? That's the question I want you to answer."

"Don't be ridiculous. It was the Cahuilla."

Pablo said, "Mr. Warner, on Thanksgiving it was exactly for Bill as it was for you in the war of '46. Remember how you were arrested by Captain Gillespie and held in jail—because he thought you should have helped him find and capture the Picos. When two friends insist on fighting, and you can't prevent it, it is best to stay out of the way. That is what you did in '46 and that is what Bill has done. The sheriff even reminds me a bit of Gillespie, don't you think?" He looked from Warner to Haraszthy.

Warner sat back, eyes cold and hard, his lips pressed to a thin line. Juan José's part in the war was a sore point with the Americans, forever thrown in his face during heated debates at the State Senate. He had told Bill this himself. Rivals still accused him of having aided the Mexicans.

"But at some point you have to choose sides," said Major Fitzgerald. "Warner has proven his loyalty. Whose side are you on, Mister Marshall?"

"The side of peace. I am opposed to the Garras and their allies."

"He is, we are all on the American side," Pablo said. "That is why we came here with the sheriff, to help you to identify the rebels."

"Let Mister Marshall talk, Mister Verdi," Haraszthy said.

Bill said. "My loyalty is to my family, my friends and my country."

"Which family?" Warner said.

"My family at Cupa, my wife, in-laws and friends."

"All Indians?" Couts asked.

"Yes, except for the Warners."

"Phaa!" spat Warner. The others looked amused.

"What about your family in Providence, Rhode Island?" said Haraszthy.

"What about them? They sent me to sea; they take care of themselves."

"Why did they send you to sea?" Haraszthy asked.

Bill closed his eyes. He saw the Nipmuck Indian village, downriver from their farm; Suski, the pretty girl he loved; her stern father; his own Puritan parents. Suski was pregnant with Bill's child. They asked permission to marry. Her father came to talk to Bill's own dad. He heard shouting in two languages.

Bill was shipped out as a cabin boy on the next whaler to leave Providence. When he returned, Suski had been sold to a Mohawk. Their boy child was dead, held by the legs and head-splattered against a tree. The Nipmuck Algonquins liked a pure race. Bill's parents agreed. He had gone straight back to sea. Now he was here.

"Someone got pregnant," Bill said. There were chuckles.

"Ah-ha," said Haraszthy. "The loverboy. How old were you?"

"Fourteen."

"That's enough family history, Marshall," Major Fitzgerald interrupted. "We want to hear everything you know about the Garras and their revolt."

"But it is interesting," said Haraszthy, looking at the other inquisitors. "Very well, tell us about the Garras. Antonio Garra, Sr., is chief of Cupeño, no?"

"Not exactly. It's a long story."

"You tell it." Haraszthy leaned back in his chair.

Bill gave them a brief history of the Garra years at San Luis Rey and Cupa. "A capitán or chief is not a dictator or a general. He does not give orders. People only follow him if he can persuade them to. And there are other important capitánes of the various clans and villages," he concluded.

"When did you last see the Garras?"

"About the twentieth of November."

"Did they tell you where they were going, what their plans were?" Couts asked.

"They said they were going to the Colorado to urge the tribes there to revolt. Their objective was Fort Yuma."

"And you didn't tell the authorities?" Fitzgerald tapped the table.

"We hoped nothing would come of it." Bill shrugged. "The Garras preached revolt everywhere, for months. It was always just a lot of talk."

"And then killing," said Warner.

"Do you know how many have been killed so far?" asked Couts.

The answer was one, five or nine, depending on what one knew. Plus four Indians at least. Bill decided to tell the truth. Pablo had advised it as the best course. There was no telling what the militia knew. To be caught lying would be bad. They had to help.

"Nine Americans, I have heard of. I don't know how many Indians."

"Very good," said Haraszthy. "Your information is very good."

"Too good," said Couts. Warner nodded.

"Do you know who killed them?" Fitzgerald leaned in on both elbows. His face was two feet from Bill's.

"The Cahuilla killed five in Valle de San José. They say the Garras, with the Yumans and Cocopas, killed four shepherds at the Colorado."

"You're sure?"

"Pretty sure."

"Do you know where the Cahuilla are?"

"No."

"And the Garras?"

"I believe they are following Captain Davidson, who fled Fort Yuma on the sixth for San Diego." Today was the eleventh, Wili's birthday. He winced. Fitzgerald refilled his coffee cup.

"Any idea how many men Davidson has?"

"There should be about twenty-seven, barring casualties. The Indians say everyone escaped the fort."

Fitzgerald sat back in his chair and studied Bill. He looked at Couts and then the sheriff. "Your information is very accurate," he finally said.

"I want to help."

"He would make a good spy," Haraszthy said.

"Yeah, if only he were working for us," Couts joked.

"Where were you when the Levi Slack party was killed?" Warner asked.

Bill had been dreading this question.

"I was there. They were at Cupa when the Cahuilla arrived from raiding Warner's store. In ten seconds the rebels had killed them. There was nothing anyone could do."

The inquisitors shuffled a bit. Bill looked at Pablo, but got no help.

"But the same rebels didn't touch you . . . ?" Haraszthy shook his head.

"Was the boy there?" Warner scowled at Luna.

"No, he didn't arrive until evening, after everyone had departed."

"So the Cahuilla rode off. Then the Cupeño left?" Couts asked.

"They were afraid, after the murders."

"Where did they go?" Haraszthy was getting bored.

"To the mountains."

"But you stayed."

"I stayed to talk to whoever might come. You came first so I talked to you. I wanted you to know what happened, to try to prevent a wider war."

"And the Cahuilla? Where did they go?" Fitzgerald demanded.

"Back to Wiliya, in Coyote Canyon. The village of Chapuli."

"They did not harm you?"

"No. They know me."

"They know me too," said Warner dryly. "Are you saying that no Cupeño took part in the raid on my ranch? I find that hard to swallow. I know some of those hotheads."

This was the other question Bill was dreading. He had to tell the truth.

"Some of them did. The Garras were very persuasive. Those Cupeño are with the Cahuilla at Wiliya."

"Would you like to name them?"

This was their death sentence. Bill strung together a few Cupeño names. Warner listened intently. No one else understood where one word ended and another began.

"All right, enough, enough," said Haraszthy, holding up his hand. "Now we will ask a question of Mister Verdi. Captain Couts . . ."

"What were you doing in Cupa?" Couts began.

"Visiting my friends."

"The Garras too are your friends?"

"Yes. Antonio Senior was with my father at the mission. I grew up with his son."

"Did he talk to you about the revolt he was planning?"

"He spoke to every Indian leader in the county. The revolt was widely publicized."

"You didn't go to the army, or sheriff, or alcalde with the information Garra gave you?"

"They already knew it. Garra made no secrets. No one believed he was serious."

"You are a U.S. Citizen?"

"I suppose so. Yes."

Couts looked at Warner, then Haraszthy.

"Did you take part in the attack on Warner's ranch?"

"No."

"Then why did you go there?"

"I already told you. I went to Cupa to see those who had opposed Garra. I wanted to bring Bill back to San Diego with me." Pablo was losing patience. "Cupa is not part of Warner's ranch."

"And you knew the difference?" Couts made a weighing motion with his hands, lifting one and then the other. "You knew who supported and who opposed Garra?"

"Yes," Pablo said simply.

No one spoke. Haraszthy drained his coffee. Fitzgerald looked bored. Bandini may have been asleep.

"Ask your boy what he knows," Haraszthy said to Warner.

Warner quizzed Luna in Spanish. Luna said Pablo had nothing to do with the Garras. He had not been to Cupa in a year. He told Warner that Bill had alerted them to be ready for an attack on Thanksgiving Day.

Couts understood. Even Bandini woke up at the Spanish exchange.

"He doesn't know anything," Warner said.

Couts whispered to Haraszthy.

Haraszthy looked at Fitzgerald, who shook his head.

"That will be all, gentlemen. Thank you."

Haraszthy opened the door—instructed the four guards: "Take the prisoners back to jail; change the water and empty the honey bucket."

"Wait a minute," Pablo protested. "You've asked your questions, now let us go. I wish to see my wife, to bathe, to get a fresh suit of clothes. You can't put us back in that filthy jail. We're not under arrest."

"Very well. I hereby arrest you," Haraszthy said. "Take them."

"What for?" Pablo was not budging.

"We'll let you know."

"We're talking it over. It won't be long," Fitzgerald told them.

In shock, they followed the guards into the plaza.

O N the way back to jail, angry shouts rose from the mob that had gathered. A crude scaffold was being assembled at the end of the plaza, near the Osuna house. They reached the cell safely. The guards emptied the shit bucket into a corner, then poured the clean water into the filthy pail, saying, "There's your fresh water; have a drink." They slammed the door in a gale of laughter.

The dejected captives sat on the floor in the stench, heads in hands. It was obvious Bill was guilty of some sort of complicity in the eyes of the inquisitors. He had known too much, said too much, been at the scene of too many crimes to be without suspicion.

But Pablo was totally innocent. It was insane to even accuse him of involvement with the Garras' revolt. And Luna had fought at Warner's side.

T H E Y heard 'Zul at the door, asking in a loud voice to see her husband.

"No visitors, them's the orders," said the guard.

"Come to the back," Pablo shouted in Pauma.

He sprang to grab the window bars and pulled himself up until he could look out.

"Wife," he said.

"Husband," she replied.

They spoke quickly in their language and he dropped back.

"She'll alert Holbein and send word to Ibarra. I asked her to find someone to look for Captain Davidson's patrol coming through the mountains. They are the nearest soldiers. Ibarra can send word to Heintzelman in Los Angeles."

He sat and rubbed his itchy scalp hard.

"We need to stick something in the wall to stand on. I can only hold myself up for a minute."

He searched the room. Bill produced his dirk, still stuffed in his moccasin. Pablo sniffed it. "It's finally lost the smell of whale guts." He scratched a hole in the adobe, about five feet off the ground. When he could insert the knife, he vaulted to the bars and stood on the handle. It held.

"We've got to get out of here and away," he said. "Or delay, delay until the army comes. Davidson's been on the march for five days. He should be here soon. Maybe Heintzelman has already left Los Angeles. We'll be hanged if help doesn't come."

"Hanged?" Bill said. That dreadful word floated on the fetid air, as though supported by the rising stench.

Pablo dropped to the floor. "I know their plan now. How could we be so stupid? They plan to charge us with treason."

He pulled the dirk out of the wall and chopped at the air with it.

"Treason?"

"Haraszthy knows all about it. He fled Hungary for plotting against the emperor. He was harboring revolutionaries at his family estate. If caught, he would have been executed for treason. Just what he thinks to do with us.

"It is a charge impossible for us to defend. All they need to prove, we have already admitted: We are American citizens. We didn't help Warner; we didn't help the Slack party; we didn't go to the authorities with the knowledge we had of hostile activities . . . the Cahuilla didn't harm us. They plan to hang us for what we didn't do. For what didn't happen! In their minds, they don't have to prove a thing." Pablo's eyes were wild and scared.

Bill slumped to the floor and dug both fists into his tense jaw. Falling Star was waiting for him. Wili and Shadow were waiting for them.

"'Zul said Lugarda will try to do something," Pablo told him.

I N the late afternoon, Haraszthy came. When he walked in, the stench assaulted his nostrils.

"What have you done?" he cried, holding his nose.

"Your guards kicked the shit can over," Bill said. "Then they put the drinking water in it."

Haraszthy sputtered, screaming at the guards in a mix of Hungarian and mangled English. He hustled Bill and Pablo to Bandini's where they were seated at the dining table. Leandro Osuna had joined Couts, Warner and Fitzgerald. Leandro grinned and shook their hands.

Fitzgerald read from a stack of papers.

"You are hereby charged, William Marshall and Pablo Verdi, with the crimes of treason, murder and robbery. There will be a court-martial at ten o'clock tomorrow morning, the twelfth of December, in this room."

"You will be supplied a lawyer, if you so desire," added Haraszthy.

"I would like to have Father Francisco González de Ibarra of San Luis Rey as my lawyer. Please send for him at once."

"Church cannot mix in state matters, Mister Verdi. You know that."

"Your father can't save you now, putito," Leandro leered.

Pablo glared at him.

"Then I'll be my own lawyer, and act for William Marshall as well, if he agrees." He flitted his eyes at Bill.

"Yes."

"Well, that is all," Haraszthy told them, slapping the table.

"Who heads the court-martial?" Pablo stood flightily.

"I do," Haraszthy said.

"The others?"

"Colonel Warner, Major Fitzgerald, Captain Couts. Sergent Osuna is an alternate."

Pablo sat back down. "This must be a joke," he snorted.

"No joke, you will found out tomorrow."

A S they were escorted back to jail, Pablo asked Haraszthy, "What about the boy?"

"He will be a witness. If he cooperates, nothing."

The cell was clean. Fresh blankets were neatly stacked in a corner with a roll of thick cowhides to spread on the cold stone floor. There was a basket of tortillas with a hunk of cheese, two little chiles and two lemons.

"Thank you, Count, this is extremely kind," Pablo said.

Haraszthy gave them a lit candle. By the flickering light they could see Luna, huddled in a corner.

"We breakfast before court-martial. Good night."

The door slammed shut; the lock clicked; orders for the night guards were given. Exhausted, Bill and Pablo arranged their beds and fell to fitful slumber. The evil wind howled the night long, but they heard it not. They were elsewhere.

69

THE TRIAL

S O M E T I M E S life asleep is better than life awake.

They rose before daylight, ate the leftover tortillas and paced the cell. Pablo leapt to the window at the slightest sound. He managed to speak to Holbein, who promised to summon some of the Indians from Mission San Diego and the rancherías who might be helpful as witnesses.

They resolved to defend themselves vigorously. Pablo had spoken against insurrection at tribal meetings. The Indians could verify this to a fair court. Luna could speak for Bill. Warner might even support him. The charges were refutable.

A T Bandini's, near the hour of ten, Holbein and some Indians were waiting. Lugarda and 'Zul stood with them. Lugarda waved shyly but did not speak. There were only a few other loiterers. It appeared the trial would not be public. Only the accused and Luna were allowed to enter.

Bandini offered breakfast, but the nervous defendants declined. The panel was uneasy too. Leandro Osuna never looked up from the table. Warner looked everywhere but at Bill. Fitzgerald was bored. Only Haraszthy and Couts showed any enthusiasm for the proceedings.

Haraszthy read the charges. He recited testimony from the interrogation, consulting his notes when necessary. His conclusion: They were guilty by their own admission—of association and probable participation in the attack on Warner's ranch and robbery of his store; of the murder of Levi Slack and three others; and of the attack on Fort Yuma, a U.S. military garrison. As United States citizens, they were guilty of treason, for aiding and abetting the Indian nations in Garra's war.

Haraszthy swore in John Warner as his first witness.

"You will tell the court what you know of William Marshall's involvement with the Garra war."

"Things started to go wrong on my return from San José last summer. Marshall quit work at the ranch and the Indians wouldn't come to work either—they had been poisoned against me."

"They quit because of the miserly wage you paid them and because the tribe had plenty of money from selling cattle," Bill objected.

"Do not interrupt the witness; you'll get your turn," said Fitzgerald.

"I knew they had money," Haraszthy said to Couts.

"The cattle were stolen from me," Warner shouted at Bill. "Garra put his brand on every calf born while I was gone and you let him."

"Anything else?" Haraszthy asked.

"Just before I left, Bill came to me, saying he represented Cupa, to ask about the Cupeño rights to land around the hot springs. He was pressuring me on Chief Garra's behalf to promise them the land."

"That's a lie," said Pablo. You've been promising land to the Cupeño since you first got the grant, before Bill came, way before Garra was chief. They wanted to find out what your plans were for the land court."

"Enough," said Fitzgerald. "This is not the land court. Stick to the war, John."

"I invited him to Thanksgiving dinner and his wife declined. She said he was busy. I saw her brother, Jacobo, watching the house in the afternoon. That night the Indians attacked. Bill knew of the plan and neither warned me nor came to help."

The court was silent for a moment. Warner traced the grain of the table-top with his fingertips.

"After the attack, Bill stayed on as though nothing were amiss. I think he incited the revolt, along with Pablo Verdi and the Garras. He betrayed me; he betrayed his country." Warner turned his baleful eyes on Bill. "My father-in-law warned me not to trust a ship deserter."

"What about Pablo Verdi?" Haraszthy asked.

"He has always been an agitator for Indian rights, since the Mexican days. The Cupeño were peaceful, before he came in '46, after Kearny's defeat at San Pasqual, and incited them to kill eleven Californios. Pablo consulted General Joshua Bean on Garra's behalf. He stirred Garra to war—by telling him Judge Bean advised not to pay the grazing tax—when what Bean really said was that tribal Indians don't have to pay."

Leandro was fidgeting, glaring at Pablo.

"Mister Osuna?" Haraszthy acknowledged him.

"I have known Pablo since we are little, niños." He struggled for the English words. "He is always making troubles, always hating whites."

"You're not white, mestizo," Pablo whispered.

"You see . . ." Leandro twisted his hands. "He killed my brother." Leandro could barely say the words.

"Wherever there's Indian trouble," Warner concluded, "you can be sure Pablo Verdi is involved."

"Thank you," said Haraszthy. He called Santos Luna and swore him in. When he learned that Luna only spoke a few words of English, the sheriff dismissed him. "You should learn the language of your masters," he said.

"Anything else?"

Fitzgerald shook his head.

"You may defend yourselves." Haraszthy piled his notes. He adjusted the tight pants of his uniform, sat back in his chair and sipped at his coffee.

P A B L O began by refuting Warner's warped version of recent events.

"Mister Warner forgets that Willian Marshall worked faithfully on his ranch for more than six years. He forgets that only the diplomacy of his foreman, Bill, kept the Cupeño from driving the Warners from the valley, as they had Pico and Portilla before him. He forgets the months and months he spent away from his ranch, when his wife and family were kept perfect and safe by Bill and the Cupeño.

"John Warner forgets that while he was in jail in '46, for suspected treason, Bill hosted General Kearny at the ranch, feeding the troops, supplying horses and convincing the tribes to support the Americans, allowing the weakened Mexicans to be defeated by Kearny's pitiful army."

"Those broncos he gave the dragoons nearly got General Kearny killed," Warner said dryly.

"On your orders John," Bill shouted. "You told me to drive all the good stock to the hills."

"Warner forgets, "Pablo continued," that while he was in jail in Los Angeles for mule thievery, William Marshall nursed his family through the worst winter in memory.

"Warner forgets that I too aided in turning the Indians against the Mexicans; that in the war's darkest hour, I brought a herd of sheep to feed the U.S. garrison at San Diego; that the eleven Mexicans we killed at Cupa were Kearny's enemies from the battle at San Pasqual.

"The court forgets that both of us opposed the Garras at every turn, at considerable risk to our own lives. You forget everything but that I am an Indian and Bill is married to one. We are patriots, not traitors."

"Is that all?" Haraszthy said.

"With the court's permission, I would like to call my witnesses."

"Call them then. Keep it short."

Pablo called Luna to testify.

Luna defended Bill and Pablo in crisp four- or five-word sentences, coaxed by Pablo and translated to effective English. The translations were grudgingly acknowledged to be accurate by Couts and Warner. The prosecutors did not challenge this exonerating testimony, nor comment.

Pablo called native witnesses from San Diego and Las Flores, and Manuelito, who had arrived from Pauma. All could testify as to Pablo's opposition to the Garras.

The court listened, but dismissed their testimony as ineligible, because they were not citizens.

"How can you say Antonio Garra is a citizen, and Manuelito Cota, who grew up with him at the mission, is a tribal," Pablo protested. "No Indian was ever as Mexican as Manuelito. He is more American than I am. Or you are, Sheriff."

"Indians cannot testify in a U.S. court," said Fitzgerald.

"What about Santos Luna, the Yuman boy who just testified?"

"All my Indians are Americans," Warner said. "I educated them to be citizens."

"Every Indian is more American than any of you. At least our forefathers were born here. Whatever you may call this land of ours."

"Are you done?" asked Haraszthy. The entire panel was bored. Couts and Leandro were nodding.

"No, I call Father Juan Holbein."

"Can priests bear witness?"

"If he's American," Fitzgerald grunted.

Holbein swore that he had never heard Pablo speak in support of the Garras. Pablo had always condemned the revolt. He had been at San Luis Rey at the time of the alleged crimes.

The panel did not cross-examine the priest.

Haraszthy said, "Thank you." The guards escorted him out.

Pablo summarized the defense: "We both opposed the Garras' revolt from the beginning. Neither of us took part in any warlike action. We did no spying for the Garras. I was hundreds of miles from the scene of any crime at the time of commission. We did not rob Warner's store or receive any stolen property. The two allowed witnesses have testified to these truths. You have presented no positive proof. We are innocent as charged."

He sat beside Bill. The look he gave his friend was devoid of hope—but not resigned—angry.

Haraszthy then read the charges: treason, murder, and robbery.

Each member of the court called out "Guilty" to the charge of treason, first for Bill and then for Pablo. They were both found not guilty of murder and robbery. Only Couts, with his rodent's smirk, looked at the accused. Haraszthy kept his eyes on his papers. The others studied the table.

Sheriff Haraszthy faced the convicted and pronounced sentence: "At two P.M. tomorrow afternoon, Saturday the thirteenth of December, William Marshall and Juan Pablo Verdi shall be hanged by their necks until dead."

Bill gasped for breath, fighting back tears. The room whirled.

Haraszthy was not finished. "Court found the boy known as Santos Luna to be guilty of false testimony. Sentence will be twenty-five lashes of the whip, to be administered at the same time and place."

Pablo roared to his feet. He swore at the panel in all the languages he knew. He lunged for Leandro with Bill's dirk, conjured somehow into his right fist. Leandro pushed himself back from the wide table but Pablo managed to stab the pushing hand, pinning it to the tabletop.

The sheriff yelled, "No." Fitzgerald struck with the alertness of a fighter, grabbing Pablo's wrist. The knife came out and rolled down the table. Warner grabbed it. They wrestled Pablo, screaming and kicking, to the polished wood floor. Leandro was cursing, sucking on a bleeding gash between his thumb and forefinger. Neither Luna nor Bill had moved.

They held Pablo until he was still, then another minute.

"You can let me up now," he said in a normal voice.

Haraszthy called the four guards, who led the condemned men out, pistols drawn. They were taken back to the cell and locked in.

B I L L stretched out on a blanket and stared at the thick plank ceiling. He needed to lie flat, to surrender himself to earth's greatest force. But rest would not come. Even gravity would be turned against them on the morrow.

"I'm sorry I threw your knife away. That was stupid, stupid, stupid." Pablo yanked at his hair.

"That's the second time Leandro's been nicked by that dirk."

"He insulted Ibarra and I didn't like him calling me a little whore. But

Luna's whipping sent me over the edge. We didn't need his witness. No testimony could have saved us."

"I don't care," Luna said.

"I do."

"It made me feel good to tell them, Pablito."

T H E Y heard the door unlock and Holbein jumped in. The door slammed behind him.

"Haraszthy has agreed you may have visitors, food, books, whatever you need for your comfort until tomorrow."

"I would like some paper and a pen to write a letter," Bill said. "And please ask Lugarda Osuna to visit me, if she will."

Holbein nodded and looked to Pablo.

"Since Haraszthy has decided to be generous, we would like to dine here, in our own company."

Pablo looked around the room.

"Please invite my wife and Lugarda Osuna to sup with us. Ask them to bring a change of clothes for me, something a caballero would wear on his last day on earth. Also fresh clothing for Bill."

He spoke quickly to Luna.

"And a nightshirt for Luna."

When Holbein had departed, Pablo spoke softly, as though to himself.

"I have never been able to forget Alipas, the boy whose life I took that night at Cupa—it has now been five years. I could just as easily have let him live. He had done nothing to me, or to anyone else. Remember what he said?"

Bill shook his head. He didn't want to think of that night.

"What is the use of crying. We can only die once; let us die like brave men."

Bill remembered—the chanting, naked bodies, lances stabbing.

"The single thing that I have been able to do, that makes it bearable, is to promise myself that when my time comes, I will die as bravely as he did." Pablo's voice grew stronger. "Now my time has come. I intend to keep that promise.

"Tonight we will wring as much fun as we possibly can from our few remaining hours. I will not die beaten into the dirt, broken and teary, begging for mercy. Neither shall you, mi amigo. We have lived well and we will die well, with clean clothes, a laugh . . . and a prayer for our loved ones."

"I barely said goodbye to Falling Star," Bill said, distressed. "She is waiting for me."

"The letter you write to her will be better than a thousand goodbyes. It will be passed from hand to hand, worn, then torn, finally carried as scraps in a locket on your great-grandaughter's throat."

Pablo had talked himself into a good mood. Bill began to feel a bit better. It couldn't possibly be any worse. To die tomorrow?

"Maybe Lugarda can save us," Bill moaned.

70

A LAST SUPPER

BILL wrote his letter to Falling Star that afternoon, cramming it with as much love, hope and regret as he could express in words. He signed the letter and sealed the envelope.

Bandini brought a bowl of steaming water with a cotton cloth and a bar of scented soap. Washing felt as luxurious as an immersion in the hot springs. They were excited, expectant, melancholy, happy: dreading the morrow yet relishing every single second of the intervening time. They vowed not to sleep until death.

HOLBEIN came at dusk with two jugs of wine, a flagon of brandy and one of sherry, all from San Luis Rey's vineyards. He had no news of the army. Haraszthy provided all that Pablo had asked, including candles, a tablecloth and linen napkins, but no knives or forks. Lugarda and 'Zul were preparing the food and had sent clean clothes: a caballero's suit for Pablo, the nightshirt, and a stiff new pair of blue denim pants, with a blue and red checked, long-sleeved flannel shirt for Bill.

Holbein presented the wines and opened the brandy. He proposed a toast, pouring it into Bandini's glazed clay mugs, sniffing the heady fumes and downing it in a gulp. "To life," they all said. It was too strong for Bill. Luna's eyes rolled. Pablo pounded his back, his own eyes watering.

Holbein opened a pale white wine that was easier to swallow. It had just been poured when the door lock rattled. Everyone froze. The guards ushered in Lugarda and 'Zul, set some baskets on the floor, touched their hats with a curious glance and shut the door. The bolt snapped in place.

The women were dressed in black velvet gowns, with black lace shawls. They were made up for a party, but it was obvious they had been crying.

Pathetic and miserable, they stood meekly next to their baskets. The candle-light flickered. Pablo and Bill were speechless, all spruced up, grinning like shy suitors on a date. It had not occurred to them that anyone could be more devastated by their imminent deaths than themselves.

While they had been relishing their last hours, looking forward to this evening, Lugarda and 'Zul had suffered every moment from the announce-ment of the sentence. Even before the trial, the building of the gallows and digging of two fresh graves had filled them with dread. All the frivolity Bill and Pablo had planned now seemed cruelly shallow.

Holbein rushed to the women, and then they all moved, holding, com-forting each other.

"Death is a selfish thing," Holbein told them. "The survivors live with the pain and guilt, the suffering and missing, the memories and longing. It is you two who will be free."

He rescued the evening with a prayer. He asked God to take them, if He must, straight to heaven—where they surely belonged—not to prolong their suffering. And to give these friends the gift of this last joyous evening together; to allow them to take bread and wine in His name, with His bless-ing, and to rejoice with Him in their ascension on the morrow.

He poured two cups of brandy, broke a chunk from a loaf of bread, placing a little piece on the women's tongues, and asked them to wash it down with the wine. The women did this obediently, draining the brandy.

The drink made their eyes stream, but the real tears ceased. They were soon laying out the food, chatting and laughing, trading gossip and giggling over the jailhouse accommodations.

They had prepared an unforgettable meal. Pablo and Bill had wished to duplicate the delicious meals taken together at Encinitas. Fortunately, the war refugees had not denuded the sea. There were fresh clams, still wrig-gling, squirted with lemon, topped with a dab of chile. Thinly pounded abalone from Point Loma, dipped in corn flour and sautéed in olive oil, were finished with the pale wine.

Mussels, scallops, chunks of corn, lobster, chayote and celery made up a creamy stew—like a spicy New England chowder. More of the yellow wine and hunks of chewy bread accompanied this dish.

Yellowtail they ate cooked whole, wrapped in bacon and baked to a dark brown. It was sprinkled with ground chile. When you cut into it, the center was still pink. This was served with a salty green tomato sauce. 'Zul rolled warm fresh tortillas with creamy butter to eat with the tuna. A murky Span-ish red filled the cups and stained the white tablecloth.

As the meal progressed, Luna became talkative. By the time the tuna was eaten, he was a raucous comedian, allowing no one to utter a word without a funny rejoinder. Wine and the nature of the occasion had transformed him into his polar opposite. In the pause before dessert, he sprang from his chair to act out his life with the Warners. He mimicked each member of the extended family brilliantly, including Bill and Zippy the dog. He could prance like Anita, whine like Mary Ann, cry like Andrés, stride and grumble and collapse into a chair like John, make himself invisible like Fanny and her sister (who was so invisible no one even knew her name) and pad silently after Warner as himself. His face, full of emotion, would go blank when Warner turned to bark an order. He would do the bidden task, his exterior in perfect doglike obedience, interior giggling with humorous rebellion.

Pablo laughed so hard it made his stomach ache, and 'Zul tried to calm him, placing her cool hands there, under his shirt.

"The silent man sees everything," Pablo pronounced, when he could speak.

For some reason this set everyone to laughing again. Luna choked on a gulp of wine and had to lie down. During the break, Lugarda served dessert.

"I made this lemon tart myself," she said.

Bill laughed at her. "We know you never cook." Pablo nodded.

"I did," she protested. "I was too nervous to sit still."

'Zul backed her claim. "She really did. I was busy collecting seafood with the Kanakas."

The pie was delicious, just sweet enough with the sugary crust and frothy meringue to offset the lemon tart. They each ate two pieces and left not a crumb in the pan. Lugarda glowed in a shower of compliments. They toasted her with a glass of sherry.

"I'm so happy you came," Bill said, beaming at her.

She took his hand. "An army of soldiers couldn't have kept me away."

Everyone took a breath. Where was the army when you needed them?

Holbein broke the dreadful spell.

"I pray the army arrives. Wouldn't it be wonderful to hear them come clanking into the plaza? Let us offer a prayer to that effect."

They joined him in that short prayer.

"We must never give up hope," he said seriously, when silence again descended.

"One of the things I didn't like about the mission was the kind of hope they taught us," Pablo said shortly. "Do not take offense, I know you mean well," he assured Holbein, "but none of the many things we were told to hope for have happened. Just the opposite.

"I believe we must accept what is and not hope for things that are not, and will not be. Otherwise life is too disappointing, and we are prevented from enjoying it fully. Life can only be good in the present. The present is real, and the continuing present—that is what makes up this entire life on earth."

Bill nodded. "That is what I too believe. Enjoyment must be found in each individual moment as it happens."

"I am not even sure that hope is a good thing," Pablo said. "Save hope for the absolutely unbearable moment. Life is joyful, if we will let it be." He tapped his cup with Bill's.

"I believe in hope," 'Zul declared stubbornly in English. "It is the past we must forget, not the future. Then our lives will be better. That is why No'ka kept Bill in Cupa (she pronounced Bill's name perfectly)—to prepare us for the future, as the padres did for Pablito. My child will learn to be American first. Then he may enjoy the moments as he likes. That is a realistic hope."

They studied her. She remained defiant. Her English was better than Lugarda's. She thrived among her enemies. She couldn't be refuted.

"It's not so easy," Bill protested, waving his hand at the cell and what lurked outside. "What if the past is better than the future? What does that say for hope?"

Pablo's face moved to speak, but he held his peace.

"Not even God can turn back time," said Holbein, his eyes on Pablo. "Your wife hopes for what must happen. It is she who confronts reality and makes the best of it."

"And she is right," Pablo said resignedly. "I don't think we have a choice. It is that or death." He held her hand. 'Zul leaned against him.

They had been avoiding that word. Now there it was, swirling about the room like a trapped bat, looking for a place to land.

Lugarda sprang from her chair, spilling her half-filled glass. "Let me tell you a story about forgetting to be Indian. Bill is right. It is not so easy."

She paced the little room. Her short boots tapped the stone floor. She had dropped her shawl and her hair fell half unpinned, brushing one shoulder. She removed the tortoiseshell comb and let it all fall with a shake of her head.

"My father's grandmother, Lugarda Quis Quis, was Yaqui, all Indian. I am named after her. She was my abuela, my nanny, my teacher; the first person I loved. From her, I learned everything, all I hold dear." Lugarda put both hands to her breast and took a deep breath.

"Did you know that Pablo and I were childhood friends? We would meet every time my family went to the mission. He was the handsome and dashing prince of my youthful dreams. No young man ever wore a Spanish gentleman's cloak with more élan. When he made me laugh, I felt as light as a moonbeam.

"Pablo was the one I should have married—impossible, I know, even if he would have had me. My brothers would have killed us both. But he was there. There to contemplate, like my great-grandmother.

"Once, he gave 'Zul, his sweetheart—and therefore the object of my jealousy, but also my continuing link to him—he gave 'Zul a short, red, pounded-bark skirt with a shell-studded belt: a native woman's dress from the time before the missions.

"When you put this skirt on, he said, braid your hair in shells, and dance with me in the noonday sun, then I shall marry you. He used that sweet mocking tone he has . . . but he was serious. It was a challenge."

Pablo smiled. 'Zul rumpled his hair.

"You must understand, 'Zul was desperate to marry him, but of course she dressed as Spanish as I did." Lugarda held her skirt and curtsied.

"When Pablo had gone, we went to my room, locked the door. 'Zul took off every single piece of her clothing and put on the skirt. It was short. It barely reached her knees. She looked at herself in the mirror. Her hands flew to cover herself, here and here." Lugarda passed a panicky hand over breast and thighs. "'I could never go out like this. He is mad. I hate him,' 'Zul cried. She dashed the skirt to the floor, dressed in haste and fled in tears.

"I took up the rejected skirt and swished it; I held it to my waist. I decorated my hair in shells. I removed all of my clothes and put the skirt on, fastening the waistband. Then I looked in the mirror. What I saw was an Indian self; my shackled spirit adorned instead of concealed. I saw my abuela as a girl. I stared at this person who had become another."

She met Bill's eyes. "Indian women have many more freedoms than we Spanish ladies. They are more equal. They do not need permission from a man for every little act. Brazen, the priests say of them. Brazen is how I felt.

"I imagined myself walking through the dining room, out into the courtyard, to the stable, bridling my horse and leaping upon him. I would ride bareback with Pablo into the far hills. We would dance in a sunlit meadow.

"I rose on tiptoes to look out the bedroom window. My mother was sitting on the veranda in the shade, reading. She was completely covered in cloth, from the tips of her fingers in white gloves, to the toes of her red-laced shoes. She had a scarf over her head. She was my jailor; the jailor of my free soul. I hated her.

"I wanted to run out; to shout, Mother, look how pretty this new skirt is. I'm going to go show it to Pablo, to thank him. I'll be back for lunch.

"I wanted to do it; to see her jump out of her pale skin; to see her shriek, clutch her throat, faint. I stomped in frustration. I did a furious war dance. I screamed in silence. I killed everyone.

"Then I took the skirt off, folded it carefully and hid it at the back of my deepest drawer. I removed the shells from my hair. I dressed and prayed for forgiveness."

Lugarda returned to sit beside Bill, a little breathless. She took a sip of brandy from her refilled glass. She had acted out every bit of her experience marvelously. Bill felt he had been there in the mirror, watching her—only the woman she had become was Falling Star, in her own red tule skirt. She was waiting for him, and he ached for her.

"You didn't tell me you did that," 'Zul was saying. "I want that skirt back. Pablo gave it to me."

"Yes I did," Pablo said. "But you never wore it and I married you anyway."

"You can't have it," Lugarda waggled her finger, "unless you wear it."

"More brandy?" Holbein offered.

"I didn't know you were Yaqui," said Luna with interest, taking up his glass.

"I never knew you fancied me," Pablo said with a sly grin.

Lugarda shot Pablo a sharp look and he gave her a lightning kiss on the cheek. She sprayed brandy and slapped him. 'Zul was giggling. Lugarda laughed between coughs. Pablo handed her a glass of water.

"I didn't," Lugarda told him. "I made it all up to amuse Lunito, who was in danger of falling asleep."

"No danger now," Luna slurred, nose-diving onto a pile of blankets and lying still. "I'm not sleeping," he mumbled. "This way I can't fall over."

"A wise man," tinkled Holbein.

Someone outside called Pablo's name. He leapt to the bars and pulled himself up to look. It was the Kanakas.

"Pablo, what dey gon' do wit' you, bra?" It was Makua. "Dey wan' hang you?"

"I guess so," said Pablo.

"You like I broke da kine door? Dis jail stay weak. Blah wen' bust out easy, one time."

"They'd just hunt us down."

"We can take one ship to da Islands. I get uncles Lanai-side. Da haoles no can find you there."

"Thank you, Makua. You'll only get in trouble. There are the guards, and the whole town is armed. I don't see how we could escape."

"Mo' betta you try, bra."

As Pablo dropped down, Makua smashed his fist against the adobe wall.

"Stinkin' haoles!"

"Maybe he's right," 'Zul said.

Bill sighed. "I wish we were on the *Hopewell*."

71

DEATH

W H E N Bill awoke, light streamed through one high window and the dusty cracks around the door. Luna snored in a corner; Pablo was gone. Holbein had donned Pablo's clothes and pretended to sleep, while Pablo walked out with the women, wearing a priest's smock smuggled in under 'Zul's dress and Holbein's wide-brimmed hat. Holbein had then stuffed Pablo's clothes with blankets, and departed alone after the change of guard.

Bill quickly checked Pablo's pockets for anything useful or incriminating. He found a little rosy boa in the caballero jacket, curled into a tight ball. It was winter and she should be hibernating. He put the pretty snake in his shirt pocket.

The door rattled and opened. A guard brought in a breakfast tray with tortillas and coffee. Others stood behind him, rifles pointed in.

"Shit." The guard spun around, spilling the coffee. "One of them's gone." He kicked the stuffed jacket. He kicked Luna too, just to be sure.

He backed out without leaving the tray. The door slammed.

" I K N E W that little snake would wiggle away somehow," Leandro said.

"This makes me look bad," Haraszthy fretted.

"Couldn't we find another Injun to hang in his place?" Couts wondered.

"I know where Verdi went. I'll go after him," Leandro told them, grabbing his hat. "You could try to find that mal hombre half-breed, Juan Verdugo. He's married to a Cupeño woman. If I don't catch Pablo, you can hang him. He certainly deserves it."

"That would do," said Haraszthy.

"No one will know or care the difference." Couts yawned.

"I will," said Leandro, jamming his hat viciously onto his ears and striding out Bandini's door.

T H E   jail door opened and two guards thrust in Juan Verdugo, a man Bill knew. He had always been friendly when he was at Cupa.

"What are you doing here?"

"The cabrones want to hang me for helping Garra," Verdugo spat.

He went to a corner and slumped against the wall, swearing quietly to himself.

Bill lay back and rolled in his blankets. It was cold. He was glad he had his leather jacket. Wind whipped under the door and through the windows, dusting the beams of light. He pulled a blanket over his head and thought of Pablo, riding north from Pala, where he had planned to visit Friar Ibarra; racing north to see Judge Joshua Bean—too far north—racing away against time that had already run out.

"I flee as once I fled Aguanga," Pablo had said drunkenly. "Not for fear of death, or because I believe I can save you, but because I must flee to survive. I flee for my life."

"To escape is also courageous," said 'Zul, ironing the creases in his smock with the flat of her hand.

"Only for Holbein, who risks to help me. My own courage is that of the coward, whose bravest act is to rise each morning to face himself. I only flee because I can, therefore I must. It is Bill's courage that is true."

B I L L   dozed, dreaming he was at sea.

The door burst open and Haraszthy and Leandro pushed Pablo in with a mighty shove.

"Your lucky day," said Haraszthy to Verdugo. "Out you get. We'll see you two at two."

The door slammed shut on Leandro's grin.

Pablo staggered to the water and drank deeply. His hat was mangled. His black smock was dusty, shredded at the elbows, knees and breech. He lay on his back next to Bill with a groan.

"Ibarra is dying. Heintzelman will return too late. I was coming back to try to rescue you—I had a plan—I galloped right into Leandro and Ramón."

"They dragged you?"

"Roped and dragged, but not too far. They want to see me hang."

Blood had caked dry on Pablo's elbows and knees. He sat up to take another drink and washed them with a wet napkin. He winced.

"I'm tired. I rode all night drunk, then all day hungover."

"You should have kept going."

"I came back because I found out that the Garras are with the Cahuilla, at Anza. Juan Antonio and Baupista are holding them captive, negotiating with Judge Joshua Bean to turn the Garras over to him, in exchange for their own clemency. I thought I could pass this information without showing myself. I might buy your freedom—or at least a delay until the Garras are in Judge Bean's custody and can be brought here. Then I was caught, and I had to tell Haraszthy directly."

"And . . ."

"Haraszthy said, good, good, this is good, then we can hang them too."

Bill groaned. Pablo put the wet napkin over his eyes and rested his head on the stuffed dummy. He was glad it was still dressed in his good suit.

"I'm happy I got to see Father Ibarra once more, to say goodbye."

H O L B E I N came to tell them it was one o'clock, time to prepare. Pablo had asked him to bring an enema and some warm water. He had convinced Bill that they should wash their bowels. Hanged men defecate at the moment of relaxation. Pablo didn't want to soil his death suit or give the crowd the satisfaction of smelling their excrement. The art of leaving must be practiced to the very end.

They washed, dressed and waited. Holbein heard their confessions and gave the final sacraments. The priest had baptized Bill the night before, with Pablo and Lugarda as the godparents. A noisy crowd was gathering outside. They heard marching feet and military commands. Bill chinned up to the window, his heart racing, but it was only the volunteer militia, on parade under a wind-shrill sky. He dropped back, silent, defeated.

The door finally opened. Their hands were tied behind their backs. They were led out to a wagon. Bill and Pablo were pushed up to sit on the backboard. Holbein clambered in and sat facing them. Luna vaulted a sideboard and rested on the bed. At the Machado house, the wagon stopped and Holbein helped Lugarda up. She sat next to him facing Bill. 'Zul waved from the covered doorway; she came out to touch Pablo's hand, all the sadness of that day etched on her sweet face.

Bill's stomach felt panicky. "What are you doing, Lugarda?"

She was dressed all in black, her face white as parchment.

"You asked me to accompany you to the gallows. I told you I would."

"I did? Are you sure?" He eyed the mob. Every eye was upon her.

"Yes, I am sure." She smiled and patted his hand.

They rode in silence. Bill thought of the gossip she would suffer. Her husband was still at the gold fields, but this day would be remembered. A tear came welling but he blinked it away. The crowd was yelling but he heard no words.

At the gallows, the wagon was wheeled back until the ropes dangled above the condemned. Haraszthy asked if they would like to say anything. Bill had nothing to say. Pablo did.

He stood. The noose swayed in the wind and slapped against his shoulder. He was dressed in his dark blue caballero's suit: golden buttons shining, white shirt, red scarf, boots polished to a black gloss. He had discarded his mangled hat.

In a loud voice, Pable declaimed, "I am not guilty of any of the charges brought by this false court. I did not attack Warner or the Slack party or Fort Yuma, or encourage an uprising or spy for any enemy. I was at Mission San Luis Rey continuously on the days of these crimes."

He paused to examine the crowd. About half of them were migrant miners. The wind swirled little dust devils around the wagon wheels.

"As for William Marshall, he is even more innocent than I. He tried to stop every criminal act for which he is charged. And this young boy, who has testified to support Señor Marshall's innocence, is to be whipped for telling nothing less than the truth."

"Shut up and die," someone yelled, followed by raucous laughter and more yelling.

When all were silent, Pablo spoke again. His voice was deadly, threatening.

"There is not one shred of evidence against us. If you allow us to be wrongfully punished, you shall suffer the consequences. You shall be cursed. You and your brethren shall be cursed."

"Get a rope on him, Sheriff."

"May you poison the land with your own filth; the rivers flow dark with your detritus; the very air reek with the foulness of your million breaths; and a burning sun coax up flames from hell to consume you. To this fate I condemn you."

Pablo glared defiantly into the jeering crowd. His gaze found Warner, who reddened and looked away, only to catch Bill's eye. The lips of the one man who could have saved them were pressed to a razor-thin line.

Bill decided to speak, just to let Pablo sit back down, to delay the noose a bit. He stood up.

"I am prepared to die," he said softly into the noise.

"Speak up, squaw man," someone yelled.

"I am prepared to die," he said again, a bit louder. In the crowd he saw Leandro, Ramón, Señora Osuna, Couts. Some Indians from San Pasqual, Bandini and a few other friendly faces stood out in the sea of scowls. There was no sign of Anita, the one friend he thought might save him.

"I hope my friends and the People will forgive me. I trust in God and in His mercy, and hope to be pardoned for my many transgressions." He took a big breath.

"But I am not guilty of the crime for which I am about to die. I have taken up the life of the Indians, but I did not incite, aid or encourage this revolt. I did not help the Garras. I chose to live with the Cupeño because I admired them. For them I am willing to give my life. But I am not a traitor."

Another breath.

All eyes were upon him, all silent. He saw the solemn Kanakas standing still, heavy arms crossed like guards at a temple. There was a space around them into which the crowd dared not press.

"But why should I be forced to choose? By what right do you say that you are Americans and they are not? You who came to their country to be free of tyranny? You who revolted against England and Spain in the name of liberty and justice, freedom and equality: beautiful words, exalted ideas."

Bill fought for air and held up his hand.

"But not for the Indian—these rights and ideals upon which our country has been founded. Not for the natives, from whose land this country has been carved; on whose land you now stand; on whose ideas your free life is based." He was shouting now. In the wagon, high above the throng, he felt like a giant.

"It is you who have betrayed your country, not I. Look at your feet. That ground you call your country; that ground is Indian country. One nation, indivisible . . ."

The crowd growled and stirred, grim, hateful.

Bill shrank back and spoke quietly.

"You have caused this war, not I. The Garras were peaceful people, who loved their cattle and spent their days among them, watching them grow. It was you and your sheriff who turned them into warriors.

"You do not understand the pride or soul of the native. You cannot move the rocks, cut the trees, kill the animals, take their land and restrict their movement, without killing their spirit. The People in revolt are already dead. They only await the final bullet, and hope to take a few of you with them."

The throng roared in angry waves of sound: "Hang 'em." "String 'em up." "Let's see them swing."

Pablo stood with Bill to face the snarling music.

Haraszthy mounted the wagon and fitted the two flapping nooses tightly around their necks. There was hardly any slack in the ropes. There would be no fall, as Pablo had predicted; no quick broken neck; only a slow strangulation.

Luna was taken down. His wrists were lashed to the scaffolding, the nightshirt, which he still wore, lifted up over his head onto his arms. The flogging would be an intermission; a whetting of the appetite for blood.

Warner came forward, dragging a long horsewhip. Haraszthy read the sentence: "For giving false testimony, twenty-five lashes."

Warner began to whip Luna across the back and shoulders. The spectators counted out the strokes. Luna uttered not a peep. By fifteen lashes, his little back was patterned by welts. Blood oozed from a couple of abrasions.

Couts tapped Warner on the shoulder—as though he were cutting in on a dance—and took over. He laid into his blows, striking with the fat part of the whip, the tip curling all the way around Luna's narrow chest. The welts went pulpy. The crowd kept shouting out the strokes, egging Couts on. Luna did not so much as flinch.

At twenty, Couts handed the whip to Leandro Osuna. Leandro looked up at Bill and Pablo, then at Lugarda. He stepped back three paces and expertly cracked the whip, raking the split tip across the welts with such force and velocity that bits of flesh flew and blood splattered the crowd. They pushed away to give him room, exclaiming with each stroke. Lugarda closed her eyes. Luna was as still as death.

When the last scrap of flesh had been torn from the boy's flayed back, Leandro returned the whip to Warner. A rumbling cheer arose. Couts untied Luna's hands and pulled the nightshirt down over his wounds. A dark red stain instantly soaked through, spreading to cover the back.

Luna stood up straight and turned to his friends. "No duele," he said with a crooked smile. "It doesn't hurt." He walked erect to the wagon and held on to the sideboard. The crowd went silent.

"Cretins," Pablo screamed into the silence. "Cowards, cockroaches, coños." He spit at the crowd. "May the devil take you—take you all to hell."

Haraszthy left the wagon; Holbein and Lugarda stood. The priest gave a final absolution, holding up his crucifix, which both kissed several times.

Lugarda took Bill's hand. He heard bets shouted out and taken, as to which hanged man would live the longest.

"Goodbye, Lugarda," he said inaudibly. She kissed his fingers but he was already gone. She crossed herself and sat back down. The wagon pulled away.

Bill tensed his neck and locked his eyes on Pablo's. Then the noose tightened, their feet angled off and they left the wagon. As the weighted ropes untwisted, they slowly swung 'round, unwound, the crowd revolving by, once, twice, three times. There was a rush of noise. People surged toward the gallows, their mouths open, moving. They seemed to be a single organism, waving, flowing. The Kanakas were punching those who came too near, clearing a hole in the engulfing humanity.

Bill looked at Pablo with each revolution. Pablo was smiling, holding his breath, neck muscles straining to keep his head straight. He had told Bill to take deep breaths before the drop, then hold and hold the final one, only exhaling when it was absolutely impossible to hold it more. The stranglehold on their throats would not allow in another breath; they would slip directly into unconsciousness.

Pablo closed his eyes and exhaled. Bill relaxed and let his breath go. He looked up into the sky. The wind had stopped. The blue was very deep, the sun white-hot on his cheeks. The clamor of humanity faded and quit.

He was skimming o'er grass, shady oak ahead, a picnic spread 'neath sheltering branch. Shadow running, Wili after him, Falling Star watching, waiting. White Fox stood arm in arm with No'ka. Stomping Deer and Big Bear waved; Melones called but he couldn't hear. He could feel the beat of a heart, pumping wildly. He flew to his wife. He held her in glowing brightness, until all was still and white.

EPILOGUE

FALLING STAR

A H I I I !" My heart summoned me, up-up, up-up, up from delicious dream. My husband was back. "Bill," I cried. Breath flew from my chest. My heart leaped. The hand that had touched me was no hand.

I sat up, careful not to wake the child. All was silence, but for the pounding in my breast. The wind had stopped. The sound that had aroused me was no sound.

I ran to the door and walked into new afternoon. No rush of wind. I heard the creek gurgle, birds chirping and calling; my own footsteps on the sand. Around the house, clouds pushed up against the side of Mount Palomar, rain slanting from heaven to earth.

The sky is crying, my husband is dead.

Doves cooed, a covey of quail scurried from the brush, pecking at uncovered delicacies. My mare nickered. I went to see what she wanted. Sulta licked my hand. My heart was calming. I whistled to the guards and Quil-sil came trotting.

"The wind has stopped," he said, looking toward the mountain.

"The sky is crying; my husband is dead," I said aloud. "Please go to Palomar. Ask my father and mother to come, to bring my son and the big dog. Tell them Bill is dead. And still I wait for him." Quil-sil did not move.

"You may bring my horse some water. She is thirsty." Quil-sil ran.

Inside, I picked up Cano and gave him a breast. "Your father is dead, little Eagle. Now it is our turn to be brave." Then I let loose my tears.

When Cano finished suckling, I shed my clothes. I walked with him into rain falling softly from a shrouded sky, dripping from the eaves. The smell of dampened earth and breathing leaves filled the air. We went to the hot pools to play. Let the rain wash a life away.

///

M Y parents came, bringing most of the tribe. 'Zul, Manuelito and Luna arrived the same day, with Bill's body on a fourth horse. Bill was hard to the curve of the gelding's back. Shadow sniffed at him and whined, confused. He looked to me for the answer he did not want to hear.

"My father?" Wili said. He touched a stiff leg.

"Yes, Wili. We must be brave, as brave as he was."

"I'm brave." His lip trembled and he rushed to my arms. Shadow howled and howled.

We took Bill from the horse. He would not unbend. We dug a hole among the Christians in the chapel yard. With him we placed his bow, the arrows Luna had made for him, his lance, rabbit stick, pocketknife, a handful of acorns. 'Zul stuffed a silk scarf from Lugarda into his shirt pocket, and found Pablo's rosy boa there, curled in a tight ball. She had somehow survived the hanging and made it all the way to Cupa.

I spread the soft French night dress Bill had given to me over his face. It smelled of flowers. White Fox covered him with a flannel blanket. No'ka put Bill's pillow under his head. I hacked hunks of my beautiful hair with a long knife and threw it into the grave. Melones did the same. Then dirt filled the hole. The men rolled a big flat boulder, a handsome stone, to mark the place.

Shadow leapt upon the stone and lay there at watch. I lay with him. We were two shadows on the fresh earth.

L U N A had come to Cupa with a bloody nightshirt stuck to his lash wounds, like a new layer of skin. "When my back is well, it will fall off with the scabs," he said. We were happy nothing worse had befallen him.

He gave me a letter from my husband. I kept it at my breast. I did not dare to open it.

They had buried Pablo in the chapel graveyard at San Luis Rey, as he had wished. Manuelito had made the prayer. At Pala, they found Father Ibarra so weak, they did not dare to tell him Pablo had died. The friends would find each other soon enough.

'Zul and I could not look at each other without crying. We gathered deadly plants we could hardly see—to concoct a painful poison for Leandro Osuna. Our tears ran until the soldiers came.

The Cahuilla had betryaed the People once more, handing Antonio

Garra, Tonio and eight of their followers over to Judge Bean. Heintzelman and Magruder had returned to San Diego, then moved out to Santa Ysabel. Their troop numbered fifty men. The volunteer militia joined them with fifty more. They came to punish us.

Quil-sil rushed at a gallop, to shout the warning.

"Many men, the militia, coming this way. They stopped at Warner's burned house. Heintzelman led the other soldiers on the trail down to the desert."

Everyone hid in the rocks on Eagle's Nest. No'ka and I stayed at the village. Shadow, who had become my own shadow, refused to leave me. Cano, my little Eagle, I kept too. We were afraid, deathly afraid.

Colonel Magruder, who knew my husband, rode in the lead. Heintzelman had lent a real soldier to command the militia. Behind him I smelled the murderers: Warner, Haraszthy, Couts, the Osunas and many other men.

Shadow growled. I held his collar. Magruder dismounted.

"Good morning," he said. "Mis' Marshall." He touched his hat.

"Good morning," I told him. "I present No'ka, my father. He is now capitán at Cupa."

They shook hands.

"We're looking for those who raided Warner's ranch and killed four immigrants here."

"They are not at this place," I said quickly.

"Do you know where they may be found?"

I looked at No'ka, as did the colonel. Chapuli was in Coyote Canyon, lying low like a lizard on a rock, pretending to be invisible.

"Wiliya," No'ka said.

"They are at the Cahuilla village of Wiliya, in Coyote Canyon," I said.

"That is the information we have," said Colonel Magruder. "We are on our way to that place. Warner says there is a trail from here, through the mountains. We would like to have someone show us the way."

I translated for my father. This was a test we had to pass.

"Yes," No'ka said after a time. "Call Quil-sil."

I whistled. Quil-sil came from behind one of the houses. The men gripped their guns and looked into the rocks.

"You will show the soldier the way to Wiliya," said No'ka in our language.

"Take them this way." I described the long path. Quil-Sil was still.

"He will take you. Are you ready?"

"Yes, thank you." Magruder mounted easily. His uniform was very clean and stiff, with shiny buttons. "I'm sorry about your husband."

He tipped his hat. Quil-sil trotted ahead on foot. On that twisted trail he could walk as fast as a horse.

When they were gone, No'ka said, "I hope Chapuli kills them all."

"I will go to warn him. No one will harm me."

At the house, I unwrapped my wedding dress and put it on. I buttoned my coyote coat tight over it. I stuffed the veil inside the coat. I carried Cano in his pack on my back. While No'ka held Shadow, barking protest, I departed by horse down the shorter trail to Wiliya.

It was still a long way. When finally I descended into Coyote Canyon, there were shots and shouting. Soldiers were attacking up the arroyo from the desert.

Major Heintzelman yelled, "Chapuli," and pointed at the little capitán. Many guns fired at once and Chapuli fell.

The Cahuilla retreated up the side of the canyon, toward me. I left my horse in the rocks, placed Cano on the ground, let fall my coat and the veil. I took Cano in my arms. My chest thumped like a dancing drum.

I looked up into blue, felt the sun hot on my cheeks, felt the weight of the baby in my arms. Joyous power leaped from my heart to tingle the hairs of my skin.

I stepped as light as a cloud. I floated down the rocky slope, hardly touching the ground. I passed through the retreating Cahuilla into gunfire. I held Cano before me like a shield. We flew toward death.

The shooting stopped. Silence spread to the top of the sky. The mouth of every gun gaped upon me. I crossed the sandy arroyo toward Major Heintzelman. I offered myself and my child to his guns.

"Marshall's wife," I heard someone whisper.

"Ground your weapons," the major ordered.

"Major Heintzelman," I said in English, loudly and clearly for all to hear. "I will command the People to surrender if you will order a cease-fire. Then we may speak."

For a moment he stared, his mouth fallen open. He was very big, a hairy giant.

"I am Falling Star, daughter of No'ka, chief of the Cupeño, and wife of William Marshall. They will do as I command."

"Very well," he replied. "Tell them to put down their weapons and return to the arroyo. They may attend to the wounded while we talk."

I shouted out this order in Cupeño and Cahuilla. I added that another army of equal size was coming, only minutes behind me. Some of Chapuli's men immediately threw down their bows, spears and guns. They went to their fallen capitán. He was limp, broken by bullets.

We sat in scant shade by a shriveled oak. More men came out of hiding to sit with us by the huts.

"Four must die," Major Heintzelman told me. "For those four who were murdered at Cupa."

"Warner killed four. You have killed Chapuli. That is five."

"They died in battle. We have a lesson to teach here." He waved to include the soldiers and Indians.

"Two more were hanged, as a lesson."

He searched my face. "It might be worse."

I remembered Aguanga; the Pomo massacre. I looked away.

"Yes, it might be worse. Which four?"

"Whoever are the rebel leaders. Any four will do."

I knew that Warner would soon arrive to finger the capitánes.

"Four must die," I told the men. "The leaders."

Stomping Deer stepped from behind a rock.

"Bi' is already dead," I said.

"I know, my sister." His eyes were soft. "I am the alcalde of Cupa. I will gladly die."

"As you wish, my brother."

He touched my arm but I had turned to the others. I was a warrior. I did not wish to cry.

Stomping Deer called clearly, so I had to hear, "Tell No'ka he is my father, and I am not afraid to die. Tell White Fox my mother yet nourishes me: My heart is strong. The song I sing is her song, and I am not afraid."

Francisco Mocate, capitán of Wilakalpa, whom I knew as a drinker and gambler, also came forward. Coton, one of Stomping Deer's friends, then volunteered. He and Stomping Deer began to chant.

We heard shouts. Quil-sil and Colonel Magruder rode into the arroyo, followed by the militia. Quil-sil came to squat by me. When I told him what had happened he stood up.

"I will die," he said. "I am without wife. The People will never forgive me for leading the army to this place."

"No. You have done nothing."

"I shot arrows into the travelers at Cupa."

"Yes, you did."

I presented the four to Heintzelman. "Thank you," he said. "You must tell the others to surrender. They will not be harmed."

Without consulting anyone, Major Heintzelman spoke out in a big voice. "Due to the peculiar state of the country and the absence of all civil authority, I hereby convene a council of war. The order of duty of the council of war shall be to try Jacobo, Coton and Quil-sil, of Cupa, for the murder of the Levi Slack party on the twenty-first of November, 1851.

"Capitán Francisco Mocate, of Wilakalpa, is to be charged with the destruction and despoiling of Warner's ranch."

The council met immediately. Warner translated. He was poor in Cupeño, he was worse at Cahuilla. The four were found guilty. The council announced the date, December 25, 1851. They recommended execution. Major Heintzelman ordered the men to be shot in the presence of the troops and Indians.

The warriors were made to dig their own graves. Then every man, woman and child in the valley was called before the long holes. The soldiers stood in lines on one side. We were in a crowd on the other. Twelve soldiers with rifles knelt ahead. The four condemned men stood straight in front of their graves. They were not tied. Someone yelled, "Fire." The rifles roared as one. All four People fell deep into the earth. We leaned over to see them dead. I looked on my brother and would not weep.

"Shovel detail," a soldier shouted.

Gravel swished. Spades clinked on stone. Earth thumped on soft bodies. Horses snorted and stamped. The shovel men grunted. A blue jay screeched and scolded. Cano gurgled in my arms.

When the holes were full, the mounds were tramped and filled to level. Then the arroyo was smoothed over with sage branch brooms. When they were done, the graves, and the People in them, had been erased.

Major Heintzelman thanked me again. Then he said, "I'm sorry about your husband . . . you have a beautiful baby."

He was being kind; he had been fair, even saved us. I thought of Pablo. Pablo would say . . .

"Merry Christmas," I said sweetly, as sweetly as I could. It echoed in silence.

The Major quickly turned away. "Mount up," he shouted. "At a walk by twos." They filed down the canyon toward the desert, the militia at the rear.

A T   Cupa, the entire village emptied to greet me. Shadow leaped to lick me, sending my horse racing. When she stopped, and I slipped off, I was surrounded, welcomed back as from the dead, questioned, answered, celebrated.

Not until I told of my brother's death, did I remember it. When I saw my parents' faces break, their grief engulfed me, swallowing me in a cold, bottomless embrace. Melones choked. We sank down, down, into dark shivering tears. I didn't try to come up.

When I awoke, I was another person in another lifetime. I had slept the sleep of the dead. We were together in my parents' house, a fire glowing: Shadow snoring, Cano and Wili at my side, with Melones, Primo, Papi and White Fox.

That was the afternoon I opened Bill's letter. My reading in English is poor. I had to say the words aloud, one by one. Shadow listened with me. We sat in the sun on Bill's stone, by the chapel next to the creek, in that valley where we had lived: Kuupiaxchem.

Dear Darling and Most Beloved Wife,

I am writing to you in my moment of deepest distress. Tomorrow they will hang me. By the time you receive this letter I will be gone from this earth. I do not even know what that means, except that I will never see you again with these eyes that adore you so. These hands that know you as well as they know each other, will never caress you more. These lips that have kissed you until they were raw and bleeding, shall never lay themselves upon the pillows of your own. Never again.

My greatest sadness is that we parted so abruptly. No time to relearn the sweetness of you to remember forever. Or to say goodbye to Wili or Shadow, White Fox or No'ka . . . Melones. To tell them what? How to explain how precious our time together? It would not be possible. Perhaps it is best this way. I have kissed every inch of this paper, front and back, so that you may kiss them all for me. Dissolve this letter in their kisses.

Shadow rolled onto his back. He lay with bent paws in the air, showing his lion's fangs and dark purple gums. I scratched his belly as I had seen Bill do, until he groomed my arm with his short front teeth.

I picked up the letter and found my place.

I am a fool and worthless and do not deserve the love you have given me. But I accepted the blessing of your love, and loved you more than I ever knew possible. Before you, I had only caught a glimpse of what love can do, of where it could take you. Now I know there is no place it cannot go.

There are things I would redo or undo. I would not have worked as hard for Warner; I would have been with you and Wili, Cano and Shadow. I look upon those days away from you as . . . as days of nothing. And here, on my last day, they are clearly that. I don't even remember them. I only remember those we spent together. And there were not enough of them; not nearly enough, my mountain princess — my gorgeous princess of the peaks. I have not yet had my fill of you. I am yet hungry for all that you are, for the unexhausted bounty of your life and love.

I never told you of my parents because they mean nothing to me. My life with them is like a story told about another person. I will not tell this story now. Only that when I was a boy, living at home, I fell in love with an Indian girl from the nearby village. Our parents violently forbade us to marry. She was sold away. I was sent to sea. That is how I came to you.

I came in sadness; I came adrift, unattached, free to set anchor where I pleased, to try another life on a new shore, in another land.

When your father offered me your hand in marriage, with purpose to create a child, it was a heaven-sent reprieve. No'ka believed, as I did, that we were one people. I could not refuse his offer.

Then I came to love you. The rest you know. And now my past has crossed the continent in a thousand wagons, to haunt me and drag me down and destroy me as it did before. I see my parents among the jeering faces. I see our neighbors, my father's friends, my friends now grown. I should have sailed farther. I did not foresee that this shore was attached to the other, forever more.

And yet, yet I would not trade this life that I have had with you and the People for any other. I would not trade a minute of my time with you for a year of life in any other place. I would not trade places with those that kill me, or those that came before, or those that follow. These seven years together have been a lifetime, a perfect, happy lifetime for me.

I pray that it has been the same for you. I gladly give my life so that you and my children shall live at peace. I hope my blood will satisfy these vampires' lust for the time at least. I hope my death will turn their evil eye away from Cupa and the Kuupiaxchem, to seek its victim and cast its foul spell in other vale, in other dell.

I Pray the railway goes north, this could be. Warner will not return. This he told me. The valley could be yours another fifty years; our children grow old in the ancient way, without fear. The grass wave green and tall, to tickle the belly of cow and deer, under the watchful eye of Palomar. And the hot springs flow eternal, to wrinkle your nose and warm your toes, clean the acorns and wash your clothes.

That is the blessing that I have asked of all the gods that Pablo can name for me.

I do not know what kind of life there may be after death, but if I may visit you in your beautiful valley, I will. I will inhabit any creature that will have me, any bush or tree, rock or stream, so that I may be near you. When you hear the quail call in the morning, it will be me. When a rabbit jumps for Shadow to chase, that will be me. If an oak bough bends low, to shade your bed, that too will be me; and in the hot pool, the bubbles that tickle your legs will have me inside, and burst against you to end my ride.

When you turn your head up to deepest blue sky, there I will be on eagle's wing, circling slow with watchful eye. And if danger should come, I'll call the crow, and say to him, "Down, my black friend, down you go, to warn my wife of approaching foe, and warn her well, caw loud and long, or fear my wrath and feel my claw."

I am forever with you. Your loving husband,
William Marshall

I sat for a long time with Shadow, gently pulling on his silken ears. Then I went to my family.

The next morning, we awoke to crows cawing madly. We ran to hide in the rocks. The militia roared up the street with torches lit and set every house ablaze. Then they pounded back down the trail and across the plain, screaming like savages. They were still yelling when they got to San Diego.

That night, heavy snow fell on the valley. It kept falling until all was white, even the ashes of Cupa. We sat in the hot pools. We were camping again. We would start anew as soon as the snow melted. There was nothing more they could do to us.